YOURS, MINE & OURS

BY
JENNIFER GREENE

All the characters in this book have no existence outside the imagination of
the author, and have no relation whatsoever to anyone bearing the same name
or names. They are not even distantly inspired by any individual known or
unknown to the author, and all the incidents are pure invention.

First published in Great Britain 2011
by Mills & Boon, an imprint of Harlequin (UK) Limited,
Eton House, 18-24 Paradise Road, Richmond, Surrey TW9 1SR

© Alison Hart 2011

ISBN: 978 0 263 88934 5

23-1211

Harlequin (UK) policy is to use papers that are natural, renewable and
recyclable products and made from wood grown in sustainable forests. The
logging and manufacturing processes conform to the legal environmental
regulations of the country of origin.

Printed and bound in Spain
by Blackprint CPI, Barcelona

Jennifer Greene lives near Lake Michigan with her husband and an assorted menagerie of pets. Michigan State University has honoured her as an outstanding woman graduate for her work with women on campus. Jennifer has written more than seventy love stories, for which she has won numerous awards, including four RITA® Awards from the Romance Writers of America and their Hall of Fame and Lifetime Achievement Awards. You're welcome to contact Jennifer through her website at www.jennifergreene.com.

For Lilly: Get ready, you sweetheart.
A life of wonders is just waiting for you.

Chapter One

Mike Conroy pulled down the tailgate of his white pickup. Brilliant May sunshine gleamed on the revolting heap of supplies in the back. He started unloading—first, the gray plastic bins. Then came the burlap, the shredded newspaper and the bags of soil.

Last, of course, came the worms.

He wasted a few seconds, rolling his stiff shoulders, mourning how his life had come to this. Even when he was a teenager, he'd had precise, clear dreams of what he wanted from life. He'd always wanted to be a successful lawyer—and he'd done that. He'd always wanted to live in a big city—and he'd done that. He'd always dreamed of living with a sexy, beautiful woman—and God knew, he'd done that, too.

He'd not only done all those things; he'd thrown that entire life away. But even at his lowest, he'd never anticipated wanting to start a worm farm. Ever. Even remotely.

"Hey, Dad. Isn't this *great?* Isn't this the best thing ever? Where are the worms? Can I see the worms?"

"Not yet, Teddy. We need to get them out of the sun, into the basement. You can help me set everything up."

"How soon do you think we'll have worm poop, Dad? You think *soon?*"

Mike knew well that when his four-year-old said *soon,* he was hoping the event would happen within the next three seconds. "The plan is to get all the supplies into the basement. Then to come upstairs, wash our hands, chill out with a glass of orange juice. And after that, the two of us can get our hands down and dirty creating our worm farm."

"Hey, Dad." Teddy, whose thatch of brown hair never looked brushed, who could put a hole in a new pair of jeans faster than lightning, who had a Tough Guy T-shirt with four separate food stains on it, looked up at him with adoration. "Worms are my favorite thing in the whole world. This is the best thing that happened to me in my whole life. I'm not kidding. I mean it. I'm not telling a story this time. It's *true,* Dad."

"I believe you, sport. In fact, that's exactly why we're doing this."

"And we're gonna make a pond. And have frogs and stuff."

"You bet."

"Mom would never let me do this."

Mike yanked the T-shirt over his head, tossed it on the truck seat.

Chicago springs were usually perfect, but this May had been a furnace. All afternoon, it'd been hot enough to choke. Sweat prickled the back of his neck. And no, he didn't respond to Teddy's comment about his mother. He was getting good—not perfect, but good—at refraining from criticizing Nancy in front of their son. He'd sworn never to make Teddy prey to those kinds of divorce battles.

"Hey, Dad—"

Thankfully he was saved another set of questions by the arrival of a white SUV zipping into the drive next to theirs.

He looked up. Teddy looked up. Even Slugger— the bassett hound snoozing upside down on the front porch—was curious enough to open one droopy eye.

He and Teddy had moved from downtown Chicago just two weeks before. Living anywhere near suburbia was another thing Mike had never planned to do, but that was another life-compromise emanating from the divorce. At least this neighborhood didn't look like Clone City. Silver Hills was a new suburb on the far west side, with all kinds of architecture and at least a half acre between most homes. His place was a modified A-frame, primarily redwood and glass, and richened up by a two-story stone chimney. The best part was being at the end of a cul-de-sac, with a serious deck and woodsy ravine in the back.

The closest house to the east had a Sold sign in the yard when they first moved in, but Mike hadn't seen any sign of life there until a few days before, when a moving van had pulled up and unloaded. Still, there'd been no sign of the owners until now.

The neighbor's house was fancier, built of field-stone, with two dormer windows upstairs and huge casement windows framing the center door. To Mike, it was a little pretentious, had kind of a fake country-estate look—not that it made any difference to him.

He missed a glimpse of the driver, because his attention was drawn by a child skipping around the back of the car. It was a girl. An ultra girlie-girl, about the same age as his Teddy. She was dressed to the gills in pink—a pink top with sequins and shiny beads and more shiny stuff attached somehow to her wildly curly red hair. The white pants had pink edges, and she had shoes that lit up with pink lights when she skipped around.

Teddy looked thunderstruck—but not necessarily

by the girl. The problem was that Slugger—who never moved fast unless a steak bone was in sight—spotted the girl and started baying nonstop. The little girl happened to have a dog next to her. At least, Mike was pretty sure it was a dog. It was white, possibly a cross between a miniature poodle and schnauzer, and just like the girl, it was gussied up beyond belief with a pink rhinestone collar and other jewelry items he'd never imagined on a canine before.

Slugger flew off the porch step and trundled over to greet the poodle with a cascade of more baying and howling. The poodle promptly squatted down and peed. Then Slugger peed. Then the dogs started chasing each other. All that might have gone fine, except that Teddy—his ever-friendly son—galloped over to the girl and began telling her all about their brand-new worm farm.

Teddy only had to say the four-letter *worm* word once for the girl to launch into a long, versatile scream that could have—should have—wakened the dead. For a kid who couldn't be three feet tall, she had the vocal range of an *American Idol* winner.

Abruptly, a woman charged out of the house, leaving the front door flapping open, making it pretty clear she feared her daughter was in imminent danger. Mike, of course, didn't know it was the kid's mother. But it seemed fairly obvious.

She had the same curly red hair. On her, it was a rich, dark auburn, dancing around her shoulders.

Unlike her daughter, she was wearing mostly green, but she had the same put-together thing going on. Her shirt was green and white, her jeans white, sandals green. Everything matched. The woman just had a few fewer sequins and rhinestones.

Mike took one quick look, but then had to do a double take.

That fast, he told himself it was a damned good thing he'd given up sex for the rest of his life. Redheads were trouble, every guy knew that. And undoubtedly she was married. Still, he'd have to be dead not to recognize she was beyond attractive. She was built lithe and long, lean like a runner, yet still had an upstairs rack compelling enough to glue his gaze there. The green eyes were gorgeous, the long face fine-boned and arresting. The mouth…man, that mouth, was not just luscious in shape but darned near riveting.

The whole package moved way past beautiful and into the stunning range.

Thankfully there was no time to dwell on it—both of them were distracted by all hell breaking loose. An elegant, long-haired pure-white kitten stepped out of the lady's open front door and promptly sat in the sun to delicately wash a paw.

Cat—the scarred-up old tomcat who'd shown up in a rainstorm a year ago and refused to leave him—suddenly shot out of the cat door and beelined for the kitten.

The mom promptly let out a shriek that verified forever where the daughter had inherited her vocal cords.

The kitten disappeared inside the open front door, followed by Cat. Both dogs, now that felines were in the picture, chased right in behind them. Teddy and the little girl pushed elbows, both trying to barrel after their respective pets.

Which left him—at least for a second—with the stranger.

She seemed to do a quick size up, which made Mike ultra conscious that he was shirtless, dirty and sweaty. But he couldn't tell from her expression what she thought of him. What she thought of the situation was more clear.

She was still gasping for breath. "I'm afraid we'll have to exchange names another time. I mean, I'd hoped to meet my neighbors under a little less chaotic condition—"

"Same here, believe me."

"Even though I'm tempted to cry right now, I have a feeling by tonight I'll be laughing about all this."

"Me, too." He liked it. That she wasn't turning hysterical—at least, once she'd realized her daughter wasn't hurt or in danger.

"Unfortunately…" Finally she caught her breath. "My cat hasn't been spayed yet. Neither has our dog. We hope to breed them."

"Uh-oh," Mike said, and that had to be the end of

the conversation. He hadn't run track since college, but in a crisis, he could always pour on the coals.

This definitely qualified as a pour-on-the-coals moment.

Amanda Scott sprinted right behind her new neighbor, calling for the kids, dogs and cats as loudly as he did. She'd had a moving company deliver the heavy boxes and furniture days before, but she hadn't planned on seriously moving in until today. Naturally, the house had a post-cyclone decor. Packing boxes and cartons and furniture were strewn every which way, creating obstacles that impeded their progress… but that wasn't the only reason she couldn't catch her breath.

It was him.

She'd known the transition from city life to the suburbs would be challenging, but she wasn't expecting *this* kind of challenging.

For five years, she'd lived her dream of a life—a gorgeous condo in downtown Chicago, an advertising job she thrived on and marriage to a perfect guy, Thom. Then came their precious baby. Then came the divorce.

The first thing she'd done—because it was the most critical issue—was give up sex for the rest of her life. Her inability to judge character in men was the reason, and Amanda was never one to duck from the truth. Although she'd moved to the suburbs solely for her daughter's sake, Amanda figured it'd work like a charm on the celibacy thing. After all, what males was she likely to run into but married men, dads and guys heavily into their families?

Her new neighbor was undoubtedly one of the married herd. She couldn't imagine any sane woman letting him run around loose and single. It was just…he was an unexpected jolt to her senses. Nothing unusual about the dark brown hair, but his chin had several days of disreputable unshaven whiskers. His brown eyes looked her over like a sip of warm Southern whiskey. The naked chest was smooth and sculpted; the jeans low-slung, his skin had a gleam of sun and sweat… The whole package wasn't just a prize male specimen. He was a whole bucket of testosterone.

He hollered again for his son, his dog, his cat. Even his voice had that guy-tenor thing going on.

It wasn't as if she was going to do anything about it. She'd just really hoped to have a little old lady for a neighbor. Or a family with a half dozen kids and a harried-looking father with a paunch.

Beyond the living area was the kitchen with its fresh birch cabinets and wonderful bay window—partly why she'd fallen in love with the house. Right now, boxes were stacked there every which way. The kitten was on top of one. Amanda saw her neighbor swoop up Princess—who immediately curled up on his shoulder as if she'd finally found her Prince Charming. Of course, she should be happy. He'd saved her from the tomcat prowling around the boxes for her.

"I'll take her," Amanda told him. He promptly handed her over in a cloud of white cat hair, and she quickly carted Princess to the nearest bathroom and closed the door.

One cat safe, now just two dogs and two kids to catch.

The dogs had quit barking—which struck Amanda as an ominous sign. The sound of crying was another bad sign—she wasn't sure which of their kids was unhappy, but the noise came from the second floor, where there were two bedrooms and a bath.

Amanda reacted to the crying first, took the stairs three at a time, and found her sweet, delicate daughter sitting on top of the neighbor boy, pretty much pounding on him. She was half his weight, but as Amanda knew, when her darling lost her temper, she seemed to gain the strength of Goliath. She pulled Molly off the boy, scolding her for hitting.

"Never hit," Amanda said firmly. "You know better. No one hits in our house. Ever. If you have an argument you can't solve, you come to me. But we don't hit. Apologize right now."

There followed a noisy dialogue of "But he…" and "She said it first…" and "No, it was him. I couldn't help it…" and "You were the one who was mean, mean and mean." Et cetera.

It took a few minutes to get the tears stopped, to

check both kids to make sure neither was actually hurt. The neighbor's boy looked just like his dad—rugged, pure male, a kid-adorable version of the grown-up.

Her new neighbor showed up at the top of the stairs. "I found the dogs."

"Where?"

"In the room I think is going to be your living room. Behind the couch. Slugger is now outside—I closed the front door, by the way, so we won't have any immediate repeat of this. And it's been fun, but I wouldn't want to overstay our welcome." He held out a hand, and his son immediately climbed up and did a stranglehold on his dad's neck. The other arm held his tomcat. Amanda could hear the hound baying and scratching at the front door from two stories up.

"Um…" She scratched her neck. How to end this impossibly awful first encounter? "Nice to meet you?"

"Actually we haven't met. Which is maybe a thank-God." He was already barreling down the stairs with both arms mighty full. His son was talking nonstop. The godforsaken cat was yowling in his other ear. "If you need help moving in, give a shout."

"Thanks," she said. She figured, after this, she'd ask him for help the day it rained money. "Same here."

His brows arched as if he couldn't imagine he'd need help from her or her household…yet his grin was still evident. A cheeky grin. A grin that said, "Hell, if you're going to have an awful day, might as well do it full bore."

An interesting man, she thought. The whole household looked slightly on the rascally side. The cat had more scars than a derelict. The dog had that hound smell, and its ears trailed the ground. All four of them could have used a bath and some clean clothes and a hairbrush.

But he could have yelled—the way most men did in a crisis. Or lost patience. Or made a point of finding blame, making it someone's fault—undoubtedly hers.

Instead, he'd just kind of charged in and started solving problems.

Maybe he wouldn't be such a terrible neighbor.

"Mom!" Molly tugged at her hand. "I don't want to see that boy again as long as I live! I hate him! And I'm thirsty! And I want to watch TV!"

Amanda almost laughed. For a few seconds there, she'd been worried about a personal connection to her neighbor. But her real life erased that worry lickety-split.

Right now she had all the chaos she could possibly handle—and then some.

Chapter Two

"I don't get it, Dad. Why she hit me. And did you see? I didn't hit her back."

"Yup, I saw, Teddy. You did the right thing. It's never okay for a boy to hit a girl. Or for someone to hit someone smaller than they are."

"But I wanted to. I wanted to *really, really* bad."

"Of course you did. She wasn't behaving well. But you just can't hurt another person. If you feel mad, you have to let it out other ways…like running as fast as you can for a while. Or punching a pillow. Or getting your mind off it by doing something else, something you like, like a puzzle or your trucks or something like that."

When Teddy stepped from the bathtub onto the

white-and-black-checked tile, Mike was waiting with a man-size black bath towel. Teddy might be squeaky-clean, but the bathroom now had more water than a lake. His son thought he was *way* big enough to take a bath alone. Maybe he was. But Mike wasn't sure the house could survive the aftermath. Even with him right there, everything in sight and vicinity tended to get soaked.

He covered Teddy's head, heard him giggle, swooped the damp package in his arms and carted him down the hall into the only room in the house that was decorated—seriously decorated.

The bed was shaped like a car. The wallpaper was a mass of trucks and cars and tractors. Mike had laid down thick, soft brown carpet, both to suck up extraneous noise and because four-year-olds—at least, his four-year-old—tended to accumulate bruises and bumps, so the carpet needed serious cushioning. No curtains. "We men," as Teddy put it, "don't need girl stuff like that."

Half the room was toys. Because Teddy's favorites tended to be moving vehicles, Mike had set him up with a "garage" for the diggers and tractors and haulers, and a couple of bins for the fifty million cars that reproduced every night. Mike had told him flat out that he didn't care—at all—about being tidy. But the cars had to be put away before bed, because Teddy could be hurt if he got up in the night to pee and stumbled over them.

Teddy considered that rule to be reasonable, which was a relief. When Teddy didn't like a rule, he could spend four hours asking "But, *why?*" questions to exhaust his father.

"I didn't say good night to the worms, Dad," Teddy suddenly worried.

"I'll say good night for you." Off went the towel. On went the football pj's.

"Why didn't she like me?"

"Who?" Silly question, Mike thought. It had to be the girl next door, from his son's mournful tone. "Maybe she did. Sometimes girls do strange things when they like a boy."

"I offered to show her my worms."

"That was very kind."

"We're going to dig in the backyard tomorrow, right, Dad? Make a big hole?"

"That's going to take some time to set up, sport. We'll be headed to the hardware store for supplies first. And Grandma and Grandpa want you to come over. But believe me, you and I are going to get into all the dirt and water and messes you could possibly want."

"I can't wait."

"We'll have fun," Mike promised him, and started the ritual tucking-in process.

"Dad?"

"What?"

"I bin thinking about why Mom doesn't want me

anymore. Maybe it's like that girl. Even when you're nice, some girls just don't like boys."

"Anyone who didn't like you would have to be really, really lame. And your mom loves you." Mike bent down, bussed his son's forehead. They weren't calling it a good-night kiss anymore. They were calling it a Night Connect.

"You're going to leave the bathroom light on?"

"Hey, it stays on 24/7. You know that."

Mike finally switched off the bedroom light and aimed for the living room. Teddy had barely said a word until he was three. Ever since then, he made up for it by talking every waking moment. Mike vaguely remembered working fourteen-hour days, poring over law books and briefs, skipping meals and sleep, never too tired to party.

To caretake a four-year-old all day—now *that* was tiring.

He grabbed a longneck from the fridge, the newspaper from the counter, sank into the easy chair by the window and propped up a foot.

He'd made the place as easy to care for as he could. Nothing in the living area but the big stone fireplace, a couch, a chair, the big TV. The open kitchen area had an eating nook, where you could see the TV whether you were eating or cooking. Mike had dibs on the west corner for his desk and computer and work setup. Teddy had dibs on the north corner, where he stashed his downstairs toys. Four-year-olds, Mike discovered, never seemed to have enough toys.

The silence now was more valued than gold. He didn't even get the paper opened before Slugger and Cat climbed up—Cat by his neck, Slugger taking up all available space on his lap. They promptly went into snooze mode.

The last of daylight blurred into sunset, and then true darkness came on. He never turned on a light. A full moon was just rising. He leaned his head back, taking a lazy moon bath in the open window. He scratched under Cat's chin, hearing him purr like thunder, and used the other hand to rub Slugger's belly, who loved that attention to the point of bliss.

He was just plain enjoying the simple evening, until his gaze accidentally glanced next door. Abruptly he stopped relaxing, stopped moving, stopped breathing.

Next door…in a second-story window…there appeared to be a navel. A naked navel.

Separating from the dog and cat, Mike climbed to his feet to take a clearer gander from the front picture window. Yup. There was a definitely a bare body in the window. Of course, he couldn't see the whole body—just the wedge between rib cage and midhip. Still, he could clearly see in the indentation of waist. The swell of curves over the hip. The belly button. An innie belly button.

Navels had never been his particular fantasy. He'd

always tended to be a leg man. And a breast man. And a fanny man. Hell, he'd always been a sex-crazed adolescent who'd turned into a wildly enthusiastic lover as an adult—until he'd recently given up sex, of course. But this was the first time he could recall ever noticing or being attracted to a belly button before.

What on earth was she doing?

Ah. Painting. He figured it out when she bent down—apparently from a ladder, because he could see her hand now holding a dripping brush. She pressed her belly against the window for support again, as she hand-painted the edge around the ceiling. Not that he could see the ceiling. But the dance back-and-forth motion of her arm pretty much told the story.

He told himself, okay, he'd figured it out, time to get away from the window. She might catch him being a navel voyeur. Worse yet, the longer he stared, the more he started worrying that maybe he really was a navel voyeur. Or that he could turn into one.

He was about to turn away except that he suddenly saw a blur of movement. Even with windows open in both places, he heard only a vague sound coming from the second story in her place, but something had obviously happened. She suddenly disappeared from the window. So did the ladder.

He didn't *know* she fell.

But there was suddenly no sign of life or movement

up there. And a fall from a ladder could be darned serious.

He couldn't leave his son, of course. He never left his son alone. Teddy had occasional nightmares, besides. Still…how long could a quick check take?

He didn't even bother with shoes, just sprinted out the front door, already calling himself every flavor of dumb. She undoubtedly locked the house, so he wouldn't be able to get in…but it was open, he discovered when he turned the knob on her front porch. Where was her head? A woman and little girl alone in the house after dark, and she hadn't locked the door?

He considered knocking, but was afraid he'd rouse the prissy white dog into a fit of barking that would waken her daughter. He just called quietly, "Hey…it's me from next door. Mike. I was in my living room, thought I saw you fall from upstairs. I'm not trying to be nosy. I'll go right back home. I just wanted to make sure—"

Abruptly he quit with the bumbling greeting. Even from her living-room foyer, he heard a groan coming from the second story.

He vaulted upstairs, had no problem identifying which room she was in, because night-lights reflected in the bathroom and kid's room. It was the room with the ceiling light shining in the hallway where the redhead had to be.

He pelted in, took in the mess at a glance—the

wobbly ladder on its side. The newspapers spread over the painting area, with the usual gambit of brushes and rollers and blue tape and supplies. It wasn't hard to tell what color she was painting the room, because there was now baby-blue all over her, the floor, the walls and everything else.

He didn't give a damn about the spilled paint. She was lying in the middle of it. He knelt down, fast, and saw with relief that her eyes were open—even if they did look dazed.

"Don't move," he said.

"Are you kidding? I couldn't move if I tried."

"At least you're talking. And I don't see any blood." He just saw a whole lot of baby blue. In her hair. On her chin. On her halter top. On her tummy. On her shorts. On the floor, too, but the gleam of baby blue on the floor wasn't interesting. "Where does it hurt the worst?"

"How am I going to get this out of my hair?"

"How about if we worry if you need an ambulance before we let vanity into the picture?"

"It's not vanity that's killing me. It's pride. I *just* bought that stupid ladder!"

He'd already noticed the pip-squeak–quality ladder. "You bought a girl ladder. Instead of a sturdy, practical one."

"I couldn't carry the sturdy ones! They were too heavy! Besides, it wasn't the ladder that caused the fall. At least, not exactly. My mom called. If you knew my parents, you'd understand why I fell."

It was pretty obvious that the fall had unleashed her ditsy side, because she started babbling nonstop. While she ranted on, he looked her over more seriously. Obviously her head and spine would be the most serious worries, after a crash like that, but she could also have broken or sprained something. He started by examining her feet—which were bare except for the neon-painted toenails.

"My parents are wonderful. Both of them. It's just that they raised me to be spoiled. To believe that I deserved everything, from Prince Charming to a perfect life. You have no idea how useless I am."

"Uh-huh." The calves were perfect. No fat. Just those perfect curves, leading to delectably soft thighs.

"My mom—her name is Gretchen—she wanted to hire painters for me. And a decorator for the house. And to pay for a summer program for precocious four-year-olds."

He figured, since she was conscious if not exactly lucid, that he'd better keep his hands off her belly and breasts. Technically he supposed he should check things like ribs and all. But since he was already mightily turned on—against his will—he knew perfectly well that the wrong kind of touching was on his mind. He'd lost all interest in checking for injuries.

Still, he tried to get his attention back on track. Her

neck was fair game. Shoulders. Hands. Wrists. And she'd stopped talking—for the few seconds it took to carefully and touch and probe those areas—he followed through with a question. "So what did you tell your mother when she wanted to do all those things for you?"

"I told her—*and* my dad—that Molly and I moved closer specifically so they had a chance to be more active grandparents. I know they wanted more time with Molly. And I wanted that, too, for it to be easier for them to be a regular part of her life. But I also told them I didn't want anything else."

"And this was a problem somehow?"

"Hey." Apparently she forgot the conversational track. Her fingers suddenly banded his wrist, and her gaze met his, clear as daylight. "Quit right there. No touching below the neck. For Pete's sake, we haven't even been introduced."

"I'm Mike Conroy."

"I'm Amanda Scott." There was humor in her eyes now. He *had* introduced himself quickly. "I can get up. I'm pretty sure."

"Let's do it slowly."

"You know, I would *really* like to stop meeting like this. We could try it all over again. You know. Behave like real neighbors. Knock on the door. Show up with cookies or a beer or a bottle of wine. Say hi, welcome to the neighborhood. I mean, we could try meeting without a disaster. Oh, no, no, Darling!"

Startled, Mike couldn't fathom where the endearment came from—but then he realized the half-breed white dog had shown up, clearly realizing something was wrong with her mistress. She was aiming straight for the puddle of paint on the floor.

"Got it," Mike said, and lurched for the dog. The poodle or poodle mix—whatever the devil she was—didn't object to being hauled up in the air. She seemed to expect being carried. He suspected going home would entail Slugger giving him hell—and howls—if he showed up smelling like girl-poodle, but there was no help for it.

"Could you put her in Molly's room, and then just close the door without latching it? She loves sleeping with Molly."

"Got it. Only, you don't try standing up until I get back."

A night-light was the only illumination in the girl's room, but Mike could readily make out that it was a girl's version of what he'd done for Teddy. Amanda, though, had gone even more overboard. Shelves were jammed with stuffed animals. A bitsy dressing table had a matching bitsy chair. The kid was swallowed somewhere in a canopy bed, and it was hard to find a path to walk between the flounces and little chairs and dolls. *Lots* of dolls. Dolls in cradles, dolls in various states of undress, dolls on shelves, dolls on the floor, dolls without heads.

Finally he located the little doll—the real one—on

the pillows under the canopy deal. The rosebud mouth was emitting a few teensy snores. The red hair curled all over the pillow. She'd kicked off half the covers. Mike set the poodle down, who promptly circled and settled at the foot of the bed, then tugged up the covers. He discovered a clearly sacred blankie had fallen on the carpet, and retrieved it. He knew about sacred blankies. Anyway. The kid was fine. The dog was fine.

But on returning to the empty room next door, he discovered that Amanda wasn't remotely fine.

She'd made it to a sitting position. Was sitting with her knees up, one hand on her forehead, making choking sounds as if she were holding back tears…only, tears were flooding her eyes in thick clear drips, turning her pearl-cream skin blotchy, turning… Aw, hell, she wasn't just a mess. She was a complete mess.

"Something hurts that bad?" He crouched down.

"Go away. Thank you for helping. But go away. I'm fine."

Yeah, he knew that female twist. No matter what he did now, he'd be in trouble. She wasn't fine. But she didn't want him here—and he sure as hell didn't want to be here. But he sure as hell couldn't leave a woman crying her eyes out.

"I'll tell you what," he started to say.

"No. I mean it. I'm fine. I'm just having a meltdown. People have meltdowns. I'll get over it. But

I really don't want to do this in front of a stranger, okay? So just go away."

"I will, I will. But here's the thing. What if you have a concussion?"

"I don't."

"It looked as if you fell partly on the side of your head, because I felt quite a bump—"

"I don't care."

He squinted, scratched his nape, thinking that was another female comment that was invariably booby-trapped. Obviously she had to care if she had a concussion, if she needed medical attention—for her daughter's sake, if not for her own. She wanted him to disappear. He got it. But if he went back to his place, he wasn't going to sleep all night, worrying whether she'd collapsed over here alone.

"I've got a plan," he said firmly. "You head into the shower. Clean up. Get the paint out of your hair and all that. And I'll be downstairs. Nowhere near you. You come out of the shower, call down that you're all right, then I'll lock your door and go home."

She was still sniffling hard, but she let loose an almost inaudible "All right. Only because I'm worried about Molly."

"Got it." He didn't care why she agreed. She agreed. He helped her stand up, trying to think like a big brother, not an adult man who was handling attractive female flesh, but it wasn't that simple. When a woman was vulnerable, a guy instinctively reacted.

It was a sick instinct, a stupid instinct, an instinct that got a guy in trouble every time, but whatever. The brush of her body against his provoked an unfortunately magnificent hard-on. He'd just touched her side, her arm, her hair… That was all it took. Some baby-blue paint came off in his hand when he touched her hair…which she saw.

"It's just latex," he assured her. "It'll come out with plain old soap and water."

It seemed an innocent enough comment to him, but, par for the course, he must have picked just the wrong thing to say, because her eyes welled up all over again. Still, she stumbled off, disappearing into master bath right off her bedroom, and closed the door.

That left him staring at her mess. It wasn't his problem, of course. And he'd the same as promised her that he was going downstairs, away from her personal space. But it really *was* a mess. It wasn't just the overturned paint can, but the wet brush lying on the floor, the overturned ladder, the roller and pan still soaked with that same sissy-blue color.

If she had to come out of a fresh shower and clean all this up…well, he could just picture her breaking into tears all over again.

It's not as if that was his problem, either, but he was stuck hanging around until she came out of the shower. She could still fall. She could still have a concussion. He wasn't about to leave Teddy alone next door much longer, but he was probably committed for another ten minutes anyway.

So he started to clean up…except that when he picked up the paintbrush and actually looked at the project—well, she had only a couple of square feet to go near the ceiling. It was downright silly to seal up and clean up, when just that little bit was left to do.

He finished the bit of wall in two shakes. She still wasn't out of the shower—he could hear the water running from beyond the closed door. She was making noise—some might call it a frightening attempt at singing the blues—but the noise at least verified that she hadn't keeled over.

He'd just do a little more cleanup. And then split.

Amanda couldn't *believe* it took so long to wash off all the paint.

She shampooed and soaked and shampooed all over again. She scrubbed her skin practically raw, then conditioned and rinsed and soaked some more.

Eventually she had to climb out. She just didn't want to. She wanted to stay holed up in the bathroom until her neighbor was gone for sure. How humiliating, to have a meltdown in front of him. She was a crybaby. Always had been, always would be.

But she'd hoped her hunky neighbor would never have to know that.

She toweled off, pulled on a clean T-shirt and shorts, opened the door a peek to let out the steam—and to listen. No sounds. She'd have heard Molly—she'd been known to hear her baby from two floors away from behind closed doors. But in this case, she only listened for the clump of a heavy footstep, a tenor sigh…the hint of testosterone in the air.

Nothing.

Still rubbing the towel through her hair, she tiptoed across the hall to her bedroom…or her bedroom-to-be. Until the room got painted and carpet was put in, she'd been camping on a couch. The point, though, was that Mike was definitely gone.

But so was her disaster area. The paint can, newspapers, roller and pan, brushes—everything had disappeared. He'd finished painting the rest of the wall. A few splotches of "Clear Skies" blue still marred the floor, but there was nothing else in the room—except for a note.

"I stole your ladder—so you wouldn't use it again. Mine's hanging in the garage. Borrow it anytime you want. I'll have your painting supplies back on your porch by tomorrow—it was just easier to clean up in my basement than mess up your new place."

There was no signature, no personal comment. He'd just come to her rescue out of the complete blue. Did the whole silent take-care-of thing.

She flipped off the overhead light, stalked over

to the window—carefully avoiding the splotches of paint—and stared down at his place.

There were no lights on that she could see. No dangerously good-looking adult male in sight. But he was going to be a problem, she could just smell it.

All her life she'd needed a hero.

Except for now. Right now she needed to stand on her own—to learn to stand on her own—or die trying. She was running out of chances to feel proud of herself and her life. The suburbs was it. Her foxhole in the battle. Her line in the sand. Her Custer's last stand.

She wasn't going to *need* a man. Ever again.

Chapter Three

The next morning, keeping his eye on the time, Mike clattered down the basement steps just ahead of his son. Teddy was running in circles—even on the stairs—chanting, "Hoboy, hoboy, hoboy!"

His joy, naturally, was about the worm-farm project. And before Teddy had woken up, Mike had hustled downstairs to set it up. The "ingredients" needed for the farm were all laid out—the plastic drawers, newspaper, garbage, burlap and, of course, the worms.

"Now, both of us have jobs," he told his son. "Your job is to tear up the newspaper. Like this. That's to make the bed for the worms."

Teddy took to ripping up paper like a nun took to

prayer. "I'm doing this really, really good, aren't I, Dad?"

"You sure are. And then…we're going to add just a little water. That'll be my job." Mike wasn't born yesterday. A "little water" to his son was like inviting Armageddon. "But you get to do the next thing. The worms need food. Something we call 'organic waste.'"

"What's that?"

"Organic waste is the stuff we usually put down the disposal. Like old lettuce. Maybe some carrots and carrot stalks. We could try a little broccoli."

"Dad," Teddy said earnestly. "I think we should give the worms all the broccoli in the whole world."

"That's precisely how I feel about brussels sprouts. Okay. Now…we add the worms."

"Can I do that? Can I? Can I?"

"Are you kidding? The worms are *totally* your job."

"Thanks, Dad!" The thrill on his son's face was almost as good as Christmas.

Finally, the project was finished, and Mike could put the lid on. "Okay. Your grandma's coming in fifteen or twenty minutes, so we've got just enough time to get you cleaned up. But remember, we can't look at the worms for at least two weeks."

"Except for peeks."

"No. No exceptions. No peeks. No looking at all. Light can hurt them. Okay? Promise."

"I promise with my whole life. I promise, hope to die."

While Mike was dunking Teddy in the tub and then getting him brushed and dressed, he took advantage to give his son the bigger worm picture. "Even though we have to wait two weeks to see the worms again, we have lots of good things to do in the meantime. Like building our water garden in the backyard."

"For the frogs." Teddy lifted his hands so Mike could thread a fresh T-shirt over his head.

"Yeah, for the frogs. The frogs are going to love those worms. And there'll be extra worms for fishing. And we can even use the worms' waste besides that."

"What waste?"

"Their castings and tea." Mike should have known his son wouldn't let him off that easy. "That's their poop and urine. It works like a fertilizer. So we can dump that in another part of the yard, like where we plant bushes or trees… Hey, I hear the doorbell. That'll be your Grandma Conroy."

"No! Do I *have* to go, Dad? I want to stay with you."

His parents may have been unhappy about the divorce, but both were thrilled to have their one and only grandson suddenly within three miles of them. Barbara Conroy had always tended to dress on the

formal side, but today she wore snug jeans and a long
T-shirt—a perfect getup for surviving the day with
a four-year-old. "Hey, you." She snagged a kiss off
him first, gave him a motherly look over. "You doing
okay?"

"Couldn't be better."

She said something to him—but his attention was
diverted when a car pulled up next door. It was a
meeting of the Lexuses. His mom's was lipstick-red,
Amanda's mom favored a custom-painted sapphire.
Apparently it was a mutual grandma-pick-up-grandkid
day.

Both grandmothers looked alike—blondish hair,
great bones, slim and both appearing energetic and
younger than their years. They spotted each other,
about the same time Molly skipped out the door and
saw Teddy.

Molly stuck out her tongue at Teddy. The insult
was returned. Then Slugger started baying because
the poodle next door started an excited-barking thing.
The grandmothers started talking and laughing at the
commotion, but for one whole, long second, all he
saw was her.

Amanda.

The grandmas herded their respective grandkids
into their respective Lexuses. Mike heard Amanda
tell her mother, "Mom, please don't call her princess" and then a minute later, "Mom, no buying her

a million toys. Just be together, okay? Have a good time."

And her mom responded with a chant of "uh-huh, uh-huh" as if they'd had this conversation a zillion times before, and the whole while she was winking at her granddaughter. Molly appeared to need several suitcases to be gone for a few hours.

Teddy just galloped to the car and climbed in. By the time the cars pulled out and all the noise disappeared—even the dogs quieted down—suddenly there were just the two of them with nothing more than a spare stretch of driveway separating them.

Lightning arced between them, even though there wasn't a single cloud in the sky.

"I owe you a big thanks," she called out.

"No sweat." He'd put her painting stuff on the back porch before daybreak, hoping he wouldn't have to run into her. But now, the more he looked at her, the more he relaxed. Last night, there'd been something… off…between them. An intimacy, because of being alone at night, the dark, her not wearing much and then nothing while she was in the shower, her crying, the whole thing.

It wasn't as if that chemical-lightning thing had disappeared. If anything, the charge was more intense—but now he was braced for it. And looking at her this morning was reassuring. She looked… well…prissy. Not vulnerable and cute, like last night, with the naked navel and the wild heap of red hair.

Today, her hair was scooped up, a spotless yellow shirt paired with white shorts, sandals with yellow flowers. And she had on makeup. At this hour of the morning.

He hadn't shaved in three days now—hadn't brushed his hair in two. No reason to spruce up—he wasn't trying to please or attract any female again. Still, he was glad to admit he had a heap of things he had to do—she hastily admitted the same—and they both took off in opposite directions.

It was the truth, besides, Mike thought self-righteously. With Teddy gone, it was a perfect chance to make a trip to the hardware store.

Amanda let Darling out for a quick business trip in the backyard, petted Princess, grabbed her car keys and list and headed out. She'd had a spiffy Austin Healey before the divorce. Now she had a white SUV, which looked like a clone of all the soccer moms' transport vehicles up and down the neighborhood.

Mike was gone, she noticed. At least, his garage door was open and his truck nowhere in sight. She hadn't forgotten what a hero he'd been for her last night, but thankfully, she'd wakened this morning certain that he was a resistible hero. They both had their hands full with major life changes right now. And she wasn't about to forget the major life lesson that had been battered into her by the divorce.

She wasn't going to be the needy one in a relationship ever again.

She backed out of the drive and turned left—then immediately realized she should have steered right. It was going to take a while before she got her bearings in the neighborhood, and hardware stores were hardly her normal milieu. This morning, though, she had a major hardware-store type of list. She wanted bricks, to make a brick walkway in the back. Mulch. Stones. Eventually she wanted a porch swing back there, too.

In the meantime, she needed just *stuff*. Gardening gloves. A little spade. A little shovel. She didn't even have a flashlight in the house. Somehow she had to figure out a way to mow the grass. And Mike—not that she wanted to keep dwelling on her neighbor—had intimated she needed a sturdier ladder.

She located the store—after only a couple of wrong turns—and even found a reasonably close parking spot. She'd been in one of these warehouse hardware stores before. Once. But she didn't have a clue where anything was, so she just grabbed a cart and pulled out her list. She figured she'd get the boring stuff over with first—the household tools. Hammers and screwdrivers and flashlights. Picture-hanger doohickeys. Things like that.

Thankfully that chore didn't take long, but once she wandered into the garden center, there seemed a million choices, a million things to look at. She slowed down. Absently started humming…

Moments later, she realized someone else was humming, too. A man's hum. Not in the same aisle where she was looking at bricks and stones, but somewhere not far. When she stopped humming to listen, he stopped, too.

When she started humming again, so did he.

She glanced around the corner into the next aisle. Saw nothing. Shaking her head, she continued on. She would have to find some help, get someone to carry the bulky items for her. In the meantime…well, she wasn't sure how she ended up in the plumbing aisle, but suddenly there he was.

Mike.

He spotted her about the same time she spotted him. He had a faucet set in his hand. She was still holding her list. But for a petrifying second, she forgot what she was doing altogether.

She told herself swiftly that it was nothing like the night before. Granted, he'd come across as this handsome, wonderful white knight, all sexy eyes and protectiveness and strength…but she so wasn't about to believe in the fairy-tale thing again.

And once she caught her breath, she realized it was okay today. Better. He was just an oversized scruffy mutt, after all. And as long as she didn't look directly in his eyes, she didn't feel any of those…well, zingers. As if she'd been prodded with something electric and compelling. As if she was somehow meant to move closer to him.

She tried a light laugh. "I swear, we keep meeting in the oddest places!"

He finally looked away from her, too, and lifted the package in his hands. "I've been looking at faucets. Nothing exactly wrong with what we've got, but there's a new kind..." He showed her. "You can turn it on and off with a wrist, never have to touch a handle. Which means that little boys—and big ones—don't necessarily have to wipe out a whole sink when they're cleaning up."

"Now that would be a miracle," she said with another laugh, this one more natural. "I'm new at the yard-and-gardening business. Never had any 'green' to work with in the city. So I've just been shopping for some general tools and landscaping stuff."

"Yeah, we're getting into that kind of trouble in our house, too."

So much for small talk. She took a breath, knowing she really needed some things to be said. "Look. I can't thank you enough for last night. You certainly didn't need to finish painting the wall or doing the cleanup—that was way over the top. And after I cried all over you, too."

"Yeah, that was really awful. Don't do it again."

She was startled, then realized he was teasing. His crook of a smile momentarily disarmed her, but then, blast it, she realized she was looking at him again, feeling the pull of, say, an earthquake or a tsunami.

"Well, I owe you a payback." She hoped her voice came out sounding normal.

"Forget it. No problem."

"I was thinking of bringing you a homemade lasagna—"

"Whoa. Complete change of mind. You *do* owe me a payback."

This time they both laughed. "So you like lasagna. Okay. Done deal. I'll bring it over tomorrow, around 5:00 p.m. or so." She pulled her cart, as if she were going to go back to her shopping, but then couldn't seem to resist asking, "Was that your mom who picked up Teddy?"

"Yeah. Barbara. And my dad's name is David. They're over the moon we bought the house here. Teddy's the first grandchild. Their place is just a few towns over, in Lisle."

She pulled at her cart again, as if she had the good sense to cut the small talk and go back to her shopping chores. Somehow, her feet seemed rooted right there, temporarily, though. She couldn't seem to quell a second round of nosiness. "How about Teddy's mom?" When Mike lifted an eyebrow, she said swiftly, "I know, I know. It's none of my business. But if we're living next door, I don't want to accidentally say something hurtful or difficult for your son, so… you know."

"Yeah, I know." His arched brow suggested he knew perfectly well she was being nosy. But he answered. "Right now I've got primary physical custody. My ex-wife hasn't remarried yet, but she's about to be." He lowered the brow. "Truth is, Teddy's real bent out of shape about his mother. He doesn't get it. Why his mom would take off. He seems to believe that she personally abandoned him."

Amanda shot him a sympathetic look. "I'm sorry."

"I didn't tell you to solicit sympathy. But it's like you said—if we're living so close, we should probably know what the situation is with our kids."

She nodded, and immediately came through with her stash of baggage. "My ex is Thom. He has regular visitation rights, although he only makes it half the time. I had a job in advertising—we lived downtown Chicago—but after the divorce… Well, Molly's about to start preschool, so I figured it was time to move to the suburbs, settle where there were good schools and families and other kids for Molly to play with." She added wryly, "To be honest, I'm finding the move a little bit of a culture shock."

"Hey, you're not alone. I never envisioned living in suburbia, either. But I felt the same, for Teddy's sake. Wanted the kind of neighborhood where he could grow up, go out and play, meet other kids, do the good-school thing. And the clincher for me was living closer to his grandparents." Abruptly he straightened, as if he feeling he'd shared too much. Or that he'd found too much in common with her. "Well, I'd better—"

"Me, too," she said instantly, and did a quick U-turn with the cart. "I need to move on. Just remember, lasagna tomorrow. If you're not there at five, I'll just leave it on the front porch. See you later."

She couldn't seem to escape the store that fast, though. She just seemed to need so much *stuff*. The weight kept adding up, for the bricks, the mulch, the stone. And once she hooked on to one of the store's employees, she asked for his help picking out a lawn mower. All the bulky and heavy stuff had to be delivered; there was just no way she could get it in and out of her car.

By the time she edged into the checkout line, her cart was full, and she was daydreaming about some lunch and a nap. As she reached down for her purse, though, she noticed something odd. The items she'd chosen had somehow changed. Somehow, the pink gardening gloves she'd chosen had metamorphosed into a heavier, ugly gray pair. The pretty little spade she'd picked out had turned into a set of gardening tools with sturdy steel handles. Instead of one shovel, there was now both a pointy shovel and a flat blade, neither particularly huge, but definitely sturdier than what she'd originally picked up.

For a second, she thought she had the wrong cart, but there were so many other things that she recognized—like the matching dishtowels and the porcelain drawer pulls and the shoe organizers and the picture-hanger doohickeys. She glanced behind her, around her. Mike was nowhere in sight. He'd undoubtedly long finished his shopping before she did.

But he was the only soul in the universe—at least, that she could imagine—who would have done this to her.

He couldn't keep pulling this white-knight thing on her.

This time, there would have to be serious payback.

Mike should have known that putting in the new faucet would turn into a federal project. Bad plumbing always led to more bad plumbing, even in a new place. Conceivably, the work was hampered by his being a *lot* better lawyer than he was a handyman. And by the dog, who wanted to sleep on his foot while he was lying on his back under the kitchen sink. And by Cat, who crawled up his leg and sat purring on his damned stomach while he was trying to wrench in the new connection.

Several phone calls interrupted him, adding more complications to the sweat-fest chore. The first call, he jumped for—hit his head, then his elbow. But it was Teddy. "Hey, Dad. Grandma said to tell you I'm being good and she wants me to stay overnight."

Mike could hear the tiny wobble in his son's voice. Teddy wasn't comfortable, being away from him at night. At least for now. "Not overnight, sport. I want you home. But if grandma wants you to stay for dinner, you can."

His son ran off, then called back three minutes later. "Okay. I'm having dinner here. Grandma says do you want to come?"

"Tell her no, thank you. But call me again if you'll be later than 7:30 p.m., okay?"

"Yeah. Grandma says she's gonna get me my own cell phone."

"No, she's not..." Mike shook his head. The connection was severed. There were possibly going to be a few complications, living this close to grandparents. Four years old? A cell phone? Not.

The other two calls he let go to the answering machine. Working with water and grease and heat under the sink was a whole lot more fun than talking to his ex. Nancy wanted to arrange a time to be with Teddy.

He'd call her back.

When he got around to it.

Even hearing her voice put a snarl in his mood. He was long over Nancy, but still testy on some of the divorce details. He was working on moving on, getting past it, all those stupid slogan words that divorced people used. But it was one thing to have a failed marriage...another to have your marriage end because your wife took off with a germ-freak nerd who couldn't weigh more than one hundred and fifty pounds.

That she could desire such a jerk was part of what festered. Even if the marriage had long lost its luster before the divorce, Mike never had any reason to doubt his ex was happy in bed. It wasn't losing her that hurt. It was losing her to such a ninny. His sexual pride still felt stomped on by a bulldozer.

Anyway. He'd had enough of chores by four o'clock. He showered, put on old shorts and his Harvard tee—his favorite, as exhibited by the frayed neck and holes—called the hound and aimed for the deck. Teddy wouldn't be home for a couple of hours. He figured a half hour of slouch time in the shade was just what the doctor ordered.

He opened the door to the deck—and almost tripped over a twelve pack of beer. Cold beer. Dripping, sweating cold. A fancy longneck brand. Bottles.

It was enough to make a warrior weep. Since he only hit a grocery store when he was desperate—those places were terrifying—he hadn't picked up beer or any other side goodies. He glanced around for a note, but he already knew who'd done this to him—even before he turned his head.

One glance was all it took to identify the slim, bare foot perched on the white lawn chair next door.

Her deck was smaller than his, with a lattice

privacy half wall—which was why he couldn't see the rest of her body. But he could see the foot. And the curve of her white calf.

The Sissy Dog was snoozing on her lap, but as if sensing testosterone in the air, she jumped to the ground and sat at the edge of the deck. Slugger was too tired to move—his position on life, twenty-three hours out of twenty-four—but his tail started wagging like a metronome.

Mike ignored the critters. He could hear Amanda talking on a cell phone, even if he couldn't see it. He opened a beer. He didn't want or mean to listen. He just figured he'd hang for a few moments so he could thank her once she finished her call. Except, she kept talking.

"Mom. Come on now. You know I love you, and I didn't mean to hurt your feelings. I'm just asking you not to call her princess... Yes, I *know* the kitten's name is Princess, but that's entirely different— Molly named her, and I couldn't talk her out of it. Mom..."

The foot lifted. Disappeared from sight. He heard the clunk of a glass, as if she'd poured something and then set the glass down on a metal surface.

"I *know* you called me princess. And you were a wonderful mom. The best. Dad was a wonderful dad. The best. But you two spoiled me rotten. I really want to raise Molly more independent than I was. I don't want her expecting..."

The foot showed up moments later with sex-red color on some of the toes. So. She was drinking, talking to her mother and repainting her toenails all at the same time. Obviously she came from the estrogen side of the species.

"…I didn't mean that, Mom. I'm just saying…I don't have skills. Skills I need. Skills I want. I don't know how to mow a lawn. How to shampoo a carpet. How to do anything *practical*. I knew how to behave at a cotillion, a country-club dance, a symphony. But I never saw Thom coming. He bamboozled me. I should have been too old to be bamboozled. He was cheating right in front of my eyes, and I never noticed the clues. *Mom*. I *know* I'm not stupid. But just because I was smart in school doesn't mean anything now. I need to be smart in life, and I'm a dimwit!"

The left foot was done, raised to be examined, then the right foot was started on. She was drinking wine, he identified, when a bottle showed up on the deck floor.

"No, no. I *love* how you raised me. I had the most wonderful childhood a girl could have. I'm just saying that times are a little different. I want Molly to be more self-reliant. To not expect a prince to rescue her, or to think she *needs* a prince to be happy. I want her to be able to rescue herself. No, no, I swear, I didn't mean it that way…*Mom*…all right! All right! I give up! You can pay for the riding lessons! But no buying her a horse! And I mean it!"

It seemed possible the phone call rather abruptly ended, because there was suddenly a series of muttered swear words from the other side of the lattice, all said in a tone of utter exhaustion. He finally had a chance to speak and he took it.

"Hey. Thanks for the beer."

There was a moment of total silence, and then a face showed up from the other side of the lattice. She wasn't completely naked, contrary to what his imagination had tried to lead him to believe. Her T-shirt read *Duke*. Maybe it was hers, maybe an old boyfriend's, but whichever, it was even older than his, more frayed, more holey. He gained respect for her right then and there. Of course, he also noticed the shortest shorts he'd ever seen. My God, she might be a redhead, but she did have a set of legs. En route, he did happen to glimpse she was shooting fire from her eyes.

"Were you *listening* to that conversation?"

"Me? I don't know what you mean. I just walked out on the deck a second ago, saw the beer, couldn't imagine anyone who would have left it but you. Appreciate it. Want one?"

"No, of course not. I… Yes."

He was going to have to rename her the whirling dervish. She put the Sissy Dog inside, grabbed her icer and wine bottle, her wineglass, and zipped down the steps and into his yard faster than he could retract the offer.

Slugger took one look and rolled on his back, assuming she'd want to pet him. She did. Then poured another glass of wine for herself. "I started with wine, so I don't want to mix it with beer, but I'm more than up for sharing a drink." She took the chair across from him—another Adirondack chair, nothing fancy. Her Duke T-shirt was so oversized that when she bent down again to rub Slugger's tummy, he could see the tips of a lace bra. The view suggested that there was a lot more bra than boob in there. The red toenails shined like Chinese lacquer. Her hair was swooped up, all messy, all wild, held off her neck with some clips.

It was hard to define why he liked the whole package. But he did.

A lot.

"What do you think?" She motioned to the space between their houses. "Do we need a fence? Because of the dogs and kids and all? I like the open space between the properties…but I don't know. A fence still seems like a good idea. At least if you think so. The point is that we should agree on the nature of fence, don't you think? And just for the record, I know perfectly well that it was you who sneaked the tools in my cart this morning."

He was having trouble following her fast changes in subject. Particularly when his attention was so zealously focused on her bare legs and inadequate neckline. "There was no point in your throwing away money on tools that weren't going to hold up. As far as I could tell, you weren't worried about price. You were just choosing stuff that had pink handles."

"Well, yes."

He wiped a hand over his face. No point in discussing that any further. "If you want a fence between the yards, naturally, I'll spring for my half."

"I'm not trying to be difficult. It was just an idea. If we both wanted a fence…I just didn't want to act unilaterally. For one thing, there are all kinds and types of fences—"

"I get it. You're not being difficult." She was. He wasn't sure why. He wasn't sure why they were talking about fences, either, except for the obvious reason. They wanted protection from each other.

"I've just had a really long day."

He thought she was trying to explain why she was being difficult again, but then he heard the old song "I Will Survive," and realized it was her designated cell-phone ring. She lifted a hand and, apologizing to him, said, "This'll be short, but I really need to take it."

"No sweat." He took another pull on his beer, put his bare feet on the deck rail and let his head fall back. In two seconds, he realized the caller was her ex-husband.

"I wasn't ducking your calls, Thom. We were busy with the move this week." And then, "I think it's a little ridiculous that you're pushing for equal custody when you couldn't even make the last two visitations. This isn't about Molly, and you know it. You just want the child support cut. It's not as if you can't afford it, for heaven's sake—"

She bounced up from the chair, turned her back—as if turning around would make it harder for Mike to hear her. Not.

"I'm not listening to yelling, Thom. Not now. Not ever. I expect you to pick her up on Saturday at noon. Have her back here by seven. I have nothing else to say."

Once she snapped the phone closed, she whirled around, her smile brighter than glass. "I'd turn off the cell phone but I can't. There could always be a call related to Molly."

"Same problem here. I can duck calls with the answering machine, but I don't want Teddy to have any problem getting hold of me." He felt a sudden restlessness. The kind of thing he felt when he was about to do something he shouldn't. She sashayed back to the chair, crossed her legs, all her movements classy and elegant—not a put-on, just apparently how she always was. The call from her ex should have been another turnoff. She was complicated, and so was her life and problems. Every encounter he'd had with her so far indicated she was high-maintenance, trouble, no one and nothing that he could possibly want in his life.

But damn it. She was so upset her hands were shaking.

She noticed him looking at her hands, and immediately said, "It's no secret to anyone. I hate confrontations. I'm terrible at them. My job used to be in advertising. Everybody called me tough. I *was* tough, I swear. But that was my business life. In my private life, well, you could say I flunked the course in fighting altogether."

"Amanda—?"

"What? Oh. I know. I'm talking too much. I pretty much don't drink at all for just that reason. One glass of wine and out it all spills. My life. And this was such a trying day—"

"And you're nervous around me."

"—and I'm nervous around you." She blinked. "I'm not. I don't know where that came from."

He hunched forward, motioned her closer.

She hunched forward with a curious frown.

He said, "Here's the thing. I've got one priority for this summer. Teddy. To get him set up. To make this a home. Check out the preschools and pediatricians. Find some kids in the neighborhood, locate the parks, the library, the stuff he can get involved in. That's my whole job this summer. And there just can't be any women in that picture."

"Okay."

"He's still ripped about the divorce. Sometimes I think it's because he never saw his mother and I argue. We never did, not in front of him. I thought that was how you were supposed to behave, but now—crazy as it sounds—I think it's part of the problem. He's got it in his head that Nancy left because of not wanting him, that he was somehow at fault. What Nancy pulled was a downright turkey move. But I can't change that or fix it. All I can do is try to settle my kid into the happiest, most stable life I can. To put it in blunt terms—"

"Do," she encouraged him.

"I've given up sex forever. Now it has occurred to me, in the past couple of days, that 'forever' might not be a precisely achievable goal. But through this summer, I really need to do the celibate thing. No entanglements. No distractions. My world has to be my kid."

"Whew!" She let out a long breath, tossed him a smile—not that glassy, classy smile but one so real it jammed the air in his lungs. It was that sexy. That natural. "You have no idea how glad I am to hear you say that. Mike—I'm in exactly the same boat."

"Yeah?"

"We're on the same page. I just made the no-sex vow the same way." She laughed, inviting him to. "The best thing about the divorce was figuring out how many wrong roads I'd been taking. I had every advantage a girl could have, was pampered and spoiled from the get-go, fell for the whole fairy tale that I was something special. I could have had a sign on my forehead that said Me-Me-Me."

"That sounds pretty harsh."

"It's the total truth. I thought my ex was the Prince Charming in the story. Never once looked further than the surface—until it all crashed. So…I'll likely look for a job in the fall. I don't know what kind. I'll work that out after Molly starts preschool. But I'm determined that this summer be about her. I want her to be about everything that I'm not. More self-reliant. More capable. I want her to take more pleasure in accomplishments than in material things. Which means…"

"Somehow I sense the punch line is coming."

"Yes. No men for me. Indefinitely probably—but definitely not this summer. I need to figure out the stuff I was doing wrong. Change. Change into being more of the person I want to be. Oh, God, it's so boring hearing someone talk about this kind of thing, isn't it? I'm sorry. I just wanted to be clear—"

"Amanda."

"Yes." He'd leaned forward, with such a serious expression, that she leaned forward, too.

"It's pretty obvious we've been worried about the same thing, don't you think? Both of us have these… life plans. About not getting involved with anyone right now. About needing to concentrate on nothing but parenting for a stretch. So we both agree…it'd be a real pain in the keester if you and I…" He motioned with his hands.

She nodded vigorously. "It would just be completely awkward."

He filled in more. "It'd be complicating. Unsettling. Exactly what neither of us want right now."

"I couldn't possibly agree more!"

He nodded. "So let's get this over with, okay? We'd better find out how dangerous the problem is before figuring out how to handle it."

Chapter Four

Granted, Amanda had had almost two glasses of wine—and before dinner, besides. So she realized she was a little addled, but she was still astonished when Mike—out of the complete blue—pulled her onto his lap.

The last she knew, they'd been talking, not flirting.

The last she knew—positively—they'd been talking about celibacy. His intention to be celibate. Her intention to be celibate. Their completely agreeing with each other.

So the fire started from nothing, came from nowhere. The smolder and snap of sparks suddenly caught, and just as suddenly spread. The heat startled her nerves, her skin, turned her senses incredibly tender. Smoke clogged her brain and fogged her vision. Sirens echoed in her ears—not sirens communicating danger, but a siren song calling mesmerizing, wicked things to her.

It was just a kiss, for Pete's sake.

She'd been kissing boys since she was fourteen. She'd been married. There wasn't a reason in the universe that this one should be so different.

But it was.

He was.

He'd kind of tumbled her onto his lap. His mouth had found hers before she'd found her balance. It was just all suddenly…there. The solid warmth of his body. The strength in his thighs and chest, the manly smell of him, the swoop of his arms creating a natural cradle.

And then there was the whole problem with his mouth. His lips were softer than butter. He offered a skim of a taste, then settled in, in a tangle of his taste and hers, the combination unexpectedly explosive.

She figured she should raise her hand and express a little outrage…but she couldn't seem to conjure any up. Objections appeared in the back of her mind, but never showed up at the front door.

This wasn't *nice*.

He didn't kiss *nice*.

He kissed as if he wanted to swallow her whole.

As if no touch, no kiss, no woman had ever ransomed his attention as she did.

Thrills shot through her blood as if she were on a roller-coaster ride.

She shifted, accidentally jamming her elbow into his ribs—but she had to look at him, had to catch her breath. His eyes were as glazed as hers. His breath coming as heavy. His frown just as dark.

But that made no sense. She went back for another kiss, to figure out what was really going on. A kiss—a few kisses—couldn't rock a girl's world. It had to be something else. Maybe some unusual kind of allergy attack. Or maybe pheromones were raining down from the sky. There had to be *something* that could be logically explained if she just studied it long enough.

So she studied a long, deep, eyes-closed kiss on him. The experiment failed. It seemed… Well, it seemed that she couldn't argue with a tsunami. She wrapped her arms around him, held on and just hoped she didn't drown—or if she was stuck drowning, that he was going down with her.

She felt his fingers tangling in her hair, holding her still, felt the sudden hard tumescence against her thigh, heard the shuddering breath coming out of him as he lifted his head…then dove back for more of that tsunami business.

A few hours later, she lifted her head.

Conceivably only a few minutes had passed, but

definitely long enough for her to feel both exhausted and energized. Exhausted, as if she craved a nap. Energized, as if the only thing she could think of was jumping him.

He had dark brown eyes. Liquid brown. The bad-boy disreputable attitude was gone. Now, she suspected that attitude thing was just a defense. This man, the Mike so close she could see every line and bone on his face, was as serious about life as she was.

Maybe even as vulnerable.

"I think," he said slowly, "that we just both found out how big the problem is." He helped her off his lap. They were both standing against each other for a millisecond, but Mike swiftly retreated to the side of the deck rail.

"A major uh-oh," she echoed, trying to make her voice sound light and easy. She didn't want him realizing how wild she'd felt in his arms. How crazy. How totally unlike herself.

"I wasn't trying to start trouble, I swear."

"I wasn't, either."

"But I did think…there was chemistry. That we'd both likely feel easier with each other once we figured out what was what. We'd already tried being honest with each other—about where we were in our lives."

"I'm always happier with honesty. No pretending. Not for me. No faking, no denying, none of that nonsense." She meant it. She'd lived the Prince Charming/princess fantasy her entire life. She was through with it.

He caught his breath. Or most of it. "Amanda. I'd appreciate a friend. I mean it. It'd be good for Ted to be around another woman besides his mother. I'd appreciate hearing how you think he's doing, from another single parent's perspective."

"And I'd appreciate a friend just as much. You've already proven to be a friend, Mike. And it sounds as if we're both going through a lot of the same problems. Grandparent issues. Ex issues. The same culture shock of moving to the suburbs. There are things we could laugh about. Talk through."

"As long as we don't let sex get in the way." Again, those fierce brown eyes met hers.

Again, she saw a different man than the rascal she'd first met. The sharp lines on his brow hadn't come from a devil-may-care type of guy. "Then we won't," she said firmly.

"We're agreed?"

"Completely, totally agreed," she said. "You know the lasagna I promised you?"

"Yup."

She motioned to the rough wood table on his deck. "Let's try it tomorrow. All of us. Give me a chance to spend a little time with your Teddy. For you to see my daughter. Let's see if they can be friends together, as well."

"Good idea," he said.

She thought so, too. Until she woke that night in the darkness, her whole body turned on by a wildly romantic dream. He was her prince. She was his princess. They were in a wild, erotic, exotic lovemaking fest, chasing each other through the sky, mating in sunlight, then moonlight, then snuggling together on a tuft of clouds.

Oh, no, she thought, too exasperated to sleep now. She got up, got a glass of water, checked on Molly, prowled the perimeter of the house. That kind of dream was not for her. Ever again.

"Okay. Now here's the deal." It was all Mike could do to subdue his excited son. Teddy had already run outside naked this morning, completely forgetting his clothes. He'd been conned into dressing—at least putting on a pj top and shorts—before galloping back out again.

They were digging the water garden—alias frog pond—today. The parts that appealed to Teddy, in order, were mud, shovels, water and frogs.

Mike had set up the design as simple as he could. "So…this is how we're going to do it. We're both going to dig inside this triangle area. *Nowhere* else. The dirt we're going to put in those wheelbarrows." He pointed to the two wheelbarrows. "*Nowhere* else."

"Got it, Dad. Can I dig now?"

"In a minute. When the hole's deep enough, I'm going to put in a liner. You can help me. And then we're going to set out rocks as a border, kind of make a triangle-shaped place to sit, where we can watch the frogs."

"Ok. Can I dig now?"

"There'll be a motor. To keep the water aerated and clean."

"Yeah. Can I—?"

"Yes." Mike gave up and let him loose.

He heard voices from next door, figured out immediately that Amanda and her daughter had yard work on their Saturday-morning agenda, too.

Their setup was slightly different from his.

For one thing, Molly wore a pink tutu, and had a pink crown on her head, and she did a lot of twirling. On his side of the driveway, Teddy was covered in mud and water inside of three minutes, and had managed to throw dirt everywhere but in the wheelbarrow.

The same sing-song refrain echoed from both yards, all variations of "Look at me, Dad!" or "Look at me, Mommy!"

Her yard had a pitcher with ice cubes and lemonade and cups and napkins.

He used a hose, both to get himself and Teddy clean enough to drink, and then to drink from.

A good hour passed, maybe two. The sun poured down, a hot liquid light. The pond got dug. All it cost were four Band-Aids, heaps of sunscreen, two or three pulled muscles in Mike's back, several buckets of sweat and a few torn clothes. The water garden was going to be darned nice when it was done, but Mike already knew it'd take eons more hours—after Teddy was in bed.

He stood up, gauging how much more he could get done before lunch, when he suddenly heard…silence. He glanced up, and saw the two redheads standing at the border of their yard. The one in the tutu had her hands on her hips and was staring at him with both disgust and fascination. Molly's mom looked as delectably dangerous as she had last night—only, last night she'd come undone in his arms. Today, she was wearing white shorts to garden, which he couldn't believe. And the pretty little bed of day lilies she'd planted looked ready for a garden show.

"We like your water garden," she called over.

"Your mommy is never going to let you in the house," Molly informed Mike, which seemed a fair indication he was wearing half the dirt in the yard.

"Molly—" Amanda started to address her daughter, but suddenly the miniature redhead shrieked.

"Mommy! Teddy's going pee pee outside! I can see it!"

Aw, well. Teddy undoubtedly hadn't wanted to waste time going all the way in the house to the bathroom when they were having so much fun. It likely never occurred to him that squirting on the back fence might not be the best idea. Mike rubbed a hand over his face, trying to figure out what to say or do, accidentally got a piece of dirt in his eye.

Then the barking started. Slugger had been outside with them, but pretty much he'd just been basking in the sunlight and snoozing—that was, until the Sissy Dog somehow escaped a tether on their back porch and came prancing over, a diamond-studded leash trailing behind her.

Slugger could move fast. It just wasn't usually his choice.

The girls took off after "Darling." Mike took off after Slugger. How her dog knew about dog doors, he had no idea, but the little squirt shot into his house, followed immediately by his lovesick hound. Molly tried to crawl through the dog door. Then Teddy showed up and the kids tangled in the doorway.

Normally Mike would have let Amanda through before him, but just then he figured that chivalry was less important than preventing the dogs from having an inappropriate hookup. He might have wished he'd had a fresh shower. That his house looked a little less like a tornado site. That the path wasn't littered with shoes and toys. Cat screeched from the top of the mantel at the hullabaloo.

The kids were circling, calling for the dogs—at least, until her Molly got sidetracked by a toy. Naturally Teddy stopped to explain the toy to her, and that left only the two adults searching high and low for the dogs—who'd suddenly turned quiet.

"Not a good sign," Mike admitted to her.

The canines weren't in the laundry room—which had wash heaped to the ceiling. Clean wash, not dirty wash. All the same, Mike so far hadn't thought of a reason why it had to be folded or put away when they could both just take stuff off the pile when they needed clean clothes. Amanda shot him a look.

"What? What?"

"Someday your son's going to get married. Which means you'll have a daughter-in-law. And she'll blame you if your son expects her to pick up after him."

"Huh?"

He pushed into his bedroom first—worried what she'd see—but it was fairly picked up. Just an unmade king-size bed, the sunlight hitting on the steel-gray sheets and striped blanket. "No dogs," he said when he spotted a jockstrap on the master-bathroom floor, and closed the door as he ushered her out.

There was no sign of the dogs in Teddy's room, either, but she got a good look. "You decorated to beat the band in here," she noted.

"I wouldn't call it decorating."

"I'm just saying—you went to a lot of trouble. And it shows. What a great room for a boy."

Maybe so, but that wasn't solving their dog-disappearance problem. Mike shut the bedroom door to close off another potential egress—or exit—depending on which the dogs tried for next. "There's nothing upstairs but a big loft—it's the playroom," he told her, and then stopped talking, because he heard sounds. Odd sounds. Very odd, yowly, canine sounds.

"Stay here," he told the kids, which had all the effect of a whisper on a flood. He took the steps two at a time, but the kids still beat him to the top.

Molly, who could outrun a quarterback, even in her tutu, let out a scream that could have shattered glass. "Mommy! Slugger's hurting Darling! He's being mean! Make him stop it!"

"He *isn't* being mean," Teddy told her, and tugged hard on Mike's arm. "Dad, I don't get it. What's Slugger doing?"

The loft was divided into father and son spaces. On Mike's side, there was a computer and desk, battered couch, pool table, wall-mounted TV. On Teddy's side, there was a town of trucks, a train set, a washing-machine box with doors and windows cut out, shelves with games and books.

Slugger and Darling were pretty much on the line between spaces, getting it on with abandon. Well, maybe not abandon. Darling looked fairly bored. Slugger looked more animated than Mike had ever seen him.

Amanda looked at them—then him—with horror.

"You didn't tell me she was in heat," Mike said.

"I didn't think she was. There was no sign. And I thought she was too young!"

"Um. It'd appear she's definitely old enough." Mike struggled to find a positive. "At least she wasn't a thoroughbred."

"That's not the point! She was mixed to be mixed with her own kind! Because it's such a good—"

"Mix. Yeah, I got it." Mike scraped a hand through his hair. "Kids, go downstairs."

"Mommy, make him stop jumping on Darling!"

"Can't you do something?" Amanda demanded.

"At this point, they look pretty well…hooked up. I'm not sure how to de-hook them. If it'd hurt them."

"I just can't believe this," Amanda said with despair.

"Neither can I." Mike sighed. "I'm guessing this means that I won't get that lasagna tonight, huh?"

Princess, Darling, Molly and Amanda were all crowded into the downstairs bathroom. Someone had originally painted the room green. As soon as Amanda could get the supplies purchased—there was so much to do in a new house—the girls had decided it was turning into their butterfly room. The grape-and-aqua butterfly wallpaper had already been decided on. But that subject had already been thoroughly discussed, and they were on to the next.

Dinner next door.

Because Molly no longer wanted to go, Amanda was determined to turn the occasion into a solid parenting lesson…but so far, that was challenging.

"I don't see why we have to eat with them, Mom."

Molly, in spite of her current scowl, looked downright adorable in her purple-and-white shorts set. Because she claimed she was way too old for a nap these days, she'd been coaxed into supervising a rest period for Darling and Princess. All three had conked out for a good hour's snooze.

Amanda wrapped a purple scrunchie in Molly's hair, making a tidy ponytail that matched her own. She was also wearing a purple-and-white shorts set. Personally, she was a little freaked to do the matching mom-daughter clothing thing, but Molly had claimed it was the "most important thing to her in the whole world."

"We're going over there for dinner," Amanda explained, "because we want to show Mr. Mike and Teddy that we're gracious."

"What's *gracious?*" Molly studied her mom as Amanda put on mascara.

"Being gracious means… Well, things weren't going too well between us all this morning, right?"

"You're not kidding. I couldn't believe Teddy peed in the yard. I didn't see his penis, but I still saw him peeing. And then his dog hurt our dog. And then they were so *dirty.*"

"Well, honey, Darling wasn't really hurt by their Slugger. That was something else. But the point—about our going, about our being gracious—is that strong girls don't run away where there's a problem."

"Why not?"

"Because the problem's still waiting for you when you stop running. So it's just a whole lot easier if you just deal with a problem right when it happens."

"But I don't have a problem. *They* have a problem. Can I put on that stuff on my eyes, like you?"

"Not mascara, lovebug. But we'll do blush together." Molly immediately lifted her face and closed her eyes, waiting for her mom to brush her cheeks. Immediately she peered at herself in the mirror.

"I look beautiful," she said with awe.

"Yes, you do. You look beautiful, but even more important, you're going to be gracious, and polite and on your best manners."

"Why do I have to be on my best manners again?" Molly insisted.

"Because they're neighbors. And we want them to be good neighbors. So we're going to show them that we're nice people. Everybody has problems come up, honey. Friends, neighbors, family. Disagreements don't disappear if you ignore them." She'd been an expert at doing just that, all her life, and particularly in her marriage. So for damn sure, Molly wasn't going to make the same mistakes. "We're going to be on our very, very, very best behavior, okay?"

"Got it. We'll show 'em. I'm going to be so good you won't believe it. I'm going to be so good you'll probably want to get me an outfit for my American Girl doll. I'm going to be so good that you'll let me stay u—"

"We're both going to be on our best manners because it's a good idea. But we'll talk about that other stuff when we get home." Amanda didn't want to commit to bribery. Unless she had to. In the meantime, there was still a ton to get ready before heading next door. Darling had to be walked—on a leash. Princess expected a treat right before dinner. Amanda had to unearth the picnic basket, then start stacking the dinner—the hot plate of lasagna, silverware, napkins, a warm towel-wrapped loaf of Italian bread, a chilled bowl of fruits for salad. There was also carrot cake with a butterscotch sauce, but she couldn't carry it all at once. Truthfully, she couldn't carry what she had now.

"I'll help, Mommy." Using her most virtuous voice, Molly reached for the napkins.

"Thanks, honey." Amanda tried to keep the irony from her tone, took a breath, and off they went.

"Good grief," Mike said when he opened the back door. "Amanda, I figured you'd bring a pan, not a whole feast. You didn't have to go to all this trouble—"

Oh, yeah, she did. Looking at that sweaty, oiled man all morning—shirtless, muscles gleaming, laughing with his son—well, the whole morning had put bad ideas in her mind, that was all. Unacceptable ideas. The trauma with the dogs was just a different layer of tension. She was living next door to this guy. She had to make it all more comfortable—a *lot* more comfortable—than she was feeling right now. And food seemed the best way to do it, because he was a guy.

Food always worked with guys.

"It was no trouble," her daughter informed him, in her best grown-up voice.

Mike, to give him credit, didn't laugh. "Well, we sure appreciate it," Mike told Molly with due seriousness, and then herded them all onto the shady back deck.

Not that Amanda wanted to dwell on it, but Mike definitely cleaned up well. A white polo set off his ruddy skin; the denim shorts even had a belt.

His hand touched her lower back for only a second, yet it was enough to put a tick in her pulse.

Teddy had been spruced up, too, his unruly hair still damp and hard-combed. The dog was completely out of sight, although there was a hint of mournful baying coming from the second floor. The deck table had been cleaned off. The view overlooked their almost-finished water garden.

The kids sat across from each other, while Mike

and Amanda unpacked the picnic basket. "That's an amazing project you took on," she said, wanting her voice to come out as cheerful as a stranger's. Specifically, she wanted to sound like an unfamiliar woman he'd never kissed, and for damn sure, never rattled.

"It's going to take a lot of hours of blood, sweat and tears, but I'm hoping it'll turn out."

His son piped up, "We're gonna put frogs in the pond. And then we'll feed them our own worms."

"Yuck! Mommy," Molly said.

"Remember. Gracious." At Amanda's reminder, Molly bobbed her head in exuberant agreement. And that was when the whole dinner started a crash-dive that just never recovered.

Her sweet daughter looked up at Mike. "We're going to be gracious to you two even if you're complete pigs."

Amanda winced.

"Well. We'll try not to be pigs for you," Mike told her. "What would you kids like to drink?"

"Root beer," his son answered, where Molly said, "Iced tea with a little sugar and a little lemon and two small ice cubes. But not too big a glass because I could spill it. And I can't spill it because I'm being extra polite today. Thank you. Oh. I mean, please. Right, Mommy?"

Amanda glanced under the table. Nope, no room to hide there.

Teddy said to his dad, "What's wrong with her?"

"Nothing's wrong with anyone," Mike said firmly, and stopped choking long enough to deliver drinks. Everyone but her suddenly impossibly fussy daughter were easily pleased by having only to pop a top.

For a short stretch, food captured everyone's attention. Molly sat next to her, crossing her legs exactly as Amanda did. Teddy looked at them both across the table as if they were as fascinating—almost—as dead animals. He started a steady round of kicking, only once in a while kicking Amanda—which was far, far better, she thought, than the Armageddon that would follow if he accidentally kicked Molly.

But those few moments of good luck just couldn't hold. She'd never seen anyone eat as much as Mike— easy proof he was nuts for lasagna. Both kids gained red stains on their clothes, but that was to be expected. One drink spilled. A nearby bee made Molly shriek. Their golden cat with the scary eyes attempted several times to leap on the table.

But it was almost over—and nothing too terrible had happened—until the subject of sex came up.

It wasn't exactly Mike's fault. Everybody was shoveling in food, and Mike took the occasion of quiet to murmur sotto voce, "So…did you have the chance to call your vet?"

She answered carefully. "Yes. At least, I reached her office. She's not in for the next few days. The receptionist said there's a type of morning-after pill. I'm not sure if it applies. We'll see."

"I told you I'd pay."

"Not necessary," Amanda started to say, but hearing the words *we'll see* triggered a knee-jerk response in her daughter.

"Yeah. You know what *we'll see* means. It means we'll talk about it later. That's what Mom said about what your dog was doing to our dog."

"Now, Molly, I didn't—"

Molly had hunched forward, was looking both male Conroys in the eye with her drama-queen face on. "I don't get it. Why your dog would hurt my Darling. My dog is sweet and wonderful. I can't believe you'd let your dog be so mean."

"Honey," Amanda said again, but she was drowned out by Teddy's voice.

"*My* dog isn't mean. *My* dog is the best dog in the whole world. Your dog must have done something," Teddy informed her.

"*My* dog didn't do *anything*. That's why I named her Darling. Because she's a darling. And your dog was *hurting* her."

"He was not!"

"Kids," Amanda said, "Neither dog was hurting the other. Molly, we talked about this."

"No, we didn't. You just said the dogs were playing. They weren't playing. I don't know why you're not telling me the truth, but I know what the truth is this time," Molly said, and turned again to Teddy. "I *saw* it. I *saw* your dog on top of my dog. I think your dog should say he's sorry!"

"Hold it, both of you," Mike said firmly. "Neither dog was being mean. Neither dog was hurting the other. What was going on was…"

He glanced at Amanda, as if asking permission. But as much as she wanted to make the situation better, right then, she was busy wiping up lasagna spots from the table.

So Mike said, "Listen up. That's just what a boy and girl dog do when they really, really like each other."

"Why?" Teddy asked.

"Yeah, why?" Molly echoed.

Again Mike looked at Amanda, this time more desperately. She reached for a spoonful of fruit salad. "Okay," he said, "but you owe me for this." And to the kids, he continued, "Because that's how dogs express when they love each other and want to have puppies."

"But I love puppies," Molly said.

"Everybody loves puppies."

"But you and Mommy were all upset. Why were you all upset if we were going to get puppies!"

"Because," he said, and almost for sure Amanda felt a big bare hairy foot tapping her ankle, "your dog is very young. And we adults felt that maybe she was too young to have puppies quite yet. That it wouldn't be good for her until she was a little older."

"I know what you're talking about now," Teddy piped in. "It's sex. I know all about it," he informed Molly. "I've got a book and everything. I can't read yet, but it's got pictures of frog babies and duck babies and stuff. I'm probably going to learn to read next year."

"I don't care about sex and reading! I care about puppies!" Molly said.

"That's just because you're a girl and you're stupid."

"Stop right there!" Both parents said simultaneously. The potential for war simmered in the air, the kids glaring at each other nonstop...but then Teddy said he had to go to the bathroom.

"You're not going to pee in the yard again, are you?" Molly asked with horror.

Teddy looked at his dad. "You told me I had to be nice. I *been* nice. I been *totally* nice. But I can't be nice *all* the time."

"Just go to the bathroom and we'll talk about it later."

When Teddy headed into the house, Amanda jumped up and started heaping dishes back in the picnic basket. Her daughter was trying to engage Mike in a further discussion of sex and puppies— Molly had a backbone of steel, and when she wanted something, such as puppies, she could be relentless.

There'd be another chance. Hopefully. Maybe. Conceivably. But right now, keeping the kids together any longer was like rubbing poison ivy on bare skin. The gathering tonight needed a fast curtailment. Amanda figured that the faster they got out of there, the better.

"So," Molly continued to grill Mike, "how come people have babies? How come people can't have puppies instead?"

A crash from just inside the house startled the three of them. Mike shot out of his seat, and Amanda was right behind him. Crashes and four-year-olds were never a good sign.

Chapter Five

Amanda only had to step into Mike's living room to grasp the big picture. Near the fireplace, a table lamp had fallen to the ground, its shade askew, its lightbulb and ceramic base in pieces. A tennis ball was in sight. And Teddy was standing in the bathroom doorway. The instant he heard his dad bang through the screen door, he started crying.

"It wasn't me, Dad! I didn't do it! It wasn't me!"

Amanda watched Mike charge over to his son—initially, she was unsure whether he was angry or annoyed or frustrated. But his response conveyed none of those things. He just swiftly scooped up his son and lifted him away from the sharp shards.

Teddy heaved sobs in between extensive explanations to his dad.

"It was a woman who did it. She came in the front door. I said who are you and you'd better get out of here. But she picked up Slugger's ball and threw it at the lamp just like that. I couldn't stop her. I wasn't strong enough. I said, I'm going to get my dad! But then she ran away! It wasn't me, Dad! It was her! The woman!"

Mike set his son on a chair—firmly—with a glance at Amanda.

"Where's your broom or vacuum?" she asked.

"I'll take care of it."

"I'm telling you the *truth,* Dad. She had yellow hair. And she was tall. And she had a big purse. And big, big, big earrings."

"Teddy," Mike said quietly, sternly. "Your mother was not here."

"It wasn't my mother. It was just a woman who looked like her. And had earrings like her. I told her and told her, go away and I'll call my dad. But she still just picked up Slugger's ball…"

Amanda figured it was an ideal time to tiptoe away. She grabbed Molly and the picnic basket and took off for home.

It was another four hours before she could call the day quits. All through the kitchen cleanup and story reads and putting Molly to bed, she kept thinking about Mike—about how he was with his son.

They both had their share of parenting challenges. But she liked how he'd handled Teddy with gentle, calm firmness. How his first thought was to rescue his son from potential harm, not to scold. And how Teddy showed no fear of his dad, only absolute, secure trust, even when the squirt had been inventing an incredibly wild story and had to know there'd be some punishment for throwing the ball in the house and breaking the lamp.

She folded the dish towel, poured a glass of sun tea, turned off lights and ambled outside. Instead of choosing a chair or the chaise, she perched on the deck steps.

The sun had just dropped out of sight, but there was still ample light to see the backyard and the plantings she'd done that morning. Robins pranced in the grass. A dove cooed from the shadows.

Slowly, the sky deepened, softened, darkened. She sipped her tea, set it down, stretched out her legs, relaxed. Stars popped into the sky, which was hardly a surprise on a cloudless night…but suddenly there seemed to be stars in the grass, as well. She sat up, confused, figuring the twinkling lights on the ground had to be some kind of optical illusion. The tiny lights switched on, off, one after the other, all through the yard. Five, then a dozen, then more.

It was crazy. She wandered into the yard, feeling the tickly brush of soft grass beneath her bare feet, and extended a hand...something touched her, then lit up. Another one of those impossible "stars."

"Fireflies. Amazing, aren't they?"

She whirled around, saw Mike's shadow from his deck, and immediately felt her pulse kick up. It was because she wanted to talk to him, of course. It wasn't chemistry. It was that debacle at dinner that she wanted to discuss.

He aimed down the steps, into her yard. Her heartbeat did more of that frisky thing...but there were stars floating and dancing around them, on an evening turned velvet dark, and the man looked downright magical, coming out of the shadows like a prince in a fairy tale.

Obviously her mind couldn't be trusted.

"I've never seen them before. Fireflies? So they're an insect?"

"And ugly in daylight. But they don't bite or sting or hurt anything. They're just putting out flashes to attract the opposite sex."

Like him, she thought. The damned man kept putting out flashes, forcing her pulse to do that thrum thing, making her somehow want to lean closer to him. Not that she did any such thing. "You recovered from dinner? And just for the record, I think you're a hero for taking on the sex-education questions."

He gave a short laugh. "Your daughter had me stumped with the question about why humans have babies and can't have puppies. Not that it's a hard question. Just hard to think up an answer that works for a four-year-old."

"Speaking of four-year-olds...I swear, Mike, my daughter can be absolutely wonderful."

He chuckled again. "I think she is. She's honest. And she stands up. My guess is that all that character comes from the red hair. Your set of genes." And then it was his turn to clear his throat. "And speaking of the other four-year-old...I swear, my son does know how to tell the truth."

"Of course he does. That's just what four-year-olds do. Invent. Imagine. It just gets out of control sometimes."

Mike scraped a hand through his hair. "Well, in my time, we called it lying. The tricky part is that the villain in all his stories is never an ogre or an alligator or a bad guy. It's always a woman who looks just like his mom."

Amanda winced—for both of them. "Touchy." She didn't motion him toward the steps, but they both seem to aim back there. He took one side and she took the other, neither touching...neither even looking at each other. She thought they were both being seriously smart this time.

Besides, there were those magical fireflies to look at.

"You weren't kidding about Teddy having mom issues, were you? Or mom-desertion issues."

He sighed. "I keep trying to turn it around, but I'm

not sure how. I was a lawyer by profession, did I tell you that? Right and wrong questions are supposed to be easy. But even when a divorce is right…even when both sides do their best…it's never so easy for the kids."

"Totally agree." She tried not to turn her head. "You're not working now?"

"No. When I left the downtown firm I was employed by, it wasn't just the divorce, but wanting something with less pressure, less hours, for Teddy's sake. I really wanted to take a couple months off, go after a healthier life here. A kid's life, rather than an adult's city life. All the stuff we talked about before. Speaking of which…do you know what you're doing for preschools?"

She started to laugh…and then he did, too.

"I know," he said wryly. "I can remember when I had the spare time for music, restaurants, a show, whatever. Now it's analyzing what makes a four-year-old fib and deciding whether he needs vaccination shots for preschool. What happened to my real life and will it ever show up again?"

Amanda felt a heart tug…she could have asked the exact same question, and she couldn't believe there was someone else who understood exactly what she was going through. This kind of talk…it wasn't like leaning. It wasn't like counting on a white knight to rescue her. It was just…incredible…to find someone else who needed to reach out for the same reasons.

A friend.

A plain old real friend.

What a wild concept.

"What?" he said, as if trying to read her expression.

"Nothing. I just… It's nice to laugh. Just laugh. Just be with someone else," she said honestly.

"Yeah. No strings. No weirdness. No worrisome anything."

"Exactly," she said, and in that peaceful moment, her sanity took a complete nosedive. There was no explaining it. Mike lurched up from the deck steps to stand up, and start for home. She stood up at the same time, thinking it was time to turn in. Screen doors were open; it's not as if they couldn't hear their kids, but it had been a long day. She suspected he was as ready for an early night as she was, and started to say so.

Only, their shoulders accidentally grazed again, when they were both in motion. And because it was dark, she stumbled on the bottom step. He caught her, kept her from falling. They were still laughing…but then she lifted her laughing face up to his, intending to say something warm and friendly.

Suddenly there was a second of silence. As magical as the firefly night. As compelling as water and food and shelter. As restlessly disturbing as the air just before a thunderstorm.

And then the storm hit.

These weren't like the kisses before. This was Gorilla Glue. Once he pulled her into his arms, she couldn't pull free. Once her mouth found his, he either couldn't or wouldn't let go.

He spun her—possibly just an instinctive moment to protect them both from falling. Whatever the reason, he whirled her down the step, into the grass, into the dark shadows of the yard. A simple turn somehow escalated into a wild, crazy dance. A dance of kisses. A dance of stolen laughter. A dance of silliness at first, yet transformed by the rhythm of silk and shadows into something darker, richer. Sexier.

He murmured something, into her hair, onto her throat, a whisper that tickled her skin, tingled her senses. She lifted her arms to loop around his neck, wanting to look at him, to understand what was going on.

He looked back, but his eyes were too dark, too mesmerizing. His palms skidded down her sides, taking in ribs, waist, hips, shaping her, learning her. Then he bent down for another sweep of a kiss, this one involving teeth and tongues and pressure.

She curved closer, spine bowed, so her breasts and belly could rub against him. She hadn't felt this ignition charge since…since he'd first kissed her. But that was controllable. This wasn't. The divorce had brought on an epic stretch of sexual deprivation. But desire so fierce, so luscious, that she couldn't catch her breath?

He made her feel it. The desire to risk all. The brand of need that tangled every nerve in the body. Abandonment. That's what she wanted. Just once in her life. To abandon all reason, all good sense, and just give into the power of this man, this moment, this incredibly powerful wildness.

A dog suddenly barked. Not his hound. Not her Darling. A neighbor's dog…reminding her—and apparently Mike—that they were in the middle of a neighborhood. His head shot up. She lifted hers at the same time.

This wasn't a Shangri-la with fireflies.

It wasn't a fantasy.

It was real life. With both their kids behind screened doors mere yards away.

"Good grief," she murmured, aware that her shorts seemed to be unbuttoned, her tee dragging off her shoulder. That his tee had been pushed up. Possibly even by her…since no one else appeared to be glued to him.

"Hell," he responded. Then, "You want to hear I'm sorry?"

"No, of course not. It just…happened. I don't believe you planned this. And I sure as heavens didn't."

He nodded, relief in his face as he stepped back.

"Good thing we understand each other. Nice to have a friend where you don't have to sweat guilt or regrets or explanations all the time."

"You said it," she said. Somehow her voice came out oddly hollow. "Thank heavens we're just friends."

Thankfully, sanity returned with daylight…and more sanity shored up after days passed without seeing her neighbor. The mosquito bites faded. The mark on her throat slowly disappeared. The raw feeling in her heart… Well, she banished it. As she was sure Mike had.

They'd been a pinch away from making love. Outside. In the grass. With the fireflies and mosquitoes. In public.

Well.

That certainly wouldn't happen again.

"When's Daddy coming?" Molly asked—for the fifth time in the past five minutes.

Thom had been due a half hour ago. "Any minute now."

"He said we were going to do something special. He said it was a surprise."

"I know, sweetheart."

"Daddy said he's going to buy me a bunch of stuff."

"Did he?" Amanda lifted the brush. They'd already done Molly's hair. Twice. But Molly wanted it "perfect."

"Daddy said we'll have so much fun that I can stay overnight next time."

"I'm sure he believes that's true, lovebug." And it would happen when hell froze over, but Amanda didn't say that to Miss Priss. The outfit for the day, after long deliberation, was a panda-bear tee in purple and pink, pink capris, sandals with panda-shaped bows and, of course, sunglasses with the same motif. Molly, naturally, had coordinated it all.

Amanda contributed a bag with bug spray, sunscreen and a variety of healthy snacks to hand to her ex. The jerk wouldn't think of any of that. He'd be too busy buying off his daughter.

Just a half hour before, the mail had arrived— and she'd gotten the letter from Friend of the Court, expressing Thom's request for full joint custody. She knew why he wanted it. So he could cut her child support.

"Can I go outside, Mom?"

"Sure. We'll wait outside."

Thom was just pulling in. The car was brand-new, a gleaming black hybrid. The devil stepped out, looking handsome as sin—white smile, cool shades, the same elegant posture and walk that had drawn her attention to begin with.

It was embarrassing to remember how naive she'd been back then.

Molly yelled, "Daddy!" And he swung her up and around in his arms as if hoping the whole world was watching—with a camera—so he could prove how much his daughter adored him.

Which Molly certainly did. She chattered ten for a dozen as she crawled into the backseat, automatically strapping herself into the child's seat. He glanced up, said, "Amanda" as if he'd just noticed her.

"You'll have her back by seven?" Amanda said.

"I'm sure you'll call me if I'm five minutes late."

His tone was snotty. She let it go.

Still, seeing him invariably provoked some icky memories. Discovering all Thom's cheating had been a blow—but the worse blow had been his explanations. He actually believed that he was entitled. That casual sex with others "didn't take anything away" from her. He believed they had a terrific life, including a great sex life, so what he did in his spare time would never have mattered, if she just hadn't found out.

Oh, yeah. He'd also mentioned that becoming a mother had made her less physically attractive, less attentive, less adventurous and fun.

He must have thought she needed that extra kick in the teeth.

Now she thought…maybe she had. Because that fight had given her the momentum to kick him out.

She waved goodbye to Molly until the black car turned the corner, then whipped around. She had tons to do today. Drapes. Closet organizing. Rug issues. All the kinds of new-home projects that were boring for Molly, and Amanda could accomplish twice as fast if she were alone.

She'd just reached for the front doorknob when a car pulled into Mike's driveway. Two people emerged from the steel-gray Volvo. The woman, stepping from the passenger side, was a stunner. Salon blond. Tall and sleek, doing the safari linen and khaki style thing. A toned figure that made any normal woman want to slap her.

Mike's ex, Amanda assumed.

But the car's driver was the shocker. The man climbing from the driver's seat was sneezing into a handkerchief. He was a little guy with a sweet face and a comb-over. He wore an immaculate white polo, with creased shorts that unfortunately revealed bony, ropy legs. Possibly he weighed in at one hundred and fifty pounds, after a stuffed dinner. Possibly.

She wasn't *staring*. She'd have gone right back in her house, except that Mike's front door opened, and out zoomed the hound, the cat, Teddy and finally Mike.

The hound and cat looked excited to see the visitors. Teddy was hanging on tightly to Mike's hand.

The driver of the car took one look at the animals, and dove back in the car, sneezing several times in succession. Mike, who had a disreputable look to start with, looked even less shaved, less brushed, less kempt than usual. More sexy. But he definitely had made a point of looking just-woken-up and didn't-give-a-royal-fig.

The blonde crossed the walk, bent down, took Teddy's hand. The squirt was holding back tears, but he talked to his mother and was eventually coaxed into the backseat of the Volvo.

"I'll have a cell phone on all day," Mike told her.

"He'll be fine with me." To Teddy, in a sugary voice, she said, "We're going to have a great day, honey, I promise. And George is really looking forward to our day together."

When the Volvo backed out of the driveway, Mike was still standing there, flanked by the hound and the cat. He spotted her when he turned.

Amanda had a flashback of fireflies and a wild, erotic mating dance…but she tamped that memory down. "*What* was that?" she asked.

"You mean, the guy?"

"Yeah."

"He's one of the main reasons I gave up sex after the divorce."

She'd done a fine job of steering clear of him for almost a week, but shoot. There were some things she could resist. This wasn't one of them. "I'm bringing fresh coffee," she said, went into her house, refilled her mug, filled one for him and crossed the driveways to his front porch.

He was sitting on the front step, with his critters. Cat wasn't about to budge, but the hound made room for her.

He accepted the mug, took a long deep slug of it. Said, "George is a germ freak. He's afraid of dirt and germs. Or about everything important in a little boy's life. Teddy can't do anything right when he's over there—and I'm going to worry about him the whole damned day."

"I would, too."

"I don't want to talk about it," he said firmly, and then, "She's not pushing for custody. Good thing. Because I'd fight her to the wall. But I can't deny her time with Teddy. I mean, she's his mother, for God's sake."

"I understand."

"I don't want to talk about it," he said again, took another gulp of coffee, hunched elbows on his knees and then went on. "I couldn't believe it when I found out she was cheating. I know this sounds damned egotistical, but I honestly believed that part of our lives was fine. Better than fine. So the worst part was finding out she was cheating with *him*."

Since he'd already finished his mug, she handed him hers. She wasn't drinking more coffee anyway. She tried not to breathe. She didn't want anything diverting him from telling her more of the story.

He shot a gesture to the sky. Not the middle-finger gesture. Just a frustrated gesture. "If she was going to cheat, at least it could have been with a better-looking guy. A richer guy. Someone who had some appeal, I could see. But Mr. Dork there? Talk about a kick in the nuts. Not that I want to talk about it."

"I can see you don't."

"But then and there, I voted for celibacy for the rest of my life. I mean, I admit, I worked long hours. But I also made good money. When Teddy was born, I brought in help for her, with the baby and the house. Made sure she had private time to see her friends, take on projects, not always feel tied down. And she was a good mom. I thought. And I thought I was making time for the two of us. We still went out. Did things. Hell. I didn't even know she was unhappy. She just said out of the blue that she was leaving. For George. And told our son that we hadn't gotten along, but Teddy never *saw* us not getting along. So he keeps saying he knows it was because he was too much trouble."

"Yikes," she said gently.

"He's *not* too much trouble. But that bozo makes it all worse, because Teddy can't please him. He really, really tries, but sooner or later, a glass of milk is going to spill. Or he'll forget to flush. Or he'll pick up something he's not supposed to touch. Or he'll do something wrong, on George's terms. Nobody yells at him. He just hates it there. You know what he tells me?"

"What?"

"That going there makes him sick to his stomach. *That's* why I did the worm farm. And dug the water garden in back. I just wanted to let him do certain things—make messes, get dirty. If he spills some water, putting water in the dish for the dog and cat, it's like, so what? He's learning to take care of pets, to look out for them. He's four. How is he supposed to do anything perfect when he's four?"

"Mike?"

"What?"

"It kills me, too. When I have to give up my kid for the day. And I had a huge list of stuff on the day's plate, from curtains to wallpaper to organizing closets. I still have dishes in boxes. And—"

"Good grief. I could get tired, just imagining you trying to accomplish all that."

"I'm tired, just thinking about it. Which kind of sparked a new thought." She hesitated, certain a bad idea was about to surface, yet for that precise second she couldn't analyze why it was so bad. "How about if we spend a few grown-up hours together? Have lunch out. Someplace you'd never take four-year-olds. Then see a movie. Something—*anything*—that's not a cartoon or has Disney anywhere in the credits."

He looked at her. She looked back. He said, "I'll change shoes and get my wallet."

"I have to take the dog out."

"Speaking of which—"

"No, she hasn't been to the vet yet. The whole

thing got kind of complicated. I had an appointment, then their office called and said the vet had a family emergency. But she's seeing Darling in two days. The appointment's made. So that's not a problem on the table today."

"Okay, then. Five minutes. Back here. My car?"

"Fine by me."

Chapter Six

Six hours later, Mike left the Dan Ryan—the expressway where faint-of-heart drivers were tortured at rush hour, a uniquely Chicagoan sport—and turned into the curve toward the western suburbs. They still wouldn't be home for another twenty minutes.

He didn't want the day to end.

He glanced at his passenger. Amanda had never said a word about riding in the pickup, but she was obviously comfortable. Even strapped in, she'd managed to curl her legs under her, had slipped off a sandal.

"This has been the best day," she murmured.

"You're not kidding." He'd been both wary and willing of playing hooky with her. Wary, because she already inspired too many wrong ideas and hormones. And yet willing, because...well, because after his ex-wife drove off, he'd still felt the rug burns on his ego.

Nancy had never said the exact words, but her opinion of him was clear. Lawyer or not, great education or not, he was still hopelessly rough-edged. Too earthy. Too physical. Too sexual. Her choosing 'George' pretty obviously underlined everything she'd found wrong with him. Maybe he'd achieved stature in a notable law firm, but that didn't give him elegance or taste by her standards.

Amanda was distinctly a woman of elegance and taste. So chances were she'd discover those rotten qualities and back off...or his own rug burns would make him too wary to get further involved.

All of which was to say...he'd been able to relax with her today.

Maybe even more than relax. They'd had just plain old ordinary fun. She'd picked the lunch spot, a place where she got to choose lobster bisque and he could vote for a raw red steak. Their entrees echoed how different they were, but that didn't seem to matter. The restaurant was packed with a professional lunch crowd. All adults. No spills, no screams, no, "I don't want this!" or "Are we done yet?" or "I'm bored, Dad!"

The movie was even better. She'd picked the restaurant, so he'd picked the movie. It was the first flick he'd seen in ages that had some skin, some blood, some action. She could eat the chocolate she wanted. He could have his own popcorn. No one whispered in his ear. No one claimed they had to go to the bathroom three times. He actually got to see a movie from start to end.

It's not as if this were a date….

He wasn't aware he'd spoken aloud, until Amanda chuckled. "Of course it wasn't a date. We're not *dating*. We just had a grown-up afternoon." She sighed with contentment. "No Bambi. No comic-book characters. And I had the whole chocolate bar."

He laughed. "You had two, I believe."

"Yeah, I admit I went overboard—but I haven't had a whole chocolate bar to myself in…well, in years. I'm always trying to think about setting the right example." She smiled at him again. "That's the best part. A whole afternoon without any 'shoulds' or 'have tos'."

Damned, if he didn't feel exactly the same way. It was funny, but he hadn't been easy in his own skin for a long time now. Certainly not when he was married. There always seemed to be something he was doing or saying wrong, something that was going to get analyzed and criticized.

It seemed unbelievable—if not downright crazy— that he could feel that rare sense of easiness with her.

By the time he pulled in his driveway, she was still

smiling...and so was he. "We have a couple of hours before the kids are due home," she said.

"Yeah. Both of us might even catch a nap or some reading time." He climbed out at the same time she did, stretched. Cat and Slugger burst out of the pet door as if they hadn't seen him in a decade. Cat slapped Slugger with a paw when the hound tried to reach him first. Slugger immediately howled, but he couldn't have been hurt too badly, because he kept galloping, ears flapping in the wind.

Amanda laughed and then kept on laughing. "I'm afraid I'll be greeted the same way when I walk in the door."

And she turned that way...but she didn't seem in any rush to race home. They both seemed to linger. Just standing there. He'd tried not to pay attention, but the warmth of late-afternoon sunshine brushed her shoulders, turned her hair into fire, and her eyes—he swore—were as emerald-green as the jewel.

"Well...thanks for a great afternoon," she said, and bounced up—as if she intended to give him a friendly, neighborly hug.

He thought that fast hug was a great idea—a way to underline how easily they were going to maintain the friendship thing. Only...once she lifted up on tip-toes, she seemed to hesitate. The shine in her eyes seemed to darken. He felt the brush of those sassy high breasts, the graze of her pelvis, the scent of her skin take over his air space.

In that spare second, he couldn't seem to breathe—except for her. Couldn't seem to move—because those basic touches ignited a maelstrom of furious wants and noisy needs. Couldn't seem to control the hunger—to kiss her again.

He didn't.

She didn't.

For a good, long three seconds.

It was her fault things changed, he was pretty sure, because she was the one who swung her arms around his neck. But then…hell. He couldn't keep his mouth off hers, and the kiss became a banquet of tasting, taking, wooing. He had to touch her. Had to. He stroked down her spine, the route not familiar, just familiar enough so that he knew the curve in her back, knew a palm on her fanny brought a groan… and encouraged her to lean even tighter into him.

Invitations hung in the air, unseen, invisible, but real as the sunlight. *Maybe* suddenly seemed the longest word in the English language, analyzed between her lips and his, between the silken brush of her hair in the breeze, between the heat he could feel rising in her skin, through her skin…into him.

She lifted her head, opened stunned-soft eyes, looked straight at him.

She swallowed. He got his breath back. She remembered to drop her hands from around his neck. He remembered to drop his hands from around her back. The flush on her cheeks—there was no changing that.

There was no changing the brick inside his jeans, either.

But suddenly she turned her head, said out of the complete blue, "We really do need a fence between our yards, to keep our pets separated."

"Yeah, you mentioned that before." Since she created the diversion, he was more than willing to embellish it. "Instead of a barrier kind of fence…what would you think about an electric one?"

"What a great idea. Then your dog and my dog can't cross over. But then it won't be an unfriendly fence. It'll just…you know. Help."

Exactly what he thought. Maybe their dogs didn't need it—but he sure as hell did. He needed something that would zap him—electrocute him if necessary—when he felt the urge to touch her again.

The electrocution idea seemed to gain momentum all on its own, because when he heard the sound of a car pulling in his drive, he jumped back from Amanda as if the foot between them was electrically charged.

The man climbing down from a tan SUV was a complete stranger. He was short and plump, sweating under his golf tan. He wore the usual suburban uniform of polo shirt and shorts, and approached them with a waxy smile and a hand raised to shake. "Hello. I live in the first house at the top of the cul-de-sac. I know you're Amanda Scott and Mike Conroy. I hope you both got a note from me when you first moved in."

If Mike had, he didn't remember it. Amanda did. "From the Home Owners' Association?"

"Yes, that's right."

"I thought it was nice of you to welcome a newcomer to the neighborhood that way," Amanda said warmly.

"I thought we'd better have a little talk before there were problems," Warren White said cordially.

"What problems?" Mike said warily.

"We have some rules in the neighborhood. Ordinances. Policies to keep the neighborhood to a standard we all like."

"Exactly what rules?" Mike's spine was instinctively stiffening. If this guy was going to try playing law games with him, he should have done his homework.

"I'm afraid you can't put a water garden in your backyard without permission."

"I beg your pardon?"

"And, Amanda, I'm afraid you need permission to plant trees, as well."

"What? You mean, the little dogwood I planted yesterday—?"

Warren kindly shook his head. "I'm afraid you needed permission. I'm sorry you didn't get it ahead of time."

Warren promised to put a list of the rules in each of their mailboxes. There were rules about what time a person could water their grass. Rules about recycling. Rules about noise. Rules about dandelion control. Rules about the length of grass allowed. Rules about no parking on the street overnight, no RV parking, no sheds put up in the yards—without permission. "Many people want fences, but we don't want the look of the neighborhood to deteriorate, so before putting in a fence, that's another thing you need to have permission for—"

"When exactly are these Home Owners' Association meetings, and where are they held?" Mike interrupted abruptly.

"Every third Thursday of the month. 7:00 p.m., after dinner. Because I'm president this year, I usually hold them in my family room. You're both welcome to attend. But I do assure you that the covenant rules are all legally binding."

For no apparent reason, Amanda suddenly snugged her hand in his, pressing hard, and stepped just a bit in front of him. "Thanks so much for stopping by, Mr. White. I suspect we're both likely to attend your next meeting. Thanks for filling us in."

When the superficial, supercilious jerk backed out of the driveway, she dropped his hand. "Okay. *Now* you can froth at the mouth. But try not to bellow at least until he's out of sight."

"Why would you think I was angry?"

"A wild guess," she assured him. "Although seeing you exhale fire was probably the first clue."

"Well, who elected him God? Did we suddenly land in a dictator state, or is this still America? What possible reason can there be why I can't have a water garden? And if he thinks I'm taking it out, he's about to find out why I made law partner when I was still in my twenties."

"Mike."

"What?"

"Try and remember that we're in a foreign country. I think they call it the suburbs."

Okay, okay, so she made him laugh in spite of himself.

And right then, Nancy and her George drove up—almost two hours earlier than planned. Teddy peeled out of the car faster than a criminal just granted parole.

Mike still wanted to finish his conversation with Amanda, but abruptly her hot-shot ex pulled in next door with Molly.

There was no more time to worry about sex or embraces or how damn much she was starting to mean to him.

From the look on his son's face, it was going to be a ticklish evening. And from the look on Molly's... Amanda was going to have her hands even more full.

* * *

Amanda didn't want to leave Mike. She knew the neighborhood "representative" had rubbed him the wrong way. Warren White struck her as the kind of ineffectual person who had no power in his real life, so he got a thrill out of imposing rules on others about their water-sprinkling schedules. Still. Mike should realize the guy was just a pompous wannabe bully... not a real problem.

In the meantime, though, she couldn't be the one to calm him down.

She definitely had her hands full with Molly.

Her daughter submitted to a bath, willingly changed into pink baby-doll pajamas, but after that, she folded her arms across her chest with a major diva scowl. "I want some mommy time and I want it *now.*"

It wasn't as if Amanda hadn't been through this before. She put a fluffy blanket on the deck. Brought out the tray of nail polishes. Molly brought her doll-size tea set. The teapot was filled with milk.

"Daddy tricked me!" was the dramatic opening to Molly's tirade.

"How, honey?"

"He was real nice and real nice and real nice. Only, then we got to his house. And there was a lady there. A *stupid* lady."

Across the way, Amanda could see lights popping on and off at Mike's house. Her attention was on her daughter, but a thick clog seemed to have settled in her stomach. Mike was probably doing exactly what she was. Dealing with a child wounded by their divorce. Through no fault of their own, his Teddy and her Molly were both still reeling from the mistakes of their parents.

Molly, temporarily, stopped her rant to study her hands, which had been soaked and filed and were now ready for the fun part. Color. "Can we do our toenails after our hand nails?"

"Sure."

"I want yellow for my toenails."

"I'm pretty sure we have yellow." Amanda didn't actually look at the basket of polishes, but since color was always a major issue for her daughter, she was almost positive they had the whole crayon set of choices.

"And I want different colors for every hand nail."

"Okay." Amanda had learned a long time ago never to sweat the small stuff. "Now tell me more about your day."

"She had on this big fakey smile. Like grown-ups use for kids. And she says, 'How would you like to go shopping with me?' And I say, 'No, thanks, I'm here to see my dad.' And she says, 'If we go shopping, I thought I'd get you an American Girl doll.' And I say, 'No, thank you, my mommy gets me all the American Girl dolls I could possibly want.'" Molly looked up with stormy eyes. "Okay. So that was a lie. And it was really hard to say no, because I *really, really* need another American Girl doll. But she was being a pain."

"Honey. Sweetheart. Now, think a minute. It doesn't sound like she was being a pain. It sounds as if she was trying very, very hard to be nice to you."

"No. She just wanted to give me a doll so I'd like her. And I'm never going to like her. She had three boxes of games. And grape Kool-Aid. So fine. I played some games with her. But you know what?"

"What?" Amanda finished one of her daughter's hands, then started on the other.

"Daddy wasn't even *there* half the time. And he didn't play any games with me. But when he was there, you know what he did?"

"What, honey?"

"He and that lady took me to the back of the house, opened the door and said, 'Ta da!' And there was this room where I'm supposed to sleep when I'm there. It had a big white chair. And a big white bed. And shelves that already had books in them. And lots of stuffed animals all over the place."

Amanda felt her heart clutch. "It sounds very pretty."

Molly glowered at her mother. "I know it's pretty. That's not what was wrong. What was wrong is that *I don't sleep there*. Which I told them. Daddy said, 'But you will.' And the woman said, 'And when you come and stay with us, we want you to have your own special place.'"

Molly started blowing on both hands, trying to dry the polish faster. "I didn't say what I wanted to say. I remembered that I was supposed to be good, so I said, 'The room's real nice. Thank you.' And then I said, 'But I'm not sleeping over. Ever.' And you know what?"

"What, sweetheart?"

"The lady called me a brat. *Me. A brat!*"

"Oh, dear."

"So then I told her she was ugly. Which she is. And I said she must be stupid, too, because she couldn't even win at Candy Land. And she didn't even know to cut the crusts off my sandwich, either!"

Amanda had to zip her mouth closed. Obviously she couldn't say what she really wanted to, such as that she'd like to whack Thom upside the head—and that went double for The Bitch. She'd particularly like to tear out The Bitch's heart for trying to win over her daughter with material crap, and even more wanted to scream at her ex for not spending parenting time with his daughter himself.

But she couldn't just agree with Molly, because that would fuel her daughter's unhappiness with Thom.

So she just listened. And once they finished all the nail painting, she cuddled her daughter on the deck rocker until Molly was sleepy enough to fold into bed. Tomorrow, when the little one was less upset,

Amanda figured she'd think of some positive, constructive things to say about the day's debacle.

Tonight, she wasn't up for it.

For a half hour, she cleaned up toys, threw in a wash load, wiped down the kitchen. The whole time she was building up a good serious brood.

The whole evening had exemplified—painfully— why she had to quit playing attraction games with her next-door neighbor. The divorce was still fresh for her daughter. Molly had to be her one hundred percent primary concern. And just as relevant, Amanda knew perfectly well that her marriage, and divorce, established her stupid judgment about men.

There was no trusting her feelings for Mike. The magic, the pull, the wonder…that was the fairy tale. The wanting to believe there was a hero, a knight, a good man just for her. The wanting to believe in "in love."

The feeling that she was already *in* love with the damn man.

This was all exactly why she'd given up sex. Because she couldn't trust herself. Because she wanted her daughter to grow up seeing a strong, self-reliant mother…not a dependent female who couldn't get along without a man.

She had to *show* her daughter that she was strong, not just tell her.

Which meant she needed to just cool it with Mike. At least, for a much longer period of time.

That all settled in her mind, Amanda started turning out lights, closing up, locking the doors. When she climbed the stairs for bed, at the top stair she glanced out the window.

Night had fallen in a whisper of dew and stardust. Mike was upstairs, in his second-story window. He'd turned off his lights, too. He was probably enjoying just a few moments of peace and silence, probably no different than she was…but then he spotted her.

She could have moved. Could have waved. Could have…done pretty much anything.

But somehow heat transmitted across the driveways, through the closed windows, somehow past all the reasons she needed to get a serious brain.

She didn't just feel a pull toward him. She felt a force field.

He put a hand on his window.

Like a damn fool romantic idiot, she put a hand on her window.

And then, before she could do anything more stupid, she whipped around and headed straight, no talking, no thinking, no deterrents, to her bed. Alone. The way she needed to be.

Chapter Seven

Rain shivered down the windows, starting at day-break. Clouds bunched and punched, building into a dark gloomy morning even before breakfast. As Mike poured coffee, he studied his son.

Teddy had come home yesterday in a rare silent mood. He'd been contentious, crabby, couldn't settle in to play anything, wouldn't talk. Mike hadn't pushed him. Hell, the kid was as male as he was. Neither of them wanted to talk about *feelings*...but Mike figured a good night's sleep might help clear the air.

He'd set up the playing field to make talk easier. Let Teddy turn on cartoons—which Mike hated; he didn't like kids doing the whole veg-out-in-front-of-the-TV thing. But cartoons and scrambled eggs invariably brought out conversation, particularly when Teddy was allowed to eat in the living room.

His tough guy was curled up on the couch, still wearing his dinosaur pj's, Slugger glued to his side—a sure sign that Teddy was upset. Still, the kid had the remote. And a deep bowl of the scrambled eggs—this, because Mike had learned early on that the deeper the bowl, the less chance of spilled eggs all over the house.

Mike took the recliner with his plate and a mug of coffee. "So, hey. You never said anything about the zoo yesterday. You did go, didn't you?"

"Yeah."

"So, was it as fun as you thought it'd be?"

"It was fun for one whole second. Until George started sneezing and sneezing." Teddy, who rarely had power over the remote, was channel surfing at dizzying speeds. "He was the one who said he *wanted* to go. That was the thing. He kept saying we'd have fun. Only, he already *knew* he was 'lergic to animals."

Mike was already forming a wincer of a picture. "Okay. Then what happened?"

"We had to leave. That's what happened. Because he couldn't stop sneezing. But he said he'd make it up to me. We'd go to a nice place for lunch." Teddy froze on a different cartoon, then hit the trigger again.

"And?"

"And I thought he meant McDonald's. Chuck E. Cheese. Burger King. Someplace *good*. Instead it was this place where you had to wait and wait and wait. It had a tablecloth, and I didn't mean to pull it, but it was itching at my knees. So his drink got acc'dentally spilled. It wasn't my fault."

"What else happened?"

"We went back to their place. Mom played cards with me. Go Fish. Crazy Eights. Then I said, 'You wanna go swimming?' She said, 'Maybe another time.' I said, 'You wanna do a movie or something?' She said, 'Sure.' Only, she just turned on the TV. Not like going to a movie. And when she got a movie on, then she just left, started doing things. Talking on the phone. Talking to *him*. Cooking. Junk like that. Dad?"

When Teddy left the trigger at a news channel, Mike knew exactly how upset his tough guy was. "What, sport?"

"Mom doesn't want to be with me. She doesn't even like me. I want to be *here*. With you. All the time. I don't want to go with her anymore. And you know what else?"

"Tell me."

"George said I was rude. And he said I wasn't 'siplined."

'Siplined? Mike thought. "Disciplined?"

"That's what I *said*," Teddy said crossly. "And I said to mom on the way back, 'I don't get it. Why you're with him when you could be with Dad.' That's when he said I was rude."

Mike winced. "You asked your mom while he was right there in the car, huh?"

"Well, yeah. I didn't ask before. I wasn't thinking about it before. I asked her when I was thinking about it." Teddy put the bowl on the floor, then burrowed deeper into the cushions. Slugger burrowed after him. Cat suddenly leaped on the couch, looking fierce and lionlike. "This is how I like it, Dad. Us guys together. No more girls."

Mike remembered last night…whenever it was… when his house and Amanda's house were both closed down for the night, and he'd just stood at the window for a moment, inhaling the quiet…and there she was.

He wasn't touching her. Wasn't thinking about her. He'd been thinking about his kid. And her kid. And what divorces did to kids, and why he needed to get back to the Celibacy Principle. But then he'd looked at her and felt that…yearning.

Yearning to be with her.

To talk to her. To touch her. To hold her and be held.

This morning, of course, turned into another wake-up call. Yearning was just yearning. Sex was just sex. It wasn't the time. Period.

"Did you hear that?" Teddy grumbled.

"Yeah." Mike bounced up from the recliner, not certain if the sound was an actual knock on the back door—but something had provoked Slugger into going into his nose-to-the-sky warning bay. Of course, some days, a purr of a breeze could do that.

In this case, though, a pint-size rock star stood at the back door—at least Mike thought Molly's getup was about that. The sunglasses were unnecessary for a stormy morning, but the little shirt was full of glistening stars. Her red hair was all braided and pinned up with sequins or jewels or something. Her nails were painted like rainbows and her shoes had flashing lights.

At four years old, she had a petrifying amount of estrogen.

She might even be as bad as her mother in a few years.

Right then, though, he figured they had a more immediate problem on their plate. Molly was out of breath from running. Her lower lip was trembling, her big eyes spattering tears. "Mr. Mike. I need a punger. Right now. Right *right* now. For my mom!"

"A punger," Mike said blankly.

"A punger! You know! A punger!" Quickly she said, "*Please! This is serious!*"

"A punger," Mike repeated, but then he got it. Plunger. Plumbing problems. Some kind of major uh-oh. "Tell your mom I'll be right there."

"It needs to be *now*."

"I understand, Molly. I just need to get a tool kit and the plunger."

"But don't tell mommy I told you. She told me to

sit in the living room, that she could handle it. But there was water *everywhere*. And she was saying bad words. I'd tell you what the words were, but I can't say them. My mommy says that nobody says those words in her house. Or my house. My mom—"

"Okay, honey. We're going to stop talking now, and start moving." He pushed on shoes, then grabbed tools, locked up the baying Slugger and herded Teddy out with him. He suspected Amanda might just guess that someone had "told" on her—particularly when he showed up with a plunger and tools—but that wasn't remotely relevant.

Keeping his hands off her was one issue.

Not helping her if she was in trouble was completely different.

He yelled a hello when he opened her back door. "Oh, it's you, Mr. Mike!" said the rock star in her loudest voice. She was still wearing the shades. "What a surprise! It's Mr. Mike, Mom!"

"Molly Ann! Did you go next door and—"

"Me?" But to Mike, she lifted her head and whispered, "I'm in trouble."

"I'll fix that. You and Teddy either play or watch some TV for a little while, okay?"

It wasn't hard to locate Amanda. The place had deteriorated since he saw it last. There seemed to be a whole bunch more purples and pale blues. Pillows. More pillows. Stuff to run into, stuff on top of tables. Flowers all over the place. But the main downstairs bathroom—where the descriptive vocabulary was coming from—had water seeping into the hall.

She must have heard him set down the tool kit, because she started talking—even though she hadn't wasted a second turning around. "Go away, Mike. I can fix my own problems! I am not looking for someone to save me every time I get into some stupid mess!"

"Okay."

"This would *not* be a good time to laugh."

"Okay."

"Don't say one word! I mean it! Just go back home!"

Weeellll. He couldn't quite say okay to that. The bathroom had definitely been redefined since his last visit. Now it seemed to be covered in butterflies. Butterfly wallpaper, butterfly pictures, butterfly toilet seat, towels embroidered with butterflies. It was almost enough to give a guy a rash—if he'd had the time to itch.

Amanda was pretty wet. Knees, feet, clothes. Towels had been used to sop up the water—or some of it. A few rolls of paper towels had been used for the same purpose. At some point she'd had a book open—*Basic Plumbing Repairs*—but that likely wasn't helping her a whole lot at this point, because it was like learning to sail after your boat had already capsized.

"I do *not* want advice. Don't you say one word!"

"I won't, I won't." He was still trying to evaluate the situation. Not the plumbing problem. Her. Amanda was the only problem that mattered. She wasn't crying, exactly. At least there were no sissy, sad tears leaking down her cheeks. This was more…a major, furious, sputtering type of crying.

He said carefully, "Behind the toilet is a shutoff valve."

"You think I didn't know that?" She huffed. *"Where?"*

"Just behind there. Look. You'll see it. Turn it off—against the clock. If it's too tight or hard to move, I could—"

"Do not touch anything. *I will do* it. And don't tell me any more, either!"

"Okay." It was amazing…almost from the minute he'd met her, he'd been tensed up. It was that relentless attraction thing. But now, finally, he could relax. He didn't have to worry about falling in love with her anymore. She was a shrew. A witch times ten. She had a completely unreasonable and irrational side.

"Do we know what went down the toilet that shouldn't have?" he asked delicately.

"An American Girl doll shoe."

"A doll's shoe," he repeated.

"Possibly both shoes. She was dressing the doll when she went potty. Now the shoes are gone. And right after she left the bathroom, this all—" she motioned "—started."

"Okay. Now, has the toilet run before? I mean, constantly run?"

"I just moved in this house. It was new, but not brand-new. Is there some reason in the *universe* I should know that answer for sure?"

"No, no," he said in his best tiptoe voice. "It's just that the more we know, the better chance we have of understanding the whole problem."

"*I'm* the *only* one who has to understand *anything*."

"You're so right." Hell, his pulse was practically humming. At the moment, she was as easy to love as a stingray. A splotchy-cheeked, furious, unmanageable stingray. "Amanda, I don't know if you have an auger, but I happened to bring one over. I wasn't going to use it myself. But you could. If you wanted to."

"I don't even know what a flipping auger is! Go home, Mike!"

"I'm going. I promise. In just a second. I just want to show you the auger… See? On one end, it has a corkscrew. So you push that end down into the hole… then you turn the handle—clockwise—until the entire spring has been fed into the pipe as far as it'll go. The idea is to reach the obstruction…"

She tried. The first time she didn't quite get it, and shot him a look filled with venom. Probably snake venom.

"I won't offer to do it, I swear," he promised, hands in the air. "It's just…you could try it again. In fact, you could try it a couple of times. If you wanted to. And when this is all over, you might want to put some ice on that elbow."

"I'm not hurt."

"I'm sorry. I didn't mean to say anything nice. It just slipped out…and yeah, you've got it now. That's the how of it. So when the auger's all the way in, you could try—only if you want to!—to slowly, slowly pull the spring back. If that doesn't free up the doll's shoe, you could try it a second time."

Thank God it worked. Out came a little white shoe. Amazing how much trouble a shoe less than two inches long could cause a person in life.

She started breathing a little better. Not a *lot* better. But definitely an improvement over the hyperventilating, crying, fire-breathing dragon she'd been a half hour ago.

"Okay now. I'm leaving. I'm going to take a wild guess that you don't have an indoor-outdoor vac— why would you? So I'll just bring mine over, leave it on your deck. It should suck up this water in no time. But before I leave…maybe you might want to turn on the water again. Remember? The shutoff valve? This time you turn it the other way."

"I hear patronizing in your voice."

"I swear. There isn't a patronizing thought in my head." His tone probably sounded virtuous because he was telling the complete truth. There was nothing on his mind but fear. He just wanted to get out of the house alive.

When she did the shutoff-valve thing and the crisis was finally completely over—except for the cleanup—she started crying again.

This time, he just backed away. There was a time to hold a woman. And a time when a man knew he'd sure as hell better get out of Dodge.

He was in bare feet by then, but he picked up his sandals by the back door, went searching for Teddy and Molly. The two were lying on the floor, leaned up on their elbows, watching TV. Only not cartoons. They were watching a mother give live birth. Apparently the event had just happened.

"Holy mother of…" Mike got calm, fast. In three long strides, he grabbed the remote, clicked off the TV and set it high on the mantel. "Molly. Do yourself a *big favor* and don't tell your mother what you were just watching. You can tell her another day. Just not today."

"I won't, Mr. Mike. Princess and Darling and me are going stay out of Mommy's way for a while."

"Good. Teddy. With me."

"But, Dad. Did you see all that blood? Wasn't it gross? Can we watch it at our house?"

"Zip it, Theodore. Not one word until we're back in our own house. Not *one*. Not even a little one. You have no idea how serious I am."

"Me, too, Dad," his son assured him. "I'm *really* serious."

Mike wanted to laugh...and then did. When a day started out this rough, it could only go up—because it sure couldn't get any worse.

The morning couldn't possibly get worse, Amanda was sure. But of course it did. The bathroom was still going to take hours to clean up, and Darling had an appointment with the vet at 10:00 a.m.

And then, out of the blue, her mother showed up. Gretchen regarded the whole plumbing mess, offered to hire a cleaning service to immediately come and take care of it, and that caused an argument. It wasn't a *bad* argument, or a mom-daughter sniping event, nothing like that. It was just that her mother couldn't hear a "No, thank you" with a megaphone.

Eventually Gretchen mentioned the reason for her visit—she wanted to take Molly swimming. That was totally a *good* thing, except that it took time to get gear together for an afternoon at a pool. And her mom was barely out the door before the phone rang.

It was her attorney, who wanted a meeting related to Thom's filing for joint custody. That wasn't exactly *bad*. She wanted to be prepared for the court date. It was just that any thought of Thom's sharing custody put a worried dent in her heart.

As if the morning didn't have enough complications, she'd barely finished with the floor and had a first load of towels and rags in the washer when there was a knock at the front door. A large truck had backed into her driveway. All the heavy things she'd ordered were being delivered—from the bricks to the patio stones, to the shiny green riding lawn mower.

The delivery guys took nearly an hour—but Amanda's mood brightened immediately.

It was the lawn mower. She'd almost forgotten about it. Her parents hadn't moved to the suburbs until she was in college; she'd just never been exposed to lawn-care issues. But now, the machine immediately made her think of Mike.

Ever since he'd come over that morning—and damn him, been a hero for her yet *again*—she'd wanted to gallop over there and heartily apologize. Only, darn it, it wasn't that simple. It was probably a good thing that something happened to force distance between them.

He'd seen her at her worst. That was good. It'd stop him from looking at her with those…well, with those eyes. Those eyes that communicated that he thought her damned incredible. Not just attractive, but compelling. Interesting. That he valued being with her. That he went crazy when he touched her.

So. Possibly her behaving like the witch of the universe was a secret godsend. But the lawnmower was another godsend—because it would give her the chance to make up.

Once the delivery man left, she sat on the lawnmower seat with a coffee mug and the instruction manual. Then turned her new baby on. A few stripped gears later, and she had the hang of it...or she would, once she got the speed thing under control.

Her mood moved from low to a reasonable soar. She didn't need a man to do work. Just because she wasn't mechanical didn't mean that she couldn't learn—or teach her daughter to learn.

She'd show Mike competence. She'd *be* competent. He didn't have to know what it was all about—how desperately she wanted to change, how much she never wanted to lean on a man again. Maybe plumbing crises were never going to be her thing, but this adorable riding mower was downright fun.

She finished her lawn, which she had to admit, represented a little learning curve. A few spots were higher than other spots. She'd sort of bumped a couple of trees. There was one small strip of grass in the front yard that she'd sort of missed. But she'd learned. And now she headed next door.

His yard was bigger than hers, but simpler. Naturally she wasn't going anywhere near the water-garden construction site, but he had a long, long backyard. For once, she was doing something for *him*. Not just making up for being a bitch this morning...but actually doing something nice. Decent. Something a friend would do.

Best yet, he was gone—so he'd come home

to a freshly mowed lawn—and not even know it was her.

She was within a few swipes of finishing in the front, when her brand-new baby started coughing. Then sputtering. Then gave out a death sigh and just plain stopped.

She'd run out of gas.

Chapter Eight

When Mike pulled into the driveway around two o'clock, Teddy's mood shifted from cranky and whiny to ecstatic. His four-year-old hadn't appreciated his first visit to the dentist, even though they'd done a fast-food lunch and a romp in the park afterward.

"It still hurts, Dad," Teddy whined, as he unsnapped his seat belt. But then he saw the tractor. That was the last Mike heard about the dentist. Now it was all, "Oh, wow, oh, wow, oh, wow!"

Mike may have climbed from the pickup more slowly, but his son's oh-wow opinion echoed his own. Certainly he'd never seen the behemoth of a lawn mower parked in his front yard before.

"We don't climb on equipment that isn't ours,

Teddy," he admonished. But hey, he couldn't resist doing a leisurely stroll around the thing, giving it a thump and pat and an admiring general look-see. Slugger ambled out of the dog door to greet them—well, mostly to greet Teddy. The hound hadn't appreciated having his man parts clipped at the vet's, and he was still letting Mike know about it. Still, all three boys slowly circled the machine with equal reverence.

"Is it ours, Dad?"

"No."

"Why not? If it's in our yard? Whose is it?"

"I don't know. But I'm pretty sure I can make a good guess."

"Maybe I could just sit in the seat for a second."

"Maybe we never do that without the permission of the owner."

Mike wanted to shake his head. Not at his son. At the mower. It was a John Deere. A beauty. One of the X700 series. Forty-eight-inch mower deck. Color-coded buttons, cruise control, CD player, four-wheel steering.

It was the kind of riding mower that a landscaping company owned. Or maybe a golf course. Not that Mike knew much about tractors, but he was pretty sure this one checked in at several thousand. No one—that is, no one normal—would buy such a thing for a regular-size yard that he could imagine. So that was the first clue to its owner.

The second clue was that *his* yard had been mowed. It would recover, of course. Grass always grew back.

The third clue was when he figured out why it was sitting in his yard. It had run out of diesel.

Add it all up, and Mike glanced next door...only to see Amanda bouncing into her drive. She pelted out of the car, popped the lid on the trunk. "Hi, guys!" she called out. "I'll get the mower out of there! Would you believe it? I ran out of fuel! So I had to run to the gas station, but I've got it, I've got it—"

"Miss Amanda? Can I sit on it? Can I?"

"Yes, honey—but *only* if your dad or I'm there. Okay? No one else can give you permission but us."

"Okay. I love you," Teddy mentioned, and that was the end of his talking to her. Amanda kind of stopped dead when he said the word *love,* but instead of looking at his son, her eyes shot straight up to his.

Mike's response was identical. To make eye contact that instant. It was one of those rare mind-meld moments. As if they were the only two people in the universe who realized there was an avalanche big enough to destroy them all. Maybe no one else saw it. But they did. Maybe no one else had a clue. But they did.

All morning he'd tried to reassure himself that he wasn't falling. It should have helped that she'd been as unreasonable as a shrew with PMS that morning. But it hadn't.

After a morning of major plumbing messes, apparently lawn mowing, then running out of diesel, Amanda was still Amanda. Her scoop-neck top had grass stains; her shorts looked almost wrinkled… but they matched. Pale blue and dark blue. Her hair hadn't seen a brush in a while, which meant it was like copper on fire in the sunlight, pretty wild…but she still had on lip gloss, cute sandals, earrings.

She almost fell under the weight of the diesel can, but she managed to pluck it out of the trunk, her smile fifty times more powerful than a kilowatt. "You don't have to thank me," she chattered on. "I owed you, for all the stuff you've done for me. I was totally happy to find something I could do the other way around! I just didn't realize how much fuel it would take to mow both yards. Or how much fuel they put in to start with. And it took me a little while to figure out how to run it. I've never mowed grass before! Would you believe it?!"

He believed it. It just didn't seem wise to agree with her, much less while she was still struggling with the fuel container. "You want me to do that for you?"

"No, no sweat, I can do it!"

"Amanda."

"Huh?"

He tried to make his voice sound light and conversational and delicate—although possibly he was incapable of managing "delicate." "Who sold you this mower?"

"Oh. The hardware store. The guy was wonderful. Seriously. Gave me exactly what I asked for."

He aimed for the same ultralight tone. "And you asked for…?"

"I told him that I only wanted to buy one mower in a lifetime, so for sure I didn't want junk. And I wanted one with power, because I'm not particularly physically strong. I wanted quality, serious dependability, nothing that I'd have trouble servicing…"

Okay, he was beginning to see how she'd gotten in so much trouble. She'd asked good questions. She'd just asked the wrong salesperson. "Did he ask you what size yard you have?"

"Sure. But it's not as if I had the exact dimensions. I just told him straight. *Big.*" She shot him another grin, as she finished feeding diesel into the mower and screwed the top back on. Suddenly, though, her smile faded. "Why all the questions? Do you think I made a bad choice?"

She'd made a terrible choice. It wasn't just the money, but that it was way too much machine for what she needed. But suddenly that wasn't the point. Her breathtaking smile had completely disappeared now, and in its place was a look of uncertainty… fragility.

In a flash, he realized he'd seen that look of raw

uncertainty before. This morning. In between moments when she'd more or less been chewing him up,
no matter what he said. Still. There'd been glimpses
of That Look.

He remembered her saying more than once that
she'd been raised as a spoiled, sheltered princess.

But he hadn't added it up before. How much she'd
been life-crippled by her background, and how much
that bothered her. The basic practical information
most people knew, she just plain didn't. Common
sense wasn't common, not the way she was raised.
And she was trying. Watching her with the plunger
and the "Dare To Repair" book that morning…
watching her in the hardware store, picking out tools,
painting on her own, and yeah, now, diving into the
mechanics of lawn mowing and mowers.

"What?" she said impatiently. "You think I didn't
pick the right machine?"

"I think you're brilliant. That you picked the
best."

The shoulders eased. The smile went back to being
shiny and disarming…and sexy. "Well. I know I
didn't know what I was doing. But I tried to ask the
right questions—"

"You're going to be the envy of the neighborhood."

"I don't care about that. But I can do this. My lawn.
Your lawn. That kind of maintenance. There's no
reason I should have to ask for help. Or hire it out."

He didn't look back at the butcher job. And if anyone else made a remark to her, well, he'd just have to kill them.

As if suddenly realizing he wasn't the center of attention, Teddy edged forward and said to Amanda, "Guess what? I went to the dentist this morning. For the first time in my whole life. The dentist let me squirt the water. It was really cool."

Mike stared at his son, astonished at Teddy's volunteering such a creative version of this morning's events. But then, men seemed genetically programmed to reinvent certain events or truths, if it meant impressing a female they cared about.

Damn. It was getting harder and harder to deny it. It wasn't just his son who cared. Mike was sinking in deeper and thicker than quicksand. He just didn't know what to do about it.

Clouds bunched in fists. Thunder grumbled, bringing on another session of wild, slashing rain. Amanda glanced next door as she raced to the car.

She'd barely seen Mike in the past two weeks, except in passing.

They waved when they saw each other. One morning, Teddy had popped in to ask for a couple of eggs. One afternoon, she'd sent Molly next door with a fresh strawberry-rhubarb pie.

She'd mowed his lawn. He'd sent over quotes for electric fences.

She'd sent a response to his fence quotes. One night, Thom had stopped by—to fight about custody, naturally—and she'd stepped out on the deck so Molly wouldn't hear the heated words. Across the way, she'd seen Mike choose that time to put a foot up on his deck—he was ostensibly holding a bottle of beer, but she had no doubt he'd have charged over if Thom had gotten out of hand.

She was invisibly watching over him, too. For instance, she'd bandaged Teddy's knee when she'd seen his son take a tumble on the concrete drive.

They were taking care of each other—and avoiding each other at the same time. That couldn't go on forever, obviously, but as far as Amanda could tell, they were both being smart. Why stroll in woods that was filled with poison ivy?

She turned the windshield wipers on full, glanced at her GPS, tried to take her mind off Mike. Her father had kidnapped Molly for a day at the Fields Museum, so storms or no storms, she needed to take advantage of the free time. June was sneaking into July. She'd already researched preschools and pediatricians, but she wanted to do an eyes-on before committing to either for sure.

Ten minutes later, she parked in front of Denise and Dan's Play School—and got half soaked just running the few steps from the car. Sandals squeaking, hat dripping, she opened the shiny red door. Naturally she'd called ahead to tour the facility. Dan—the dad of the D&D team—was waiting for her. His easy smile was the first thing that won her over. Everything about him—and the place—radiated a love and understanding for little ones.

She loved what she saw. There was a music room, a plant room, a "critter" room—a place where live animals were either borrowed or housed, from aquariums to turtles and spiders and hamsters. The last door on the right was clearly an art room, where smocks hung on hooks, and the walls were exuberantly finger painted.

The bathrooms were spotless, the facilities all miniature-sized—yet there were also high shelves that stocked underpants and other emergency replacement clothing in a variety of sizes. A central room included a locked refrigerator, where milk and fruits were stored. Available snacks were listed, fruits, nut bars, no cookies allowed except for special occasions.

A gigantic bathtub, near a window, was piled high with pillows and blankets. "Not for naps," Dan explained. "But kids sometimes get stomachaches. Or just want to curl up and have some quiet time. When a four-year-old gets out of control, our philosophy is…of course, to remove them from the situation and give them a chance to control themselves. But before we make that into a penalty, we try the curl-up in the tub thing. Most of the time, a child wants to get under control. They just don't know how yet. So…"

He opened the front door for her, still talking. Outside, rain still sluiced down, turning green leaves emerald and putting a sting of freshness in the air. She reached in her jacket pocket for her hat, still listening to Dan, but trying to hurry along now. "So you need me to let you know within the next couple of weeks."

"That would be best. We're almost booked up now—"

"Well, it's yes, I can tell you right now. I'd have brought the checkbook if I'd known for sure what a terrific facility you have."

She turned around, stepped down, and…*wham.* Another burst of thunder and lightning startled her— not coming from the skies, but from Mike.

He was headed up at the same time she was headed down. Their eyes met, and there it was, the chemistry of the century. Even with her hair frizzing up and her face washed of makeup, she felt conscious of her breasts, her pelvis. Her skin, the beat in her throat.

The preschool owner was still talking, as if he had no clue Armageddon was taking place on his school steps. Mike smiled, slow and easy, but he was still taking a lazy sip of how she looked, and she was drinking in his damp hair and sassy eyes and long, lanky frame just as zealously.

Naturally, she got a grip. "You're checking out the preschool?"

"Yeah. Been making the rounds all morning."

She gave him a thumbs-up, to show him her vote on the facility, but Dan immediately engaged him in conversation, so she had every excuse to continue on her way.

There, she thought. Both of them had managed that beautifully. Easy. Comfortable with each other—but neither risking a step closer to harm's way.

Maybe Amanda wasn't strong, but she was getting stronger. Maybe she hadn't learned self-confidence yet, but she was getting there, too. She was coping. She was making a life. She was being the best mom she knew how to be.

She just had to refrain from jumping down any well pits.

Okay, Mike kept telling himself. So he'd run into her checking out preschools. That wasn't so odd. Certainly not prophetic. They both had four-year-olds. They'd both just moved. They both had a lot of parenting things to do.

Besides…preschools weren't sexy. Parenting wasn't sexy, either.

It was in his head. That she belonged with him. That he belonged with her.

He had to get it out of his head. He was too damned old—and smart—to let his hormones do his thinking.

Stopped at a red light, he glanced again at the address. In another minute, he'd be at Dr. June Weavers, who was one of the five pediatricians he'd researched. He could still take Teddy into Chicago—it's not as if they lived hundreds of miles away from his original pediatrician. But it made no sense, to trek a sick kid on freeways and through rush hours. Finding a closer doctor was the more logical option.

It finally stopped raining after lunch, but the sky was still drizzling. The trees looked waxed-wet and shiny, but humidity hung in the air like a blanket. He parked, noting the expensive landscaping at the doctors' complex, took the stairs up two at a time.

And paused.

Amanda had just pushed through the door and was bolting down the steps. She'd have barreled straight into him if he hadn't put out a hand.

The simple touch made her head shoot up. She sucked in a breath before she found a wry smile. "Pretty unbelievable, huh? Two places in a row?" And then, "Don't waste your time. This one's a no vote."

"Really?"

She listed her concerns. "Four crying kids in the waiting room. The receptionist was frazzled and out of patience. Dust in the corners. Just…no."

"The doctor had hefty credentials."

"I thought so, too. And maybe she's brilliant. But it's just not a well-run place."

"You have more on your pediatrician list?"

She nodded. "Oh, yeah. Dr. Alan Rivers is the next on mine—"

"He was at the top of my choices, but I was doing a circle, hitting the geographically closest ones first."

"Well…"

"Well…"

Since they both had cars, it seemed a foolish idea to leave one, but they both liked the idea of checking out "Dr. Alan" together. Two sets of eyes were always better than one. The office was just five blocks from the first doctor—but a major difference in worlds.

Mike stalled in the waiting room. The setting was a kid's dream. A big-screen TV carried a whole selection of programs, from reading shows to movies like *Free Willy.* An aquarium took almost a whole width of wall, with all sorts of colorful fish darting around, the setup no higher than his knees. There was a lot for a kid to do besides wait and worry, he thought.

Amanda tracked down Dr. Alan for both of them. The doctor emerged from the exam rooms as soon as he was free. The guy was almost as little as his patients, big glasses, floppy hair, a bright blue stethoscope. Amanda remarked on the bins near the doorway—a child could pick out a pair of slippers, if he or she wanted to wear them in the office. And another bin held small, washable stuffed animals. A sign read Pick a Friend to Take in the Room with You.

The doctor gave them a full ten minutes. Neither

needed more. On the way out, Amanda said, "For me, this is a cut-and-dried. He's my guy."

"Because the place was so kid-friendly?"

"Yeah. That mattered. And it was spotless. And no one was in uniform."

"And nobody looked scared."

She smiled at him. "Yeah. That was the biggie. I don't doubt kids cry when they're getting a vaccine, but I liked it, that none of the kids looked afraid, even though they were at the doctor's."

His truck was parked next to her car, where both of them hesitated again. "So we've got two things marked off the parenting list for the day?" he asked.

"Yup. And I'm exhausted."

He laughed. "You think there's a chance we can refrain from running into each other for a few hours?"

She stopped smiling, cocked her head. Something passed between them—something that muted the sounds of traffic and voices, that intensified the rustle of wet leaves and hint of lilac in the air. Something that made her eyes look mesmerizingly honest. That made him want to look and never stop looking.

"I'm not sure we're going to manage it," she said suddenly, softly.

"Manage what?"

"Staying out of trouble."

She turned around, ducked in her car. He stood

there even after she'd backed out of the parking lot and zoomed down the street.

He was about eighty-eight percent sure that she'd just given him a dare. She hadn't *said,* "I want trouble." But her tone had a whispery dare in it. Her eyes had a fever-bright dare for damn sure. Her body, her smiles... Oh, yeah. She was all about danger and dares.

It wasn't a good idea to dare a guy who was at the end of his hormonal tether. He'd been good as gold. But like his four-year-old said—his *male* four-year-old—nobody could be good *all* the time.

Amanda arrived at Warren White's house at ten to seven. As she'd expected, the White decorating scheme was beige. As in, beige, period. No bright color had seen a surface in the White house. The setup for the Home Owners' Association meeting was a gathering in Warren's great room...which opened onto a deck, where teenagers were supposed to watch over the little kids who came with their parents. Amanda wasn't about to trust strangers with Molly, but she could see there were a ton of kids there, all having fun.

Still, she sat next to the door, with an eye on the yard outside. The older kids started a game of Mother, May I...and Molly, being the competitive tiny over-achiever that she was, instantly joined in.

Amanda relaxed—a little—and scoped the room,

trying to pick up names, friendly faces, who had which kids of what ages. She'd worn a scoop-neck top with white slacks, sandals, just a scrunchie pulling her hair back…while she knew the dress code for a city job with her hands tied behind her back, she wasn't so sure of the rules in the suburbs. Most seemed to take her in as "one of them" from the start—a relief.

At least until Mike walked in.

Warren took center stage in front of his fireplace precisely at 7:00 p.m. He even had a little gavel. Cute, she thought. Pompous and silly, but still kind of cute.

Mike wasn't. The women all silenced when he walked in—Amanda suspected they hadn't seen that much testosterone in one package in a *long* time. He'd brushed and showered, done the whole cleanup thing, but he still had that look—the cross between ruffian and quarterback. He was a bad boy with charm. They could all smell it.

He spotted her in less than a millisecond. And there it was again. The Dare. Just like this afternoon. She'd been a perfect lady, hadn't done a thing to entice or invite him, had been keeping to her celibacy pledge like a damned saint.

But at the preschool, then the pediatricians' offices…well. He'd been daring her, Amanda thought darkly. And he was still daring her. She'd *tried* to be honest with him. She'd *tried* to stay out of his way, to avoid temptation, to just be a good neighbor and a good friend. But he had to quit looking at her that way. Had to quit sending out those hungry, hungry vibes...as if he wanted to eat her up, and to spend a whole long night doing it.

He was sending out dares.

As if she'd sucker into that childish double-dog-dare kind of thing. Well, she was smarter than that. She smiled at him, crossed her legs at the ankles, went for the ladylike posture. *She* wasn't the one who was asking for trouble. It was him. Every time he looked at her. Every time he came close. Every time he breathed.

"Calling the meeting of the Home Owners' Association to order. Lucy, would you read the minutes from the May meeting?"

Warren started the meeting in a voice that resembled the drone of flies in the summer. Lucy—a woman with cotton-candy hair and a girl's swim-team logo—dutifully read the minutes.

Mike quietly crossed the room to sit next to her. Since Teddy wasn't with him, she glanced outside—and yeah, there he was, already teamed up next to Molly in the crowd of kids in the big backyard. The game had changed to "Simon Says." The kids looked happy.

She wasn't.

For a man who had almost no hips and no butt, somehow he took up a huge amount of room. He smelled like fresh soap and vanilla ice cream. And yearning. He definitely smelled like yearning. He carried a folder.

"New business," Warren announced.

Mike raised his hand.

"Well. It's nice to have a newcomer so willing to participate in our group. Welcome, Mr. Conroy."

"Mike," he said as he stood up.

There followed a gasper.

She knew the neighbor who raised worms for his kid, who dug in mud, who neglected to shave for days at a time. But she didn't know the lawyer. She'd never have guessed Mike could turn into a powerhouse who tapped into authority and command the minute he opened his mouth.

He was wearing sandals, for Pete's sake.

He didn't talk for long, just said he wanted to respond to issues raised by his putting in a water garden in his backyard…and a proposed electric fence he wanted to install. He handed a legal-looking document to Warren, but to the group of home owners, he laid out the gist of it more simply.

"I didn't realize the Home Owners' Association had 'rules' until Warren expressed them to me. My response is that document. I guarantee that I'll return the property to its original condition, if or when I sell the place. I also guarantee that the water garden I've been putting in will exceed any standard of good landscaping set by your association…"

There was quite a bit more. When he finally sat down again, Warren had the expression of a major suck-up. "Mike, Mike, Mike. None of us were objecting to the water garden. We think it's a wonderful idea. We just wanted you—and anyone else who's new to the neighborhood—to *ask* first."

When the meeting was over, the group of neighborhood women swarmed Mike. Amanda might have gotten a cup of lemonade with the rest...except that her mom's ear, the left one, picked up the sound of crying.

Not her Molly's crying.

But Teddy.

Chapter Nine

Mike would have chosen to stay a few more minutes at the infamous Home Owners' Association, partly to shake hands with a few more neighbors—but mostly to walk home with Amanda. But Teddy's brouhaha forced an immediate exit.

Teddy held his hand on the short walk home. He didn't talk. Couldn't. There were no tears now, but his eyes were still blotchy, his mood still stormy. Teddy didn't want to cry in public. Mike understood that guy kind of pride.

Once at home, though, Mike lifted him to the kitchen counter, plucked ice cream from the freezer, got them both spoons. "So just say. What happened."

"There was this stupid girl."

"Yeah, when I was your age, a lot of stories started that way." There were more ice cream cartons in the freezer than meat. Mike pulled the cover off the Cherry Vanilla. One spoonful for Teddy. Two for him.

"We were doing Simon Says. And I took four steps like I was supposed to, only that meant I sort of ran into this stupid girl. So she turned around and slugged me."

Mike did the next round of ice cream, this time with a wet dishcloth ready for the spill he knew was coming.

"I didn't *do* anything, Dad. I was just playing the game like I was supposed to. Only, I won the last one and I think she didn't like that. When she punched me, I really, really, really, *really* wanted to punch her back. But I didn't. You tole me a million times. You never hit a girl."

"You did the right thing," Mike assured him. "So then what?"

"So Molly hit her."

"Molly?"

"That was the thing. I told her I couldn't hit a girl. She said fine, but nobody ever said she couldn't. So she hit her. But, Dad. It's a bad thing. A very bad thing. When a girl has to do your hitting for you. I was so mad I started crying. It wasn't *fair.*"

Mike put away the ice cream, hooked his arms to

make a seat for his big guy, and they moved into the bathroom, then the bedroom. Slugger and Cat both knew Teddy was upset. The critters climbed on the bed first, so there was almost no room for Teddy.

Mike was still trying to figure out what had upset Teddy more—that a strange girl had hit him, or that Molly had been his hero instead of his having the chance to be one himself.

Apparently his stress level wasn't all that great, because he zonked out before Mike could pull up the covers or turn out the light. "Cat. Slugger," he called, thinking that the critters needed one more let-out that night...but neither acknowledged him in any way.

They weren't leaving the kid.

Abruptly the house turned silent...and Mike turned restless. He cleaned up in the kitchen, because he'd learned early on that ice cream spills were easier to deal with when they happened, rather than waiting for the next day. After that...well, there was always stuff to do. Start a load of wash. Hit the mail, go through bills.

Instead, he just...sort of aimlessly paced. Overall, he wasn't unhappy at how the Home Owners' meeting had gone. He'd gotten what he wanted. He just had a real bug about other people imposing rules on him...but most of the neighbors were nice enough. A bunch of the guys invited him to a Wednesday-night poker game. A few moms had clustered around him, talking about preschools.

But the only one he'd wanted to be with was Amanda. He wanted to know what she thought of the group. He wanted to tease her—she was supposed to be as afraid of suburbia as he was—yet she'd fit in so easily; both men and women warmed to her right away. Not that he was surprised. She gave off a quiet friendliness, an honesty and warmth.

His prowling around eventually led him to his front window, where he just stood there, staring at the windows in her place. Her household looked shut down. Molly had undoubtedly been put to bed by now. He saw no movement in any of the rooms, nothing but some distant light.

She definitely wasn't finishing her evening on the deck tonight. The firefly-night rolled through his mind on slow replay. The fireflies, the dancing in the grass, the moonlight, her soft silver laugher... He remembered every minute of that crazy evening.

Abruptly realizing how long he'd been standing there, staring at empty windows next door like a complete fool, he pivoted around. Kicked off his shoes. Headed for the shower.

When Molly was finally asleep, Amanda left her daughter's bedroom with a major sigh. They'd had quite a discussion before bedtime—brought on by the shiner in her daughter's left eye. It wasn't a bad bruise, considering the other little girl in the altercation had been a hefty second grader. But it invoked a torrent of talk about when "wrong is wrong" and when "wrong is right."

It was always wrong to fight, Molly knew.

But it was always right to stand up for a friend against a bully.

So which was the rightest answer? If you had to act really quick and your friend was hurt *right then* and there was no time to go in and ask your mom?

Amanda wasn't about to agree that hitting was an effective answer for anything, but by the time she wandered into the kitchen, her head was spinning. In the next life, she wanted to be her daughter. So passionate about life. So full of spirit and love and absolutely certain of what she felt about everything.

Without turning on a light, Amanda opened the fridge, then a cupboard. There didn't seem to be anything she wanted to eat or drink. Nothing she wanted to do. She was definitely too antsy to watch a show or read…and positively too wide-awake to sleep.

But then she froze.

Mike was awake. She could see him across the way, a tall dark silhouette. The distant sink light provided the only illumination, or she'd never have caught his shadowed frame. He couldn't see her. He was facing her windows, but she had no lights on. So it was unlikely he could see her, yet he stood there, as if he were searching, and then suddenly turned away and disappeared back into the darkness.

Her pulse started thrumming…and wouldn't

stop. A lump filled her throat…that refused to be swallowed.

It was his loneliness that struck her. An invisible loneliness, nothing he'd say or admit to, nothing anyone was supposed to see.

But he'd been looking at her house, her windows. For *her*. Even if he never said it. Even if he never intended to do anything about it.

And something abruptly snapped in Amanda. She couldn't explain what exactly. She just felt suddenly, oddly…angry. Vibrantly angry. Impatiently, infuriatingly, zestily angry.

She tore around the house faster than a wet cat, brushing her hair, brushing her teeth, unearthing the monitor she used when Molly was a baby. Then she charged outside, barefoot, prancing fast because the grass was wet and the night damp-cool and ghostly.

Before she lost her nerve—before she got scared—she zipped up his deck steps, didn't knock on the back door, just pushed open the glass and charged in. Immediately she stubbed her toe—on heaven knows what, probably a toy—made a groan of a sound, loud enough to wake the dead, but his watchdog didn't even come out to see her, much less bark. Mike couldn't possibly be sleeping yet; she'd seen him from the window less than ten minutes ago. But he didn't show up, either, no matter how much noise she was making, stomping around.

Of course she realized why, when she aimed

toward a flicker of light, and finally heard the sound of water coming from the master bath.

She took a step into his bedroom, and in the dark, for just a second, she lifted her foot because the toe was still stinging. She was acting crazily, she knew. She was behaving completely out of character.

She was taking a risk she was terribly afraid of.

On paper, this was just an impossibly wrong thing to do. On paper.

She took a breath, turned the knob on the bathroom door. Steam engulfed her, dancing on the mirror, shining up the tile floor. A giant gray towel waited on the counter. Mike was in there, beyond the smoked-glass shower doors.

She put the monitor on the counter, pulled off her cowl-neck top, pushed down her green cotton slacks. Opened the door and stepped in.

Mike turned around on a spin at the sudden burst of cool air. There was soap in his hair, water in his eyes. Mostly what she saw was somewhere around two hundred pounds of wet, naked man.

His first reaction was shock. That shocked silence lasted somewhere around a short millisecond. Initially his mind was clearly on something unrelated to sex. One look at her, and his body altered faster than a millisecond, too.

Before she'd taken a second step, he'd pulled her in and closed the glass door with the two of them inside. Before she could conceivably explain why she was here, he layered her against his hot, wet body and leveled a kiss on her.

If she'd just *known* she was going to do this crazy-fool thing, she'd have worn her black lace bra and matching panties, definitely not the pale yellow set from Target, on sale. She'd brushed her teeth. She just hadn't remembered the right clothes. She always remembered the right clothes for the occasion.

Only…well, it seemed the bra and thong were soaked in two seconds anyway. So was the rest of her. If she was going to drown in there, what possible difference could it make if she wasn't wearing her best bra?

And then the bra was gone. Tossed over the shower door.

Warm water splashed in her eyes, forcing her to close them…while Mike kept kissing her, swinging her against the warm, damp smooth wall, pinning her there. He held her hands flat against the tile, using his body to touch, to stroke, to incite. He groaned when his mouth left hers, only to trail a wreath of kisses down her throat.

He lifted her as if she weighed nothing, making it natural for her to wind her legs around his waist. When the nest between her legs rubbed against his belly, he swore. Then swore a second time when he nuzzled his cheeks between her breasts.

She recognized the tone in his voice. He was making that anger sound that she'd experienced earlier.

That vibrant anger. That infuriating, impatient, zesty anger.

Who knew he'd feel the same? Her heart opened in a shattering crack. She hadn't let anyone inside in forever. Hadn't trusted anyone, possibly ever, not this way. He'd been strung tight with denying what he needed, what he wanted. That ferocious hunger and yearning, to touch and be touched, was better denied than answered from the cold distance that came from failing marriages. Sex without trust had made her heart sore and scared.

But with Mike…it was right. The way it hadn't been right in a long time. He *liked* her. He valued her. It showed in his touch, his taste, his tenderness…his wildness.

He came up for a hoarse breath, asked, "Molly?"

She motioned outside the shower. "Brought monitor."

"Birth control?"

"What, you don't store condoms in the shower, waiting for me?"

He laughed, but it sounded a whole lot more like a groan. She rewarded him with a tiny bite from his ear. "I was giving up birth control, since I never planned to need it. Ever. Again. Until you. But for now I've got the long-term patch."

"Good."

That seemed to end the conversation. At least, he lost interesting in talking. So did she.

The damn man found the showerhead hose. She saw his sudden grin, saw his hand shoot up, grab the attachment by the showerhead. He eased her onto the tile floor, crossed her legs over his, and then played, pelting her throat, her tummy, her spine, between her legs...with warm, pulsing water.

Well, if *he* was in the mood to torture and tease... she was more than capable of stealing the hose and taking her turn. His laughter provoked another shattering crack in her heart. He was laughing with her. Sharing with her. It wasn't *using*.

It was giving.

And suddenly, as much fun—and teasing—as their playing had been, suddenly she wanted his hands. His skin. Him. Nothing between them.

His eyes darkened, sharpened. The water was still warm, blindingly warm, when he palmed her fanny, snuggled her closer, aimed inside. He slid in slowly, all slick slippery warmth, watching her reaction as he began a careful stroke...until he was all the way in. Slow turned into a canter, than a galloping hurry. She had a fearsome sensation of falling, a buildup of want so explosive, so consuming that she feared it would never end, never be over, never be appeased.

He whispered encouragement, praise, promise. When she peaked, her head fell back on a near scream...and he followed with an exultant groan as deep as hers.

She tried to breathe again, but couldn't. She stayed

wrapped around him like a scarf, her head in the crook of his shoulder, her body limp and wildly sated, not wanting to move…but the water started turning cool.

They both let out a yelp. He lifted his head. "I wondered when we'd run out of hot water. Darn it."

She was suddenly freezing. He was, too. He flipped off the faucets, helped her to her feet, and grabbed the thick gray towel to wrap around her. He had to step outside to find another. Towels were heaped in a basket on the floor; he took a black one for himself, but he wasn't concerned with drying himself off.

Instead, he rubbed her down until she was warm, kissing her brow, her neck, her shoulder en route. "I'm not afraid of much, Red. But I was afraid of this."

"Afraid of…?"

"Afraid that we'd be this good. I was hoping—if we did this—that it'd be kind of a clunker. Good, but not crazy good, so we could just get it out of our heads, go back to the friend thing, knowing the chemistry wasn't that bad of a problem."

She said, "For me. I'm afraid it's a mighty big problem."

For that, she got another kiss. On the nose. And a shine in his eyes that could have kindled fire. "You're not kidding. That was beyond anything I remember, Amanda. So now you've made our whole chemistry dilemma even worse."

"Hey. You were the one who dared me!"

His shaggy eyebrows arched. "Huh? You were the one doing all the daring. The way you walked. The way you looked at me. The way you smiled. The whole thing."

"I never did *anything*. It was you. Sending me those looks all the time."

"Hmm. So…is that what suddenly made you… come over here to climb in my shower out of the complete blue tonight?"

She looked at him, through wet hair and a smile that refused to stop coming. "No, Mike," she said softly. "I came over because…"

Startling both of them, Molly's voice suddenly crackled from the monitor on the counter. "Mom! Mommy! There's a lizard in the door! He's coming in here!"

Amanda sucked in a breath, but Mike was already shaking his head. "Don't worry about it for a minute. Of course you have to go. But I'd like to finish that conversation."

"Breakfast. My deck." But that was all she had time to say. Still wearing his towel, she plucked up her clothes, sprinted through his house and out the back door. Outside, it was darn near freezing on her bare feet and wet hair—but she ran like lightning, pelted into her own house.

"Mommy!"

She'd forgotten to bring the monitor back, but it

didn't matter. She could hear Molly's voice for herself now.

"I'm coming, honey!" She traded Mike's gray towel for a butterfly one from the downstairs bathroom, and scooted up the stairs. Out of breath, she paused in Molly's doorway. "I was taking a shower, honey. I need to put on a nightgown and I'll be right in."

"It's a horrible lizard. Purple and orange. With glasses. And pointy feet. *I'm* not afraid. But he was going to hurt you, Mommy. So I have to come sleep with you."

It wasn't how she hoped to end the evening, snuggled in a narrow twin bed with a four-year-old, Princess and Darling. Yet her daughter and the dog and kitten all slept as soundly as zombies.

She didn't. Her heart was still racing, her mind spinning, Mike's name humming in every beat of her pulse. Maybe she'd done the wrong thing. Maybe she'd done the right.

She was frighteningly unsure how this could possibly turn out well for both of them.

But she didn't regret what happened. Didn't, wouldn't, couldn't.

Amanda woke up in a tantalizingly high mood... until she glanced at the clock. Molly, Princess and Darling were already out and about somewhere, but the princess clock beside her daughter's bed claimed it was eight. Which meant she could have company from next door for breakfast before she'd had a chance to brush her teeth, much less to make anything to feed the four of them.

She flew out of bed, hurtled through drawers to find the appropriate dress-for-success attire—a frayed sweatshirt, old yoga pants. In the bathroom, she did the wash-face, brush-teeth thing, then swiped on two splashes of blush, braided her hair with a long scarf, loose, not tight, and didn't bother with shoes because there was no time. She hoped she looked like he usually did. Casual. Honest. Natural. Definitely not overly put together.

Molly, Princess and Darling all crowded her in the kitchen. She whipped up eggs, added a dab of cream cheese and cheddar, fresh chives…dropped a fork, then the spatula. Princess leaped on the counter in a cloud of white fur; both pets wanted to be fed and loved; Molly wanted a change in hairstyle *right now*. She started the toaster, pulled out the marmalade, poured OJ into a glass pitcher…chased outside to wipe down the glass table on the deck…chased back in to find Molly sampling the marmalade with a spoon.

Panic didn't set in. Not then. At least not totally. It was just that during all that frenzy of activity, a few teensy needling thoughts squeezed into her mind.

Such as…Mike had given her serious reasons why

he'd voted for the celibacy route. Her showing up in his shower wasn't exactly fair.

Such as...last night, it seemed terribly important that she not sit back, not be the kind of princess who needed a man to take charge. But by light of day, courage didn't look like courage anymore. It sort of looked brazen. It sort of looked like a pushy, brazen woman had shown up in his shower, specifically when he'd said he didn't want to be involved.

The more she thought...the more she wondered whether it was too late to hide under the nearest bed with heaps of blankets over her head.

She ran silverware and napkins and place settings out to the deck, ran back inside, cracked a nail on the door, shook it, turned the eggs, popped the first round of toast, heard the knock on the door.

Then panic set in.

"I know we're late," Mike said.

"That's okay, we're running just a tad late here, too." She smiled brilliantly, hoping he couldn't see that there was a gulp in her throat bigger than the state of Nevada.

He and Teddy were cleaned up, spiffed up. Teddy had a tucked-in shirt. Mike had a white polo that set off his tanned skin and a totally naked chin. He not only looked handsome beyond belief; he'd shaved. For her. And here she looked scruffier than his dog. He had to think she'd made no effort, where he so clearly had.

Their eyes met, and she almost dropped the eggs. Would have, if he hadn't swooped in and taken the bowl. "Let's help, guys," he told the kids, which was an outstanding idea.

He not only looked jumpable; the look of him brought on more nerves, because she was afraid she would. Jump him. At the earliest opportunity. Apparently now that the Brazen Gene had been let out of her closet, it was going to be tough locking it back in.

Mike and the kids carted everything outside. She brought up the rear with the OJ pitcher and glasses—which Mike took out of her hands before she could drop them. The morning still had a sting of a chill, but the grass was diamond-studded with dew, the sun soaking-bright.

The kids dove in as if no one had ever fed them… but that didn't last long. They started making faces at each other. Molly, ever the lady, exposed a mouthful of scrambled eggs. Teddy pulled his eyes apart with his fingers. Both of them pulled out their lips.

"It's hard to believe they're going to be part of civilized society in another twenty years, isn't it?" she asked Mike.

He laughed. Not a loud laugh. But a throaty, sexy laugh. Turned her on all over again. "You promise it'll only take twenty years?"

A forkful of egg arced in the air, landed in the

lilies. "Hey, guys. That's over the top. Who did it?" Amanda demanded.

"Not me," Molly said.

"Not me," Teddy said.

She pretended to buy into that bologna, turning a stern expression on Mike. "Mr. Mike, if you throw food again, you're going to get a time-out, and I'm not kidding."

That set the kids to giggling again. It was a lot easier, entertaining the four-year-olds than facing Mike alone. But eventually they got too squirmy to sit still, and Amanda gave them permission to go inside and play a game.

Unfortunately, once the kids deserted ship, the insanely messy table was the only thing between her and Mike. She'd felt his eyes on her, his smile on her, all through the picnic breakfast...but it was the first time she could really look back at him. At least in that naked way. That raw-nerves honest way.

"Did you sleep okay?" he asked her.

"Slept good. Just not long enough. You?"

"Like a log. Although I wish you hadn't had to run home. Was Molly all right?"

"Yes. It was just her lizard nightmare. But I still needed to be there."

"Of course you did."

Conversation stalled like a dead battery. Mike's eyes never left hers. Finally he put his elbows on the table, hunching forward. "My guess is the kids'll interrupt us in two minutes or less. So either we dive into talking about last night. Or let it be. You have a vote?"

"Better talk."

"Ok. The last thing I expected was a naked woman in my shower last night. Was there maybe something that triggered that happening? That I should know about?"

"Well…" How could she explain something that just all clicked in her head all at once? "It was because of Molly. In the fight yesterday with the second-grader."

Mike frowned. "I saw the shiner. But somehow it's hard for me to imagine how the two issues could be connected."

"Because. When I was talking to Molly—about fighting and violence never being a good answer—she got her back up. Some days she is *such* a red-head. And even though I'm not condoning her hitting anyone…later, it just kept occurring to me. Molly's viewpoint was right. Sometimes it's the girl who has to take charge."

"Amanda. Try to concentrate. Because I'm getting more lost instead of less."

Why did she have to be such an incoherent mess this morning? When it mattered? When everybody told her she was articulate in a crisis, how come she had such a hard time with Mike?

She clasped her hands together. "This is the thing.

We've had this…connection between us. Neither of us want our kids hurt. Neither of us want it to go too far. But I just kept thinking, Mike, we're *friends*. We're both smart. I think there's a level where we trust each other. So why couldn't we do something we both want—and maybe need—as long as we're both careful? But then…I thought…you really couldn't be the one to take the plunge."

"And why would that be?"

"For the same reason my daughter hit that little girl. And your son didn't. Because you're raising your son to be a gentleman. The same way you are."

Something cooled in his eyes. A ruler stiffened his spine. "Trust me, Amanda. I'm not."

"You are. In every way." Her voice was warm, sincere…but from his expression, she seemed to be hitting him totally the wrong way.

"So." His voice turned softer than butter. "*You* made the first move, because you didn't think I had the guts to?"

"No. Good grief, Mike. No. That wasn't what I meant at all—"

"I think it's pretty clear. You and Molly think we're the kind of guys who can't do our own fighting."

Now she was getting confused—as well as palm-cold anxious. "This wasn't about fighting. Neither of us want our kids to fight. Both of us are teaching our kids that violence is not a way to solve anything—"

"I'm not talking about the kids. I'm talking about

us. And if the only reason you showed up last night is because you didn't think I'd ever find the guts to—"

"Wait. Just wait. That's not what—"

Teddy and Molly barreled out of the house at the same time, shrieking and laughing…and soaking wet.

Amanda couldn't remember what they said they were going to play—fish? Candy Land? A marble game? So she wasn't sure which culprit had unearthed the squirt guns from the closet in the back room. Of course, it didn't matter who.

She shot an unhappy look at Mike—who didn't look back. He grabbed his kid. She grabbed hers.

There wasn't going to be any more private talking. Not now. Amanda felt a sinking sense of loss. She told herself that you couldn't lose what you never had.

But Mike's expression had become starched, his posture rigid.

She'd hurt him. Really hurt him.

She'd bumbled a moment that seriously mattered— and she had no idea how to make it right.

Chapter Ten

A half hour later, Teddy didn't object to a ride in the truck, but he kept sneaking peeks at him. "Dad. Molly and I didn't break anything or hurt anything. We just got wet."

"I know."

"But you look so mad."

"I'm not mad."

"Then how come you keep looking mad, if you're not mad?"

Mike declenched his jaw, rolled the iron out of his shoulders, smiled at his son. "I think you and I have earned a big day off."

"I think so, too!" Teddy agreed, and then added, "What does 'a day off' mean?"

"It means you and I are going to have a guy day. We're going fishing. In a lake. In a boat. Where there are no phones and no doorbells and no one can reach us. You like that idea?"

"I love it! I love fishes! I've always loved fishes!"

The whole afternoon, Mike tried to get his head back on track. There were tons of places to snag a rental boat, buy some live bait, set Teddy up with a fun afternoon. The sun was blazing, the lake silvery-calm, the sky a pure blue canvas without a single cloud. Teddy caught a little bass that fought like the devil, then a bigger one, a catfish, one pretty pike.

The whole time, Mike felt lower than a skunk, although he did his damnedest to hide the clunky mood from his son.

But he was hurting.

From the day he'd met Amanda, he warned himself not to fall for her.

She was the wrong woman—the most contrary redhead he'd ever come across. And it was the wrong time—for all the reasons they both knew and had commiserated about.

But last night, when she'd shown up in his shower... he'd known.

He hadn't just fallen. He'd leaped straight off the cliff, so deep, so hard, there was no climbing back. She'd scraped past layers no one else ever had. She'd *touched* him...because she'd taken that kind of huge emotional risk. With him. For him. And for all their play, he'd tried to lavish her with tenderness and care and skill. The best of who he was as a lover.

So when she'd pulled the "friends" on him this morning, it ripped. But the details—that she thought she'd had to seduce him—as if he weren't man enough to do the seducing…it just sent him into a crash funk.

He'd been *trying* to play by her rules by not touching her. He'd been *trying* to be a decent guy, for once.

Amanda was nothing like his ex, Mike knew, but suddenly it felt like new song, old refrain. Amanda was the cultured, classy type. She thought he was fine for a roll in the hay—but not good enough to fit in with her image of a long-term mate.

Teddy snoozed the whole way home, and Mike had the quiet sunset drive to put it all in perspective. That's it. He'd shut up from here on. Go back to the rules they'd agreed on to begin with.

He'd be a *friend*.

Nothing else.

His resolve lasted a whole four days. When the phone rang, he had thick gloves on and was working in the basement with Teddy's worm farm—knee-deep in a project that didn't smell good, didn't look good and needed to be done.

He'd have let the machine pick up—Teddy was with him, and there was no other emergency that couldn't wait five minutes that he could imagine. But when the machine clicked on, he heard Amanda's voice.

"Mike? I'm pretty sure you're there. You probably just can't come to the phone. But...I had a problem come up, and I was hoping—"

That's all that went down before he'd taken the stairs three at a time and grabbed the landline in the kitchen. "I'm here. I was just downstairs. What's up?"

He knew from the way she said his name, from everything in her voice, that she was stressed and strung tight.

"I hate to ask you. But I have to be in court at one. I didn't ask my parents to babysit, because frankly, I'd rather they didn't know until afterward. They get all upset, and this was something I didn't want spilling on Molly inadvertently. Anyway, I called an agency. They sent over a babysitter with fabulous credentials. She got here at ll:00 a.m. I kicked her out three minutes ago. There was just no way—"

"You need me to watch Molly."

There. He heard her take a breath. *Breathe.* "Yes. If you could. It's too late for me to set up anything else. I have to be in the car before ll:30 a.m. And—"

"Hey. Molly'll be fine with me. You know that. Don't even think twice."

The girls arrived five minutes later. Amanda was dressed like he'd never seen her, wearing judge-sober navy, nothing like her usual put-together thing. Just a navy skirt, white blouse, all tidy and meticulous, makeup on the spare. Her hair was rolled up in some kind of coil in back; God knew how she'd tamed it, but it was pinned and straight within an inch of its life. She had a smile on. He didn't know whose smile it was, but it sure as hell wasn't Amanda's.

"Thanks, Mike," was all she said.

"You need someone to go with you?" He couldn't take his eyes off her strained face.

"No. Everything's fine. I just needed help with Molly—" she shot a reassuring smile at her daughter "—because she would have been completly bored all afternoon, stuck sitting in a chair while I was at this little meeting."

It wasn't a little meeting, but Mike got it. That was the story for Molly.

"Hey, she'll have a good time with us. Right, Mol? And don't worry about the time. We'll be here."

She took a breath, thanked him again, gave him a house key in case he needed anything for Molly… then bent down to kiss her daughter and she was off.

He turned to Molly. It appeared to be a Cat Day. She wore a top with pastel cats, carried two stuffed cats and had a purse the size of a half dollar that looked like a cat. There were two jelly beans inside the purse. She gave one to Teddy right off, so she

could have the other, but so far she wasn't talking
to him.

He hunkered more to her height. "Here's the deal.
We're not doing something you're likely to have fun
with, right this minute. We're bringing the worm farm
up from the basement, because they're ready to live
outside in the shed. And there are enough worms to
start feeding the frogs in the water garden. But that's
all pretty dirty work. Nothing you'd probably like."

She nodded.

"But you could sit on the table in the yard and just
watch us for a bit, okay? We'll get this done as soon
as we can. And after that, Teddy and I'll get cleaned
up. And then we could all go for an ice cream cone.
Or to the library. Or watch a movie. Or go to the park.
Or…"

"Go shopping," Molly supplied.

That hadn't been on his list, would never have
been on his list, but he nodded. "That's just what I
was hoping you might like to do."

"I really don't want to do anything. My mom did
not want to go to this meeting. Something is *wrong*
and I don't like it. But I guess I could sit here for a
while." She perched on the deck table, crossed her
legs like her mother and motioned like a princess for
the boys to proceed.

Mike hesitated, thinking maybe he should get her
to talk if she was upset. But without knowing what
Amanda was dealing with exactly, he figured he'd

better try a wait-see before trying to dive into Molly's little head. As it happened, he didn't have to worry about either choice, because she'd ambled down to the water garden, holding one of her stuffed cats, before two minutes had passed.

"Mr. Mike, your stones are all wrong."

He'd framed the kidney-shaped water garden with stones, both to keep down the liner and to make the project look "done." "What's wrong with them?"

"You just didn't put them in a pretty way. They don't look right."

He looked at his brilliantly designed minipond, then raised an eyebrow at the pint-size diva. "So how do you think they should look?"

She showed him, and damned if she wasn't right. After she'd rearranged all the stupid stones, the whole setup looked better landscaped.

"You're pretty smart," he told her.

"That's what my mom says. But grown-ups never listen to me. I don't know why." She was ignoring Teddy as if he didn't exist, but that was possibly because his son had his hands full of worms and was dying to get her attention. "Only, now you need some lights."

"What kind of lights?"

"You know. The kind of little lights that you put outside. They don't have cords. They have to get sun during the day to make them work. Then they'd make your pond look pretty at night." She frowned.

"I think you need four." She motioned where she wanted them.

She *was* a miniature of her mother. "I think you're right again."

"I could give you more ideas, if you want." Once she opened up, of course, she couldn't shut up. She supervised lunch, which included how to properly wash hands, how Mike should cut the bread crusts and how napkins were folded. Once they all sat down—including Slugger and Cat—she opened up about Amanda.

"I've been thinking about it," she said, "and I think I know where my mom is. It's all about heat."

"Heat," Mike echoed.

"Yup. Heat. I'll bet her meeting is with the vet. Because when we took Darling to the vet a while ago—the new vet, the one we're going to now—he said it might be too late. And then my mom sent me out to the waiting room. And when we got home, that's when we had to start locking Darling up in the laundry room. Or she had to wear a diaper when she was walking around. It's all about in heat."

"I see."

"Darling doesn't have to wear a diaper anymore. So I thought everything was okay. But then Mom had to go to this meeting. And that's the only thing I know she was worried about."

Okay, he just couldn't completely let that go. "You know what? Your mom may be worried about something, just like you're thinking. But you might want to remember, she's really strong and smart."

"Yeah, she is," Molly agreed.

"Being smart doesn't mean you'll never have a problem. Everybody has problems. But I think you can stop worrying about your mom. She's so strong and smart, that I'm positive she'll find a way to work it out."

"I sort of know that." Molly sighed. "I just don't like it when she doesn't tell me everything."

Teddy, clearly tired of being cut out, interrupted to say, "If you get to talk to my dad, then I get to talk to your mom."

"Yeah. So?"

"And if you get to come over here, then I should get to go over to your house sometimes."

"Sure," Molly said.

"And I worry about my dad, too. All the time."

"Yeah? What about?"

Teddy had to think. "Just things. Like when my mom isn't nice to him. Things like that."

The kids had a competitive argument over who was the best kid/who worried most/who took best care of their mom or dad. Mike felt like a humorous fly on the wall; they battled back and forth as if he weren't even there. The afternoon filled up. He took the kids for ice cream, then had to find a potty. A trip to Target thankfully solved Molly's shopping need, where he bought exactly the lights she told him to—that required another potty break. By three o'clock in the afternoon, he brought out cards on the deck and played fish forever. At least twenty minutes.

About then he started glancing at his watch. It might be too soon to start watching for Amanda, but he figured whatever had gone right—or wrong—about the custody hearing had already happened. She was either hugely relieved...or hugely upset.

His mother called. She wanted them over for dinner on Sunday. The phone rang again. It was a headhunter who specialized in attorney positions and wanted Mike as a client. The kids settled on the rug with the dog in front of a Disney flick.

Mike told himself to get the mail, get some bills paid, use the quiet time to tackle some chores.

But it was four-thirty by then, and Amanda still wasn't home.

He knew how courts worked. How custody hearings went. Amanda had no way of knowing how long she'd be gone, and she'd have called him if she expected to be crazy late, or if anything had happened. She'd never have left her daughter hanging.

So there was no reason for him to worry.

And he wasn't worried exactly.

He was just glued to the window.

At ten to five, her white SUV zoomed into the driveway. The sound of the car sent Slugger baying and Cat snarling at the dog door to confront the arrival. Molly and Teddy didn't budge—they were near the end of the movie—but when Mike said, "Your mom's just pulling in, Mol," the little one bounced to her feet.

Slugger and Cat beat everyone else out the door to greet her, then came kids, with Mike bringing up the rear. By the time he got a look, she was bending down to give Molly a giant hug and kiss, so he couldn't see her face.

Teddy got in there, to start explaining that he thought he should have time at her house, too, and Amanda was agreeing with him. "I was thinking of something we could do that would be fun for you. You like getting your hands dirty, don't you?"

"Yeah, I do," Teddy confirmed.

"In fact, Teddy, I was thinking…maybe you could come over when we have a baking afternoon. Lots of flour all over the place. Lots of messes. Lots of squishing butter between your fingers. We could make pies or cookies or something. That sound okay to you?"

"That sounds like something I've wanted to do my whole life. And nobody ever let me before."

After Teddy's turn, his hound had to be petted, and Molly was still talking to her mom nonstop…but finally, finally, she lifted her head. "Hey, neighbor. Did you survive?"

"We had a blast."

"Uh-huh. What do I owe you? A day in a padded

cell? Brownies? Cookies for the rest of your life? Slave labor cleaning floors? Pizza?"

She made the kids laugh...he did, too. "Let me think on it."

"Yeah, you probably need a five-hour nap, huh?"

He chuckled again at her teasing, since she clearly wanted him to. "Everything go okay for you?"

"Sure did," she said heartily. "Tell you about it when I get a chance. In the meantime...I'd better get Molly in and my brood fed and watered. Thanks, Mike. I really, really appreciate it."

"Hey, no sweat. Anytime," he said, and meant it. She looked at him, her expressions, her words, as if he were seriously a cherished friend, sincerity radiating from her tone and smile.

They were doing the friend thing really well, he thought.

And wished he could kick a mountain in the shins.

Something had whipped the hell out of her in that custody hearing. He didn't know who won what—or who lost what—but Amanda's eyes had the fierce brightness of a lioness. She was hurting. Bad.

Mike felt a sudden, sharp ripping sensation. Her hurting wasn't supposed to be his business.

She didn't want a hero. She wanted a friend. She didn't want someone to beat up her enemies, to protect her, to watch over her.

She wanted a friend. She didn't want him in the

parts of her life that involved pain or fear or any of that other rotten life crap. She just wanted a friend.

Those were her rules.

Well, they'd played it her way. Now they were going to play it his way.

Chapter Eleven

Well, Amanda thought, she'd handled that reasonably well. Or as well as she possibly could have. Mike
hadn't guessed she was upset. Neither of the kids
sensed anything was wrong…although Molly was
still sneaking questions at bedtime.

"I think you're going to be a prosecuting attorney
when you grow up," Amanda said as she snuggled
Molly in fresh sheets and her favorite doll of the
week.

"I don't know what a prosecutor attorney is."

"It means someone who's really good at asking
questions. And at finding ways to get the answers
they want." She bent over to kiss Molly good-night.
"Did you have a good time next door?"

"I told you that already. I had a great time. I didn't scream about the worms. I just ignored Teddy when he was being awful that way. And I helped Mr. Mike in a whole lot of ways."

"You did, huh?"

"He thinks I'm smart."

"Everybody thinks you're smart. Because you are."

"I know. But he *listens* to me. Like I wasn't a little kid. Like I was somebody you want to listen to."

"Well, that's really good." The fairy night-light stayed on, but Amanda switched off the pink lamp with the fringe shade

"Mommy. Don't go. I need some mommy time."

"We can have all the mommy time you want tomorrow. But it's late tonight."

"Just a couple more minutes!"

Amanda wasn't positive she could hold it together for a "couple more minutes," but she sank back on the bed and said, "Okay, whiffer-sniffer."

Molly giggled. "Thank you very much, Bonkle-wonkle." It was an old game, always worth some smiles, but then Molly got more serious. "I don't know what a meeting is. But I don't like it, when I don't know where you are."

"A meeting is just a word to describe when people are getting together for some reason. And you may not always know where I am, Mol, but you will always, always be able to reach me. No matter where I am or what I'm doing, I'll always have the cell phone on for you."

"But something could happen to the cell phone. It could break. Or fall in the sink. Or drop in a lake. Or a car could run over it."

"You're right. Even having a very, very, very good cell phone isn't totally foolproof. Things happen. But I would never leave you with anyone who couldn't find another way to reach me."

"Okay. I think. Mom."

"What?"

"You were at the vet today, weren't you?"

"No. Where'd you get that idea?"

"It just came into my mind. I don't know how it got there. But if you weren't at the vet's, where were you?"

Amanda had prepared that answer before coming home, so it could slip off her tongue, fast and easy. "I was talking with some attorneys about some business."

"Well, don't talk to those attorneys again. Just talk to Mr. Mike. He's an attorney. We don't need any other attorneys. And then you wouldn't have to be gone for a whole afternoon."

"Hey. I've been gone lots of afternoons, and you never had a sweat before. Think of swimming with Grandma. And the Curious Kids Museum with Grandma and Grandpa. And you used to do mornings in daycare when I was working. You know I always come back."

"I know."

"I can't be with you every second. And you can't be with me every second. But that's okay. Then we come back together and can tell each other about our adventures. Right?"

"Yeah. Right."

"So are we square?"

"We are very, very, very square. But, Mom."

"What, hon?"

"Just don't go wherever you went today, okay? Anywhere else is okay. But not to that *meeting* again."

"I'll try my best, ragamuffin. And now, you try your best to sleep really good, okay?"

"One more kiss?"

"Three more kisses, and don't you dare try to escape a great big old hug, too."

There. A few more giggles, more hugs, and finally, Amanda could ease the door closed and tiptoe out into the hall.

Her smile died; her shoulders sagged, and she lifted a shaky hand to pull the pins out of her hair. Her mother had left a message on the machine. An old friend from high school had left another message, said he'd be in town over the weekend, and hoped they could get together.

She turned the volume off the phone, switched off the light in the kitchen. She wanted a shower, to shake off the dirt of this terrible day. She wanted a glass of something alcoholic, too, but couldn't work up enough ambition to actually get it.

Feeling boneless-tired, she sank into the blue chair in the living room and leaned forward with her head in her hands.

Most women she knew felt destroyed by a divorce. Maybe she'd been there, too, but she'd tried to see it as an opportunity to build herself into a better woman. A stronger woman. The kind of competent woman who wouldn't just *let* bad things happen to her because she wasn't strong enough to face the facts.

Well. She'd faced some facts this afternoon.

She'd failed to protect her daughter.

The only job in the universe that mattered.

She felt a claw on her ankle, sighed, and lifted Darling to her lap. A heap of purring fur leaped to the top of the chair and then delicately tried to wind herself like a scarf around Amanda's neck. She loved both pets. Hugely. And they were overdue attention today, but just then, all she wanted was some nice, long, wallowing silence.

Somehow, someway, she had to get up the next morning.

Somehow, someway, she had to find a way to say the right maternal things to Molly.

Somehow, someway, she had to find a way to believe she hadn't failed in everything that mattered to her.

"Hey. I knocked. But I wasn't sure if you heard me…and the back door wasn't locked…"

Her head shot up. The last person she expected to see was Mike, much less standing in the arch of her kitchen, holding a two-inch kitty-cat purse. The purse looked downright funny, hanging from the beefy wrist of a six-foot-two hunk.

More to the point, she'd assumed he'd be comatose by now, after dealing with two four-year-olds for most of the day. For sure he was wearing torn old jeans and a tee that looked as if it lost a wrestling match—it was that wrinkled and ragged. But he wasn't.

He looked like the Mike she'd fallen in love with. Brash and unbrushed, a smile as natural as sunshine, that easy, earthy way of moving that was so purely male. It wasn't hard to imagine him fighting down and dirty. It was easy to imagine him cleaned up, in a navy suit and white shirt, fighting to win with a force-ful presence, and slow, quiet words. It was just as easy to imagine him being there, through thick and thin, no minor irritation like earthquakes or avalanches keeping him from those he loved.

He was just a bigger-than-life kind of guy. It wasn't his fault.

But she wasn't going to be on the list of loved ones he dug through those avalanches for. As often as she remembered the night they made love, she winced every time her heart replayed the messy hurts that showed up the next day.

And faster than pride, she straightened. Possibly she couldn't find another fake smile today to save her life, but she tried for a normal, pleasant expression. "Aw, Mike, I'm sorry you went to the trouble. You didn't have to bring over Molly's purse. We'd have gotten it tomorrow."

"Yeah, right. I've spent one-on-one time with Molly now. Once she realized she'd forgotten something as important as this—" he carefully removed the purse from his wrist and set it on the couch "—I figured there'd be hell to pay for someone. I didn't want it to be me."

She still couldn't smile, but darn it, almost. "Uh-oh. Am I sensing she was a tad difficult this afternoon?"

"Are you kidding? She was perfect. I'm in love with her. She is absolutely honest. Just says everything like it is. That was cool," he said, as if they were starting another conversation, "about the two jelly beans in the purse."

"What? Oh. Yes. I told her, one for Teddy, one for her. I figured they'd be a conversation breaker when she first came over—"

"Great thinking, Mom. It really worked. And in the meantime…" From behind his back, he produced a sturdy box with fancy lettering. "I had something to celebrate. Had a bottle of Talisker hidden away for the past couple of years, needed an excuse to bring it out. Share a glass with me?"

"Thanks, Mike, but no. Honestly, I'm half asleep. Just really, really tired—"

"Just one short glass."

"I'd like to, really, but just not tonight—"

It was like talking to a brick wall. Maybe he didn't hear her, because he went into her kitchen and returned with two glasses. And maybe he couldn't see her shaking her head.

"Very short. I promise," he said genially, not looking at her face, just gathering the box, the glasses, some paper towels for napkins, and then settling—not on the couch or other chairs—but on the ottoman right in front of her. "You hold the glasses, okay? It'll take me a minute to get this open."

It was going to take him longer, because Darling leaped off Amanda's lap and headed for Molly's room. Princess, on the other hand, decided she'd rather sit on Mike's lap than hers.

She loved them. But just then she wasn't up for the cuteness of pets, or Mike this close, or Mike here at all. She'd put on a strong face all day. For Molly, she could do that. But for Mike…she wasn't sure she could fake anything with Mike.

He didn't act as if he noticed anything wrong. Just kept talking. "This cat has more fur than a coat. And I thought she was a kitten. You're turning into a little white pumpkin, aren't you…? Teddy's at my parents'. His first overnight. It's a big deal. He's been afraid to be away from me at night ever since the divorce. Had nightmares when we've tried it. But…out of the blue, he said he wanted to, so I called them up…and they both leaped at the idea. I'll be glued to a cell phone all night, but hoping it'll work out okay."

"Is that what you wanted to celebrate?"

"No, not that. I'm up for celebrating that another time—assuming he makes it all night without my being called to come get him. Okay, here you go…" He'd opened the blue box, produced the bottle and opened it, all without making the purring machine on his lap even budge. He poured equal amounts in two glasses, just filling them halfway, and handed her one, but with a caution.

"Now, this isn't a drinking drink. It's a sipping drink. A slow-sip-and-savor drink. The only place this is made is on the Isle of Skye. Aged ten years plus. And there's no talking or discussion when you take your first slow sip. You just close your eyes and let it happen."

He wasn't talking fast; he just kept on talking in that slow, easy way of his. She couldn't get a word in, much less an objection. She gave up, accepted the glass, and just figured she'd finish the drink quickly and *then* coax him to go home.

"Wait, wait, wait!"

She lowered the glass at his admonition, saw his grin.

"You don't drink this without a toast." He lifted

his glass to hers, clinked. "To parents of four-year-olds."

"Good one." Again she lifted the glass, but before it reached her lips, the scent hit her nose. "Hold on. What is this?"

"Scotland's most famous single malt."

"You mean, whiskey?"

He shot her a glower. "When you speak of Talisker, you speak in reverent tone and terms. It's Scotch whiskey. You've never had it?"

"Actually, no. I'm usually a wine girl. Not that I haven't had a mint julep or Manhattan at a party sometimes, but—"

"Okay. Another toast." He clinked her glass again. "To virgin Talisker tasters."

"Mike. You're acting awfully goofy tonight."

"Uh-huh. Taste."

She took a slow, careful sip. Initially the liquid felt soft and smooth on her tongue, interesting, different… but that was before the fire. Flames shot internally straight to the top of her brain. Smoke whooshed out her nose, throat and possibly her ears. Embers drizzled down her esophagus. Tears welled in her eyes. Her entire living room blurred, tilted sideways.

Eventually the smoke cleared. The pale blue chairs and blueberry-blue carpet stopped moving. The soft light from the purple-and-blue Tiffany lamp looked normal again. Mike was hunched over the ottoman, less than two feet from her face, his exultant grin just full of the devil. "I knew you'd love it."

"Love?" She opened her mouth, released some more fumes. "To tell you the truth…" She glanced at the amber liquid, considered, and couldn't think of a single reason why she needed to tell the truth. He obviously loved the drink. "I think this may possibly be the best thing that's happened to me all day."

"Atta girl. Another toast. This one to redheads. But *only* to redheads who happened to be named Molly or Amanda."

"Okay. Listen. I love the goofball thing. But, Mike. I'm not a big drinker, and I don't do hangovers, and—"

"Me, either. That stopped being fun before I was nineteen. We're not drinking a lot—I promise. Talisker is only for special occasions. You never level it. At most—no matter how much you beg—you can only have two glasses, max."

She frowned, studying him, unsure where all his high spirits and energy and foolishness were coming from. It wasn't as if she wanted to burst his bubble. If he had good news to share…well, that's what being a friend was about, wasn't it?

And especially after this afternoon, she knew she could never be more—no matter what she felt for Mike, or what she'd hoped for.

So she lifted her glass—tapped his—and said, "My turn to make a toast."

* * *

Talk about a slow drinker. It took her a full half hour just to sip through a shot, and probably the same amount of time to level a second.

Mike never wanted her inebriated. He just wanted her to talk. She was wound so tight, he was wary that she could crack into a zillion pieces.

And even after two shots, he figured the bottom line. No amount of liquor was going to loosen her up. But maybe from exhaustion, or the late hour, she curled her bare legs under her and kind of hovered inside the pale blue wing chair.

"You told me before this that your ex was applying for partial custody. So this was it? That hearing?" By the time he got around to asking, he tried to make his voice as lazy and safe as a hum in the night.

"Yup." She didn't seem to want to continue, but finally, out it came. "Thom won. I lost."

"Tell me."

"It's a real short story. I failed her. There's only one darned thing in this life that I *have* to do right—and that's protect Molly. And I failed big-time."

Mike unclenched his jaw. Maybe later he'd find out Thom's address and tar and feather the son of a seadog. But just then he was listening. And he was going to stay calm while listening if it killed him. "There has to be a little more to it."

"Thom was pushing for joint custody. Obviously I've known that for a while. And here's the thing. He's her father. I never wanted to deny him the right to be her father, or to spend time with her. She needs her father and loves him. But damn it, Mike…"

"Keep talking."

"It isn't about being a dad for him. It's about manipulation. Because when she's over there, he's somehow an absentee. There'll be some woman friend of his that does the babysitting. He doesn't actually *want* joint custody, because he doesn't spend half the time with her that he could. He just wants not to have to pay me child support."

"Keep talking."

And about then, she bolted out of the blue wing chair, as if sitting still even a second longer was impossible. She was still wearing the navy-and-white outfit thing she'd put together for the court, but it was coming undone mighty fast now. The white shirt was no longer tucked in, no longer buttoned at the neck. She'd lost the shoes. The navy skirt was twisted around. Her hands started gesturing. The hair got wilder. She stumbled and circled and ambled around in her bare feet, not crying. Sometimes her eyes spit out some moisture, but those tears were hot and mad, not soft.

"I don't *need* the child support. But I've been using that money to put together a college fund for Mol. He makes over six figures. Don't you think it's fair that he contribute?"

"Absolutely," Mike agreed.

"I told the judge that Thom cancels half the time he sets up a visitation with Molly. I told him that he's repeatedly left her with strange women she doesn't know, and that often enough she comes back upset and shaken up. The judge didn't care."

"Who's the judge?" Mike asked, thinking there was another tar-and-feather candidate. He knew a good number of judges, but not so many in the family court setup. She told him the name. Unfortunately all he knew about the guy was that he'd been on the bench for over a decade.

"The judge said…that unless there's abuse or specific proof of neglect, that Thom is entitled to more time. Initially he didn't grant equal custody. But as of right now, Thom gets an overnight every two weeks. *Mike*. I'm supposed to just spring this on Molly. After she just talked to me about not wanting to spend nights there!"

She spun around, and he saw her expression in the colored light from the Tiffany lamp. "Aw, Red. That's the worst sting, isn't it?"

"It is. This is supposed to start this coming weekend, which means I have to start talking to her about tomorrow. My job as a mom is—obviously—to make this as smooth and stress-free as I can. So I have to say something like, 'Hey, lovebug, you know your dad loves you, and you'll have fun on those sleepovers, and you know I'll be there when you get back.' So I'll *try*. But, Mike, I'm afraid it'll come out fake, because it's such a lie. She doesn't have a choice. How am I supposed to make her do something that I think is wrong? And make out like I think it's okay?"

"I hear you."

"When I got out the courtroom…Thom grabbed my hand. He said there'd be another custody hearing after this. I could count on it. And in the next one, he'd win full joint custody. That I shouldn't kid myself. He'll end up not paying a dime of child support."

"Come here."

"It's not *about* the money. It's about his using Molly in the wrong way."

"Come here."

"It's about her feeling she's lied to when she's with him. That's why she doesn't feel safe there. And I always promised her that I'd protect her. And now I can't."

"Come here."

She heard him, because she finally quit pacing around like a caged cat and faced him. "Mike, you can't help me. And if you could, I wouldn't want you to. I need to fight my own battles. And I swear, I'm *trying.* This is just the worst kind of thing to lose. I feel cut off at the knees. I failed my daughter."

That was it. Mike strode over, scooped an arm under her legs, and lifted her in his arms.

He'd wanted her to talk. Well, she had. She'd spilled thoroughly. Only, now she was saying such ridiculous things that she obviously wasn't in a reasonable mood.

And no one, but no one, could be more unreasonable than Red when she was upset.

Come to think of it…he was damned good at being unreasonable when he was upset, too. And right now, he was more than upset.

For her.

And with her.

Chapter Twelve

Amanda was beyond shocked. She had no idea what triggered Mike, much less what changed him from a listening, empathetic friend into a wildly out-of-control lover. She couldn't think. She couldn't breathe.

She *really* couldn't breathe. Once she'd started talking about the afternoon in court, the story had burst out like a runaway freight train. She hadn't cried, but her throat was thick with unshed tears... and Mike, out of nowhere, took her mouth in a deep kiss.

He'd picked her up as if she were lighter than pearls and just...taken off. He seemed to be careening up the stairs to her bedroom, because the pale lamplight in the living room had disappeared and they were galloping somewhere in the darkness. His shoulder bumped into a wall.

That didn't stop him from kissing her.

Nothing seemed to stop him from kissing her.

She was a disaster. Surely he'd noticed? She was unbrushed, undone, un-everything. She felt sick, anxious, lost. Her self-worth index seemed to be hovering around a negative ten.

And still he kissed her. He lifted his head for a gulp of air, smiled at her as if they both had something to smile about, then dipped down again. The last time he'd seen her bedroom, she—and the room—had been covered with paint. Moonlight streamed through the froth of curtains, ribbonlike on the thick, soft carpeting she'd put in.

The next time he came up for air, he dragged his T-shirt over his head, then started stripping her. He didn't seem to notice that she had drastically low self-esteem issues. He seemed to esteem every part of her quite thoroughly. He pulled down the zipper on her navy town skirt…popped off the button on her proper white blouse.

She should have smacked him from here to Timbuktu.

She considered it.

Temporarily, she seemed to be kissing him back and fumbling for the snap on his jeans…but she was still considering it.

He groaned as if she were killing him…when he was the one being the devil. He backed her to the bed edge, slipped her bra straps down, then laid her down on the poufy, soft comforter. The comforter didn't last long. He pushed away the covers and the pillows in one long swoop…then swooped back on her.

"You prepared to suffer?" he asked her.

The question made as much sense as anything else he'd done, but it wasn't like he gave her time to answer. His face dipped in and out of moonlight, and he made her giddy, the way he looked at her. As if it was his first time with a woman, and he'd waited a hundred years—not just for this—but for *her*.

That tongue of his. His hands. He made it seem like no woman ever had more gorgeous knees. More delectable elbows. More fascinating navels. It didn't seem to occur to him that these weren't erogenous zones. You couldn't seduce a woman by kissing her elbow.

Except her.

He seemed to be seducing her, no matter what he touched, no matter where, no matter how. She wasn't sure how a woman who could have been so, so low earlier in the evening could somehow, someway, now feel more powerful than any woman alive.

He seemed to be the somehow and someway.

He played and kept playing, until her skin had a silken sheen, and her heart was thundering a symphonic drum and she couldn't stop touching him back.

She felt on fire, inside and out, with need, with want, with…love.

"Enough," she said.

"I haven't even gotten started."

With the sudden superwoman power she'd developed, she twisted and miraculously moved him around until she was on top of him, and he was lying at her mercy on the rumpled sheets. "I've had it with you, Mike."

"I'm sorry."

"Oh, no. You're not sorry. But you will be."

"Hey. Red?"

"No more talking."

"I just wanted to mention. I'm in love with you. I don't know if it's right or wrong, sane or insane. This isn't going away. It's *bad*. The worse case I've ever had. Times a hundred. I thought I knew what love was. Until you."

"If you think that's going to get you out of trouble, think again," she said. Being a man, he probably wanted to go fast. Tough.

She sipped in a sigh as she closed around him, feeling how he filled her, how they connected, perfect as a lock and key. She was the lock.

He was the key.

No one else had ever brought out the redhead in her. She'd always been laced up. Liked being laced up. Except with Mike. She had a terrible feeling it would always be that way with him. That she wouldn't be able to hold back. That he'd bring out the lusty and earthy side of her, even when she had always, always liked everything tidy.

She lifted, sank…testing a rhythm, then finding one that seemed as natural as flying. "I love you right back," she whispered, and then couldn't talk anymore. Her heart took off in a soar, past earth, past sky, into a place where she felt weak with yearning, fierce with wanting. On fire, with need, for him, with him.

Finally, release came on a whoosh of a cry. She collapsed on top of him, breathing hard. She closed her eyes, felt his long strong arms cuddle around her. Felt his kiss on her brow.

That was the last thing she knew…until the rock-and-roll ring of his cell phone startled them both.

Amanda didn't know what time it was. Only that Mike popped awake as if shot with a bullet. Still, he took the time to ease her on her side before jerking across the bed, patting the floor until he located his pants, found and flipped on the phone.

She knew it was about Teddy. What else? Her blurry eyes eventually made it to the bedside clock. 3:00 a.m.

Definitely Teddy.

The conversation was hard to transcribe. Someone on the other end was talking; Mike's voice sounded as if he were talking through mud. "Okay. Okay. Okay. I'll be right there."

When he snapped off the cell, she said, "Ill? Or scared?"

"Ill. Just woke up. Rash and a fever." He was already out of bed, pulling on jeans. "At least he didn't wake up from being afraid. He was making it the whole night. My mom's best guess is chicken pox. I could have sworn he had every vaccine known to the universe. I thought kids couldn't get any of those 'spot' diseases anymore."

He'd immediately gone into dad mode, which she completely understood. When a child was sick, parental instincts took precedence over everything else. She didn't expect him to be thinking of her... yet the minute he pulled on his shirt, he leaned over and kissed the side of her neck. Slowly. Tenderly. Softly.

Before swearing, and grumbling that he had to go.

"But we have unfinished business, Red. And don't you forget it."

She smiled in the darkness, closed her eyes.

She thought she'd sleep...not only had Mike completely worn her out, but the day had been long and traumatic before that. Yet moments later, her eyes popped wide-open.

The day *had* been traumatic, the custody hearing agonizing. She'd been building character and strength and some skills, she'd thought. All blown away when she couldn't get the judge to listen about Molly. She'd left the stupid hearing feeling beyond inadequate.

Now, though, it occurred to her that was kind of how she'd felt after Mike bailed her out of her plumbing mess. She'd been so clueless. Because she'd *been* clueless. He'd been a hero for her that day.

The blackest night slowly brightened, turned into a pre-dawn dusty charcoal…then finally the pearl fog of a new day. It was still only five o'clock. She faced the window, from the pillow where Mike had laid his head, curled up tight. Now she got it. He hadn't stopped over by accident with that god-awful whisky.

He'd been her hero.

Again.

He hadn't changed the outcome of the stupid hearing. But he'd made her put it in a different perspective. He'd known perfectly well what he was doing. He'd planned it.

By five-thirty, she was biting her nails…and she hadn't bitten her nails since she was six. This was precisely how they'd screwed up before. That's what happened when you had kids, of course. Instead of being able to cuddle and talk things out and just *be* together after making love…they'd had to separate. And in the hours apart, they'd both frozen up.

Both of them. Not just her. He'd frozen up, too.

She felt as if she were on the cusp of grasping it

all—grasping what really mattered, about her, about him, about the two of them…when suddenly she heard Molly cry out.

There was no way Teddy was staying at his parents' house. None. Teddy was beside himself crying when Mike showed up…and burning up, as well.

His mom never freaked in a crisis, but she was clearly upset. "I know what to do for a sick child, Mike, for heaven's sake. It has all the symptoms of chicken pox. Nothing worse. But I just couldn't seem to comfort him. All he wanted was you."

"It's okay. I'll get him home." Teddy immediately simmered down—at least temporarily—once Mike picked him up.

Except, Mike was the one shaken up after that. Teddy's little body was so darned hot. Mike wrapped him in the sheet he'd been sleeping in, added a blanket, strapped the whole bundle into the truck and took off for home.

Before daylight, he'd called the new pediatrician, the old pediatrician, the E.R. They all gave him the same answer. The pinpoint-size spray of spots on Teddy's chest and tummy were symptomatic of chicken pox. So was the 102-degree fever. And a mild case of chicken pox was running through the county. They gave him the rundown on the course of the disease, things he could try, what to expect for the next ten days.

They all said the same thing.

This was a normal childhood illness, nothing to worry about.

Right. His kid was miserable, threw up the child's fever reducer, didn't want to sleep, just wanted to be held on his dad's lap in the recliner. Eventually Cat joined them. Then Slugger.

He wanted to call Amanda. Couldn't—without dislodging his entire family. And then she called, sometime early in the morning. He couldn't reach the phone fast enough, and the answering machine picked up.

"Mike…Molly came down with chicken pox. I'm guessing if you're dealing with a rash and fever, your Teddy has the same thing. Call if you need a hand." Then her softer voice. "We'll catch up. You can count on it."

He brooded on that. For him, their night together had been an Armageddon…but there was every reason to fear she wouldn't take it in a positive way. Hell. It could look to her like he'd plied her with liquor and been insensitive to the custody hearing thing she'd been through.

He made red Jell-O soup and scrambled eggs, then blue Jell-O soup, then finally got the hang of making the Jell-O gel. But then it gelled so tight that you could turn the bowl upside down and it wouldn't come out. Teddy asked for peanut butter and jelly—which he promptly threw up. Mike microwaved chicken noodle soup. Then more scrambled eggs. Then he ran out of Jell-O and scrambled eggs.

The tiny dots formed blisters two days later. Teddy's fever broke, but now he was itching and miserable and crabby.

Mike played trucks. And watched cartoons. And read books. And played fish. He coated the kid with everything he had in the medicine cabinet to stop the itching.

When he heard the knock on the door, he wasn't sure if it was Tuesday or Thursday, what month, what year. It was daylight. That's all he was sure of.

He opened the door, squinted at the sudden sharp sunlight…saw Amanda. Well, mostly what he saw was her flaming hair and shocked expression.

"Holy kamoly. You look *horrible*. Why didn't you call me? I was—"

He wasn't coherent. Wasn't going to be coherent again. Maybe ever. So he just blurted out what he needed to say. "I wasn't trying to get you drunk."

"I never thought you were."

"I didn't mean to be so…physical."

"Of course you did. That's you. You'll always be more fantastic with action, especially that action— than talk. Chitchat isn't your thing. No sweat." She closed the door and took a long gander at his living area. "You are such a dimwit. Why didn't you tell me you were in trouble?" Then she took an even longer gander at him. "You haven't shaved. You look as if you haven't slept. You look as if—"

"It's been horrible," he confirmed.

"Molly's taking a nap. My mom came over to watch her for a couple hours. I needed to get out to the grocery store, and I came over to see if I could pick up anything for you two." She raised her eyebrows. "No point in asking, I can see. It's obvious you need everything. Let's see how good you are at following orders."

"What orders?"

By nightfall, Mike figured she was akin to a cyclone. They were at her house by then. The kids were in pajamas in front of the TV. Both had had oatmeal baths, rubdowns, a liberal application of calamine, then dressed in their pj's. They'd gobbled down toasted cheese sandwiches, then lemonade, then small bowls of sorbet.

Nobody was crying. Nobody was whining. Both kids looked a pinch away from going to sleep for the night.

"I think," Amanda said quietly, as she handed him a serious bowl of chili sprinkled with sour cream and melted cheddar, "that you and Teddy should take the spare room tonight. Molly can sleep in with me. My guess is that you really need a night's sleep, and I can handle a round if the kids need someone in the night."

She could handle both kids behind her back. And him. They'd stayed at his place until she'd transformed it. The dirty dishes went away. The Jell-O bowls disappeared. The heap of messy cutlery seemed to all fit in the washer. She'd stayed with Teddy while he showered and found clean clothes. Then she'd herded them to her place—kicked her mom out—and started in with the little ones. The baths, the cooking and feeding. The calm, no-nonsense orders. Even Slugger and Darling obeyed her. They were sacked out by their respective charges by the couch.

"I think that's too much trouble for you," he said.

"What's the trouble? Both of us will end up losing sleep if we stay in separate houses. This way we can run relay for each other. Each get a solid stretch of sleep."

She sounded totally reasonable, but Mike wanted time with her. *Real* time. Not time like this. He couldn't guess what she was thinking or feeling—about him. About them.

But he caved about the sleepover, and when he settled Teddy in the upstairs room around eight o'clock that evening, Teddy begged him to sack out next to him. He did, for just a few minutes.

The next time he surfaced, Teddy was still sleeping soundly, and the wall clock claimed it was 6:00 a.m.

He'd slept ten solid hours.

And there was only one thing he wanted or needed—and that was to find Amanda.

Chapter Thirteen

Mike was quiet, descending the stairs, unsure if Amanda or Molly were sleeping—not wanting to wake either of them if they were still asleep. But when he glanced outside…there was a slim, white, unforgettable leg stretched out on a lawn chair.

The morning was cool, with a wispy mist dancing over the grass, hiding in and out of bushes. The sun had a beat of warmth, more promise than reality this early. She'd put a bowl of strawberries on the glass table, a carafe of coffee with a spare mug that he strongly suspected was for him. Both his dog and hers were snoozing at her feet.

She was wearing easy clothes, that kind of green

she liked, in a loose, soft top paired with jeans. Her feet were bare. So was her face.

When he opened the door, she immediately looked up and smiled. Then motioned to the mug.

"I figured coffee might be the first thing you wanted."

"That's it," he said firmly. "I love you forever. Don't fight it. You're going to have to marry me."

"You know what? I was thinking the same thing."

He almost sputtered on the first sip—when he was downright desperate for that caffeine. She clearly liked it that she so easily rattled him. She watched him sit in the chair next to hers, put a foot up before speaking.

"When I woke up three mornings ago," she said quietly, "I thought…maybe you were into payback. That you were doing the same thing to me…that you believed I'd done to you."

"Run that by me again. A little slower. A *lot* slower, Amanda."

So she went slower. "The first time we made love… you thought I was doing a hit-and-run. That I was willing to sleep with you. But still keep a distance."

He wasn't sure what the balance was between quicksand versus honesty. So he just motioned her to go on.

"So when I woke up three mornings ago…I started worrying…at first…that you were doing just that.

Startling me with a seduction. You didn't ask first. You just took charge."

"Amanda—" He got it. Quicksand or not, he had to get the whole truth out there, no matter what it cost him. Too much was at stake to risk less.

"Hear me out. I figured it out, Mike. Your coming on to me took a ton of courage…just like the night I came on to you was the biggest risk I'd ever taken. I've been trying to be a different woman than I was before. So that first night, it wasn't about sex. Or just about sex. It was about my being strong enough and honest enough to admit I wanted you. And to ask for what I wanted and needed, loud and strong."

His turn then. "Three nights ago, I knew something bad had happened at the hearing. I could see it in your face, your eyes. I didn't how to help. I just knew…I wanted you to turn to me when something bad or sad happened. No matter when or how or what it was. I *hated* it. That you felt so bad."

She put down her coffee, leaned forward. She lifted her hands toward him and he took them. Their knees touched. Their palms nested together. She said carefully, "Mike. I don't want to be a leaner. Or a needer."

"I know that bugs you. But I don't see it. I never saw it. You're smart. You're a general and a diplomat in a crisis. You're the best mom on the planet. When a situation's tough, you don't run, you dive in—wherever, whenever. Do whatever it takes."

She frowned, as if it never occurred to her that someone would see her that way. "I was just raised... so helpless."

"That may be true, Red. But that's not character. It's just circumstance. A person doesn't start out the first day of medical school doing brain surgery. It takes some time and practice."

"You respected that before I did."

He hesitated, long and hard. Reached for more coffee. Still hesitated. Her eyes were on his face, her expression patient, waiting. Apparently she wanted him to lay out something tough. Offhand, he couldn't think of any way to avoid it—particularly if he wanted to win her. And he wanted that more than life.

"Okay...from my side of the fence now...I let something loose the other night."

"I know. You shared some of your precious Talisker."

"That's true. But not that. I was worried about... Well, I don't know how to say this. I just don't seem to do certain things...in a fastidious way."

"Fastidious?"

Okay. So he didn't know the right word. The delicate, ladylike word. "You know," he said edgily. "There's a place for *please* and *thank you*. Maybe even a place for that language in bed. But I can't promise any aptitude for...finesse."

"This is about your ex, isn't it." She didn't frame a

question, because there wasn't one. She already knew that answer.

"Yeah. When she picked up with George… I don't know how to say it. But she made me feel like I was a bull. Insensitive. Not the tidy kind under the covers. It's my reality. I like the smells, the sweat, the sounds."

"Mike?"

"What?"

"I'm sorry your ex is such a prissy woman, handsome. But personally, I think it's obvious that you're always going to be dark French roast, not decaf."

"Well…maybe I need to know if you're into that dark French roast thing."

"Hmm." She appeared to consider. "After the two intensive samples I've had…I have to say I can't ever imagine wanting decaf, ever. Why settle for bland when you can have it all?"

"That's it," he said, and pulled her from her chair onto his lap. He couldn't wait any longer to touch her. Hold her. "I told you I loved you, Amanda. And I meant it from the heart and soul both."

She lifted her face, anticipating his kiss. That first connection was so sweet, so needed, so cherished that he felt his heart opening, wide enough to let the sun in.

His sun was her.

Naturally, seconds later, the dogs got up and barked. Then Molly stormed outside, followed by

Teddy. Both their kids were still polka-dotted. Neither seemed to find it strange that their parents were snuggled together. They just both climbed on. Then came the dogs. Darling fit on top, but Slugger couldn't jump that high, and started baying his unhappiness.

Amanda started laughing...then so did he.

"How on earth are we going to keep all this straight?" he demanded.

"That's easy," she murmured. "Everything is yours, mine and ours."

And kissed him again.

The August afternoon was crazy-hot...hot enough that Mike felt justified hiding in the basement. That was, until Amanda found him.

"Out," she said simply.

"I don't think I can do it."

"Out," she repeated. He gave in—Amanda knew he would eventually. "I can't believe a big strong guy like you would be afraid of a few kids."

"I never heard of a meet-and-greet for four-year-olds. And as far as I can tell, the whole thing's terrifying."

It wasn't. It was a super way for the kids to meet some other children their age before preschool actually started. Both yards were decorated with balloons and tables, both places had snacks and drinks. Precisely between the houses, there was a hired balloon maker...making animal balloons for each child. In

Mike's yard, groups congregated who wanted to do the worm-and-frog thing. In Amanda's, there was a twirling contest, requiring a lot of girls wearing tutus and crowns.

Amanda had hoped a good handful would come to the impromptu gig. Instead…she counted over thirty kids, not counting moms and neighbors. "Talk about a success," she murmured.

"All your doing. I still can't believe we're both surviving suburbia."

She lifted her head, saw his expression. "You've come to love it, haven't you?"

"Love it—yeah. In spite of myself. But we have an awful lot to sort out, Amanda. Which house do you want to live in? Are both of us going to work? How are we going to manage all the grandparents? The ex's?"

"Yes," she said, as if that were an answer.

"Yes?"

"Uh-huh. There was a time I wanted perfect, Mike. Now I realize what I was looking for back then was shallow and boring. Never again. I want complications. I want messes. I want challenges. Are we going to have fun creating our lives together, or what?"

"You said it. Bring it on, Red." He grinned, bent down to kiss her nose…and naturally, was interrupted by the sound of a scream. Molly's.

In her most dramatic voice, Molly announced to

the world in general, "Guess *what!* Princess just had a kitten. On my bed!"

"Uh-oh," Mike murmured.

Amanda laughed again. "Just one more thing that's going to be yours, mine and ours. What could possibly be better than that?"

"Nothing in this world," he agreed, and swung his arm around her shoulder.

* * * * *

BURNING AMBITION

BY
AMY KNUPP

First published in Great Britain 2011
by Mills & Boon, an imprint of Harlequin (UK) Limited,
Eton House, 18-24 Paradise Road, Richmond, Surrey TW9 1SR

© Amy Knupp 2011

ISBN: 978 0 263 88934 5

23-1211

Harlequin (UK) policy is to use papers that are natural, renewable and
recyclable products and made from wood grown in sustainable forests. The
logging and manufacturing processes conform to the legal environmental
regulations of the country of origin.

Printed and bound in Spain
by Blackprint CPI, Barcelona

Dear Reader,

During my research for THE TEXAS FIREFIGHTERS series, I was more than a little surprised to learn the status of women in the fire service. It's the twenty-first century, right? Women have made big strides in attaining equality in the workplace…in most occupations.

They're still fighting for respect in fire stations, though. When I first considered writing a female firefighter character, I knew this would likely be an integral part of who she is. Faith Peligni is the first woman in the history of the San Amaro Island Fire Department, and she's driven to prove herself—because of that and because her dad is the fire chief. She has to fight not only the image of being a weaker female but also of being favoured because of her father's position. The worst thing she could do is fall for someone in the department—especially an officer. Captain Joe Mendoza can't afford to have feelings for Faith, either, as her dad is his mentor, his boss and has heavy influence on the promotion Joe hopes to attain.

But she does…and he does.

I hope you enjoy Faith and Joe's journey from off-limits to happily-ever-after! Thank you for picking up my book. If you'd like to learn more about my other books, please visit me online at www.amyknupp.com or contact me at amyknupp@amyknupp.com. I enjoy hearing from readers!

Happy reading,

Amy Knupp

Amy Knupp lives in Wisconsin with her husband, two sons and five cats. She graduated from the University of Kansas with degrees in French and journalism, and feels lucky to use very little of either one in her writing career. She's a member of Romance Writers of America, Mad City Romance Writers and Wisconsin Romance Writers. In her spare time she enjoys reading, college basketball, addictive computer games and watching big red fire trucks race by. To learn more about Amy and her stories, visit www.amyknupp.com.

Acknowledgements

Thank you, yet again, to the most patient retired firefighter ever, for talking me through countless fire scenarios and answering another thousand questions for this book.

Thank you to Denise McClain for answering my medical questions so willingly (and to your dad for giving me an enjoyable glimpse of a hard-core, old-school firefighter).

Thank you to Doug McCune for educating me on the finer points of baseball spring training.

Thanks to Tasha Hacaga, Emily Becher and Kay Stockham for the brainstorming, the inspiration and the motivation. And for accommodating my sudden odd music 'needs.'

To my parents, thanks for being the best unpaid promotional team a girl could have.

To my boys, thank you for putting up with a less-than-spectacular summer when every other phrase out of my mouth was "after my deadline"!

And as always, thanks to Justin for having an extremely high tolerance for midnight plotting sessions and an uncanny knack for knowing when to slide a margarita in front of me.

CHAPTER ONE

FAITH PELIGNI FELT AS IF she was being thrown right into the fire her first day. And that was just how she liked it.

Everyone on duty at the San Amaro Island Fire Department had gathered across the street from the station at the city-owned training facility. Captain Joe Mendoza, whom Faith had known in passing since she was three feet tall and running around in her father's too-big standard issue helmet, was currently explaining the drill. It was a two-person relay that involved dragging a hundred-fifty-pound dummy, climbing the four-story tower while carrying a heavy coil of hose, then rappelling down the outside wall. Each pair would be timed, with the fastest team the winner.

There was enough trash-talk going on between some of the guys to fill the Houston city dump. Faith had been introduced to a few of them, and so far, everyone was leaving her alone. On the one hand, she was grateful for the peace, but on the other, it meant she didn't fit in. She wasn't one of the guys. Standing by herself as Cale Jackson, one of the lieutenants, demonstrated each stage of the drill, she wondered if she ever would be. Did she want to be?

Maybe. What she really wanted was their respect. To be able to walk through the department and be confident that no one still believed she wasn't here on her own merit.

"Listen up, men. And women." Captain Mendoza sought out Faith's eyes with his coffee-black ones. "Sorry, Faith. Old habits. I'm going to pair everybody up and then we'll get started. Any questions?"

No one responded, so the captain began calling off names. Instead of worrying about who she'd be partnered with, Faith walked closer to the tower to scope it out, looking for any pitfalls, since she wasn't familiar with it.

"Peligni, you're with me," the captain said, finishing up his list.

Faith didn't glance at him, afraid she'd betray her annoyance. Was he putting her with him so he could "help" her? A charity case? She bit down on any protest and turned to face him.

"I have a reputation for winning this," Captain Mendoza said as he approached. "You think you're up for it?"

She studied him, searching for a hint of bullshitting. He was a big man, well over six feet tall and wide in the shoulders. His eyes were gentle, kind, yet he had a look about him that said you definitely didn't want to get on his bad side. His black hair was short, his face tanned. Strong. Handsome. The kind of face you wanted to trust. As far as she could tell, he was being sincere.

"I'll do the best I can," she said.

He likely thought the activities this drill involved put her at a disadvantage. The first two legs depended mostly on upper body strength, which, of course, women were lacking compared to men. However, Faith was confident that she was stronger than most people gave her credit for, thanks in large part to extra workouts every week. Even on her days off, she put in one to two hours of physical training. While it would never make her stronger than some of these guys, she could definitely hold her own.

The third leg, rappelling, was one of Faith's favorites. She loved the feeling of flying downward and bouncing off the wall. One of her brothers, Lou, had taken her skydiving once, and it had been just as fun but with less control. Lou teased her that she'd missed her calling, and had tried to get her to join him in the military.

She watched intently as the other teams took their turns, trying to pick up tips, spots where they lost time. The men watching paid attention in a general yelling and cheering way, but they'd obviously been through this drill numerous times and weren't worried about shaving off every possible second like she was. Of course, they didn't have the stakes she did. If they didn't win, it was just another day. If she didn't win, there'd be rumblings that she shouldn't have gotten the job, that a woman couldn't hack this career, and on and on. While she didn't want to let such talk get to her, she had no doubt it would. Maybe she was shallow, but she wanted her fellow firefighters' respect.

Captain Mendoza leaned in close to her and she caught a whiff of his masculine, sporty scent. "The last two stairs before the top are wobbly as hell. Watch your step up there."

She nodded, debating internally. She considered being stubborn and working things out herself. But that wouldn't serve the bigger goal of winning, would it? Though she didn't like the idea of getting help, she liked losing even less. "Any other tips?"

"You're asking for something I've never given away before," he said, watching her with those dark eyes.

"Not even to your teammates?"

"None of them has ever been smart enough to ask."

They shared a brief grin, and Faith said, "Well?"

"Avoid the handrails. They'll slow you down."

"Got it. Thanks."

"We're up next. You ready?"

"Ready as I'll ever be."

"I'll go first."

Faith nodded, and followed him to the starting line while the second-to-last pair finished up.

"Faith," the captain said, making her look up at him. "Show me what you've got."

With that, he turned around and started suiting up in full gear. Faith did the same.

"Time to beat," the official timekeeper called out as the man before them—she couldn't remember his name—crossed the finish. "Four minutes, fourteen seconds."

"Can we do that?" Faith muttered to Captain Mendoza as they continued to prep.

"Have to push it," he said. "I think we can."

She knew it was up to her to pull her weight. No sweat.

Yeah, right.

The captain finished putting his gear on, and the whistle blew for him to start. Most of the guys were loud in their support of him as he lugged the dummy over the ground, but Faith kept her cheering silent, willing him to make up for any time she might lose ascending the tower with the heavy hose.

She put her last glove on, transfixed by the sight of him. She'd guess he was around forty, based on the lines of his face, not the way he moved. He was one of the biggest men on this shift, all solid muscle, and yet his grace and speed mesmerized her. He made it look as if the hose weighed three pounds instead of thirty. When he got to the top, he quickly fastened the rappelling gear and went over the edge. Like the rest of the guys, he took the wall in four rhythmic bounces.

Faith's adrenaline kicked in as he ran toward her.

"Go for it," he said as he tagged her hand.

She took off in a sprint to the spot where he'd dragged the dummy. The thing weighed more than she did, but she was used to that. No excuses in her world. She toted it back to the starting line and then sprinted to the tower.

When she reached the coil of hose, she stumbled a bit and almost fell. Just what she needed. She caught herself at the last moment and avoided ending up on her butt, but lost a couple seconds. She heaved the hose up and took off, eyes on each step, focusing on balance, avoiding the handrails.

By the last flight of stairs, her lungs were screaming, and she wondered if the air was thinner up here, because she sure wasn't getting enough oxygen. She forged on, preparing herself for the last two wobbly steps before unloading the coil.

Now for the fun part.

She attached her rappelling equipment and, without hesitation, climbed on top of the wall and lowered herself over, her back to the group of firefighters. Instead of hitting the wall four times, she flung herself out and made it halfway down with her first release. Pushing off with her legs, she flew the rest of the way, hitting the ground hard but intact. She unfastened the rope and sprinted to the finish line, ignoring the burning in her lungs.

JOE NODDED SLOWLY to himself as he watched Faith's final approach. This woman was going to cause an uproar in the department, not only because of her looks but because she could teach several of the men plenty when it came to busting one's ass.

He didn't know if she'd make the time they needed to win, but she had nothing to be ashamed of, given the way she'd gone after it. Her rappelling was beautiful—seemingly wild, yet she'd been in control the whole descent, pulling off the time-saving move. The woman could run, too. If this was how she performed in every aspect of the job, he'd be thrilled to have her working for him.

When she raced over the finish line, he held his hand out for her to slap again and praised her effort. His eyes were on the timekeeper as he hit the stopwatch, read the results to himself and then looked up with an unreadable expression.

"Let's have it, Olin," Joe said, caring too much about the results.

"Four minutes, eleven seconds. Congratulations, Captain. You and the new girl are the champs."

"Yes!" Faith whispered her response so most of the guys couldn't hear her, as if she understood celebrating would egg on some of them. She was young—only twenty-six—but Joe could tell she had a lot of street smarts and experience dealing with animallike males from her tenure in the San Antonio Fire Department the past few years.

Her glossy, sable hair was straight and reached below her shoulders. Her eyes were the brightest blue he'd ever seen, making him think of the Gulf of Mexico on the clearest day. She'd shown up to work that morning wearing no makeup—she didn't need any to highlight her striking features.

She met Joe's eyes, her blue ones overflowing with excitement and pride at their achievement. It was impossible not to catch some of her enthusiasm, regardless of how well she tried to hide it.

He nodded at her, grinned, then looked away, seeing her father's penetrating gaze in his mind and hearing his plea, just a couple of hours ago, for Joe to take Faith under his wing.

Joe wanted to see Faith succeed, not only because her father, Fire Chief Tony Peligni, was a good man. Not just because she was the department's first woman and had to carry that burden on her shoulders. Joe wanted her to do well because he liked her and felt lucky to have her on his team.

Professionally speaking, of course.

FAITH ABSOLUTELY, positively was not going to make coffee today.

Any other day, she'd do so willingly, because she was all about sharing duties, from meal prep to cleaning the rigs. But if she brewed coffee on her first day, it could be interpreted as a statement she didn't want to make. It'd be far too easy for one of the men to see her as the coffee girl, and who knew how long it would take to outgrow that derogatory title? Didn't matter that she'd been part of the winning team in training and had gotten a couple of compliments from the others about her rappelling skills. Some of these guys were Neanderthals at heart, she suspected. Lieutenant Ed Rottinghaus, for one—the man who'd fought to prevent her from being hired. There were likely others who felt the same. All it took was one moron following her around with the coffeepot. That wasn't the way to win respect.

The bitch of it was she was dying for a cup of hot, strong caffeine. She'd missed her morning dose in her rush to get out the door, and needed it even more than she needed the lunch she'd packed.

"Hey, new girl. Nice showing at the training drill."

She turned warily to look at the man with dirty-blond hair who'd just walked in. She'd probably been introduced earlier, but all the stacked-with-muscles bodies were starting to look the same to her.

"Thank you," she said. "I'm still trying to remember names."

"Derek Severson." He held out a large hand and she shook it. "Nicest guy you'll meet in this place."

"Is that right?" She laughed. "Good to know. I'll try to remember your face if that's the case."

"Hundred percent unbiased truth. So… Awful big shoes to fill, being the chief's daughter."

At least he didn't beat around the bush or talk behind her back. "I'm not trying to fill his shoes. Just here to fight fires."

He picked up the dirty coffeepot and went to work cleaning it in the sink. Thank God. A second point in Derek's favor.

"How many scoops?" she asked, taking the bulk can of coffee grounds down from the cabinet above once he'd finished scrubbing. Helping was inherently different from making the coffee herself.

"You like it strong?" Derek asked. "Or girlie?"

She shot him a look and realized he was joking, not singling out her gender. "I like it to wake me the hell up."

He was married, she guessed. Or taken. Good-looking, if slightly shaggy, he had an easygoing, friendly manner and warm, blue eyes that put a person at ease. Impossible that a man like him would be single. Not that she was looking for someone. Not here.

"Five. Six if you want to screw with the others. They like it girlie."

Once the coffee was brewing—with six overflowing scoops—she wandered around the kitchen, snooping absently, waiting for her pick-me-up to get done. Derek poured himself some health-nut cereal and added milk from a carton that had a Don't Use My Damn Milk sign taped to it.

She unwrapped her microwave dinner, started it cooking and then went to the coffeemaker to help herself.

Two more firefighters strolled into the kitchen. One had his eyes on the coffeemaker and the other made a beeline for the refrigerator.

"Hey," the dark-haired one on the coffee hunt said to Faith.

"Penn, right?" she asked.

"That's me." He smiled at her as he took down a coffee mug that said Never Do Anything You Wouldn't Want to Explain to the Paramedics on the side. "Welcome to the department."

"Thank you."

"Ah," the second guy, a redhead, said, walking up to her at the counter. If she remembered right, his name was Nate Rottinghaus, the son of her not-so-favorite lieutenant. "You."

Faith tensed and met his eyes. "Me."

"You know, the captain would win that competition if he was paired with a three-year-old." He poured his coffee, walked to the long table that ran up the center of the room and sat down across from Derek.

"What the hell, Nate?" Derek said.

"Careful or she'll figure out what an ass you are," Penn added.

Faith moved to the end of the table to force Nate to look at her. "I like to know what I'm up against. Got anything else you want to get off your chest?"

He perused her with lazy, smug eyes, as if he was silently calculating how long she'd last in the department. She'd bet the idiot couldn't count that high.

"There are lots of jobs where your looks could help you get ahead. The fire department isn't one of them."

The microwave beeped and Faith spun around, her appetite suddenly gone.

"Ignore him," Penn said. "He's used to it."

Faith gave a forced smile. "Already done."

"I was going to track you down." Penn hoisted himself up on the counter and ripped open a protein bar. "As the new kid on the block, you've been nominated to be on the auction committee for the upcoming Burn Foundation fundraiser."

"Nominated, huh?" She pulled out her meal and set it down to cool. "I feel honored."

"You lucked out. Not only do you get to work with me, but the auction's in a month and the bulk of the planning is already done. Easy way to get volunteer points." He took a drink of coffee. "You know, in case you need points with the higher-ups." He said it with a conspiratorial grin, taking the sting out of his words.

"I'll probably need twice as many points with my dad," she joked.

Granted, it was only her first day, but getting her colleagues to think of her as something beyond a female, beyond the chief's daughter, was going to be a constant battle. She could handle Penn's friendly jibes. Hell, she could handle Nate's asshole remarks, as well. But she couldn't wait for the day when she wasn't the newbie trying to prove herself.

CHAPTER TWO

JOE HAD COME TO DISLIKE the cheery, "sunshiny" couch in the sunroom of his mother and stepfather's house in Corpus Christi.

His mom was almost always resting there whenever he visited these days. Carmen loved the bright yellow with ivory pinstripes pattern, but the mere sight of it made Joe's shoulders tense and his mood go to hell. As if it was the couch's fault she was stuck there.

He softened when he zeroed in on her face. Even as she slept, her features weren't peaceful. Her skin creased between her eyes and her lips turned slightly downward. To see such solemnity on the face of a woman who'd lived her life full of joy was jarring.

Not wanting to bother her even though she slept more than she was awake these days, he settled into the armchair near her feet and picked up a golf magazine from the end table. He didn't make it through the first article before she stirred.

"Mama," he said when he saw her watching him. "How are you doing today?"

Carmen raised herself up a little, arms shaking from the effort, and leaned against the two throw pillows behind her, smiling warmly. Joe hurried to her side to help.

"Sit down," she told him. "I'm having a good day.

I'm glad you're here." She patted her short gray hair, chuckling and rolling her eyes when she discovered the left side was matted. Her face seemed puffier than when he'd visited last week.

"Did Jorge leave already?" Joe had let himself in when no one had answered the door.

"At about one. I told him to," she said before Joe could protest his stepfather's absence. "Isa's here somewhere. I'm not alone."

Isa, the housekeeper, had been part of the package when Carmen had married Jorge. It'd taken Joe's mom months to get used to the idea of having someone else clean her house, but Jorge had insisted he wanted his new wife working less and enjoying life more. To Joe, it had seemed pretentious. But now that his mother was all but bedridden due to a harsh combination of lupus and vasculitis, it was a godsend having Isa there for several hours a day. She wasn't a nurse, but the housekeeper could let one in. Though Carmen didn't yet need round-the-clock care, Jorge had hired a visiting nurse to come out twice a day when he was at work.

"How are you doing, Joey? You look tired."

"Long night at work. Didn't get much sleep." He grinned. "Why do you think I come over here?" The truth they didn't mention was that Jorge, as a partner in Smith, Vargas and Wellington, had an unavoidable business trip, and Carmen couldn't stay by herself for more than an hour or so at a time. Her body was too weak for her to get around without help, so anytime she had to use the bathroom or wanted something, she required assistance, much to her frustration.

"Did you get a good one last night?" his mom asked.

"Nah, just a bunch of nothings."

Her eyes sparkled as she told him about a two-alarm fire she'd listened to over the scanner a couple nights ago. She knew the lingo as well as he did, and they could talk for hours about the subject. "It reminded me of the one you fought at that factory a few months back."

"That was a good one," Joe agreed. Nothing wrong with his mother's memory.

"You're going to get that job, you know, Joey," she said out of nowhere. "Your professional life is an overwhelming success. I'm proud of you."

He met her eyes and nodded. He was about to thank her when she continued, shutting him up.

"It's your personal life that worries me. What about a woman?"

"What *about* a woman?" he asked in dread. It had been a while since she'd gone on this particular rant, and he hadn't missed it.

"Did you find one yet?"

He forced an image of Faith out of his mind. "I do okay on my own."

"You're a wonderful person, Joey, but you need a woman."

"When the time is right, I'll find one." Now he was spouting empty promises, but it was better than dashing her hopes or making her worry more.

"It's time to step up the search, son. You'll need someone to talk to about the good fires after I'm gone."

He shot up off the chair. "Do you need something to eat, Mama? I could use a snack myself."

"Stop doing that, Joe." Steel underlined her tone. "You know I hate it when you talk like this."

"You can hate it all you want, but you have to face the facts," she said gently. "Changing the subject every time I want to talk about the future is not only futile, but it ticks me off."

He perched on the coffee table and put his hand on her bony one. "I don't want to think about it."

She squeezed his fingers, her grip firmer than he'd expected. "Believe me, I don't want to think about it either, sometimes, but I don't have a lot of choice in the matter. It's a natural thing for a woman to want to make sure everything's in place before she goes."

"You don't know how long it will be. No need to talk like it's tomorrow."

"It could be," she said matter-of-factly, and Joe knew she was right. "If you won't find a woman who's worthy of you, my greatest wish is for you to find a place here with Jorge and his sons."

"I can't move here—"

"That's not what I mean, Joey." She gazed out the window for several weighted seconds, her eyes following the flight of a Couch's kingbird as it landed on the branch of a bush, but her thoughts were obviously elsewhere. "By place I mean…a family. I want you to feel like they're yours."

Joe leaned forward and rested his elbows on his knees, still holding her hand. He stared at the floor, debating how frank to be.

"Jorge is a good man," she continued.

"Of course he is."

"You don't like him."

Joe turned that over in his mind, shook his head.

"That's not true. I didn't like him at first, but I don't dislike him now."

"But there's something holding you back."

"Not at all. I just don't fit in."

"Sure you do. You all play golf. You like sports."

"Those are interests we have in common, yes." The grand sum of shared interests, come to think of it.

"Why can't you embrace them as your family, then?"

He stood and paced. "They don't respect me. My career. To them, I'm a bumbling blue-collar guy who has no place in their overpaid lawyer world."

Concern deepened in her eyes, twisting the blade of guilt that was perpetually buried in his gut. "That's not true—"

"Maybe it'll change if I get the job as assistant chief."

"Don't be ridiculous, Joey. Jorge doesn't care what you do for a living."

"Have you ever noticed how he introduces me? And how he introduces Ryan and Troy? I'm Joe Mendoza, his stepson. End of story. They're Ryan and Troy, junior partner and partner at Smith, Vargas and Wellington. His pride and joy. Men after his own heart, men with brilliant futures."

"They're his sons, Joe."

"I know that, and I don't begrudge them the fact. It's not the lack of a blood tie I'm talking about. It's…" He shook his head, realizing he was getting worked up, which would in turn get his mother worked up, and that was the last thing she needed. "We just come from different worlds. They'll never consider firefighting as good as law."

She studied him as he forced himself to sit on the coffee table again. "Tell me why you're going for this job, Joey. Is it because you want to be assistant fire chief or because you think it will make things easier with your stepfather or, Lord forbid, make me happy?"

"I want the job," he said without hesitation. "I've had my path planned out since I was a kid. You know that. I'm going to the top eventually, just like Dad."

But she wouldn't be there to see it, possibly not when he became assistant chief and definitely not when and if he was lucky enough to climb to the top position in the department.

"I've pushed you," she said quietly, introspectively.

"You've encouraged me. There's a difference."

"A fine line," she agreed. "Have you really given this serious thought lately? You love fighting fires, Joe."

"Hell, yes, I love fighting fires. I love the fire service. I'm a good leader. The position is perfect for me—a natural next step."

"If it will make you happy. But you won't be in the action as much."

That was putting it mildly, but he merely nodded.

"You've never been the desk jockey type."

"I wouldn't call it a desk job."

She stared at him so long he squirmed. "You listen to me, Joey. I want you to think hard about this. Think until you're purple in the face. Think about what *Joe* wants. What you want your life to be like. Don't include me or the legacy of your father or anything else in the equation. Only you."

"I want to move up in the fire department."

She made a succinct sound, a cross between a hiss and a shush. "Not today. You give it some time. Don't worry about me."

As if that would happen.

He wouldn't admit it out loud, because she'd throw a fit, but he wanted like crazy to get that promotion while his mother could still appreciate it. He wanted to share that victory with her. "I won't worry about you if you won't worry about me."

She stared at him, her strong jaw set, and shook her head. "No deal."

"How about a different deal? I'm going to get that job. And I want you to be around to see it. Can you do that?"

It was a ridiculous plea, he knew, but he had to grasp on to something.

Instead of scolding him for being in denial, his mother smiled at him and nodded, as if the two of them could conspire to fool fate. With that sparkle in her eye, he could almost believe it.

"You'll make one heck of an assistant chief, Joey."

FAITH'S NERVES WOUND tighter as she and her dad approached the front door of Ruiz's Restaurante, home of the island's best fish tacos. Food was the last thing on her mind this evening, though.

She'd spotted her mom's Ford Escort in the parking lot and thanked the powers that be when her dad didn't notice it. He'd pulled into a space about five spots down from the Escort and never bothered to look around.

Faith hurried in front of him so she would hit the host station first.

"How many?" the lanky high school kid asked as they approached.

"We're meeting someone," she muttered, and headed right past the guy, spotting her mother in a booth by the window. She didn't look back at her dad, just hoped he would blindly follow.

"Hi, honey," Nita Peligni said.

Faith smiled, bracing herself.

"What on earth—?" her mom began.

"What are you doing here?" her dad asked at the same time.

"Faith." All warmth was gone from her mother's voice.

"Dammit, Faith."

"Wait," Faith said quietly but firmly. "Dad, sit down. Please, Dad."

He studied her, as if the reason for this meeting was jotted on her forehead. Then he turned his tired eyes toward his soon-to-be-ex-wife. "Okay with you, Nita?"

"I don't know what good it's going to do, but fine. Faith, what is this about?" Nita crossed her arms, her dark hair—all natural and not a hint of gray—falling in a bob just below her ears. She wore a peach T-shirt that washed her complexion out, and the shadows under her eyes aged her. It was evident the separation wasn't agreeing with her, but far be it from Faith to point that out.

Tony slid into the booth across from Nita and Faith took a seat next to him, trapping him there.

"Well? What gives?" her dad asked her, shoulders sagging.

"I just wanted to spend some time with my parents. Together. I've been back for two months now and I'm sick of visiting you one at a time."

She was staying with her dad in the family home—which was rambling and empty with just the two of them. No wonder he'd seemed so distraught when she'd come back from San Antonio. He'd been wandering around in the echoing twenty-five hundred square foot house by himself. Her mother had moved into a sterile, colorless, two-bedroom apartment on the mainland.

"We're getting a divorce, Faith." Her mom looked at her with those unwavering dark brown eyes that could scare small children, not telling Faith anything she didn't know. Just the one fact she didn't want to accept.

"Why the rush?" Faith asked, taking a tortilla chip from the red plastic basket in the middle of the tiled table. "You have your whole life to get divorced, if it's really the right thing. What if you're making a mistake?"

"We're not making a mistake," Nita said resolutely.

Her dad was noticeably silent, crunching on chips, eyes on the table.

"Dad?"

He only shook his head. "I'm sorry, princess. I know it's hard on you kids, even though you're grown up."

"It's because of my career, isn't it?" Faith asked, desperation clawing at her to somehow find the key, keep them together, make them see reason.

"What?" her dad exclaimed with both outrage and

shock. "No. Your choice to become a firefighter has nothing to do with our marriage."

"You guys have argued about it for years," Faith said, spouting the suspicion that had been gnawing at her since they'd broken the news of their separation. "Ever since I was twelve years old and told you that's what I wanted to do."

"It's something I will never understand, Faith," her mom said, repeating the same tired chorus. "It's not a job for a woman. It's not safe. I thought maybe when you broke your collarbone it might knock some sense into that head of yours, but you're back at it. Just waiting until the next injury, God forbid."

An unfamiliar uneasiness rolled through Faith's gut, but she ignored it. The collarbone had healed. The building that had collapsed on her in San Antonio should be a distant memory. "A man would've suffered the same injury I did if he'd been standing in that exact spot when the roof caved in. It had nothing to do with ovaries or breasts."

"Faith." Her dad held his palm up, as he so often had, and waited until she pressed hers to it out of habit. That it was something they'd done for as long as she could remember, a sign between her and her dad. "Your mother will always worry about you. Can't change that. You scared us when you got hurt."

"So does that mean you think I shouldn't have gone back to the career I love?"

"No," her dad said, avoiding her mother's steely gaze.

"Did you raise me to quit when bad things happen, Mom?"

This wasn't at all what Faith had planned for their evening together, but she couldn't stop the anger and disbelief from spilling out. It'd been festering for several years since her last big blowup with her mother on the topic.

"I'm not going to dignify that with an answer."

"This is my career. It's what I love doing and want to do for the next twenty or thirty years. I plan to earn several more certifications, promotions, become an officer—who knows how far I can go? But not if I run away because of a broken bone."

"I hope the next time it's not worse, Faith." Her mom's eyes shone with unshed tears that almost got to her. Almost.

Again her dad held his large, work-roughened palm out, and when Faith completed the action, it soothed her enough to take a deep breath and realize she was about to ruin this evening. She had them together at one table, creating the opportunity for them to talk about inane things—anything *but* her career—and remember what they'd had in common forty or so years ago, when they'd fallen in love.

She opened her menu and scanned it, even though she knew it by heart. "What are you guys ordering?"

"Enchiladas," they both said at the same time.

Faith hid a grin.

"Beef," her dad said.

"Seafood." Her mother glanced at her. "What sounds good to you, Faith?"

"Fish tacos, as usual." She closed her menu.

Her dad's cell phone rang and he answered, switching to his business tone and gesturing for Faith to let him out of the booth. She did, watching him walk past the host toward the front entryway.

The waiter came by to check their chip supply and take their requests. Faith went ahead and ordered for her dad, since she knew exactly what he wanted.

That turned out to be the wrong thing to do. He strode back in and grabbed the sunglasses that he'd set on the table. "I have to go. Mayor Romero called an impromptu meeting at city hall. You two have a good dinner." He leaned over and kissed the top of Faith's head before she could say anything.

"Tell the mayor he might want to rethink holding impromptu meetings over the dinner hour," her mom said coldly.

Her dad nodded, showing no emotion.

"Dad?" Faith's plan was falling apart. "Can't you stay for a little while?"

"It's important, honey, or he wouldn't phone me at dinnertime." He walked out, waving a goodbye over his shoulder.

Faith sank deeper into the booth. As she did, she caught a look on her mother's face—of disappointment. Resignation. Just for a moment.

After a few minutes of awkwardness, the two of them engaged in small talk, which was what they did best. It was safest to stay away from topics either one of them cared a lot about. Before their food arrived, Faith spotted Joe Mendoza as he walked by their table.

He turned back when he recognized them. "Faith, it's good to see you. Hello, Mrs. Peligni."

"Good to see you, too," Faith replied.

"Hi, Captain Mendoza," Nita said. "Are you here alone?"

It was impossible not to notice the way the captain's black polo shirt stretched to the limit over his shoulders. His long legs were encased in light blue jeans and he wore black cowboy boots. When he smiled, the corners of his eyes crinkled, making Faith think he must smile a lot. His dark eyes flitted over her for an extra second.

"For now. I'm meeting my great-aunt for dinner." He glanced around, presumably looking for her. "Are you ready to go at it again in the morning?" he asked Faith, referring to their shift the next day.

"Absolutely. Looking forward to it."

"Did you hear about your daughter's performance in the training drill on her first day of work?" he asked Nita.

"I did not."

"She was impressive. Part of the winning team."

"Pair me with a walking legend and it's hard to screw up," Faith said drily, trying not to bask in his compliment.

"Faith has some amazing rappelling skills," Captain Mendoza continued.

Nita's eyes widened and she nodded slowly, politely, but she wasn't able to hide her true feelings. "That's good, I suppose."

An awkward silence fell over them. Thankfully, his great-aunt, who had to be ninety years old, came whisking up to his side.

"There's my Joey," she said, hugging him and then smiling at Faith and her mom.

Captain Mendoza introduced them all, and then the

two of them made their way to the table the host had originally indicated, on the far side of the room. Faith followed him with her eyes, covertly admiring the view from behind. At the same time she was touched by the way he held on to his aunt's elbow, pulled her chair out for her and pushed her in at the table. He sat at a right angle to Faith, giving her the opportunity to appreciate his profile. He was good-looking and a gentleman, but he was probably about fifteen years older than her and, much more importantly, her supervisor.

Their waiter delivered their food, and Faith and her mother returned to their stilted, low-stakes discussion of the unseasonable weather and Faith's four brothers.

"You know, Faith," her mom said when they were almost finished eating, "you're the one who initiated this dinner. I know you're disappointed that your father walked out, but you could give me your full attention, anyway." She smiled as she spoke, but Faith frowned.

"I *am* giving you my attention." She'd heard every word her mother had said, even if she wasn't doing much of the talking.

"Could've fooled me." Her mom scooped up guacamole with a chip. "He's attractive, I'll give you that."

A flash of alarm had Faith straightening. "Who's attractive?"

"Come on. Who have you been staring at for the past twenty minutes? The captain."

"I'm not staring at him. Or if I am, it's only because he happens to be sitting directly in my line of sight. He's my officer, Mom."

"After watching how the fire department tore up your father's and my marriage all these years, I would think you'd want to find someone with a different lifestyle, Faith."

"The 'lifestyle' is something I love," Faith reminded her, picking up her glass to take a drink. "But I have no intention of dating anyone in the department."

Her mom shoveled a bit of enchilada onto her fork. "Although…you did say advancement is your goal. I imagine getting to know the captain *better* is one means to the desired end." She chuckled, amused with herself.

Faith set down her glass. Hard. "I don't believe you just said that."

"I'm kidding. It's a joke, honey."

"It may be a joke to you, but for me it's my life." She threw her napkin onto her half-finished meal. "I have enough trouble being taken seriously by the men I work with. I would think you, a female, my *mom,* for God's sake, would see the importance of dispelling clichés that weaken women."

"I'm sorry, Faith," Nita said quietly. "But the way you were staring at him, and the once-over he gave you when he was at our table—"

"There's nothing between us. There never will be. I may be ambitious and determined to advance, but *that* is something I would never do." Faith strained to keep her volume down. "Ever."

CHAPTER THREE

"YOU MAKE A LOT of the guys here look bad." Evan Drake, an easy-to-like firefighter, was spotting for Faith as she did barbell squats. "I like that."

Trying not to smile, she closed her eyes and concentrated on the burn in her glutes and quads as she slowly straightened. When she nodded, Evan took the barbell from her and replaced it on the rack. Except for them, the workout room at the fire station was empty, though others had been in and out during the hour-plus Faith had been exercising.

"Spotters aren't supposed to make the lifter laugh," she said, mopping sweat from her forehead with a towel.

"Sorry. You can lift a lot, though."

"I have to. Not everyone is open-minded about women doing this job." She'd started weight lifting in high school, already accustomed to doubts from her own mother.

"You'll run into some skeptics here, if you haven't already," Evan said. "Ready for the next set?"

Faith nodded and got back into position, bracing herself for the weight.

Halfway through the set, the door opened and Captain Mendoza and Nate Rottinghaus came in. Faith was just starting to push herself up to a stand when the captain caught her eye and nodded subtly. She floundered, lost her focus and had to stop for a second to regain her composure.

Dammit. He was good-looking—especially in workout shorts that hinted at thigh muscles that didn't quit—but that was no reason to be distracted.

He was watching her, adjusting one of the weight machines, when she closed her eyes and tried to clear her thoughts so she could finish the stupid rep and not look like an idiot. Or a weak female.

"Think you're more than just a pretty face, huh?" Nate said once she was standing. He'd moved to the hand weights on the other side of her.

Instead of ramming the barbell into his head as she'd like to do, Faith didn't blink. She moved straight into the next repetition, counting to herself.

"Another comment like that will get you written up." The captain was suddenly right next to them, in Nate's face. "Faith's been working out for nearly ninety minutes. If you had a fraction of the work ethic she does, you might make something of your career."

Nate raised his chin almost imperceptibly, kept his shoulders stiff, his face expressionless. "Sorry, Captain. Didn't realize you'd taken her under your wing. Probably a good idea. It's tough when you're…new." She felt his eyes rove up and down her body, making it obvious that "new" was not what he meant.

Faith gritted her teeth and rose with the weight too quickly.

"Whoa," Evan said, steadying it.

"I'm done." She let him take the barbell from her

once again, her heart thundering. Technically, she still had three more reps, but to hell with them.

What she wanted to do was storm out of the room, but she still owed herself another half hour of exercise. If she stopped now, starting again would be tough. Plus, she wasn't going to let the peanut brain scare her away.

"Thanks for spotting," she told Evan. "Let me know when I can return the favor."

"You got it."

Faith went to the other side of the room and stepped onto one of the treadmills. She'd run three miles to start her workout and normally didn't go much more than that in a day, but she had anger to burn. She turned the speed up to seven miles per hour and began hoofing.

She needed to start bringing her headphones so she could block out the world, specifically when she was in the presence of idiots. Today she had nothing to quell her nerves or distract her except the even rhythm of her feet hitting the machine. After a couple miles, it became somewhat hypnotic. Calmed her down a few levels.

At the two and a half mile mark, she noticed the captain heading for the door already. She glanced at the clock. She was six minutes short of her full workout time, but she stopped the machine anyway. Grabbing her water bottle and towel, she strode out with a wave in Evan's direction.

The captain was turning the corner toward the showers when Faith cleared the exercise room.

"Captain Mendoza."

He paused and looked back at her. She walked briskly down the hall toward him.

"We're informal around here. Everyone calls me Joe."

"I need to talk to you, Joe. In private, please."

He studied her, his eyes flickering to her lips so briefly she wondered if she imagined it. She might have liked that in another time and place...with someone who wasn't her supervisor. But here and now? Right after Nate the Flake's stupidity? Not so much.

"We can go to my office," he finally said.

As they both turned in that direction, he touched her bare waist between her sports bra and exercise shorts with his large hand. Faith flinched in surprise.

"Sorry," he said, removing his hand and increasing the space between them.

When she glanced sideways at him as they walked, he stared at the floor as if embarrassed. For some reason that was almost endearing, or would be if she wasn't already halfway to irate.

It seemed eons later when they finally got to his office, though it wasn't far from the showers. The captain let her enter first, and she stood next to the door as he closed it.

"What can I do for you?" he asked in a relaxed tone that said he had no idea how ticked off she was. He walked around his desk and faced her without sitting.

"That scene with Nate," she began.

"I'm sorry, Faith. He crossed the line—"

"He's an idiot," she interrupted. "But that's not what I wanted to talk about."

"Oh?"

She clamped her jaw for a moment to let out some of her frustration in a way that wouldn't get her in trouble.

Meeting his gaze across the desk, she swallowed. "With all due respect, *please* don't do that again."

"Do what?" Joe asked, narrowing his eyes.

"Don't stick up for me. Don't jump to my rescue when a coworker acts like a pig. Just…don't. Please."

One brow flickered, hinting at his surprise. "It's my responsibility. I don't take that lightly."

"This is different."

"You think you should receive special treatment?" he challenged, crossing his arms.

"No! That's just it. I don't want any special treatment. I want you to go out of your way to *avoid* giving me special treatment." Clenching her fists, she paced in the small space, doing her best to remain calm, professional.

He stared at her, eyebrows raised.

Faith glanced at the door to reassure herself it was latched. "Can I be frank?"

"Always."

She barely registered she was picking at the cuticle of her thumb with her index finger. "In San Antonio, there were other females in the department. Even though a few of them had been there for years, we still weren't respected as equals by some of the men."

Joe nodded, acknowledging that the problem wasn't unique to San Antonio or even Texas, unfortunately.

"Here, I've got two strikes against me—my gender *and* my dad's position. I'm going to have to work three times as hard to receive half the respect. And I plan to do exactly that. It's not right, but I knew the situation coming into it."

"I have no doubt you'll succeed."

Faith shook her head resolutely. "Don't you see? If you or anyone else—officer or not—smooths things over for me, I'll never be seen as just another firefighter."

"We haven't worked together for long, Faith, but I'm certain you're not *just* another firefighter."

Was that to be taken as a compliment? She was momentarily surprised into silence, trying to read his intent. His face gave nothing away, so she continued. "I know the culture here. I grew up on the island. Practically grew up in the station. You may mean well, but I can't have you interfering."

Joe didn't immediately answer. He just watched her. Made her nervous. Antsy.

"I appreciate your dilemma," he said at last, in that low semidrawl of his. "But as a captain I can't allow certain things to go on in the station when I'm on duty."

"I understand that, Joe. I'm not asking you to bend any rules or allow blatant harassment or anything like that. But harmless comments from people like him… If I can ignore it, why can't you?"

"You know what your dad would say if he heard I let somebody treat you like that?"

She shuddered to think of it. "My dad doesn't have to know everything that goes on. He wouldn't want to."

"Everything, no. But I get the impression that when it comes to his daughter, he wants details."

"So you're going to tell him a bully picked on me at recess today?"

Joe shook his head. "I hadn't planned on it, no. All I'm saying is that I'm going to do what I need to do when I'm the captain on duty."

"When rules are broken, that's fine. When people are jerks, could you try to rein yourself in? Please?"

Something in his jaw ticked as he studied her again. Seconds dragged on, and at last he spoke. "I'll see what I can do. But I make no promises. Those men need to learn how to act."

"If their mothers couldn't teach them, no offense, but I doubt you can, either."

"You might be right."

"I have four older brothers. Three of them are decent human beings. The fourth, there's no hope."

"If neither the chief nor your mom could straighten him out, I might have to concede." Joe's mouth curved in a half smile but his stance remained tense. Serious. "Anything else you need?"

Faith shook her head. "Thank you, sir."

She'd called him goddamn sir.

As Faith left his office, Joe pressed his knuckles on his desk hard enough to crack them.

He didn't mind being called sir, and received it plenty from the rest of the men. In theory, he should be fine with Faith calling him sir as well.

But he wasn't.

Because it made him feel like an old man to a young, attractive woman.

He supported having women in the station, provided they could pass all the tests, physical and otherwise. Faith could. He was okay having her here.

He'd be more okay with it if she didn't look so good, and frankly, that wasn't acceptable.

Joe grabbed his radio and headed outside to work off

some serious steam. It was a pity he was on a short leash to the station because he could run all the way to the north end of the island right now...and back. Twice.

He'd left the exercise room instead of using the tread-mill because watching Faith run had his mind going in all kinds of places it had no right to. Twenty minutes was not a workout, but he'd been entranced by her long, muscular legs, tanned and smooth. Her perfect breasts and slender waist, the slight curve of her hips that moved just so with every step on the treadmill.

It'd been raining all day, but Joe took no heed of the steady downpour. In fact, he welcomed it. Maybe he could drown his thoughts.

Faith had been upset by him "defending" her, but if she had any notion of the things that had gone through his mind in the past forty-five minutes...

He shook his head and picked up his already burning pace.

It wasn't just her beauty and her fit body that got to him. It was her sheer competence. Her confidence and drive. The way she didn't let naysayers get in her way. He admired her determination to earn the respect of her new colleagues.

He appreciated her desire to do it on her own. Totally understood her stance. However, as he'd told her, he couldn't promise he wouldn't interfere again. When he'd heard Nate's veiled chauvinistic comment, he'd jumped in involuntarily.

He couldn't do that again. He'd meant what he'd told her about adhering to his duties, but defending her ear-lier had come as naturally as scratching to a dog. There hadn't been any thought involved. His reaction had been on a basic, elemental, man-looking-after-woman level.

There was nothing to do but admit it—and only to himself. Faith Peligni was one of the sexiest, most intriguing women he'd ever met. And he was in a position where nothing could ever happen between them.

Not after her father had asked him to look out for her.

Not if he had any hope of retaining the fire chief's trust—and having a chance in hell at a promotion.

CHAPTER FOUR

FAITH HAD BEEN IGNORING the state of the Peligni
family home for the two months she'd been back in
town recuperating.

But when she drove up in her Subaru, frazzled and
grumpy from braving the beginning of the spring break
influx at the grocery store, she couldn't help noticing
that the bushes, once neatly manicured, were shaggy and
unkempt. The lawn, though only a square patch of grass
on this side of the house, was overgrown. A broken-
down charcoal grill sat to the left of the driveway.

She pulled into the garage, leaned against the headrest and closed her eyes. Her dad had always been a
fanatic about the yard. Her oldest brother, Will, used to
joke that their dad carried around a ruler, and when the
grass hit two inches, he fired up the mower.

That was before. When their family was still intact.
When her mom still lived here. Before her dad had
started sinking into what Faith suspected could be
depression.

She realized her hand was clutched so tightly around
her keys that they were digging into her palm. Groan-
ing in frustration, she climbed out and popped open the
back.

She didn't mind grocery shopping for her and her
dad. It was a lot easier than when the seven of them

had been home at once and the trip would cost several hundred dollars. Their mom had always taken one child with her to the store, and the rest of the siblings had mobbed the car upon its return, helping to carry in the goods and then rummaging through them and snacking before anything could be put away.

Today, no one came out to greet her. Not that she needed assistance—there were only two paper bags stuffed with food. But the quiet, on top of the neglected state of the property, brought her down. Made her long for Peligni family chaos. Or at the very least, her old dad back. She needed to call Paul and Will tonight to fill them in on their father's state, sure, but also just to hear their voices.

As she made her way up the interior stairs to the main level of the house, she realized she was stomping her feet on each wooden step.

Where was this anger coming from?

She sympathized with her dad and had a hard time blaming him for being sad and out of sorts. Her mom had left *him*. Given up on their marriage after almost forty years, supposedly because of his dedication to his job. Nita had resented it for years, but no one in the family had ever thought it would come to her leaving.

So why, when Faith spotted her dad on the plaid sofa in the living room asleep—*again*—did she want to throw something? Wake him up with a crash?

She set the bags down on the kitchen counter and breathed slowly, summoning her patience. When she turned around, a photo on the top shelf of the baker's rack caught her eye. The whole family, taken three years ago at Christmas.

Everyone wore button-down denim shirts and every-one looked happy. Lou, who'd actually managed to get leave that coincided with the holidays that year. Paul and Will, the two oldest and brainiest Pelignis, who lived on either coast and didn't make it home often enough. Even Anthony, Faith's self-centered brother who usually had an excuse for everything, had made the relatively short trip home from Dallas. Her dad smiled widely. Her mom, too… Was it just a facade? How long had she been contemplating leaving? Faith wondered, not for the first time, whether her dad had had any inkling a separation was coming.

Her anger didn't go away, but it was no longer aimed at her father. He was the one who'd had his marriage ripped out from under him, who'd been hurt to the core. She was the only person he had to help him through it, since she hadn't been able to convince her brothers there was anything they could do to keep their parents together. It was up to her to be there for their dad—to sympathize, sure, but also to give him tough love when he needed it. Like now. He had to stop sleeping all the time.

"Dad?" She slipped her shoes off and walked quietly across the ceramic tile floor. "Dad. You have to wake up now."

He rolled over, from his side to his back. Snorted. Continued to slumber on. In the past, he'd been a super-light sleeper from years of being awakened by the alarm at the station, or so he always said.

"Dad, wake up. It's after one o'clock and I bet you haven't eaten lunch yet."

He woke with a start and sputtered, "What? What's wrong, princess?"

She sat on the edge of the sofa by his feet. "Nothing's wrong. You just need to get up and eat."

He looked around, dazed, then sat up slowly. "I could eat, I guess."

"Did you have any lunch while I was gone?" She knew the answer, but asked anyway.

Her dad checked his watch and shook his head. "Didn't realize it was so late. What are we going to eat?"

"I picked up a rotisserie chicken and some potato salad. Let's go get it ready."

Faith went into the kitchen, decorated with Southwestern style, but her dad moved more slowly. She started unpacking groceries and setting out their food on the oversize table that used to hold the whole family, trying not to think how inconceivable it would've been for her dad to forget a meal just a few months ago.

"Smells good," he said when he entered the less-than-tidy kitchen. "What can I do?"

"Grab us some drinks from the fridge."

A few minutes later, they sat at the table filling their plates.

"So how's the job going so far?" Tony asked as he served himself potato salad.

"Pretty good. Just learning how you do things here."

"Any problems?"

Nate's obnoxious face flashed in her mind and she blocked it out. He was a problem, sure, but nothing she couldn't handle on her own. Tattling wasn't her thing, anyway.

"Nope. Everything's fine. A little bit slow…"

"This isn't San Antonio, Faith. Never will be. You prepared to handle the less exciting shifts?"

"Yeah, it just takes a little getting used to. It makes it easier to fit in PT, though."

Her mind wandered to her workout yesterday. Joe's interruption. The way just the sight of him had distracted her from her routine.

"How's Joe treating you?"

She started. Had she said his name aloud? No. *Idiot.* It was a normal question. She just had a guilty conscience.…

"He's okay, I guess." She took a bite of white meat and chewed. "Actually, he hovers. I don't think he trusts me."

"I'm sure he does, princess."

She shook her head. "No matter what I'm doing, he shows up to check on me. Tries to help when I don't need it. He's not like that with anyone else."

"It's his job."

"To babysit? It's a fire station, Dad, not a day care."

A more perceptive person might suggest she protested too much, and that person would probably be right. For once, she was thankful her dad wasn't at the top of his game.

"Joe's a good guy. If you ever need anything, you can trust him. He'll look out for you."

Faith closed her eyes and set down her fork. "I don't need anyone looking out for me."

"You're new, Faith. Don't be so hardheaded. If someone wants to be nice, accept it."

She didn't respond immediately. Took a drink of cold milk instead.

"You don't get it, Dad. I can't afford to have an officer bending over backward to help me. I'm a woman in a man's job, fighting off perceptions that I'm the weak link every single second I'm on the clock." Her volume remained level, though she snapped out the words.

"Don't get upset. I know you can handle the job. There's no doubt in my mind you're as good as those men, better than a lot of them."

"How can I *not* get upset?" Now she got louder. "My own mother suggested I sleep with the captain to get ahead."

"She did *what?*"

Faith shook her head. "Never mind. She thought she was being funny. I'm just sick of having to prove myself to everyone, including my family."

"Faith." He reached across the table and held his palm out toward hers until she returned the gesture. "You don't have to prove yourself to me. Ever. But I will always worry about you." His voice was thick with emotion. Affection.

Faith couldn't help but be touched by his words. Her response got caught in her throat. It took a lot for her dad to show his feelings so openly, and once again, her irritation dissipated.

"I'll be fine."

He seemed flustered for a moment. Inhaled shakily. "If anything ever happened to you again, Faith,

anything worse than last time, I don't know if I could
survive it."

That did it. Tears filled her eyes. She fought them
hard, refusing to let them spill over. For several seconds,
she didn't dare breathe, afraid of losing it. Surreptitiously, she wiped the corners of her eyes and blinked
hard until she thought she could speak.

"I'll do the best I can, Dad. But you have to let me
do it my own way."

"I THINK WE'VE GOT something."

The words were nonchalant, but Joe's tone was laced
with a restrained excitement Faith hadn't heard from
him before.

The engine sped toward a hotel on the shore. *Something* meant a fire. A real one, not a trash fire that could
be knocked out in less than ten minutes.

Adrenaline pumped through Faith's system. This was
her first big fire since her injury in San Antonio.

Joe confirmed again that this one was business, and
she angled herself a little in the back-facing seat to look
at him as she adjusted one of her boots. He leaned forward slightly, eyes sparking with life as they skipped
from Derek, who was driving, to the dark smoke a few
blocks ahead of them.

He loves every bit of this, Faith thought to herself.
*Like a little boy loves seeing the big rigs speed by with
sirens blaring and lights flashing.* It didn't surprise her,
because most people in her profession lived for the challenge of a large fire. But Joe was normally so cool and
collected in the station that his tangible excitement made
her smile.

As they arrived on the scene, Joe hollered orders to their crew. He jumped out of the rig and located the battalion chief in charge, while Faith, Penn and Derek worked at the truck, getting equipment ready.

The hotel was medium-size, made up of multiple structures. The involved building was six stories high. Acrid smoke filled the air and flames showed on the second and third floors.

Joe came back with more specific directions for the crew. Penn was on the nozzle, Faith with him. Without a word, they hooked up the appropriate hose to the engine and made their way to the entrance at the end of the building that Joe had indicated.

Penn glanced over his shoulder at her with a questioning look and she nodded, but her heart hammered uncharacteristically out of control. She tried to ignore it.

He headed inside and Faith, holding on to the hose, followed—until she was just inside the door.

She froze.

The scene was status quo for a seasoned firefighter. The smoke was so thick she could barely see a foot in front of her, the temperature already climbing. Her partner continued on, but Faith couldn't force her feet to move for anything.

Her chest tightened and a scream climbed in her throat. She couldn't seem to get air into her lungs, and she checked again to make sure her breathing apparatus was functioning. It was.

She glanced up and couldn't see the ceiling. Then she noticed how hard she was breathing—for no reason.

You're losing it, Faith. Get a hold of yourself.

With effort, she slowed her respirations, closing her eyes. Gradually the need to crawl out of her skin receded, and she realized if this wasn't a heart attack, it must be some kind of anxiety thing. Whatever it was, it sucked.

The hose in her hands was yanked forward, jolting her back to the fire and the very real need to get moving. What was she doing, standing here like a probie at her first fire?

Faith reassured herself that no one had witnessed her freak-out moment. Not that anyone could see in this smoke, anyway. She hesitated again, then swore at herself and moved ahead to catch up with Penn, praying he hadn't missed her yet. If anyone found out she'd flaked, there was no hope of ever overcoming her reputation as the chief's daughter and a charity case.

HOURS LATER, Faith poured water down her bone-dry throat, surveying the fire site to estimate how much longer cleanup would take. Maybe another half hour if they were lucky.

This whole end of the resort hotel was a loss, but they'd managed to stop the fire from jumping to the other buildings. Two companies from the mainland had been called in as well, and injuries had been few and minor.

Fatigue weighed Faith down as she squatted next to the truck, leaning her back against it, finishing her drink. Ten hours was a long fight, but you never really noticed how wiped you were until afterward, when the adrenaline stopped and salvage and overhaul wound down. Once the flames were doused, the firefighter had spent time rehashing the situation as they carried out anything that could be saved, trading stories of what they'd encountered, one-upping to see who'd ended up having the best assignment. Silently questioning if they'd done the right things, made the right decisions. If there was anything they could've done better.

Faith's self-critique was easy tonight—she'd blown it. Oh, sure, she'd gotten her act together and done okay in the end. But walking into that burning building and locking up…

Unforgivable.

And the biggest problem was she wasn't sure it wouldn't happen the next time they got called to a big fire.

No one had noticed, but that didn't change a thing. *She* knew.

Derek Severson and Clay Marlow rested several feet from Faith, still talking as they rehydrated. She stood and disposed of her water bottle. She had a policy of never being the last person back from taking a break.

A few minutes later, the crews had removed as much as they could from the interior and ensured there were no remaining hot spots. Faith noticed a couple hundred feet of hose from their engine that had to be loaded. She headed over and started rolling it, though every muscle in her body was beginning to ache. She was starting to fantasize about falling into bed; it was after 2:00 a.m. and would be a short night, anyway.

She stood and was lifting the first roll of hose to take to the engine when a pain near her collarbone nearly flattened her. She sat down hard, dropped the hose on the ground, muttering swear words to herself.

When she could breathe again, she glanced around, trying to act as if nothing was wrong.

Dammit… Joe was standing near the engine and staring straight at her. If the concern on his face was any indication, he'd seen everything.

She was afraid to stand up again because it freaking hurt. Another jab of pain, on top of her exhaustion, was liable to make her cry like a girl. Instead, she busied herself with the hose, trying to make it appear as if it wasn't rolled quite right and needed to be fixed.

"Faith." Joe loomed over her in the chilly night.

"Yes, sir." She didn't look up at him, just worked intently on the nonexistent problem.

He squatted next to her. "What are you doing?"

"Fixing the hose."

"The hose is fine."

Finally she glanced up at him.

"You hurt yourself," he said in a gentle, low voice so no one could overhear. She was eternally grateful for his discretion.

"Not really," she said, giving up on the hose act.

"I saw you, Faith. Don't insult me by lying."

When she looked into those concerned dark eyes, she couldn't continue to deny it. But she could understate it.

"It was my collarbone. Just a sharp, brief pain, but it's over now." Which was the truth. So far. "Long day, I guess."

He watched her closely for several seconds, as if gauging whether she was leveling with him.

"Do we need to have Scott or Rafe check you out?" he asked, gesturing over his shoulder to the ambulance.

"No," she said quickly. "Really. It didn't hurt until just now. I must have twisted wrong as I stood up."

He wasn't convinced, Faith could tell. So to persuade him, she had no choice but to stand and prove she was fine.

She picked up the hoses, swallowed and braced herself. This time she rose more slowly. And yeah, the pain was there, but not as bad. She fought through it, refusing to let it show on her face. Because, of course, he was still staring at her.

He brushed her wrist in a touch that was probably not professional, judging by the way it got Faith's heart racing. Before she could scold herself for her reaction, he spoke—again quietly, so no one could hear. "Don't be stubborn, Faith. Let me carry one of those. You don't want to reinjure yourself."

She didn't know if it was the mind-blurring fatigue or the feel of his rough fingers so tender on her skin, but she weakened. Let him take one of the rolls from her. She walked by his side to the engine but insisted on putting them away herself. Self-consciously, she glanced around to see if anyone had noticed that Joe had helped her. A couple of guys were nearby, but not paying attention to them; maybe no one had seen. She should've just carried both hoses.

"So," Joe said, still in a private voice. "I want more information on this. Did you injure yourself tonight? Run into anything? Have something fall or hit you? Did you—"

"None of the above, like I told you. You saw the first and only episode and it's gone now. Can we drop it? Please?"

"I need to report—"

"Any injuries that occur on the job. This isn't an injury and it didn't happen on this job."

"You watch that collarbone. If you have any more problems with it, I want you to see a doctor."

"Yes, sir," she said formally.

She could almost swear he flinched.

As she turned away to get back to work, a thought occurred to her. "You're not going to tell the chief, are you?" He'd flip out and go all protective-daddy on her, which was sweet in theory, but totally unnecessary. And not at all what he needed mental-healthwise, or she needed careerwise.

Joe looked off into the distance and it was all Faith could do not to beg him.

"Don't you think he would want to know?"

"He's got too much on his mind," Faith said. "He doesn't need to worry about something insignificant like this. If another building falls on me, you can mention it, I promise."

Joe didn't seem to appreciate her attempt at humor. When he said nothing, Faith grasped her thick turnout pants in her fist until her knuckles were likely white. "Equal treatment, Joe. That's all I'm asking for."

"First Nate's treatment of you and now this. I'm keeping a lot from the head of the department."

"But the head of the department wouldn't really need to know about either if I wasn't his daughter."

He exhaled and pegged her with those eyes again. "I'll keep your secret, Faith. Again. Just promise me about the doctor if you need it."

She nodded, suspecting her definition of needing it might differ from his. "Thank you."

She walked away, pretty sure that she could trust Joe's word—but not at all happy that she had to.

CHAPTER FIVE

"SURELY YOU BIGWIGS could have found someone in the firm to be your fourth?" Joe asked his stepfather, Jorge Vargas. The black-haired man wasn't quite as tall as Joe, but stood ramrod-straight, even when he was relaxed on the golf course. It was obvious the man had power and liked to use it.

The Corpus Christi Country Club golf course was already a brilliant, well-manicured green, and the air wafting over them was warm for early March. Spring break. Hell month for the San Amaro Island Fire Department. The tournament sponsored by his stepfather's and stepbrothers' prestigious law firm fell at the worst time of the year for Joe, but he'd made a point of asking for the day off. Everything had worked out, the shift at the department was covered, and here he was. For better or worse. He reminded himself repeatedly that he liked golf and didn't get on the course enough. And really, these guys weren't too bad. This was a relatively easy way to make his mom happy.

"Come on, Joe," Jorge prodded, "the Vargas men are going to take this tournament. You're one of us today. You're the best and you know it."

He didn't want to be a Vargas...but he'd happily take a quarter of their earning power.

"Joe putts like a woman." Troy, the older of his two

stepbrothers and Mr. *GQ,* took out his driver at the second hole. He'd been out on the course regularly, as evidenced by his bronzed skin.

"You wish I putted like a woman," Joe said. "It's been weeks since I've played, though. Some of us have to work for a living."

"Speaking of work, did Maurice get you the info on that possible witness for the Sullivan case?" Jorge asked Troy.

"Left me a message. I'll touch base this evening and take care of it."

These three—Jorge, Troy and Ryan, the younger, lankier brother, who sported a goatee—weren't terrible company…until they started talking business. Then it was as if they turned into droning robots that didn't know when to shut up.

"You're up, man," Joe said to Troy as the group in front of them moved on, successfully ending the shop talk, at least for now.

Troy stepped up, spent forever and a half pondering the shot, then hit the ball onto the green. Looking smug, he turned around to face them. "Beat that, suckers."

"We're on the same team, dumb-ass," Ryan said. He was a pretty boy beneath the facial hair, with chiseled features and dark lashes longer than most women's.

"Same team, sure. But we could make things more interesting." Jorge dug his wallet out from his back pocket and waved a twenty. "What do you say a little wager among family? Twenty bucks a hole? Winner takes all."

"In." Ryan raised his chin, clearly thinking he had a good chance at collecting.

"Hell, yeah, I'm in," Troy said. "I could use some spending money."

Being the blue-collar guy, Joe had three measly twenties in his wallet. All the more reason to beat these paper pushers. "Might as well give me your cash now," he said, moving up to the tee, taking a practice swing.

"You're all talk, Joe," Ryan said.

"Put your money where your mouth is," Troy added.

Joe tuned out everything the morons behind him chattered about and focused. Maybe said a little prayer. He couldn't afford to lose more than a couple of holes at twenty bucks a pop. He swung and watched his ball arc through the cloudless sky, silently coaching it along. It made it to the green, barely, but he'd take it. Putting was his strong point, in spite of what Troy liked to believe.

Two strokes later, Joe collected his first sixty bucks of the afternoon.

"Can I write this off as a donation to charity?" Troy asked as he handed over his bill.

"Don't write too soon," Joe said, buoyed by his victory and letting the insult to his lower tax bracket slide right off. "I'll be taking more."

They traded taunts and insults as they walked to their carts, and Joe admitted to himself this wasn't so bad. Sunshine, golf and his artificial family. Soon they'd be the only family he had.

His mother made no secret that she wanted Joe and his steps to form stronger bonds. The last thing he wanted her to do was worry about him, so he was making an effort. Heck, *still* making an effort, as he had been since she remarried, five years ago. He visited her and Jorge in Corpus more often, since she couldn't get out much and no longer made the trip to the island. Spent time with these three when he could be doing other things. He would never fit in, but if it gave his mother peace of mind, he'd continue to try.

"You still planning to come for your mom's birthday?" Jorge asked Joe as they climbed out of the cart at the third tee.

"Of course." That it could be her last hung heavily on his mind, and he wondered if the thought crossed Jorge's, as well.

"You got a girlfriend yet?" his stepfather continued.

"Is my mother recruiting you for the get-Joe-married campaign?" Joe took a drink from his sports bottle and closed the top.

Ryan cackled next to him. "I hope not, for Dad's sake. It'd be easier to get a twelve-year-old girl voted in as governor of Texas."

"I don't have to tell you how much your mom worries," Jorge said to Joe, and the way his tone changed when talking about her, how it softened with affection, reaffirmed his devotion to his wife. "I remind her all the damn time that you're a grown man, but you know how women are."

"As much as I'd love to put her mind at ease, I'll go out on a limb and predict I'll be showing up by myself," Joe said.

"You could always pay for a companion," Ryan suggested.

"I might be able to pay for one night, but that's eternally better than paying a lifetime for that high maintenance glamour girl you married." Joe liked what he knew of Shelly, but he couldn't pass up the opportunity to give Ryan grief.

"I reckon he got you there," Troy said, grinning.

"Reckon he did. Price you pay to sleep with a beautiful woman every night." Ryan didn't seem too upset by his lifetime sentence. "So how's the fire department?"

"Busy as a hound during flea season. On top of spring break, I'm going for a promotion. Assistant fire chief. The current guy's retiring."

"Will you be able to stay away from the manual stuff as assistant chief?" Jorge asked. "Keep your hands clean?"

Joe shook his head and grinned. His stepfather would never understand. He'd stopped trying to explain it after the first dozen or so attempts. "That's the downside. Not being able to fight fires myself."

All three men stared at him as if he'd admitted to romancing livestock.

"You all should shed your suits and ties and try it sometime," he said, gauging the progress of the team in front of them as they finished up the hole.

"I'll leave the hero-ing up to you," Ryan said. "Charred isn't really my color."

"I don't know," Troy said. "Your heart's pretty black, bro."

"Joe," his stepfather interjected. "You got anything planned in early April?"

"The usual," Joe said. "What's up?"

"The guys and I thought we'd see if you wanted to go with us to spring training."

"Astros?"

"Of course," Troy said, as if Joe was the densest man on earth.

Joe had been a Rangers fan since he was old enough to beat a plastic bat on the living room floor. Never an Astros fan. He hadn't been invited to the annual pilgrimage with the Vargas men before. Which meant one thing. "My mother put you up to asking?"

"We wouldn't listen to her if she did," Troy said.

The senior Vargas glared at his older son.

"Okay, maybe we would, but this wasn't her idea." Troy backpedaled.

"Why don't you guys watch some real baseball?" Joe asked.

"We invited you on our trip, man," Ryan said. "No need to go injuring our team."

Joe asked several questions about the trip and racked his brain for any plans he might have made. Several guys at the station would be off that week—a regular occurrence after the intensity of spring break on the island. It'd be a hassle to get away then. However, though the Astros didn't do it for him, taking a trip with Jorge and his sons would go a long way in calming his mother's worries, convincing her they'd do just fine as a family even without her. That was a gift to her he couldn't deny just because these guys were a bunch of stuffed shirts who liked the wrong team.

"Let me check my calendar and see what I can do."

CHAPTER SIX

FAITH'S EYES WERE GLAZING over as she stared at the study manual for the hazardous materials test. She hadn't procrastinated. Not entirely, anyway. She'd studied last weekend for quite a while. But now it was the eleventh hour and she was close to panicking.

She got up from the station's kitchen table and stretched her arms over her head in an attempt to get her blood flowing. She went to the counter behind her and poured herself another cup of coffee, emptying the pot. The clock on the microwave oven said 3:14 a.m. She was the only one stirring in the place, and the silence was starting to ring in her ears.

"What are you doing up?"

Joe's voice in the doorway behind her made her drop her mug, which shattered on the tile floor. Thankfully, the coffee that splashed on her was only lukewarm.

"You need to wear a bell around your neck," she said, bending to pick up the large chunks of broken pottery and trying to ignore the racing of her heart. It wasn't caused just by having the life startled out of her. Unfortunately. It had everything to do with the man who'd surprised her. She hadn't felt this kind of nervous excitement since her crush on Dylan Morrison her first year at community college.

She glanced at Joe in time to see him smile. It must

be late, because she couldn't resist admiring how good-looking he was. Her tired mind was filled with the un-invited fantasy of him walking up to her and kissing her till her brain melted and her hands shook.

Oh, her hands *were* shaking. From too much caffeine, no doubt. Lack of sleep.

Faith found a dustpan and hand broom beneath the sink, and swept the little pieces. Joe mopped up the remaining liquid with paper towels.

"Test is tomorrow?" he asked, glancing toward the open book on the table.

"Technically today, I guess. I'll go take it as soon as shift is over."

They stood at the same time and her fantasy scenario of thirty seconds ago intensified. He came over to her at the counter and surveyed the coffeepot.

"Didn't save any for me, I see."

"Sorry," Faith said, putting space between them. "Didn't know you were a night owl."

"Always have been. Didn't know you were afraid of tests."

"Always have been."

Joe rinsed out the pot and refilled the filter for another twelve-cup supply. "That surprises me. You seem to know your facts."

"I'm somewhat of a perfectionist."

Joe chuckled. "And here I thought you were laid-back. Carefree."

"Maybe in a different lifetime. So what's up with coffee at three in the morning? Do you really have that much work to do or are you just afraid of the dark?"

"Never know what's under the bed."

"Want me to check if it's safe for you?" she teased. "I hear there can be some pretty ferocious dust bunnies in the corners around here."

"That's what happens when firefighters can't clean to save their lives."

"They need better leadership, clearly."

He didn't seem to see the humor in her comment.

"You take your job very seriously, don't you?" Faith asked, leaning against the counter next to him.

"About as seriously as you take yours."

She nodded at the truth in that. "Did you always want to be a firefighter?"

"Either that or a Jedi."

If she hadn't spilled her coffee by dropping it, she would've spit it out at his reply. "Jedi training didn't pan out?"

He cracked a grin and shook his head distractedly.

"How long was your dad the chief?" she asked. She vaguely remembered meeting Chief Mendoza a couple times, but she'd been so young then, maybe ten years old. At that point, the trucks and flashing lights had been much more interesting to her.

"Two years. That was before there was an assistant. It wasn't three months after he stopped fighting fires and became chief that he found out about the cancer." Joe's face hardened as he tried not to give away his feelings.

"Lungs, right?" Faith did remember, very clearly, when his dad had died. The funeral had been gigantic, though she hadn't been allowed to attend. It'd been on the news and the front page of the newspaper. Her dad had considered Joe's father a mentor and had been struck deeply by his death.

"Yep. No doubt from everything he breathed in on the job."

"I can't imagine growing up without my dad," Faith said.

"I was twenty-five when he died."

"Oh. I guess you were grown-up." She smiled sheepishly. "Sorry."

"Yeah." His tone lightened. "Tell me I'm old."

"I'd never say that to someone who can run faster than me."

He studied her curiously. "So how is working in the same department as your dad going so far?"

"Going well," she said, refusing to get into her worries. In general, it was an honest answer. "I always dreamed of working with him. He's the reason I got into firefighting."

"You two have always seemed close. I remember that even when you were a teenager."

"Drives my mom crazy sometimes."

"That's what she gets for marrying one of the good guys," Joe said.

"I wish she remembered he's one of the good guys. Though he does make it difficult lately."

Joe turned toward her and brushed her hair behind her ear. Her breath caught, and he retracted his hand, as if realizing he wasn't supposed to touch her. "He's kind of out of sorts, isn't he?"

She looked down nervously, whether from the personal topic or the contact, she couldn't say. "That's one way to put it."

"If there was something I could do to help, I would. I like your dad. Respect him a great deal."

Faith nodded, wishing like crazy she had a clue how to help her father. "He needs something to keep him busy. The weekends with no work just about kill him. Evenings are long, too."

"Does he have any hobbies?"

"His boat," Faith answered. "But he's been on it only once since I moved back. He seems to have lost interest."

"Maybe I could persuade him to take it out. Get him to take me for a ride or something."

"You don't have to do that, Joe."

He looked into her eyes with such concern she wanted to melt. "I want to. It's not exactly a hardship having to go out on a boat."

"Feel free to try. Don't be surprised if he turns you down."

As he gazed at her, his pupils grew wider, and the awareness between them jumped way higher than it should.

"I'm…going for Jones's position," Joe said, his voice hoarser than usual, kept low so that no one could over-hear their…discussion about work?

Had she missed something? Was the awareness all one-sided?

"I know." She blinked and tilted her head to the side. "Everyone knows. You and Captain Schlager."

"I really want the job." He didn't step back, didn't remove his hand from the counter right next to her body.

"You have a good chance, in my new-to-the-department

opinion." Then it dawned on her what he might be getting at. "Do you think I know something? Because of my dad? Believe me, he doesn't—"

"No, Faith. Even if I thought he talked to you about it, I'd never ask you for that information."

"Okay."

Still confused, she started to move away. Joe gently caught her wrist and forced eye contact.

"I want..." He didn't finish the sentence but his eyes told her exactly what he wanted.

Okay, then. She hadn't misread the signs. "I know." She nodded nonchalantly, as if he'd just told her there were fish in the ocean.

Faith picked up the coffeepot and poured the steaming liquid into her mug. After turning away from him.

The current that had sizzled between them faded to awkwardness. Joe headed for the table and pulled out the chair next to the one she'd been sitting in earlier. "So...your test. What are you working on?"

"Really, I don't—"

"Want help. I know. As your captain, I'm ordering you to sit down and let me quiz you."

"That is so wrong, flaunting your position...." She kept her tone light.

"It's in my best interest for my people to pass tests and earn certifications. Makes me look good."

"With all due respect, I really need to change out of these coffee-soaked clothes and get some sleep." She actually hadn't planned to go to bed tonight, but lying in her bunk awake was preferable to sitting here awkwardly with him.

He looked at her hard, sizing her up as if he knew she just wanted to escape. But instead of calling her on it, he nodded once and said, "Good luck on your test, Faith."

CHAPTER SEVEN

JOE PICKED UP THE PHONE from his nightstand two nights later. "Mendoza."

"Joe, it's Derek. Slight problem." The concern in the firefighter's voice shot a dose of alarm through Joe.

He sat up in bed, rubbed his eyes and checked the digital clock. Twenty after eleven. He must've dozed off since he'd hit the sack over an hour ago. A 7:00 a.m. shift came too damn early. "What's going on?"

"I stopped by the Shack to get the nightly deposit. Chief is here."

The Shell Shack was the beach bar Derek and his wife, Macey, owned. In the past year or so, it had become a regular hangout for the department, and while Chief Peligni didn't usually join in the camaraderie, it wasn't unusual that he was there.

"He's tanked, Joe."

"Chief is?" Joe was out of bed, pulling on his jeans without conscious thought.

"You got it. Kevin says he's been here since six-thirty. Came in for a burger with Mayor Romero. Been drinking ever since."

"Can you call him a cab?"

"In his state, I don't think that's a wise solution. Cab could take a while to get here, with all the spring breakers. I'm concerned about someone recognizing him."

"He's that messed up?" Joe couldn't fathom the man he'd looked up to for years making a spectacle of himself. He'd never even seen the chief tipsy and couldn't imagine how much liquor it would take to make him falling down drunk. If he knew the chief the way he thought he did, the man would be humiliated once he sobered up and realized what he'd done. But hell. Lately Chief Peligni wasn't acting like the man Joe knew.

"I'm not sure he can walk on his own," Derek said with some hesitation. "I'd take him home myself, but thought it'd be better for you to handle it. You're tight with him, right?"

Joe couldn't fault Derek for not wanting to get involved in the chief's business—especially not this business. It'd be awkward enough for Joe. "I'll take care of it. Can you stay with him until I get there?" He pulled a wrinkled T-shirt off the floor and shook it out.

"I'll be here."

"See you in five." Joe ended the call and pulled the shirt over his head, trying to wrap his brain around the situation. Either he'd been sleeping harder than he'd thought or the chief had gone off the deep end.

Without his permission, Joe's mind veered to Faith. Did she know what her dad was up to? He doubted it. She wasn't the type to sit back and let her father self-destroy. After what she'd said the other night in the station kitchen, he suspected she'd take it hard if she found out about the chief's current state. Though it wasn't his business or his place to interfere, Joe didn't want Faith to learn about her dad's bender. Didn't want her to be hurt.

He hightailed it the few blocks to the Shell Shack

and turned into the small parking lot, taking the only available spot.

He jumped out, the brisk night breeze rustling the palms that lined the hotel lot next door. If the weather didn't make a massive turnaround in the next few days, spring break visitors to the island were going to be mighty disappointed. Maybe it would scare away a few, but likely not enough to make a difference in the havoc the month wreaked on the fire department.

When Joe cleared the doorway, he instantly spotted the chief leaning heavily on the bar. The horseshoe-shaped counter curved around such that Joe had a view of the older man's face. It was red, the skin droopy. His eyes were aimed downward but Joe could tell from here they weren't focused on anything. The chief wore a light gray polo shirt—thank God he'd changed out of his uniform beforehand—and there was a wet splotch on the front.

Derek sat on the stool next to Chief Peligni, talking to him. He glanced up at Joe and shook his head slowly.

Joe walked around the crowded bar and stopped next to them. "Evening, gentlemen."

Derek nodded in reply, looking uncomfortable as he stood up and let Joe take his place. Chief Peligni didn't react for a few seconds. Finally, he raised his gaze and squinted. "That the captain?"

"It's me," Joe affirmed. The man reeked of a distillery even from two feet away.

Glancing around, Joe took inventory of the other bar patrons, relieved that everyone was too caught up in themselves and their drinks to pay any attention to the chief.

"Can I get you anything, Captain?" Kevin asked from behind the bar.

"No, thanks."

Joe sat on the stool Derek had vacated and attempted to make small talk with the blitzed chief. To his comments about the weather and the crush of customers, Joe received unintelligible mumbles.

Okay, enough bullshitting. He needed to get Chief Peligni out of here and safely home. Wouldn't be an easy task—the older man had gained weight recently and must weigh over three hundred pounds—but Joe would do it. The chief had done a lot for him over the years. Now it was his turn to return the favor.

"What do you say we get out of here?" Joe asked, standing.

More muttering he couldn't understand.

"You need to sleep it off, Chief. Let's go before things get any worse."

It was too late, though, because at that moment, Faith's gorgeous face appeared in the doorway and she looked anything but pleased.

FAITH WAS GOING TO WRING her father's thick neck.

He'd sounded more than a little out of it when he'd called her a few minutes ago for a ride. Words slurred, train of thought easily interrupted but he'd managed to say where he was. What he hadn't mentioned was that Joe Mendoza and Derek Severson were here as well, witnessing the show.

Her cheeks warmed and she stepped back out of the doorway to the Shell Shack to summon her game face. Glancing down at the exercise shorts and tank top she'd thrown on, she swore to herself. She hadn't counted on running into her captain. Hadn't counted on running into anyone. She'd foolishly thought when her dad asked her to pick him up that maybe he'd meet her in the parking lot.

Clearly, she hadn't fully grasped the situation. And it wasn't going to get any better while she wasted time out here trying to figure out how to save face. Wasn't going to happen.

Straightening her back, she headed inside, determined to hide her embarrassment and concern for her father. Those were family matters. Private.

Ignoring her colleague and supervisor, Faith went around to her father's side and rested her hand on his forearm. "Hey, Dad. How are you doing?"

The time it took him to react to her voice and turn his head was not a good sign. "Princessss."

Fan-freaking-tastic.

"I was just going to bring him home," Joe said quietly. "Derek called me. Did he call you, too?" He looked toward the back room, where Derek was talking to the bartender and cook.

"No," Faith said, trying to keep her frustration out of her voice. "*He* called me." She gestured to her father, who didn't seem to register the conversation going on in front of him. "I can handle this. Thank you for trying to help."

She felt Joe staring at her as if he had something to say, but he remained silent and she didn't look at him again. Instead, she turned her attention back to her dad. "How long have you been here?"

"Little bit." He took an unsteady drink from the glass

in front of him and frowned at the taste. "He's givin' me water."

The bartender emerged from the back room as her dad spoke, and Faith mouthed a thank-you to the man for cutting him off.

"I'm here to help you, Faith," Joe said, still stubbornly sitting on the other side of her dad.

"We'll be fine, thanks," she replied, her jaw stiff.

Again, the captain hesitated, and she felt frustration coming off him in waves, but that wasn't her concern. Her dad was.

"Did you eat dinner?" she asked him, as Joe finally walked out of the bar, turning to glance at her one last time when he reached the doorway.

The fire chief seemed to think about that for a while, then shrugged. "'Magine I did." He leaned hard on the bar, as if it was the only thing holding him up.

"We need to get you home," Faith said. "What were you thinking, Dad?"

He tried to focus on her, then turned his squinting gaze to the bartender. And started snickering like a teen-age girl in trouble, his large shoulders shaking. "I don' know, Faithy. You tell me."

He'd never been a hard drinker. A lot of firefighters were—their way of dealing with the things they saw on the job. They used alcohol to come down from a har-rowing shift or one that ended in tragedy. But not Tony Peligni. He was hard-core and intense—and usually stone-cold sober.

Faith had been flirting with acknowledging the truth for weeks, but now there was no way to deny it. The breakup of his marriage was sending her father down a path she never thought she'd see him travel. One she couldn't bear to watch. She had to find a way to get her parents back together. They loved each other—always had. Faith was absolutely sure of it. She needed to help her mom see what she was doing to this man and get her to come to her senses.

Later.

Now Faith needed to get her dad out of the bar before someone recognized the falling-over-drunk guy as San Amaro Island's fire chief.

"How much does he owe you?" she asked the bartender, pulling her wallet out of her purse. She looked around for Derek, relieved to see he'd apparently taken off, as well.

"He's clear," the bartender said. "You going to be able to…?" He motioned toward the parking lot with his head.

Faith nodded, biting her tongue. She knew most people didn't realize she was stronger than she looked. And her dad *was* big. But she didn't do the female-in-need-of-rescuing well. Never had.

"Come on, Dad. Time to take you home."

He slowly turned and narrowed his eyes at her, as if trying to place where he knew her from. Faith hopped down from her stool, acting much more optimistic than she felt, and offered him her hand.

"You shou' go home, Faith. Gettin' late."

She hid a sad smile, thinking how much easier it would be to have to look after only herself at this moment, instead of her sixty-year-old father.

"Let's go," she said gently. "You have to work in the morning."

Realization brightened his face for an instant and he turned to the bartender. "I'm the fire ch—"

"He knows," Faith said loudly, to cover his words, darting a look around behind them to see if anyone else had heard. "Come on, Dad. We need to go *now*." She tugged at his arm. "Stand up."

His movements were in slow motion, but he finally turned to the side and put his feet on the floor. He was so unsteady he slid right back to the stool, and Faith had to use her strength to keep him upright.

Okay, so this was going to be an undertaking.

"I'll help you, but you have to walk to the car," she told him.

She didn't give him a choice, just yanked at him, and he did his best to get to his feet. Unfortunately, his "best" wasn't quite enough. The bartender looked over in alarm as Faith braced herself with all her might against her father's weight.

"We're *fine*," she insisted through clenched teeth as her dad finally managed to establish some semblance of balance.

Coaching his every step, she supported him to the exit, thankful there was no actual door to open. She could feel stares at their backs, but wasn't about to acknowledge them.

"I'm parked on the street," she told him. "Just a little farther." She was starting to breathe hard from the effort of keeping him upright.

Before they could even clear the side of the building, her dad shifted his weight from her to the wall and leaned hard against it. "Princess, need to rest. I'll jus' sit here for a bit."

She fought to keep him on his feet, but there was no way. He slid down the rough wall and landed on his backside on the wide sidewalk.

Tears of frustration burned Faith's eyes as he stretched out and rested his head on the pavement.

Stronger than she looked, sure, but able to lift three hundred pounds? No way. Sitting down next to him and banging her head on the wall was the most appealing option right now.

"You really have a problem allowing someone to help you, don't you?" Joe said from the darkness.

CHAPTER EIGHT

FAITH CLOSED HER EYES and leaned against the Shell Shack's exterior wall, looking defeated. Only Faith Peligni would take it personally when she failed to carry an unconscious man three times her size. And that stirred something deep inside Joe. Something that had nothing to do with sympathy.

"I thought you left," she said, annoyed with him, but fighting not to let it show. He could tell by the set of her jaw, the tight control of her voice.

"I talked to him enough before you got here to suspect something like this could happen."

"You were just waiting to come to the rescue, weren't you?" Faith looked down at her dad and shook her head. Her shoulders sagged. "I'm sorry. I guess we do need a little assistance."

"Don't worry about it. Let's just get him out of here. Come on, Chief." Joe leaned down and roused him.

The big guy muttered something and Faith avoided Joe's gaze. The urge to touch her, to try to make her feel better, rolled through him out of nowhere.

He bent over to prop up the chief, burying his mind in the task and attempting to ignore Faith. She got into position on the other side, and together they pulled him upright. Chief Peligni came to long enough to ask where the hell they were taking him and to complain about how fast they were moving.

"To my 4Runner over there," Joe told Faith, indicating the vehicle with a nod. "It's close." When they got to the passenger side, she opened the door and they awkwardly heaved him inside.

Once the door was shut, Joe locked it. He and Faith looked at each other as they caught their breath.

"Want to follow me?" she asked.

He nodded, recalling from previous visits the flight of stairs they'd have to drag the chief up once they got him home. "I'll drive you back here to get his truck once we get him settled." He searched until he spotted the chief's Suburban at the end of the row.

Faith shot a frown toward her dad and bit her lower lip before heading toward her car, parked at the curb.

Joe went around to the driver's side of his SUV. He paused before getting in and watched her walk away. Let himself admire her curves in those tiny shorts and the yellow fitted tank top. Her hair was pulled back in a ponytail. She was dressed for relaxing, not for impressing, and still his heart thundered in appreciation.

He glanced guiltily at Chief Peligni and climbed in, making a point of *not* checking out the chief's daughter again. Not that the older man had even noticed; his head was propped against the window, eyes closed. Joe reached across, drew the seat belt over him, pulled it out as far as it would go and fastened it. He could just about get drunk off the fumes coming from the passenger seat.

While Faith was careful and deliberate with just about everything she did, she apparently didn't drive the same way, speeding off like a maniac. Joe had been to the chief's house before for cookouts, so he took his time getting there. When he pulled up, her car was in the driveway and she was leaning against the wall of the garage, arms crossed. She gestured for him to drive up close to the open garage door.

After fifteen or twenty minutes, they'd managed to get the chief up the flight of stairs, into his bed, shoes off, with a glass of water and a bottle of aspirin on the nightstand. He'd been half-awake for part of it, but Joe doubted he'd remember any of this in the morning. Joe wasn't sure the man would be able to get up in the morning.

Faith drew a crocheted blanket over him, since they hadn't had a chance to pull the covers back before laying him down. When she finished, she exhaled tiredly and nodded at Joe. Together they walked down the hall toward the living room.

When they reached the last door on the right, Faith went into the room, flipping on the light. Her bedroom, he realized, as he peered in like a Peeping Tom.

"I can wait outside," he said.

"Just a sec. I need a sweatshirt, but there's something for you in the kitchen."

Curious, he stood there in the doorway, trying not to watch her every move as she searched through the drawers of an antique-looking white dresser. Instead, he took in the details of her room, still feeling somewhat like a voyeur, but unable to resist.

The room was…shockingly pink. Her bed was un-made, but there were lacy white ruffles around the bottom of the mattress and edging the pink floral pillowcases. The walls were painted a pale pink to match. The furniture was dainty, almost little-girllike. Clothes were scattered on the floor and he tried his damnedest to ignore the silky pink and purple underthings among the jeans and fire department shirts. He did *not* need to know what she wore beneath her uniform.

He was still staring as she approached him, pulling on an orange zip-up sweatshirt.

"Welcome to the Pepto room," she said.

Joe grinned, fighting off images of those panties....

"For my sixteenth birthday, my dad's treat was to let me have my room redecorated any way I wanted it," she explained defensively.

"I never imagined you as a pink kind of woman."

"If you wear pink, they never see the knuckle sandwich coming."

"And you seem like such a peaceful person," he said, following her to the kitchen.

"It's the brothers. One in particular needed his ass kicked on a regular basis. Thankfully, Anthony lives in Dallas now, and doesn't make it home much. Here." She grabbed a plastic container off the counter and removed the lid.

"Cookies?"

"Scotcheroos. Baked them today."

He took one and bit into it. "You made these?" He couldn't keep the surprise out of his voice.

"I can do more than just put out a fire, Captain." She grinned and helped herself to one. "Not that I bake often. These happen to be my dad's favorites. Of course, he never made it home to appreciate them." The smile disappeared instantly, as if someone had thrown a bucket of water over her head.

"His loss," Joe said, trying to keep it light.

"Take a handful. Otherwise I'll eat more than my share. I made a double batch."

He took one more, not wanting to steal the chief's treats.

"You don't like them?" Faith challenged.

"They're the best cookies I've had in a long time."

She went to a drawer and pulled out a plastic zipper bag, then shoved in as many cookies as she could fit. "If you're lying, you can give them to your dog."

"I don't have a dog," he said. "And I'm not lying. Let's go get your dad's truck."

She stuffed another bite in her mouth and nodded, turning serious again. "Thank you for helping us tonight, Joe. You were right, I don't accept help very well, but…"

"It's no problem," he said, mildly amused by her discomfort. "Middle of the night rescues are what I do. But then, you can relate."

She seemed about to say something else, but only led him down the stairs and out the door.

As they drove back to the Shell Shack, he was hyperaware of the woman sitting just two feet away. Chief Peligni would have to give up the bottle, because this couldn't happen again. Joe realized he wasn't capable of spending time with Faith outside the station without his mind going in dangerous directions.

Thankfully, the drive was a short one. When he turned into the lot, he spotted a small object reflecting light next to the building where the chief had passed out. He pulled up behind Peligni's SUV and told Faith he was going to check it out.

A cell phone was lying on the ground about a foot from the rough wood wall, and he bent to pick it up. When he straightened, Faith was right behind him. He ran into her, unaware that she'd followed. He turned and steadied her, and she took a step back.

"Sorry," she said.

"This your dad's?" he asked, holding it out.

She took it from him and glanced at the display. "That's his." She dropped it in the pocket of her sweatshirt. "He's like an irresponsible teenager tonight."

At that instant, she looked unsure of herself. Just for a moment. Unsure and…so tired. And yet pretty and young with the moonlight illuminating her face. Her eyes darted around as she did her best to act as if nothing bothered her. He wanted to tell her it was okay to be bothered. Against his better judgment, he forced eye contact, feeling a jolt when she finally focused on him.

"What?" she asked defensively. "I look like hell, I know. I was in bed when my dad called me—"

"You don't look like hell," he said quietly, leaning closer to make the mistake of a lifetime and not giving a damn.

He palmed her cheek. Touched her lower lip with his thumb, caressing the moist warmth of it. Felt her breath on his fingers as her lids grew heavy.

A stray lock of her dark hair fell onto her cheek, and he brushed it back.

"Joe."

It was barely more than a whisper. Definitely not a

warning to back off. So he closed the space between them and gently kissed her lips, testing her. Tasting.

The contact shot heat straight through his body. For a woman who was so tough on the outside, she was soft, feminine. Her scent was light, with a hint of flowers.

She wound her hands behind his neck and pulled him closer. He should've guessed that even her kiss would be bold.

He deepened the contact, thrusting his tongue between her lips. She tasted of sugar and confidence…and damn, what a turn-on. He pulled her slender body up against his, his hands resting at the point where her waist curved into her hips. Her body was firm, fit. Strong and lean. He imagined that body unclothed….

Headlights illuminated them like a sudden spotlight on an auditorium stage, and they jumped apart. Faith ran her fingers over her lips, peering at the driver. The man, probably close to seventy years old, gave them an enthusiastic thumbs-up as he passed them.

"He doesn't know the least of it," Joe said.

Faith's low, nervous laugh was gratifying. Alluring.

"It's late," she said after a few seconds, sobering. "I need to check on my dad."

"I bet he hasn't moved an inch."

They started toward their vehicles, and Joe pressed his hand to her lower back. His pulse was still hammering away, his body demanding more attention from this beauty, but his brain was now fighting it, letting in the message that this was a no-win situation.

Joe walked her to the driver's door of her dad's Suburban without conscious thought. She turned toward him. "You didn't have to walk me here. I'm fine." Back to Miss Independent.

He stole a glance at those lips of hers and was considering one last ill-advised taste when she broke the spell.

"I hope it goes without saying that this can't get out," she said.

"This?" he asked, surprised. "No. It's private."

"I didn't mean the kiss…but yes. That, too." Realization flitted in her eyes, and he knew the moment her regret kicked in.

"I meant my dad." Faith made sure no one was within hearing distance. "No one needs to know about tonight. It was an isolated incident. Derek won't say anything, will he?"

Shaking his head, Joe moved back a few inches and straightened, willing the haze of desire to dissipate.

She fidgeted with her keys, seeming uncharacteristically nervous, then hit the button to unlock the Suburban.

"Gotta go." She climbed in and closed the door, effectively shutting him out.

FAITH MANAGED TO ACT as if everything was fine until she pulled into the garage at home.

Everything was *not* fine. It was nowhere near fine.

What had she done?

She'd kissed her company officer. Her captain. A man who had power over her career.

It wasn't that Joe would use it against her. It was more about what others would think if they ever found out. What she thought of herself.

And how Joe would treat her now.

He already hovered, and would coddle her at a moment's notice if she'd let him. She hadn't yet figured out if it was because of her gender, her newness to the department or something else, but the last thing she wanted was for one of the other firefighters to notice Joe's protectiveness.

And kissing a man tended to arouse his protectiveness even more.

If she could've chosen the best way to lose, or never gain, her colleagues' respect, becoming involved—physically, romantically, stupidly—with one of the department captains topped the list.

CHAPTER NINE

FAITH COULD'VE USED about four more hours of sleep after the episode with her dad. Of course, lying in bed, going back and forth between beating herself up for what happened with Joe and playing their kiss over and over in her mind like some romantic airhead, didn't help.

As she walked across the apparatus floor for roll call, the buzz of energy she usually experienced at the sight of the equipment perked her up. She hoped they got an exciting gig or two today—something to keep her awake.

"Look who it is," Clay, one of the other firefighters, said as Faith headed toward the four men already waiting.

"How'd it go last night?" asked Cale, the lieutenant with short, spiky brown hair.

Faith's heart skipped two beats before she figured out they were addressing the guy behind her, Penn Griffin.

Guilty conscience much?

"Like I'd tell you bozos," Penn said. His wide grin and the sparkle in his eyes revealed more than he intended, though.

"How's it going, Faith?" Clay said. She didn't know him well, hadn't worked many shifts with him, but his brown eyes seemed genuinely friendly.

"Pretty good. How's your baby?"

"You're thinking of Evan Drake. He's the one with the baby."

She looked at the floor, embarrassed. "Sorry."

"Give Clay a little time and he'll probably have a baby, too," Penn said. "Right now his world revolves around a couple of women."

Faith raised her brows.

"One of them is my four-year-old daughter," Clay said, smiling. "And one of these days you'll meet Andie, my wife."

"Looking forward to it."

While they waited for the captain—Faith was forever doomed to be scheduled with Joe, it seemed—she wandered over to the truck and began opening compartments. She was usually assigned to the engine instead of the truck, but just in case, she needed to be familiar with the location of each tool, every piece of equipment at this station.

She looked up automatically when Joe strode in carrying a clipboard. Their eyes met briefly, and though his lingered for an extra split second, they gave nothing away. She relaxed a little and quashed the flicker of excitement sparked by the memory of kissing him.

She joined the group as Joe began calling out assignments for the day. Once again, she was on the engine with him. Was he taunting her? Messing with her?

Just as well that he didn't make changes to the norm, she supposed. Last night shouldn't be cause for rearranging everything. She intended to go on as if nothing had happened.

"Did anybody hear if we're getting new radios yet?"

Penn asked. "Mine's crapping out. Can't trust it anymore."

"You're not alone," Joe said. "Find a spare one and see if it's any better."

"I thought Chief Peligni was going to order new ones," Clay said.

Faith tensed at the mention of her dad's possible slip-up and refused to look at Joe.

"I'll speak to him about it today," Joe assured him.

"He's sick today." Faith immediately regretted speaking up. Reminding everyone she was the chief's daughter was not the brightest move. And there was no need to inform Joe that her dad hadn't made it in—he'd find out soon enough.

"He okay?" Cale asked. "I can't remember the last time the chief was sick."

"He'll be back tomorrow," Faith said quickly, cursing in her head. Might as well just blurt out that he had the mother of all hangovers. She glanced around for Derek and was glad to see he wasn't on duty today.

She felt Joe's gaze on her, questioning, wanting her to confirm that it was a case of brown bottle flu, but she made a point of ignoring him.

"Get to work," Joe said to everyone in his captain voice. "Faith, I need to speak to you."

She'd never been sent to the principal's office, but suddenly had a decent idea of what it felt like. Attempting to hide her ridiculous nervousness, she took a few steps toward Joe.

"In my office," he said, nodding in that direction. "I'll be there in a couple minutes."

Faith walked off the floor, annoyed that he'd called

her out in front of everyone. Couldn't he have quietly pulled her aside as she went about her assigned chores?

Once in the office, alone, she crossed her arms and watched two of her colleagues out the window as they raised the flags for the day and picked up litter in the courtyard. Joe entered the room and closed the door with a soft click, startling Faith.

"Why the closed door?" she asked, wondering for the first time if she was in trouble of some kind.

He stopped directly in front of her, too close. His gray officer's shirt stretched over the bulk of his shoulders and muscular chest. "I didn't figure you wanted the whole department to hear our conversation about your father."

"He's fine," she said tersely.

Joe stared down at her, so close she could see the pores of his recently shaved chin. She forced her eyes to his brown-black ones, fighting the temptation to sneak a glance at the sensual lips she'd tasted last night.

"May I get through?" he asked, gesturing to the narrow path between the windowed wall and his desk.

Faith practically jumped out of his way, feeling like an idiot for the direction of her thoughts, when all he wanted to do was walk past her.

"I assume he's still sleeping off last night?" Joe asked, pulling out his desk chair, but remaining on his feet. He leaned his fists on the clutter-free surface.

There was no sense in lying. As out of it as her dad had been last night, it'd be nothing short of amazing for him to be up and functioning before noon and they both knew it. But instead of admitting that, she didn't answer. Waited for the next, hopefully better question.

"Are you doing okay?" he asked gently, and for some reason, that made it hard for her to swallow.

"I'm fine."

Joe shook his head. "He's fine. You're fine. Everybody's fine. What am I worried about?"

"That's *my* question." She crossed her arms.

"I'm not the bad guy here, Faith."

She noticed dark shadows under his eyes and realized he had to be as exhausted as she was. All because of her family's problem.

"I'm sorry. You're right." She wasn't even convinced her dad was the bad guy. Right now wasn't the time to assign blame, though.

She sat in the chair in front of Joe's desk, shoulders slumping, suddenly overcome by fatigue and…fear. "I don't know what to do for him."

"He's a grown man. Sometimes people have to help themselves."

"That seems kind of harsh."

"Maybe. Maybe not," Joe said sternly. He walked around to the front of his desk and leaned against it, crossing his legs at the ankles. "I don't know what to tell you, Faith. But you're doing more than anyone else in your family just by being there for him. Staying with him. That's a lot."

"My brothers all have busy careers. They think I'm overreacting, but they haven't seen him. How *off* he is."

"The chief is glad to have you there."

"How do you know?" she asked, not entirely comfortable with the personal direction of the conversation. How close *were* Joe and her dad? Had they discussed her before? That didn't sit well with her.

"He doesn't hide his opinion. He's very proud of you."

Joe's words made her squirm. She rose to her feet, intent on getting the heck out of there and back to the tedium of daily chores. She found herself close enough to catch his masculine scent.

She stepped to the side, away from him. "What did you really call me in here for?"

"Faith…" Joe had been up all night trying to figure out how to broach this subject, and he still hadn't thought of a good way.

Her eyes narrowed warily.

"I'm concerned about your dad."

Her shoulders stiffened and there was a decided change in the air. No longer were they officer and firefighter standing there, or even two people who'd shared a misguided but brain-numbing kiss last night. Now there was a current of adversity…her versus him.

"He's going through hard times," she said. "But he'll be fine."

Joe ran his fingers over his chin. "I know the separation from your mom is rough, but it's starting to affect his work, Faith."

"Like I said, he'll be back tomorrow." She swallowed hard and studied the ground, looking for a moment like a little girl who'd lost her favorite teddy bear. So uncharacteristic of her.

"He's always been a model chief. Follows his own regulations to the letter. He's prompt. Exact. Thorough."

She nodded. "It's who he is."

"That's why I'm worried. He's been late recently. To meetings. To work. He's let several issues go unaddressed...."

"He's not himself some days."

"I understand that, but..."

"But what?"

Joe didn't know, exactly. "I can't continue to ignore it. He's in too important of a position. And now this..."

"So you're going to, what—tell on him? Who are you going to tell?"

"I'm not going to tell anyone. Not right now. But I am going to keep an eye on him. If Mayor Romero needs a heads-up..."

"What is this? The depression patrol? Maybe he *is* depressed, but that's a health issue. Not a professional one."

Joe exhaled loudly, exasperated. "I'm just letting you know, Faith, that while I'm not going to say a word about carrying him to his bed last night, I don't like that I seem to be repeatedly forced to keep Peligni family secrets. It puts me in one hell of an awkward position."

She stared him down, the look in her eyes combative. "We don't need your help. Consider yourself uninvolved."

"I was involved the second you asked me to keep something from the chief."

Still shooting daggers at him with her eyes, she

grabbed the doorknob. "I'm sorry, sir. It won't happen again."

She swung the door open so hard it bounced off the wall as she walked away.

JOE SAT DOWN HARD in the worn chair at his desk, still able to discern Faith's feminine scent in the air though she'd marched off minutes ago, once again ticked off at him.

That shouldn't bother him, but it did. He'd blown it. Whether you looked at it professionally or personally, he'd said all the wrong things, in the wrong way, when she'd just confided that she didn't know what to do about her dad.

He hadn't intended to come across as an unfeeling bastard. Wasn't trying to threaten her or the chief.

On a personal level, maybe it was a good thing that he'd lacked any kind of gentleness, but if she was just another firefighter, just one of the guys, he would've handled the situation better.

She was getting to him and that wasn't okay. Even if he didn't care what the chief thought. Even if he wasn't trying to get the assistant chief job.

It wasn't okay.

It was unprofessional and somewhat embarrassing that the department had one woman on staff and the goddamn captain couldn't keep a rein on his thoughts.

When Faith had walked into the bar last night, he couldn't deny the buzz that had pumped through him at the sight of her. He hadn't thought twice about helping her out. At the time, he'd convinced himself it was something he'd do for any of his "men," but today, after making the mistake of ordering Faith into his office, he knew there'd been more to it than duty.

If he continued down this road, kept close tabs on Faith as the chief had requested, he risked getting in deeper. He had every intention of fighting off his desire for her, but look where that had gotten him last night. She cast a spell over him, made him stupid and lacking in judgment.

He was a lot weaker than he'd thought.

When it came to Faith Peligni and his career with the San Amaro Island Fire Department, he was screwed. Something had to give.

CHAPTER TEN

FAITH HATED HAVING TO ASK her mom for anything. Most days, she'd walk ten thousand miles to avoid it, but this was her dad. She was desperate.

She knocked on the door to the third-floor apartment. The building was box-shaped, nondescript. Everything her mother wasn't. She and her mom could disagree on anything under the sun, they could argue about the color of the sky, but the one thing Faith wouldn't debate was that her mother had good taste when it came to decorating. Cooking and dressing, too. Nita Peligni was well-versed in all things domestic. A year ago, this apartment would've chilled her mother's blood.

"Faith," her mom said, opening the door and looking surprised.

Some people would be insulted, but Faith could readily admit she hadn't visited here often—only twice before in the two months plus she'd been back in San Amaro.

"Hi, Mom." Faith held up the plastic container of scotcheroos. Her best attempt at a peace offering. "Can I come in?"

Her mother stepped back so Faith could enter. "What's with the cookies?" she asked suspiciously.

"I baked scotcheroos. Too many." That they were her

dad's favorite and not her mom's remained unspoken, but hung between them.

Her mom frowned and set the container aside on the high counter that divided the living room from the kitchen, without even acting tempted. "What are you doing here?"

Faith wandered in as if it were her home, even though it didn't feel like anyone's home with its taupe walls, beige carpet and total lack of personalization. She couldn't spot anything that screamed out Nita Peligni.

"You're not planning to stay here, are you?" Faith said, falling unladylike onto the cheap, used sofa.

"What?" Her mom perched carefully on the non-matching chair. She looked out of place in this room in her casual robin's egg-blue pantsuit, her hair, as usual, perfectly in place.

"This is temporary," Faith continued, waving her arm. "To teach him a lesson."

"To teach...who? What are you talking about?"

"If you were planning to stay here, you would've bought better furniture. Added some throw pillows, some artwork. Color. Your walls are bare, Mom."

"I have upholstery covers on order, Faith. A rug. And once I get those, I'll pick out some accent pieces."

"You've been here for three months. It's not like you to live in this monotone blah."

Her mom settled back into the chair and crossed one leg over the other. "Frankly, I don't know what's like me. As a suddenly soon-to-be-divorcee at the age of fifty-eight, decorating hasn't been my top priority."

She was sincere, not just saying it to gain sympathy, and somehow, in spite of Faith's anger and her tendency to be more concerned for her dad's well-being, it was impossible to be unaffected by her mother's plight.

Her mom had left him, though, Faith reminded herself.

"If it's so bad being by yourself, why not go back?"

"Is this why you came? To browbeat me? To try to get me to move back home?"

Once again, Faith had let her emotions carry her too far, just as she had during the argument at dinner. Why she couldn't just chill out, hold herself back, when it was vital to making her point, she didn't know. Her mom had always set her off.

"I didn't come to browbeat. But...Dad needs you, Mom."

Her mother looked away and swallowed hard. Smoothed down her pants with fidgety hands. "He's never really needed me, Faith. Not like he's needed his career. And that's the fundamental problem."

"Mom—"

Nita held her hand up. "Stop. I know you want us back together, but it's not going to happen." She walked over to the sofa and sat a foot away from Faith. "It's too late for your dad and me, honey. The sooner you accept that, the better off you'll be."

"This isn't about me." Faith popped up off the sofa, uncomfortable with her mother's closeness. "Dad..." She lifted her face to stare at the ugly white ceiling through tear-blurred eyes. Pacing toward the kitchen, she swiftly wiped the moisture away. She fought to collect herself for several seconds, then finally faced her mom. "He's not handling this, Mom. At all."

For a split second, her mom's feelings showed in her

eyes—concern and…love. Faith could swear to it. But then it was gone and the hardness, the hurt were back.

"What do you mean?" Nita asked.

"He's…I'm pretty sure he's depressed. Clinically. He sleeps all the time. Forgets to eat. Drinks too much." Faith was laying most of his secrets out there, but couldn't bring herself to admit how bad the other night had been. Not if she could avoid it. She wasn't even sure her dad remembered any of it. He'd walked past her this morning before she'd left, on his way in to the station after his sick day, and acted like nothing was wrong.

"I'm sorry he's having a hard time. But this isn't easy for me, either."

"So then why not try again? At this point he'd do just about anything to get you back where you belong."

Her mom shook her head slowly. Sadly. "*You* would do anything, Faith. But your father…I don't think he knows how to put me first. I've waited for thirty-eight years." Her voice wavered and she hesitated. "There comes a time when you have to face up to reality. Admit to yourself something is never going to happen."

The tears wouldn't stop filling Faith's eyes. She marched into the kitchen and grabbed a tissue to wipe them. Her mom clearly didn't realize how serious the situation was. How bad off her dad was. And short of telling her about his drunken night, Faith wasn't sure how to make her understand. The digital dots on the microwave clock blinked while she considered. Tried to convince herself to speak up. In the end, she couldn't do it. Couldn't rob her father, the person she probably loved most in the world, of his last shred of dignity. She didn't want her mom to come back out of sympathy or fear of what he might or might not do. She wanted her to come back because they still loved each other.

Faith indelicately blew her nose and threw the tissue into the wastebasket in the pantry. As she headed back out to the bland living room, someone knocked on the door. She didn't think much of it other than an inconvenience until she noticed her mom's reaction. Nita jumped up almost before the knock was over and darted a guilty glance at Faith before walking past her and opening the door.

"Hey, beautiful."

Faith couldn't see the man yet, but she'd put him in his fifties, tall and very much interested in her mom.

"Craig. Come in and meet my daughter. This is—"

"Faith," he said smoothly. Way too smoothly. "I've heard a lot about you."

She looked from him to her mom. He was indeed tall, thin, with a full head of salt-and-pepper hair. She wouldn't give him handsome, but she could see how he would catch a woman's attention. *But not her mom's.* Faith closed her eyes as the implications sank in.

Her mom had a…boyfriend? What the hell did you call it when she was fifty-eight years old and not yet divorced? Besides disgusting.

"I was just leaving," Faith said, looking around for her purse.

"Faith, don't be rude. This is Craig Eggleston. I've been wanting to introduce you."

Like hell she had. And Faith had no interest in meeting him. She didn't want to know about him, didn't want to think about him.

Were they sleeping together? God. Did people her

mother's age still do that? Faith closed her eyes for a moment and pressed her lips together. Shook her head slightly. "It's nice to meet you," she said, without offering her hand. "Really, I have to go now."

She finally spotted her purse on the floor by the sofa, grabbed it and made a sincere effort to walk instead of run out the door.

Maybe Joe was right, after all. Maybe there really wasn't anything more she could do to help her dad.

No. Faith refused to accept that. To give up would be to let her dad down, and after everything he'd done for her, including putting his name on the line to get her hired, she wasn't about to do that.

CHAPTER ELEVEN

SO WHAT IF SNACKING late at night was bad? Whoever made up that rule hadn't ever taken part in a vicious fire station round of beach Frisbee. Faith had to have burned as many calories during the game as she usually did on the treadmill. Now she was famished. She couldn't get the last slice of chocolate cheesecake—sitting in the refrigerator all by its lonesome—out of her mind.

Might as well put the cheesecake out of its misery before someone else did.

Most of the guys were in the living area watching a cheesy horror movie, and the hall that led to the kitchen reeked of microwave popcorn. That didn't sway her from her sweet objective. The swear words that were uttered in the supply room did, however.

She walked beyond the kitchen and looked into the open doorway. Joe had his back toward her, hunched over a box that must have fallen off the shelf and spilled.

She hadn't been alone with him since the other day when he'd told her he was tired of being involved in Peligni family business. She didn't really want to be alone with him now, either, so she tried to back out of the room before he noticed her.

"Midnight snack run?" he asked, shoving the last rolls of bandages into the box as he stood.

Faith halted her attempted escape. "I can hear the

chocolate cheesecake calling my name from my bunk. What are you doing in here?"

He replaced the box on the shelf and held up a syringe. "Come see."

Joe strode out of the room, not giving her a chance to reply. Curiosity propelled her after him. Instead of going toward the racket of male voices in the living area or heading toward the bunks, he took the hall to the wing of offices.

As they turned the corner, Faith saw light shining under his closed office door. "Working late again?" she asked.

"Not exactly."

He opened the door a few inches and cautiously peered in, then pushed it the rest of the way. He gestured for Faith to follow him in, and then closed the door behind her, reminding her of their last less-than-pleasant discussion in this room.

She glanced expectantly at his desk, but the surface was clean, with neat stacks of paper organized on one corner. Joe stepped across the room, toward the desk the lieutenants used, where a shallow cardboard box rested on the floor.

"You did not," Faith said, moving closer.

Wriggling furry bodies made stilted movements toward a large mound of gray fur. Cale had discovered the litter of kittens and the mama cat this morning in a corner of the apparatus floor, huddled in a spare turnout coat that had fallen off one of the hooks.

"It's loud out there when the trucks start up," Joe said defensively.

"You brought them in here?" Faith was stumbling

over the image of their burly, dedicated leader transporting the tiny critters to a safer haven. Where he could keep an eye on them.

"One of them isn't nursing right." He lowered himself to the chair he'd moved next to the kitten nest. "The little orange one over here," he said, pointing.

The kitten was noticeably smaller than the others, and while the rest of the litter were drinking from their mother, the orange one mewed, so quietly Faith almost couldn't hear it.

She had no experience with cats, but the troubled kitten seemed to wrap itself around her heart and take hold. "Maybe it's just not hungry now?"

Joe shook his head. "Hasn't eaten since I moved them in here. The others seem to nurse every hour or two."

"How long have they been in your office?"

He looked sheepish. "I brought them in before lunch. It was getting too hot."

She stifled a grin and knelt on the floor next to his legs and the box. He'd added a towel to cushion the cardboard, and a water dish sat beside it. "I didn't know you had such a soft heart," Faith said, not realizing until the words were out how personal they sounded.

"I try not to let it show." Joe went to his desk where a saucer of milk sat next to the carton with the Don't Touch My Damn Milk warning.

"Derek's going to miss his milk."

"I'll buy him more."

"Think the little orange one will drink it from the saucer?" Faith held her hand out slowly to the mother cat and let the sleepy animal sniff it.

Joe shook his head. "Too small. A website suggested

trying this." He indicated the needleless syringe again, then filled it with milk.

"Isn't there some kind of kitten formula you should use?"

"Know any twenty-four hour pet stores where I could get some?"

"Good point." The mother cat licked Faith's fingers with her warm, rough tongue, making her smile. "I think I've been accepted."

Joe returned to the chair next to her. "The cat has good instincts."

Faith puzzled briefly over whether that was a compliment or just a statement.

"Come here, Blaze," Joe said as he cupped the tiny orange baby in his large hand.

Faith chuckled. "You named it?"

"Just this one," Joe said sternly, which amused Faith more.

He gently opened the kitten's mouth and squeezed drops of milk in. Faith watched intently and tried to determine whether any of it was swallowed.

After several minutes, they decided the kitten was getting at least a little nourishment, since the level of milk in the syringe had gone down and very little had spilled on Joe's uniform. He continued to give the sleepy animal a few drops every couple of minutes.

"Faith," he said, his tone no longer the quiet, affectionate one he used to talk to the kitten. "I'm sorry for how I came across the other day."

She ran her index finger lightly along the orange kitten's back, attempting to hide her reaction to his words. She didn't expect an apology from him. Didn't need one, really, because he'd been absolutely right. As her captain, he shouldn't be put in the middle of her family's problems. She should never have asked him to keep her collarbone pain from her dad. Derek should never have called him to go get her dad at the bar.

"There's nothing to apologize for on your end." She made her own voice businesslike. "I'm sorry you had to get involved in something you shouldn't even be aware of. Things that never should've happened in the first place."

"But they did. The scope of my job goes beyond just fighting fires to making sure all my men—*people*—do what needs to be done."

"You were thrown into the middle of our family soap opera. I wish Derek had called me instead of you."

Joe put the syringe aside when the kitten refused to take more milk, and held the rumbling fur ball in his hand, against his wide chest.

"I've worked for your father for years. He worked for mine. I'd do just about anything for him, Faith. I *am* worried about him, but I said it all wrong the other day."

She nodded. "Okay. I'd offer to shake on our peace treaty but it seems you have your hands full." She sat back on the floor, supporting her weight on her arms and watching him stroke the kitten. Trying not to admire his large hands or think about the juxtaposition of such strength and gentleness. "Can I ask something personal? Since we've already got the line all grayed up between us anyway?"

Joe grimaced. "Shoot."

"Your mom is married again, isn't she?"

He nodded.

"What was it like when she first started dating? After your dad passed away?"

He leaned back in the chair and stretched his long legs out, brushing her thigh with his calf. "I hated it. She waited almost ten years, as far as I know, but I couldn't stand the thought of it."

Faith propped her elbows on her knees and ran both hands through her hair. Nodded. "Me, neither."

"Your mom?"

"I visited her yesterday. Hinted at how bad Dad has gotten. How much he needs her. She acted concerned and then her new guy walked in. He called her 'beautiful.'"

Joe set the kitten back in the box, next to its mother. "Ouch."

Faith inhaled shakily, overcome by the emotions that had swamped her when Carl or Craig or whatever the hell the smarmy man's name was had walked in with his smarmy grin.

Joe leaned forward and put a hand on her shoulder, squeezing lightly. "It does get easier."

"She's not even divorced yet," she managed to croak out, refusing to look at him for fear he'd see how upset she was.

"Yeah. That's rough. Are you two very close?"

Faith shook her head. "She doesn't approve of my career. Kind of takes all the feel-good qualities out of a mother-daughter relationship."

Uncomfortable and antsy, Faith hopped up off the floor and glanced around for a distraction. "Can I hold one of the other kittens?"

Joe shrugged. "It's okay as far as I know. I've never raised any before, but it seems like human contact would be good if they're going to be pets."

"Are you going to adopt them?"

"Not planning on it."

He plucked a fuzzy black beast from the pile and stood, holding it out to her.

"I think you already have," she said. "At least one."

His hand brushed her breast as he released the cat to her, and he retracted his arm as if she'd burned him. Faith cradled the kitten and turned away, trying to act as if she hadn't noticed. Refusing to let her brain veer in that direction at all.

"Maybe that's what the chief needs," Joe said lightly. "A kitten to take care of."

Faith laughed at the image. "I'll let you approach him on that one. He can't even take care of himself some days. When can they be taken from their mom?"

"I have no idea. I'll be dragging Blaze to the vet as soon as shift is over." Joe bent to spread out the edges of the towel. "Back to your mom. Maybe this is just a phase. Might be nothing serious. Do you know?"

"All I know is that she's seen him before and they're close enough that he knew about me, knew my name. Makes me sick to my stomach."

"I remember that feeling. Maybe the punching bag would do some good."

"Already beat the crap out of it today," Faith said. "Definitely therapeutic."

"That's my girl."

His words were extraordinarily personal, she thought.

And she couldn't bring herself to hate it. In fact, the thought of being his girl warmed her to her toes.

Time to get her cheesecake and then shut herself away in her room, where she could be alone with her inappropriate thoughts of this man who had a way of endearing himself to her with his feline rescues and late night encouragement.

"I'll let you—" she raised the kitten and looked into its tiny face "—get to sleep." She set it back in the box. "And you get to work. Or babysitting or whatever it is you workaholic captain types do till all hours of the morning, squirreled away in your office."

"It's a difficult job," Joe said with mock seriousness. "I'll actually be feeding that one every two hours." He gestured to the orange kitten. "Should make the night go fast."

Faith considered offering to take a shift, but being alone with this sexy man in the middle of the night wasn't a good idea. No matter how tempting. "Good night," she said, opening the door.

"Sleep well."

The words, though innocent and innocuous, sent a shiver through her. She'd likely not sleep well, thanks to images of him nurturing a helpless little animal the size of his palm. She grinned to herself as she made her way to the kitchen.

"What's got you so happy at this hour?" Penn asked when she walked into the kitchen.

Thank God she wasn't the type to blush. "Cheesecake," she blurted out. "There's one more—"

"Too late." He held up a plate with only a few bites of said cheesecake remaining.

The dessert had been brought in by Evan's wife, Selena, and was fair game, but Faith had counted on beating the guys to it.

"I *used* to like you," she told Penn, feigning disgust.

He laughed. "You'll learn. Best to steal it and store it in your room if you really want it."

"Clearly. Oh well. This way you get to deal with the calories."

"I'll lose sleep over it," he joked as she left the kitchen.

She was disappointed she'd missed out on the sugar she'd been craving all evening, but given a choice, she'd rather witness Joe's save-a-kitten efforts any day.

CHAPTER TWELVE

MAYBE SOMEDAY she would learn to scope out a place before putting in her food order, Faith thought as she joined her friend on the patio.

"You would choose this table," she said, keeping her tone light as she took the stool beside Nadia, one of her BFFs since grade school. "You still have a talent for zeroing in on the strongest concentration of testosterone in any room, don't you?"

"Still have it?" Nadia said after sipping her strawberry margarita. "My talent is finely honed after all these years, darlin'. Most single women appreciate my skills."

"They're firefighters," Faith said of the large, boisterous diners at the next table. And of course, not just any firefighters. She was shocked to see Joe among the group that included Cale, Turner, Penn and Clay, plus Clay's family.

"Excellent," Nadia said, her eyes sparkling. "You can introduce me."

"Like you've ever needed me to introduce you to anyone."

With her long blond hair, petite body and eternal cuteness, Nadia seemed to have people flocking around her wherever she went. Men, yes, but even women instinctively liked her.

"Introduce you to whom?" Mercedes, Nadia's opposite in almost every way, climbed up on the third stool and set down a basket of chips and a Sandblaster, the Shell Shack's signature toxic drink.

"Take your pick," Nadia said, gesturing to the group. "San Amaro's bravest, ripe for the choosing."

"Some are taken," Faith said in a futile attempt to dampen Nadia's enthusiasm. And no, she was *not* referring to Joe.

"The one with the kid, I'm assuming. Too bad."

"That's Clay Marlow."

"Tell me the rest. The ones that are available."

"Some things never change," Faith said to Mercedes, who laughed and shook her head.

"Once a serial dater, always a serial dater." Mercedes casually tossed her dark, curly hair over her shoulder. "It's part of why we love her."

"True," Faith said.

"Here's to girlfriends who understand each other," Nadia said, raising her glass. Faith held her piña colada up and nodded, appreciating the sentiment.

One of the best parts of being back on San Amaro was these two. Though they didn't get to meet often enough because of their jobs and crazy schedules, it was as if they'd been together just yesterday whenever they did make plans.

"Faith, are you and your pretty friends going to ignore us all night?" Penn of the deep blue eyes, which had no doubt caught Nadia's, had angled his chair to face them.

"I don't think that's possible," Faith said, smiling. She introduced Nadia and Mercedes to everyone she knew at the firefighters' table. When she got to Joe, he wouldn't make direct eye contact. He checked out Nadia and Mercedes, nodded at them, greeted them just as Cale did, but he didn't look at Faith once.

"And I'm betting those two belong to Clay," she continued, doing her best to ignore Joe, in turn.

"This is my wife, Andie," Clay said, referring to the tall, pretty brunette with a row of earrings lining her ear. "And short stuff here is Payton."

Faith stepped down from her stool and extended her hand first to Andie and then to the little girl sitting on Clay's leg. His daughter had gorgeous shiny brown hair and eyes that matched her daddy's. "Nice to meet you," she said. "I've heard a lot about you both."

"Faith is a firefighter, too," Clay told his daughter, which made her stare up at Faith in wonder.

"I have to hang around with noisy boys a lot," Faith told her, sensing that Joe was now watching her. "Kind of like you're doing tonight."

"Boys are smelly," Payton said, making everyone laugh.

"Don't let her fool you," Andie said. "She's got all these smelly boys wrapped around her little finger."

"As they should be." Faith held up her hand for Payton to high-five her.

"Are there more girl firefighters?" Payton asked, not even blinking at the attention from all these men.

"Not here on San Amaro," Faith told her.

"There should be," Payton said, still watching Faith carefully.

"I think we've got all we can handle with one," Penn said.

Maybe Faith's guilty conscience was at work, but she could swear he glanced pointedly toward Joe.

"I bet he's scared of girls," Faith said to Payton. "What do you think?"

The little girl giggled and studied Penn, then nodded.

"Looks like my food is here," Faith said, glad for the excuse to go back to her table with her friends. "Talk to you guys later. Nice meeting you, Andie and Payton."

"They're all hot," Nadia said once she sat down again. "Not sure I can narrow it down."

"You're not dating any of them," Faith said, digging into her cheese fries.

"Which one would you pick?" Nadia continued, as if Faith hadn't shut her down.

Mercedes surreptitiously looked over the choices as she put some ceviche in her mouth. "Have to agree, difficult choice," she said quietly. "What about you, Faith? You know them beyond their pretty faces. What do you think?"

"I think I am not going out with anyone from work."

"Not interested?" Nadia looked skeptical. "You sleep with these guys every week. I think a little fire station romance could be hot."

Faith finished chewing a bite of burger before responding. "That's because you don't work there."

"I don't think everyone agrees with you," Mercedes said. "The dark-haired one at the end—was it Joe?— keeps looking at you."

Without moving her head, Faith checked him out and, sure enough, Joe was sitting there with his arms on the table in front of him, watching her intently from behind his dark sunglasses. She glanced around quickly to see if anyone else had noticed, but her coworkers were all caught up in trying to be the funniest guy on the planet. Still, it made her nervous. Her friends had noticed. And they were watching her now, so she couldn't frown at him or give him any signal to make him realize he was being obvious.

"The captain," Nadia said, drawing out her words and smiling. "Faith's going for the big guns."

"After we eat, I'll take you over and you can get to know him yourself if you're so caught up on his position—"

"I can think of a lot of positions that would be fun with him."

Faith couldn't help laughing at her persistent, single-minded friend. It was mostly an act, she knew. Nadia was a flirt but nothing more. Which was the only reason Faith didn't feel the need to clobber her over the head with a hard object for checking out Joe so thoroughly.

"I CAN DO THAT, princess."

Faith's dad ambled out of the garage to where she was changing the lawnmower blade on the driveway.

No doubt he *could* do it, but whether he would was another story altogether.

"I got it. Almost done." She tightened the bolt that held the blade on.

"Why don't you let me mow then," he said.

"It's okay, Dad, I need the exercise." She'd still train for at least an hour, but he didn't need to know that.

She should let him do it, but she'd worked herself into enough of a lather over the six-inch-tall grass that she was determined to hack it off herself. She'd intended to finish the job before her dad even climbed out of bed. Surprisingly, it was only five to ten. Last weekend he hadn't been moving until almost noon.

He strutted up to her once she righted the mower and gripped the handle. "That's an argument you can't win. Who needs the exercise more?"

She grinned, unable to stay mad at him. "You have a cushy desk job. I need to be in top shape."

He looked down at her gruffly and she laughed.

"Go eat breakfast, Dad. I like to mow."

"I like to mow, too."

"Not to be rude, but if you like to mow so much, maybe you could do it before it hits my waist next time." She pointed toward the overgrown lawn.

He nodded soberly. "I'll do that. I hadn't noticed."

She frowned, unable to keep up the facade that everything was fine. "Dad, I talked to Mom the other day."

"How's she doing?"

"She looked tired, but seems okay."

He gazed sadly off into the distance and Faith couldn't bring herself to tell him the rest of the story as she'd intended. Couldn't mention that her mom seemed to be moving on. Before seeing the lost look on his face, she'd thought he should know about the new boyfriend. In case he ran into her mom and the smarm in public or something.

"I didn't tell her about the other night," Faith said hesitantly, hating to bring it up at all. They had yet to discuss, or even mention, his drunk fest.

He froze. Seemed to stop breathing. "You didn't?"

"I didn't think you'd want her to know."

He looked at the ground and swallowed. Avoided Faith's gaze. "I was wondering," he began in an uncharacteristically quiet voice, "how I did get home. I don't remember. Tell me I didn't drive."

"You didn't drive. You couldn't have. You don't recall calling me?"

He thought for a few seconds, then shook his head. "I'm sorry, Faith. That won't happen again."

"It better not," she said, more forcefully than she'd meant to. "Dad, Joe Mendoza had to help me get you to your room."

Tony swore and walked to the wooden bench near the front sidewalk. Sitting down heavily, he leaned his elbows on his knees and hung his head. Faith silently sat next to him.

"How did Joe get involved?" he asked.

She told him what she knew of his adventures before she'd arrived at the Shell Shack.

"I'd phoned your mother from work that afternoon," he said after another long pause. "She asked me not to call her again. Not that that's any excuse for drinking myself into oblivion."

"No," Faith said, wondering if her mom had any idea how much power she held over this seemingly powerful man. Did she even care? "Next time you feel like that, Dad, could you call me? Before you start drinking."

"I hope to God there isn't a next time. Did anyone else see me? Recognize me?"

"Not that I know of. There wasn't anyone else from the department there that night besides Joe and Derek. Just a big crowd of tourists."

They sat without speaking for several minutes, her

dad seemingly lost in his thoughts and Faith trying to appreciate the beautiful spring morning around her. Trying to figure out how to be what her dad needed right now. Whatever that was.

"I know I have to move on," he said finally. "Get over it, like she has."

Did he know about the other guy?

"Until I do that, give her some space like she asked, I'm only going to piss her off."

"I don't think you just 'get over' thirty-eight years of marriage," Faith said.

He chuckled. "When you put it like that…"

A wren landed several feet away from them and hopped across the sidewalk. It poked its tiny beak in the moist dirt of the weed-filled flower bed, hunting for lunch.

"I'm sorry you had to see me like that, princess. No daughter should ever have to deal with such a situation."

She refrained from agreeing with him aloud. "We all make mistakes. I'm sorry I had to have Joe help me. There was no other way. He said he'd keep the whole thing to himself."

Her father sighed and patted her knee. "You're a good girl, Faith. Don't know how I'd get through this without you here."

That made her think again of what Joe had said—that there wasn't much anyone could do for him except just be there. Maybe the captain had a clue what he was talking about, after all.

"I'm going to mow before it gets hotter," she said,

jumping up and cutting the awkward father-daughter talk short.

He didn't say anything else as she returned to the driveway, just sat there looking so damn sad. Broken.

Not mentioning her mom's "wonder-smarm" was the right decision, Faith assured herself. She refused to be the one to crush her dad. She might not be able to get her parents back together, but she could protect him from more heartbreak.

EVERY FIREFIGHTER LOVED being on the nozzle in a big blaze.

When Joe gave Faith the assignment as they climbed off the engine a week and a half after the fire where she'd freaked out, she tried to summon her usual excitement.

As she and Nate hooked up the attack hose and lugged it toward the back of the sprawling one-story furniture store, her heart hammered. Not in a good way.

They stopped outside of the building to make final adjustments.

She couldn't lose it. Not again. Especially with Nate, her favorite naysayer, right behind her. She could work with him even though she didn't like him, but she would not give him more reason to doubt her abilities.

She automatically checked that her flashlight was strapped on to her air pack, and pulled her gloves on more securely as she fought nausea.

No hesitation. You're not going to get hurt. Not going to screw up. Get in there already, before someone wonders what the hell you're waiting for.

She squeezed her eyes shut for a second, then forced herself to go inside.

The fire was in the front half of the building. Working toward it was like wandering through a human-size maze, thanks to what she assumed were furniture displays throughout. Nausea boiled in her gut and she felt shaky, but she kept going. Faith didn't realize she'd made the boneheaded, unforgivable mistake of going inside without her partner until she turned to check on him and found herself alone. He must've let go of the hose while adjusting his mask or something. Where the hell was he?

The smoke was thickening, but she could still see the door she'd come in. She could go back and get him but the flames were advancing quickly. She needed to knock them down. Nate would follow the hose and catch up to her any second now.

Visibility continued to tank and the temperature kept climbing. She'd just about reached the place she needed to get to before opening the hose when she tripped. A sharp corner of something jabbed into her padded coat, padded coat dulled the pain. She stumbled, trying to stay on her feet, then ran into another solid object, felt a blow to her head and found herself sprawled on her side. Disoriented. What had she hit her head on? She felt for her helmet and found it had been dislodged. She lay there for several seconds, trying to get her bearings, before she realized the flames were too close. She groped around for her helmet, the smoke black and blinding now. Having had a building collapse on her made her only too aware of how badly she needed to protect her head.

And her radio. Where was her radio? She'd had it when she'd started, she was sure.

Frantic, she slipped one glove off, hoping to find something that would help her—helmet, radio, hose. The heat was too much, though, and she was afraid she'd drop the glove as well. Swearing up a storm, she yanked her glove back on as she continued to search. Finally she located her helmet and put it back on her head.

Faith noticed she was breathing too fast, using up too much of her oxygen, about the same time she realized she couldn't find the hose. Her way out.

Her chest got that squeezed-in-a-vise feeling and she gasped for breath, even though there was nothing wrong with her supply. Sweat drenched her under her gear and it wasn't just because of the heat in the building. She crawled away from the fire a few feet, feeling for the hose on her way, unable to see a thing—whether from smoke or tears, she couldn't say.

Seconds or minutes ticked by—her sense of time was as hazy as the toxic air around her—and she stubbornly kept moving on her hands and knees, searching for the hose line. If she could just find that, she could get back to what she needed to be doing and put out the freaking fire.

There came a time—she wouldn't be able to pinpoint it later, exactly—when putting out the fire became a secondary concern and getting the hell out of Dodge took over.

Faith had known how quickly a person could become disoriented in a fire, but that didn't prepare her for the panic and terror she experienced now. All sense of direction was gone, and she could no longer see the light from the door where she'd entered. Everything looked the same—a cloud of thick, impenetrable smoke unevenly lit by flames that seemed to be everywhere. She might be five feet from where she'd originally gone down or she might be on the other side of the building. She'd tried to stay close, to avoid going more than a couple of feet in any direction as she searched. The fire was no longer on just one side of her, so she couldn't use that reference to navigate.

Why had she rushed in without Nate? If she hadn't let her panic push her, hadn't let herself wind up alone, everything would be fine. He would've seen her go down, would've made his way to her and helped her get back to the nozzle, and they would have the fire under control by now.

The fire that seemed to be everywhere. On all sides. Creeping closer.

She could die today.

The thought gripped her like a hand to her throat. She froze, unable to decide what her next move should be. Unable to even process her options, limited though they must be. The only thing that ran through her head was that those who'd doubted her—her mother, some of her colleagues—were right. She wasn't good enough for the job.

Heat at her back ripped her attention away from that pathetic line of thought, and she refused to give in to the panic that was trying to suffocate her. She crawled away from the immediate danger, feeling around on the floor for a clear path. Away from the intense heat.

When the alarm on her breathing apparatus started

beeping, signaling she was about five minutes from running out of air, she frantically wondered what would get her first, lack of oxygen or a heart attack. Her chest felt as if it would explode, and the heat now seemed unbearable. Add burning to death to the list of possibilities.

Love of God, how did she get in this situation?

More importantly, how could she get out of it?

She continued feeling for a clear path, blind, alone and scared out of her mind. She kept fighting for another breath.

When she felt something yank at her leg, she nearly wept. It was a person grabbing at her—had to be. Someone had found her. Maybe she wouldn't die, after all.

CHAPTER THIRTEEN

JOE HAD RESCUED several people over the course of his career, but he'd never felt such profound relief as when he grasped an object and realized it was Faith's boot.

Relief and other things he wouldn't—couldn't—put a name to right now. He'd been searching for too long, ever since Nate had radioed that he'd found the hose, with no Faith at the end of it.

Joe had to give her air and get her out of here fast. Penn was backing up Nate now. They weren't too far away, battling the flames. Another company had been called in as well, since the fire had tripled in size and intensity, but right now, all Joe could think of was the woman on the floor in front of him.

She was beneath some kind of obstruction, likely a piece of furniture, so he had to pull her free before he could do anything. When she raised her head, he silently thanked God that she was conscious. Her alarm was sounding and she pulled off her mask. She couldn't have much oxygen left. Bending over her, Joe removed his own mask and placed it on her face long enough for her to draw several good breaths. While she filled her lungs, he cradled her in his arms and positioned them both to get the hell out.

She held the mask out to him—a good sign. He took two big inhalations and returned it to her, then eased them along, as close to the floor as he could manage. The going was slow. He'd never come across such a cluttered, confusing layout in a structure fire before.

Faith offered him the mask again. He refused, shaking his head, but either she couldn't see him or she was stubborn, because she held it out insistently. He finally paused long enough to take a fresh breath, mostly to appease her. They'd be out in less than a minute, and though his lungs were burning, he had no idea how much smoke she'd taken in before he'd found her. She needed it worse than him.

He could tell when the guys put water on the flames directly behind them, just as he neared the exit. When he got Faith outside, Rafe, one of the paramedics, rushed over to take her, but Joe carried her to a safe spot near the ambulance himself.

Joe stepped back and let Rafe and Scott get to her to check her vitals. When they got her helmet and hood off, he could see how pale she was. Her lack of protest when the guys fussed over her told him more than anything she might have said. It'd been a close call. Too damn close. He'd never lost a firefighter on his watch, and he planned to keep it that way.

The officer of the company from the mainland came over to confer with him then, and Joe forced his attention back to the fire. They'd made a big turnaround in their fight with the arrival of the second company, and it looked as if this blaze would be knocked down soon. Then he'd be able to reassure himself he'd gotten to Faith in time, and that she'd be okay.

FAITH STEPPED OUT the back door of the beachside station at long last. The cool air on the patio was a relief after the stuffiness inside and the measuring stares most of her colleagues had tried to hide.

Darkness had fallen hours ago and the beach was mostly empty. She sat on one of the cushionless plastic chaise longues and closed her eyes, allowing the sound of the surf to isolate her with her thoughts.

It had taken a battle, quiet though it may have been, to convince Joe to let her help with the overhaul at the furniture store after the fire was out. She'd rested on her butt like an invalid for close to an hour, letting the EMTs fuss over her, appeasing her captain, soothing her raw throat.

So she'd taken in a little bit of smoke. She was a firefighter. That happened. She was lucky as hell it wasn't worse, and she knew that. But it wasn't worse.

Every muscle in her body ached, sure. She had several cuts and bruises, but everything was minor. She was fine.

Physically.

Mentally, not so much.

The sliding door whooshed open behind her and she wished she'd walked farther away, toward the water or up the shore.

Joe. He stood behind her, and she didn't turn, but she sensed him. He was one of the very few quiet men in the department; most of the guys would come out noisily and not be able to resist announcing their presence.

She could feel Joe watching her, and it made her want to jump up and run away. What did he think when he looked at her? How stupid she'd been at the fire scene? Irresponsible? That she wasn't cut out for the job?

Would he be wrong if he thought any of those things? She wasn't so sure.

A minute passed while he stood behind her, staring, not saying a word. Faith fought within herself not to acknowledge him first in this silent standoff. She willed him to turn around and go back inside—to no avail. Then decided she might go ape-shit crazy if he stood there for another excruciating minute.

"You can go—I'm fine," she finally said, cringing because of the dryness in her throat. "Feeling great."

"I know you're okay. That's not why I came out."

"Your team losing?" Faith had no idea what NBA team was his favorite, but when she'd sneaked outside, everyone had been caught up in a game on TV, acting as if the fate of the world depended on the outcome.

He entered her line of sight at last, taking the chaise next to her. And God bless him, he held out a tall bottle of ice-cold water to her. She unscrewed the lid and took a few swallows. The chilled liquid helped and hurt her throat at the same time.

"Nope," he said. "Winning."

"Then why'd you come out?"

"Heard you were alone."

She drank more water. "Nothing wrong with alone."

"Sometimes. This isn't one of them."

"Kind of thinking it is."

He stared at her hard for several seconds, making her want to squirm. "Beating yourself up?"

Damn him.

"Some." Endlessly.

"Normal."

"Sucks."

"Everyone makes mistakes," he said quietly, as if that was top secret.

"Mine could've killed me."

"That's the kind of work we're in."

She looked away, afraid her doubts would show in her eyes. Neither of them spoke for several minutes, and she was almost able to block out all thoughts and pretend everything was okay. She was starting to appreciate his company, just a little, when he ruined it.

"We can save the official stuff for later, but I'm curious…what happened, Faith?"

"I tripped," she said, knowing she couldn't avoid talking about it at some point. Might as well get it over with. "It was like a maze in there. I don't know what I ran into, but I landed on my butt. Don't think I lost consciousness, but I might as well have—I was really out of it."

She paused to take another drink.

"I've never seen an interior like that," Joe agreed.

"My radio was gone, helmet fell off. Then I realized I'd lost the hose, too."

"You weren't very far from it when I found you."

She closed her eyes. "Humiliating."

"No. Stop it, Faith."

"I don't know how long I tried to find it. I swear I was going in circles."

"Happened to me once," he said.

"What did?" She found it hard to imagine him having any difficulties in a fire, even though she knew most firefighters had stories. She'd heard plenty from the old-timers in her five years on the job.

"Lost the line once in a fire and couldn't find it to save my life, no pun intended."

"What happened?"

"I came across it eventually. But I know that feeling where you think you're not going to make it out."

Nausea welled up in her gut. She broke into a cold sweat.

"How'd you end up alone in there, Faith?" Joe's voice was low but intense. "That's not like you."

"How do you know what's like me? We've been working together for less than a month." Granted, she was with him almost every single stinking shift.

"I've seen enough to know you're a damn good firefighter. You had a respectable record in San Antonio."

Tears burned her eyes, so she closed them and rubbed her fingers over them as if she had a headache.

"That's not meant as a criticism," he said. "I'm trying to understand what happened."

"It's...I don't know." She studied the knee of his uniform pants. "The accident in San Antonio. I think it messed me up."

"The one that broke your collarbone?"

"That'd be the one." She stalled by taking another long drink. Debating how much to say. "The fire at the Sea Breeze Hotel a couple of weeks back?"

He sat up and turned toward her, putting both feet on the ground between their chairs. "I remember it."

"You sent me in behind Penn."

He nodded and touched her forearm gently, as if urging her to continue.

"I lost it, Joe. I mean really lost it. Froze up and nearly ran back out the door as soon as we got inside." She expected him to say something, but he remained silent. "I thought I was having a heart attack for a second."

"Panic attack."

"I almost didn't make it any farther."

"But you did."

"Penn didn't notice I stopped. I had to back him up."

"It's not an unusual reaction the first time back in after an injury."

"That doesn't make it okay," she said, her voice barely more than a whisper. "It was horrible."

"But you overcame it on your own."

"Today was the first big fire since that one. I was terrified the same thing would happen. Those feelings, the panic, started as soon as the engine stopped."

She swallowed hard, the same feelings threatening to overcome her now. "I had to talk myself through it. Force myself to go inside."

"You overcompensated," Joe suggested.

"Over-somethinged. I couldn't stand the thought of someone noticing me standing there like an idiot. I didn't bother double-checking to make sure Nate was ready. Didn't even think about it. Just rushed in as soon as I could move."

"I wish you'd said something before today. That's one of the basics, Faith."

She bolted off the chaise, hands clenched, and went to the edge of the patio. "Don't you think I know that? Believe me, it's killing me."

"You could've corrected the mistake if you'd radioed out or come back to get Nate."

Yeah. She could've done lots of things a hell of a

lot better. She'd been over every single option about four hundred times in her mind. She didn't need anyone telling her what she'd done wrong—she could do that herself just fine. "I'm going to the water." Maybe *into* the water. Maybe soaking her head would make her feel marginally better.

Two minutes later, after she'd sat down hard on the cushiony sand, Joe strode up beside her. She closed her eyes. Could a woman not suffer humiliation in private?

"You know I have to report it all," he said, lowering his large frame next to her on the sand.

"Of course. I can't wait till my dad hears what an idiot I am." And so much for earning anyone's respect around here.

Way to go, Faith. You deserve it.

"He knows you well enough to understand it was a fluke."

"That's just it, Joe. It wasn't a fluke. I screwed up big time because I *am* messed up. My head is wrong."

"You had a building fall on you. That can mess a person up."

"Not a firefighter." She chewed on her lip as she stared at the waves coming in. They were relatively calm right now, contrasting with a wild surf just that morning, when she and Joe had reported for their shift. Similarly, the storm inside Faith had died down and become a single nagging pulse of doubt. Fear. "Maybe my mom was right, after all," she said in a small voice.

"Right about what?" Joe asked, leaning closer. "What does your mom have to do with anything?"

"She hates that I'm a firefighter. She's always said it's not a career for women."

"I suspect you've never agreed with her about that?"

Faith shook her head.

"Then why start now?"

She pierced him with a sharp look. "Bumbling around in a fire, nearly getting myself killed. That tends to make a person doubt herself."

"Stop the doubting right now." He barked it out like a direct order.

"Sure thing. Just tell me how."

Joe locked his hands around his knees and shrugged. "Hell if I know. But I'm certain you can do it. You're smart. You told me you just passed your haz-mat certification, right?"

"That was on paper."

"Proves you know your stuff. You're a strong person, Faith."

"I don't feel strong. I feel like a fool."

He shook his head, staring out at the Gulf. Beyond "It takes strength to stand up to a member of your family who doesn't believe in what you do."

"It's not that she doesn't believe in it. She just doesn't like it."

"Same difference."

Faith frowned. "I believe that's called stubbornness, not strength."

"Your mother has really never supported your career?"

"That's an accurate assessment. She and my dad used to argue all the time when I was a teenager and insisted I wanted to follow in his footsteps."

"I don't know what I'd be doing right now if my dad hadn't been a firefighter."

"You don't think you'd be doing this?"

Joe hesitated. "No idea. My dad was the chief, my mom is a fire buff and an original member of the Burn Foundation. I don't think I ever really considered other options."

He seemed genuinely bothered by the discovery.

"You love fighting fires," Faith said. "I can tell when we get a good call."

"I like my job."

"Sure, but this is more. You…come alive when there's a fire."

Joe nodded. "Hell, yeah. Best part of the job. Don't think you could find a firefighter who wouldn't agree with that."

She flinched. Most days, she'd be the first to agree, but lately she didn't know whether to be excited or full of dread when they got some action. "Don't you think you'll miss that if you become assistant chief?" she asked, relieved to have the spotlight off her own weaknesses.

"Might. That's the way it goes." His answer came quickly. Too quickly.

She watched him in the near darkness, wondering how much thought he'd really given to what it would be like, moving up in the department. Sure, he'd planned it his whole life. But planning as a kid with big dreams and really considering something as an adult were two different things.

Who was she to point that out to him, though?

Who was she to tell anyone how to live his or her life

or do his or her job? After today she wondered if she would ever be able to do hers right again.

"We were talking about you, not me," Joe said sternly, and if Faith hadn't been so depressed she might've grinned.

"Thought we were done."

"You know I have to write you up."

That was the insult on top of the injury, as far as she was concerned. "Yep."

"There's no way around it. You could've been seriously—"

"I know, Joe." She sucked in the cool evening air, trying to calm herself. It wasn't his fault, but the way he was trying to justify it only made her feel worse. As if she'd let him down as well as herself. "I get it. I told you I don't want any special favors. Anyone else would get the same treatment."

"Correct." He glanced behind them at the station, which was lit up like a stadium on game night. He slid his hand over hers, startling Faith. "Right now, however, I'm treating you differently than I would the other firefighters."

She glanced down at their entwined fingers. Knew she should pull away, yet couldn't. Call her Ms. Hypocrite, but his hand was strong. Warm. Reassuring somehow.

"I'm going to go out on a limb here and guess that you're harder on yourself than anyone else ever could be," he said. "Speaking as your captain, we need to find a way to get you over your hesitation, because that could be deadly."

Faith nodded, her throat blocked by a lump of emotion. He wasn't telling her anything she didn't know, but his use of the word *we* made her feel as if maybe she wasn't hopeless. Maybe she could figure out how to get her mojo back.

"I'm behind you, Faith. I know you're better than what happened today."

"Is that spoken as my captain, too?"

He looked back at the water, the white tops of the waves visible in the dark. "Yes. And…as something else."

She was afraid to ask what. Her father's protégé? A friend? Something else? Something forbidden?

Yeah, definitely best not to ask.

She swallowed hard. "Thank you. I'm going to go inside now."

Before she touched him again or, God forbid, started liking him even more.

CHAPTER FOURTEEN

"GREAT DAY FOR FISHING," Joe said, leaning back in his seat in the stern of the *Hot Water,* the chief's trawler yacht. It was more a luxury boat than something meant for fishing, but it worked just fine to sit out here with a couple lines in. They were in the bay, close to where it met the Gulf of Mexico. One of the chief's preferred fishing spots. They were near enough to shore that Joe could make out some people there.

"Not too bad," Chief Peligni said, looking up at the cloudless, early evening sky through his sunglasses. "Don't get out here much anymore."

"Shame to keep this beauty tied up."

Joe had brought up the boat the other day at work, planning to get Chief Peligni out of the house, as he'd promised Faith. The chief had beat him to it, though, inviting him to an evening of fishing.

"Suppose it is. Need another beer?"

Joe nodded, and the older man stood and went into the cabin, returning a couple minutes later with two cans and a bag of cheese popcorn.

"So," the chief said, settling on one of the seats and putting his feet up. "You going to tell me what the hell happened with Faith the other day? The reality version and not some damn watered-down crap from the report."

That explained the invitation, Joe thought. Just as well. He'd been expecting to have this discussion before now. But Chief Peligni had seemed distracted, not really engaged at work.

"What do you want to know?" he asked, setting the beer aside. This could get tricky. He was sure to be straddling a fine line between what the chief needed to find out and what Faith had told Joe in confidence about her state of mind.

"How in the name of God above did she end up needing you to carry her out of a goddamn structure fire? She's better than that, Joe. What happened?"

Joe told him about the furniture store, that there had been crap everywhere, making it a bitch to get through. "She tripped. Hit her head."

"Got that from the report. Why was she alone? Did someone else screw up?"

"No. According to Faith, she thought Nate was behind her when she went in."

"Dammit. The girl knows better than that in her sleep."

Joe was in full agreement, but knowing what she'd been going through since her injury made him more sympathetic. However, he didn't dare defend her to her father without sharing that information, or the chief would be suspicious of his motives.

Granted, there was good reason for that suspicion. The dreams Joe had been having about Faith were proof enough.

He needed to do something about his attraction to her. Maybe move to North Dakota.

"She was off her game, I guess," he said vaguely. "I don't think it'll happen again."

"No. Faith's good."

Joe's cell phone buzzed in his pocket, and he took it out, surprised he had a signal out here. His stepfather, according to caller ID.

"Mendoza," he said automatically.

"Joe, I'm at the hospital," Jorge said, making Joe's gut sink. "It's your mom."

"What's going on, Jorge?" Joe stood, as if that could help him absorb the news better. His mom frequented hospitals, especially lately, but he'd never get used to it.

"Apparently she's got pneumonia in both lungs. Hitting her pretty hard."

Joe swore. That was an understatement, he knew. A head cold hit his mom hard due to her fragile health. Lupus and vasculitis weakened her system significantly. Pneumonia could... He shook his head. *Not going there*.

"You in Corpus? At Memorial?" he asked.

"Room 319."

"I'll be there. Thanks, Jorge."

"Get here safe. I'm not going to be the one to tell her you're in a car wreck."

"See you in a couple hours." Joe ended the call and swore some more.

"What's the matter?" Chief Peligni asked.

"My mom's in the hospital with pneumonia. With her other health problems, it's serious." He stared at his phone helplessly. "Possibly deadly. I need to get to her."

"She's in Corpus Christi?"

Joe nodded, pacing the deck, feeling trapped.

"Pull the lines in. I'll take you to the marina and Faith can get you up there."

"I can get myself up there, Chief." He started reeling in the lines as the chief had directed.

"You've had four beers."

"So have you."

"I've had three, and I'm not wanting to drive a hundred miles on the highway. There's no boat traffic between here and my slip." He nodded in that direction, and they were close enough that Joe could see he spoke the truth. "Besides, I got you doubled in weight."

"I'm okay," Joe said, but he knew Chief Peligni was right. "Faith has better things to do with her time."

The chief had already pulled his phone out and pressed a speed dial button for his daughter. He briefly told her what was going on, nodded repeatedly, answered her questions and ended the call.

"She'll be waiting at the marina parking lot."

"Fine." Joe was bothered by inconveniencing Faith, but frankly, he couldn't dwell on that when his mom was in grave danger. Her immune system was weak on a good day. She'd been worn down recently. After all her years of battling the autoimmune disease, he should be used to the possibility of a worst-case scenario, but he wasn't. He'd never accept that his mom wouldn't be around forever.

By the time they made it to the marina, Joe was ready to dive off the side of the boat and swim to get there faster.

He and the chief tied up the boat and he stepped

ashore. "You coming?" he asked as he walked along the narrow pier to the main dock.

Chief Peligni shook his head and waved him off. Joe didn't have time to question him. It was probably best that he stayed put and let the beer lose its effect, anyway.

Faith stood against the wall of the marina store, watching him approach. As preoccupied as he was, he still couldn't help noticing how good she looked in thigh-hugging jeans that ended just below her knees, a white tank top and denim jacket. Heels made her muscled legs look even longer than usual. Her hair was held back by a thin headband, with chin-length strands left to frame her beautiful face. She looked like…one hell of a woman. A very pretty, feminine one. Her appearance revealed nothing of the very capable firefighter she was. As he walked nearer, he noted the large turquoise pendant that hung enticingly just above her cleavage.

"Took you guys forever to get back," she said, pushing herself off the wall as he approached.

"Tell me about it. Faith, I'm sorry to interrupt your night. You look like you had plans."

"Just a movie with Nadia and Mercedes. No big deal."

"Well, thank you. I appreciate it. I could've made it—"

"Joe?" she said, clicking the doors unlocked as they approached her Subaru.

"Yeah?"

"Technically, right now, you're not my officer, since we're off duty. I'm fine with driving you to Corpus. You know I respect the heck out of you, but please, just close your mouth and get in the car."

He stopped a few feet from the passenger door and stared at her.

"Your mom is waiting," she said sternly.

He mimicked her sternness, nodded and did as she said. Unfortunately, he found her sexy as hell when she got bossy.

FAITH'S HEART WENT OUT to the four men—Joe, his stepfather and two stepbrothers—as the doctor walked out of the otherwise empty waiting room on the third floor of the hospital.

No one said a word while they absorbed the prognosis: Joe's mother was severely ill, her fever climbing dangerously higher as her weakened body waited for some powerful antibiotics to knock out the bacteria. She was in intensive care and had been sleeping since Joe and Faith had arrived.

"She's stubborn," Troy said, leaning back stiffly in one of the uncomfortable, lime-green chairs. He wore neatly tailored pants and a button-down shirt, even at this late hour. "If anyone in her condition can beat this, it's Carmen."

Joe abruptly stood and walked out of the glassed-in room to the main hall. Faith craned her neck to see where he was heading, but he paced out of her line of sight.

She looked back at the three men still in the room and caught Joe's stepfather watching her.

"I'm glad you're here with him," Mr. Vargas said,

leaning forward, elbows on his knees. "He tries to be such an island, but this could really tear him up."

"I wish there was something I could do," Faith said, detesting her helplessness.

The other stepbrother, Ryan, stood and ambled to the doorway, repeatedly rubbing his fingers over his goatee. "How involved are you two?" he asked Faith.

She shook her head. "We're not." It wasn't really a lie. Kissing once didn't make them involved. Just stupid.

Ryan angled his head slightly, thoughtfully. "Must've misread things. Too bad. He needs someone like you in his life."

"He's my officer," Faith said, sounding defensive. She stood. "I'm going to go find him."

Mr. Vargas nodded, sidetracked by his own sorrow. His affection for Joe's mom was obvious. Heartwarming.

"Can I bring you guys something from the machines?" she asked. "A drink or some chips or something?"

All three shook their heads, and Troy thanked her.

She headed down the hall Joe had taken, but didn't see any sign of him. At the nurses' station, an older woman in cartoon character scrubs must have noticed her confusion.

"Looking for the big guy? Navy-blue shirt?"

Faith nodded.

"He's out on the terrace." She indicated a glass door farther down the hall.

"Thank you."

Faith went through the door, which led to an open-air rooftop terrace. Neatly trimmed shrubs had been shaped into hearts and stars and placed at intervals around the perimeter, and a raised flower bed showed sprouts of green beginning to pop through the soil. The terrace was deserted except for Joe, who stood near the low wall that ran around the entire area. Because of the angles of the odd-shaped space, he was in partial profile to her. He leaned on the wall, looking out over who knew what, seeing nothing, she was sure.

She walked toward him, the cork soles of her wedge shoes making very little noise on the pebbled concrete. He was so lost in his thoughts he didn't appear to hear her approach. When Faith touched his forearm, he jumped.

"Hey," she said, not letting her hand drop.

He looked straight at her, a deep sadness etched into his normally stoic face. "Hey." There was no hint of the ass-kicking, confident fire captain in his voice.

"Can I get you anything? Some coffee?"

"Some grain alcohol," he said solemnly.

"I wish that would make things better somehow."

"You and me both."

"Okay if I stand out here with you?"

"Fine by me."

Faith joined him in leaning on the wall and watched the comings and goings of people below at the brightly lit entrance to the emergency department.

"You don't have to stay here. I can get back to San Amaro on my own," Joe said after several minutes.

"I don't mind."

"You go on duty in the morning. Go home. Sleep."

"So do you," she said, neither one of them admitting they didn't know what the morning would bring or if he'd be able to make it in to work at all. "I can catch a nap inside if I get tired. Right now I'm fine."

He looked down, seeming to focus on her for the first time since she'd come outside. "You won't leave, will you?"

She shook her head. "You're beginning to know me well."

"I know you're stubborn as all get-out."

"Thank you."

With a ghost of a smile, he put his arm around her and tugged her to his side. He held her there, both of them watching an ambulance pull up and unload a patient below. She figured he needed the contact, the human touch, and it felt good to be tucked into his side.

"Your steps seem like decent guys," she said after several minutes, wanting to somehow reach out to him.

"They're okay. For lawyers."

"All three of them are lawyers?" Joe didn't talk much about them. In fact, before the drive up here, she hadn't known he had any stepbrothers, and had heard him mention his stepfather only in passing.

"All three of them. Same firm. Do me a favor and don't ask them about it. They'll get to talking like a bunch of girls—no offense—and never shut up."

Smiling, she said, "No offense taken. I'm not often accused of being chatty."

"I like that about you."

"So you're not close to Troy or Ryan?"

He shook his head. "We hang out sometimes to appease my mother, but it's just for show."

"They seem genuinely concerned about you," she

said, recalling the conversation after he'd walked out of the waiting room.

"No reason to be concerned. I'll be fine."

"I was once accused of overusing the word *fine* when I didn't want to get into detail."

"Yeah?" He peered down at her with a tired but almost amused expression. "Who accused you of that?"

"Some wise guy know-it-all officer type."

"As long as you don't let those officer types hear you talk like that about them you'll be fine."

She glanced up at him to gauge whether she'd offended him. It was difficult to tell. "We're not on duty right now. Technically, you're not my—"

"Not your captain. Got it."

"My captain wouldn't have his arm around me. That could get him in trouble."

A low sound in his chest was probably as close as he'd get to a laugh tonight. "Point taken."

"Are you ready to go back in? Sit with your family?"

"Surrogate family," he corrected. "It's easier to be out here."

"How come?"

He removed his arm and she couldn't help noticing the cool breeze that blew over her. Leaning on the wall again, he said, "Don't have to put on an act."

"You would with your stepbrothers?"

Joe shrugged. "Maybe."

"It seems like they care a lot about your mom."

"Jorge would do anything for her."

"Troy and Ryan must be concerned, too, or they wouldn't be here. Do they have families?"

"Ryan's married. No kids. They're here for their dad."

"They're worried about you."

Joe studied her as if he really didn't believe that. How could he not? Faith wished he saw that he was going to need those guys in the near future, especially if his mom didn't recover.

She looked at her watch. "Almost time for the next visit." The nurses were letting them in one at a time for a few minutes every other hour. "Let's go."

Straightening, he inhaled deeply, as if bolstering himself, and nodded. As they walked back inside, he put his hand on her lower back. Faith liked the feel of it more than she should, but she shoved that out of her mind. There were more pressing things to worry about.

CHAPTER FIFTEEN

JOE LEFT HIS MOM'S intensive care room when Ryan showed up for his turn. He nodded on his way out.

His mom still didn't know he was there. He'd watched her sleep for the few minutes he was allowed in, willing her to wake up for a second just so he could tell her he loved her.

The doctor had made a point of saying there was hope that the antibiotics would take hold, but he'd also made it clear they weren't seeing any signs of that yet and couldn't predict how her body would react. It would take time for the drugs to bring about any improvement. While Joe hadn't allowed his mom to speak of worst-case scenarios in the past, he was forced to face up to them tonight. Kind of like having his head rammed into a cement wall. Painful and sure to leave lasting damage.

Achy and wrung out, he walked slowly back to the small waiting room that was starting to feel like their own personal home base. Unlike the bright-as-day main hallway, where nurses and other medical personnel hurried around like busy worker bees, the room was secluded and had lights that could be dimmed. Faith had stretched out on a row of chairs and fallen asleep, her hair cascading over the side of the thin cushion.

The urge to go to her, to sit on the seat nearest her

and pull her head onto his legs, run his fingers through her silky hair, overwhelmed him. Oddly, it'd be the most natural thing in the world to have her that close while she slept. But he sat near her feet, leaving an empty chair between them, because they weren't alone. Regardless of Faith's insistence that being off duty meant their difference in rank didn't matter, it did. What was more, she was the daughter of his mentor and the man who would hopefully support his bid for the position of assistant chief.

So instead of touching her, Joe reclined on his uncomfortable, too small chair, resting his head on the back and watching her surreptitiously. Finally admitting to himself that he was genuinely glad she was there.

"Joe!" Ryan appeared at the doorway of the waiting room. "Get in there, man. She's awake. Thought you'd want to talk to her before she drifts off again."

Joe rushed out, hollering thanks over his shoulder. When he got to his mom's room, her eyes were closed, and disappointment weighed him down. He stepped into the dim room, the rhythmic sound of the machines pulsing. Taking her frail hand gently in his, he sat on the edge of the chair that had been pulled up close to her side.

When she slowly turned her head toward him and her eyes fluttered open, he lowered his forehead to their entwined hands and said a silent prayer of thanks.

"Mama."

"Joey. You made it." Her voice was just a thread of sound, as if she hadn't used it for weeks.

"Of course I made it. How are you doing?"

In typical Carmen style, she nodded slowly, attempting

a smile. Always keeping it positive, even when she likely felt as if she'd been dragged around by a ladder truck.

His throat swelled up and he kissed her fingers.

"Your body has to fight, Mama."

"I'll be okay. I'm not ready to leave you yet. You're not ready."

"Damn straight I'm not." If her will could keep her alive, he could rest easy. She was too worried about him and how he'd get along without her, without any true family. Unfortunately, he knew all too well it didn't necessarily work that way.

Her eyes drooped and she fought to keep them open. Her face was pale beneath the oxygen tube that ran under her nose and across her cheeks, and Joe thought how unlike his mother this woman appeared.

"Go to sleep, Mama. I love you."

He held on to her until her husband came to the door. Joe had never questioned Jorge's feelings for Carmen, but the look on the man's face as he gazed at her was so full of love and heartbreak that it finally hit Joe. When his mother passed away, this man would lose his life companion, the one he chose to spend day in and day out with.

Joe wouldn't be alone in his pain. And maybe... maybe there could be more to a stepfamily than just appeasing his mother, after all.

EVERY MINUTE OF THE NIGHT seemed to last an hour as they prayed for some change, a positive sign, even though the doctor said it was too early.

Surprisingly, Troy and Ryan were still there at 2:00 a.m. Not as surprising, so was Faith. When she'd woken up from her nap, Joe had tried again to convince her to drive back to San Amaro Island, but it had only been for show on his part. He wanted her there with him. The implications of that were something he'd have to examine later.

Faith leaned close to him, allowing him to catch her scent when he turned toward her.

"I need coffee," she said. "What can I get for you?"

He started to shake his head, but she held up a finger to stop him.

"No. You're eating something. Or drinking. Take your pick. Beer doesn't count as dinner, and even if it did, that was light-years ago."

"For being such a tomboy, you've got some serious mother hen tendencies."

"Consider me well-rounded. What do you want? Coffee?"

He nodded and twisted to take his wallet out. "A package of chips or nuts, too."

"I've got it," she said, refusing the bills he tried to hand her.

"I'll go with you," Troy said, standing and stretching. "Want anything, Ryan?"

"The biggest, most caffeinated bottle of pop you can find."

"You got it." Troy turned to Jorge, who was awkwardly sprawled in one of the chairs, snoring. The younger man shrugged and led Faith out.

Ryan stood and rolled his neck in circles. Paced across the room. Joe's eyes were shut, but sleep eluded him in spite of how bone weary he was. He felt the chair next to him shift as Ryan sat down.

"How you holding up?" his stepbrother asked, his leg bouncing rhythmically.

"Holding up," Joe said. "Not much else I can do."

Ryan nodded and neither of them spoke for several minutes. Joe didn't have the energy to think of a coherent sentence.

"Did you know that our mom died of cancer?" Ryan asked.

"Knew she died when you guys were kids."

"Teenagers. Long, drawn-out deal."

"This must bring it all back," Joe said.

"Little bit. It's different when it's your mother."

Joe didn't respond. He appreciated the sentiment, but wasn't up for a heart-to-heart.

"All I got to say is it sucks and it's exhausting and I'm sorry as hell you're going through it, man. I'm going to track down my drink." As he stood, he clapped Joe on the back.

Several minutes later, Faith and Troy were stretched out on the floor of the waiting room, feasting on candy bars and mini doughnuts. Ryan had wandered back in as well by the time the doctor returned.

"Dad," Ryan said.

Jorge jerked awake and straightened slowly, as if his back was stiff or achy.

Joe watched the doctor for a sign of what news he might have for them, his heart thundering in his chest.

Dr. Zander sat on one of the chairs and smiled tiredly at them. "I don't want to give you false hope. There isn't any big news. It could be days before we really know how she's going to do."

"But she's no worse?" Jorge asked.

"She's holding her own."

"If her condition was going to deteriorate, wouldn't it have already happened?" Jorge was voicing some of the thoughts that had circled repeatedly through Joe's head all night as the hours ticked by.

"It's hard to say," the doctor responded. "Let's just focus on the fact that she's hanging in there. I wish I could give you something more concrete but…"

"Understood," Troy said.

"We might be able to rustle up a place for at least one of you to sleep," Dr. Zander offered. "Like I said, it's going to be a while for solid news of any kind."

"We might take you up on that." Again, Troy acted as their spokesperson. "Thanks, Doc."

The doctor's mouth tilted into a sympathetic half grin as he nodded at them and left them alone again.

Faith came over and sat next to Joe. She didn't touch him or let on that there was anything between them more than two people who worked together, but Joe caught her concern, the understanding in her eyes.

"Are you planning to make it to work?" she asked almost apologetically.

He looked at his watch. Quarter to four. "My interview's at ten."

"For the job?" she asked, her eyes widening.

"For the job." He considered his options, feeling torn.

"Go ahead, Joe," his stepfather said. "Nothing you can do here. You know what your mom would want if she was awake to have her say."

Joe exhaled shakily, fatigue and emotion taking their

toll. "She'd tell me to get my ass to the interview and land the job."

"I'm sure you can reschedule it," Faith said. "I'll talk to my dad."

"Hell, no, you won't." Joe stood and stretched his arms over his head to get some blood flowing. "I can talk to him myself if I need to."

"If anything changes here, I'll get the company jet to pick you up," Jorge said. "You can be here in twenty minutes."

"You going to stick around?" Joe asked.

"I'm taking the day off." Jorge crossed his leg over the opposite knee. "You can spell me when your shift is over. After you get some sleep."

"I work twenty-four hours," Joe reminded him.

"I'll stop by later to give Dad a break," Troy said.

"Go to work, man. Get the promotion." Ryan stuffed the last powdered doughnut in his mouth.

"Okay." Joe was ambivalent, unable to summon any enthusiasm for his interview, but he figured that was due to lack of sleep. What drove him to agree in the end was that his mother would, indeed, be disappointed if he didn't make it to his interview because of her. Especially if she recovered enough to find out about it. There was nothing he could do, sitting here in this dingy, ugly room, and that fact was starting to drive him up the damn wall.

"You can sleep on the way," Faith said. "I have enough caffeine in me to get through the next week." She held up an extra large paper cup from the twenty-four hour coffee shop on the hospital's main floor.

They said goodbye to the others, and Joe checked

for another update on his mom on their way out. No changes whatsoever since the doctor had been in, which was what they expected.

He and Faith rode the elevator down and walked out to her Subaru in silence. The briskness of the night air did nothing to wake him up, nor did the ambulance that whisked into the emergency area down the way, sirens off but lights flashing. That was someone else's problem. He had enough of his own.

Once they were in the car, they both sat there, not moving or speaking. Faith leaned against her headrest and angled her face toward him.

Joe exhaled slowly, coming down from the intense stress of the past several hours. Not that his worries would be over anytime soon. But just getting out of the sterile hospital and that drab room with the puke-green chairs made it easier to breathe.

"Thank you," he said. "I couldn't act like it in there, but I was glad to have you with me."

"Hmm. Do I give you the company line here or the other one?"

"What's the company line?"

"The fire chief told me to get you to your mother. I'm sure he wouldn't approve if I had dropped you at the front door and driven off."

"What's the other line?"

"I didn't mind any of it. Not that you needed me there, with all the Vargas men hovering."

Joe disagreed to himself about whether he'd needed her there. He thought back over the long night. "They're decent. Like you said. I don't think I really ever gave them a chance. Just assumed we were all making the best of an awkward, late-in-life blending of families."

"They kind of…acted like family."

"Yeah. They did." Joe was surprised to find that he genuinely agreed with her.

He was sure he couldn't have gotten through this night without these people. His stepbrothers, Jorge and most of all, Faith.

As he leaned his head against the window and drifted off, he was vaguely aware that that in itself was more than a small dilemma.

CHAPTER SIXTEEN

AFTER AN ENTIRE NIGHT at the hospital, the workday at the station had been anything but restful. They'd been running since eight that morning and barely stopped during the fourteen hours that followed. Faith couldn't remember when they'd had so many alarms in one shift. It'd almost compared to an average day in the San Antonio department.

She should be unconscious.

She should be curled up in her hard but sufficient bunk, sleeping like a baby.

She should *not* be lying here thinking about Joe. Drifting off every so often, but then tossing and turning, disturbed by her thoughts.

Last night she'd seen a different side from the in-charge, unflappable fire captain. She'd glimpsed a man who would do just about anything for his mother and was, understandably, scared to death of losing her. A man who wanted to be stoic and strong, but who felt things deeply.

The only opportunity she'd had all day to ask about his mother's condition had come after lunch, once he'd returned from his interview. The others had left the kitchen, and Faith and Joe had found themselves alone for all of five minutes before another alarm came in. By that point, he'd spoken to Mr. Vargas once, and not surprisingly, there'd been no significant change. And while it was good news that she was no worse, the lack of positive change was getting to Joe. Faith could tell by the raw fear in his eyes.

She whipped the sheets off and sat up in her bunk. Rubbing her hands over her eyes, she made a decision she might live to regret.

She knew Joe would be awake, in spite of their past twenty-four hours. Knew he was either in his office working or in his private bunk room. He'd told her he avoided sleeping at the station as much as he could because he hated being awakened by the alarm.

Knowing that he was up, alone, probably tormented by concern, she couldn't just sit there.

She glanced down at the clothes she slept in—yoga pants and a light blue tank with a built-in bra. Nothing she hadn't been seen in before whenever she ventured out of her room in the middle of the night. Her hair was probably a mess, but she didn't care. She wasn't going to him with the goal of turning him on.

When she opened her door, she peeked out like a fugitive in the night. There was no one stirring anywhere; most likely her colleagues were collapsed the way she should be, trying to get in more than a few minutes' nap before the alarm sounded again.

If it went off while she was talking to Joe, in his room, things could get interesting.

Yeah, she could live to regret this decision, but that wasn't enough to dissuade her. Once she was in the hall, she couldn't make herself turn back and not find out how Joe was doing.

She walked, acting nonchalant, past all the closed

doors, seeing no lights and hearing no signs of anyone awake. When she got to the end of the hall, she glanced over her shoulder before turning toward the officers' bunks and offices, just in case.

Joe's private room was the third door on the left. Just as she'd expected, a dim light shone underneath it. Her heart raced and she wondered again what she was doing. Would he be pissed that she'd crossed the line and come to his personal quarters? Before she could lose her nerve—or be discovered by someone—she knocked softly.

The door opened almost immediately, but only about a foot.

"Something wrong, Faith?" he asked.

She shook her head, about to speak, when he bent down.

"No," he said firmly. "Get back, both of you." When he stood, he held two kittens.

Faith tried to hide her laugh.

"Come in before the whole herd escapes," Joe said, whisking her in and shutting the door quickly. "Cinder, don't even think about it."

"And here I was worried you were all alone." Faith bent down to pet the black kitten, which clawed at the bottom of her pant leg. "I figured you'd found a home for these guys. When did you move them in here?"

"Few days ago. Sanchez complained about having them in the office. Wuss claims he's allergic to them."

"Where's Blaze?" she asked, scanning the cramped room for the orange kitten who'd had trouble nursing. The mama cat was snoozing in a fuzzy nest of blankets in the corner by an overfilled bookcase. A light gray baby was curled up next to her, but the rest of the litter were awake and ready to get into mischief, crawling all over the room.

"My aunt has her for now. Still needs to be fed by hand every few hours and I can't always do it when I'm on duty. I'm trying to convince her to make it permanent."

Faith knelt on the floor and held her hand out to the mother cat, speaking in a soft voice. "Hey, girlie, you're a good mama."

The cat raised her head and sniffed the offered hand, then closed her eyes again. Faith stroked her soft fur.

"Why don't you put them in one of the common areas?" she asked. "I bet some of those tough guys would fall in love."

"Maybe when they get a little bigger. Not sure I trust a couple of the Neanderthals with them."

The black kitten who'd attacked Faith's pants when she came in crawled up on her lap. Her tiny claws dug through the material into her flesh, eliciting a pained laugh.

"You need attention, obviously," Faith said, picking her up and holding her at eye level. "Are you getting the shaft from big, bad Joe?"

"She'd like you to think she is," he grumbled. He'd sat down on the low bed along the wall opposite the bookcase. The room wasn't much longer than the bed and there was only about three feet between it and the bookcase. The wall was adorned with posters of old cars. *Hot rods* was the term that came to her mind.

One of the two kittens Joe had picked up when Faith came in was now on his shoulder, nibbling at his ear.

The other had decided his arm was the place to be and was drifting off to sleep, cradled like a baby. He gently put the ear-biter on the floor.

"What are you doing here, Faith?" His voice was quiet, mostly businesslike, but a hint of gentleness, of the Joe she'd spent the night in the hospital with, slipped through.

She put Cinder down beside the mother cat and moved up to the mattress next to him, since it was the only place besides the floor to sit. With one leg drawn under her, she faced him.

"Checking on you. Have you heard anything more about your mom?"

"Her temperature's still high, but that's to be expected, or so they keep telling me. In other words, no real news."

"She hasn't gotten worse, though, right?"

"Not that they've admitted to." He ran a hand over his short hair. "It's damn hard to be here, but sitting in that waiting room for another night…not sure I have it in me."

"It sucks to not be able to do something for her."

He nodded and ran his large hand over the tiny kitten's back. "Yeah, it does. Work is at least keeping my mind occupied. Or it did until everything slowed down."

"You should try sleeping."

"So should you."

"Been there, done that," she said. "How'd your interview go?"

"Not too bad, I don't think, when you take into account an all-nighter and a mother in intensive care."

At that, Faith reached out and put her hand on his thigh just above his knee. "Did you tell the committee what was going on?"

He shook his head. "Your dad referred to it once, but if I can't be at the top of my game after staying up all night, then I'm not doing my job."

"It wasn't your standard up-fighting-fires night."

He ignored her statement and she self-consciously removed her hand from his leg.

"I imagine you did well in spite of everything," Faith said. "You don't seem to let things get to you."

He turned slightly and met her gaze head-on. The kitten apparently didn't like the motion and stumbled down his leg to the safety of its mama.

"Some things I can't prevent from getting to me, it seems." His look intensified, became pointed.

Faith's pulse reacted by going triple time. "Like what?"

"I think you know." He took her hand in his, wove their fingers together. "You shouldn't come to my room in the middle of the night, Faith."

She nodded, her voice momentarily caught in her throat. "I'll go."

He nodded, too, but at the same time leaned closer and gently pulled her hand toward him. With his other palm, he cradled her chin. Caressed her lower lip with his rough thumb. His eyelids drooped heavily as he closed the space between them and touched his lips lightly to hers. His fingers wound around to the back of her neck, beneath the cascade of her hair, and the kiss became more urgent. Faith wasn't sure she could pull herself away if the alarm did go off. Some things were worth getting busted for.

Throwing what little caution she'd had to the wind, she wrapped her arms around his neck, wanting him closer still. He slid his tongue into her mouth, a sexy moan coming from his throat as they tasted each other, explored. His kiss was a reflection of the man—confident, uncompromising, yet tender. Thorough. His touch made her feel…treasured.

Without breaking the contact of their lips, he leaned her back diagonally across his narrow bed. Faith's knee came up beside him, and as Joe's body covered hers, his hardness pressed between her legs, making her body ache for him. His fingers inched up beneath her tank. She ran her hands over his muscled back. The breadth of his shoulders made her feel delicate. Decidedly feminine.

When his hand slid beneath the elastic and his warm palm covered her breast, a needy sound came from her. She arched into him.

"You're so damn sexy, Faith," he said into her ear. "Tough and hard on the surface, but soft. Beautiful."

She'd never been so turned on by a voice before. Of course the words were doing their part, too…and his hands…and lips.…

Without warning, pain pricked at her thigh and she let out a gasp. Rising up on an elbow, she realized the culprit was the little black kitten, its claws sinking into her leg.

Joe scooped up the tiny animal and held it in front of his face. "Bad cat!" A grin tugged at his lips, though, and Faith started laughing quietly.

He set it on the floor and Faith sat up, her heart still racing, blood still humming. She pulled her tank down and ran a hand through her hair as the reality of their situation sank in.

"Good thing the cat interrupted," she said. She'd been on the verge of losing her mind and her judgment.

She stood and again tried to straighten her hair.

Joe rose as well and kissed her, then pressed his forehead to hers. "Your hair is fine. You look good." His voice was gravelly. So damn alluring.

He backed her slowly up until his body held hers against the door, and once again, he sought out her lips with his. Thirty seconds ago, she'd been thinking how stupid it was to come here, and now she was succumbing to him again. Loving his touch. Wanting more.

"Joe," she managed to gasp. "I need to get out of here."

He acknowledged that with a deep, sexy sound and kissed her again.

"We're at work," she said. "What if we get an alarm?"

That seemed to penetrate his brain, and he groaned in frustration. Drawing her to him, he kissed her temple and wrapped his arms around her. "Yeah. You need to take your gorgeous self back to your room and lock the door."

"Is that an order?" Faith asked, grinning, loving the feel of his rough skin on her cheek.

He stepped back from her and straightened, looking mostly serious. "Yes. That's your captain speaking."

Faith palmed his cheek briefly. "You're kind of cute when you're all in charge. Good night, sir."

She opened the door and slipped out before any kittens could escape.

JOE LEANED HIS BACK against the door, still reeling.

Damnation. What the hell had he just done?

He closed his eyes. As his body revved down, his remorse went up proportionately.

The gray kitten, who he'd started calling Smoky, had made a nest on his pillow. He picked up the little fuzz ball, stretched out on his back and set the cat on his chest. Unbothered, it closed its eyes and was sound asleep within seconds.

"At least one of us has no worries," he said, rubbing its front paw. Contented, the cat flexed its needlelike claws.

Even with all his guilt and worry, he still wanted more of Faith. He could lie here and tell himself till he was blue in the face that he couldn't touch her again, but he knew, if given another opportunity, he'd be hard-pressed to walk away.

For the first time, he allowed himself to consider the possibility of seeing her in secret. Away from work. Just enough for them to get each other out of their systems. No one had to know. His job wouldn't suffer and his chances at the promotion wouldn't be harmed. No one would be able to accuse Faith of getting special treatment from him.

God, what was he thinking? That wouldn't be fair to Faith. She wasn't the type to sneak around and deserved so much more than that.

Which brought him back to the same agonizing dilemma. He wanted her and he couldn't goddamn have her.

Faith's scent still lingered in the air and he couldn't get her face out of his mind. Holding the cat against his chest, he sat up, replaced her on his pillow and headed to his office. If work could take his mind off his mother, then maybe it could take his mind off the vexing brunette, as well.

CHAPTER SEVENTEEN

FAITH WAS PATHETIC.

She'd fully acknowledged this when she'd casually convinced Nadia and Mercedes that this was a good spot to stake out on the beach. That it was just up from the fire station, where she could watch the trucks head out on alarms, was no coincidence. But she wasn't admitting that to anyone but herself.

She happened to know Joe was on duty today, because she'd overheard her dad on the phone yesterday. Joe had taken someone else's shift, as he frequently did, workaholic that he was. His work ethic reminded her of her father. Unless Joe had traded shifts, he was also scheduled to work with her tomorrow. She wondered if he would break down and sleep tonight, and that question brought to mind his room, his bed, his kisses....

She'd seen the engine return after a call about an hour ago, and caught a glimpse of him riding shotgun. That she was acting like a teenager with a crush disturbed her on some level, but she couldn't help it, really. She'd made a mistake the other night by going to his room, but there was nothing she could do about it now.

"What is it you're not telling us, Faith?" Mercedes sipped her margarita and set the cup back in the sand next to her lounger. "Who are you stalking at the fire station?"

Faith was lying on her front, the closest of the three to the station. She didn't look at her friends. "I'm just admiring the trucks."

"You don't lie very well," Nadia said, grinning.

To prove she wasn't staring, Faith turned on her side and took the bag of corn chips from Nadia, helping herself to a handful. "Being involved with someone at work would not be a good idea." Which, though possibly misleading, was one hundred percent true.

"If it was Mr. Right, exceptions could be made." Nadia pushed her sunglasses up over her gorgeous blond hair and squinted toward the station. "I could use a Mr. Right Firefighter with Big Beautiful Muscles myself. Maybe it's time to hang out at the Shell Shack some more."

"I've been racking my brain for you," Faith said. "None of them are bad-boy enough for your tastes."

"What? No bad boys in the fire department? I don't believe that for a minute," Nadia said.

"There are a few rebels and troublemakers, but I wouldn't really call them losers. Not your type."

"Maybe she's turning over a new leaf," Mercedes said, flipping through the latest issue of *Cosmo*. "Going for someone with a job this time."

"You two are evil," Nadia said. "So I've made a couple bad decisions. I want to know more about who you've been watching for all afternoon, Faith."

"Yeah, spill it, girl. Does it have anything to do with the all-nighter last week?"

Faith shoved a bunch of corn chip crumbs from the bottom of the bag into her mouth. As a stall? Maybe. "I told you about the captain. His mother was in intensive care. We spent the night in the waiting room."

"Is his mom okay?" Nadia asked.

"She's going to be. She finally turned a corner and they think she'll go home in another week. Nice of you to ask," Faith said drily.

"So, the captain, huh?" Mercedes said. "The one who was watching you at the bar that night?"

If she'd kissed anyone else, Faith would've fessed up to her friends in a heartbeat. But it was Joe. There was too much at stake. While Mercedes and Nadia would never outwardly accuse her of getting close to Joe for professional reasons, she couldn't stand the possibility of anyone thinking that, even in passing.

"I'm going to throw this in the trash before it blows away." Faith crumpled the empty chip bag as she got up, ignoring her friends' comments about running away from their questions.

It was almost five o'clock and this part of the beach was clearing out. Most of the hard-core spring breakers were about a mile up, close to the bigger resorts and the frequent TV coverage. The trash cans were fifty feet or so away, placed out of reach of high tide. As Faith walked toward the nearest one, a man jogging down the beach in her direction caught her eye.

She knew that gait. That large, muscled body.

Her heart raced and she quietly called herself an idiot.

He's the fire captain, she coached herself. *Not the man you've been dreaming about at night.*

"Pick up that pace," she called. "You're getting soft, Captain Mendoza."

He slowed to a walk and came over to her. "'Captain Mendoza'?" he questioned, low enough that no one else could hear, and Faith couldn't help noticing—and liking—the way his eyes roved up and down her bikini-clad body.

She smiled easily, too happy to see him. "I call you soft and you take issue with the proper use of your title and name?"

He didn't smile. "Everyone calls me Joe. If you start acting different now…"

Her grin was long gone. Something about his tone, his condescension, rubbed her wrong. "No one's around who knows any differently, Joe."

"I don't think you realize—"

"I realize perfectly. I'm sorry I said anything at all, but then ignoring the captain as he runs by might raise a red flag, too."

He wiped his forehead with the bottom of his T-shirt. "You're right. I didn't expect to see you here. Like *that*." Again, he allowed his gaze to wander downward.

"My parka is back by my beach towel," she said, pointing over her shoulder.

Joe looked where she indicated.

"Not really," Faith said. "But we could go say hello to my beautiful friends. I could set you up with one of them. Then your problem would be solved."

"I'm sorry, Faith. I'm not handling…*this* well. I've never been in this situation before." He was obviously talking about more than just seeing her in a bikini on the beach.

"Considering I'm the first female in the department, I'm glad to hear that."

He still didn't crack a grin.

"Try to lighten up," she said, wishing she could kiss his uptightness away. "Nobody knows, and it's not going to happen again."

"What if I want it to happen again?"

Faith's breath caught and a weird lightness filled her chest.

"Wait," Joe said before she could respond. "Forget I said that."

Okay, then. Whiplash. She hardened her expression. It wouldn't do for him to know how much his admission had stirred her.

"I get it," she said firmly.

"I need to get back to the station. PT time's over."

She nodded as awkwardness fell over them. "See you at work, *Joe,*" she said obediently.

He jogged off with a vague nod.

She watched him, unable to deny her appreciation of that body and the way he moved it. She had a hard time staying annoyed for more than fifteen seconds.

No, he wasn't handling *this* well, but it was pretty much impossible for her to figure out how to navigate this thing between them, either.

His message was clear, though: there would never be a repeat of the other night.

She supported that decision. In theory.

So how to explain the tears that suddenly filled her eyes?

"FAITH, CAN I TALK TO YOU in private?" Joe asked, coming up behind her and scaring the crap out of her as she rinsed the engine off with the hose the next morning.

She turned to gauge the look on his face, but couldn't tell if she was in trouble again or if this was work related. She secured the hose back on the wall and shook her hands dry as she followed him outside.

"What's going on?" she asked.

"Have you talked to your father lately?"

A sick feeling swirled through her gut. "Not since yesterday. I stayed over at Mercedes's house last night."

"He hasn't showed up for work yet today," Joe said.

"It's almost noon." Faith frowned and tried to remember if he'd told her of any plans. "He didn't call in?"

"No one's heard from him."

She pulled the cell phone out of her pants pocket and checked for messages, but found none. Maybe he was still in bed. She pressed the speed dial for his cell phone.

"I've tried both his numbers," Joe said.

Ignoring him, she paced toward the main courtyard, listening to the empty rings on the line. When her dad's voice mail finally picked up, Faith swore and hit End. Then she dialed their home number, praying he'd answer and everything was fine. Trying to ignore the rising nausea and the weird, uneasy feeling that all was not right.

The family voice mail started playing back in her ear. She let it finish, left her dad a message to phone her right away and ended the call. She leaned her elbows on the mural wall that curved around the courtyard, and tried to think of where her dad might be that he would ignore his phone.

Joe came up next to her. "Did you try your mom?"

She still held her phone, so she scrolled through her contacts to find her mom's new number.

"Mom, have you seen Dad today?" she asked.

"Faith, I've been wanting to talk to you. I know you were upset by Craig—"

"I'm fine, but Dad is missing. Did he call you?"

"What do you mean, he's missing?"

Gritting her teeth, Faith briefly explained what she knew.

"Faith, I have no idea." To her mom's credit, she sounded genuinely concerned. "I just saw him last night, but he didn't mention anything."

"Where'd you see him?"

"At the grocery store, across from the movie theater. Craig and I were picking up something for dinner, and your father was grabbing takeout from the Chinese counter."

"Craig was with you?" The rock in Faith's gut sank deeper.

"We'd just gone to a matinee."

Faith closed her eyes. "Mom, did he know Craig was *with* you?"

"I introduced them. He seemed fine. What else was I supposed to do, Faith? It was awkward, but we're all adults."

How about don't move out in the first place?

"Maybe he's at a doctor's appointment or something," Faith said. "But meeting your boyfriend might not have gone over as well as you'd like to think, Mom."

"I didn't plan it that way. I'll call Will and Paul and see if they've heard from him today."

Faith doubted her dad would call her brothers, even the two who checked in most often, but it was worth a try.

"Let me know. I'm at work." The alarm sounded over the intercom. "I have to go."

She and Joe headed inside to hear the details of the emergency. It was a car accident, so the engine and the ambulance would respond. Faith and Joe were assigned to the truck for the day, so they stayed put.

"Your mom saw him last night?" Joe asked as they walked off the apparatus floor, back into the station.

"She and her boyfriend." Faith couldn't help the anger that laced her words. She followed Joe into his office.

"I kind of gathered. Same guy you met?"

"Same guy. Pretty sure my dad had no idea before that." Faith sat down hard on the chair in front of Joe's desk, racking her brain. "Did you call Leo Romero?" The mayor of San Amaro was also one of her dad's good friends. Maybe he knew something.

"Wasn't sure if I should. It might be nothing. Maybe he fell asleep in a lawn chair in your backyard or something."

"It's been hours since he was supposed to be in. But you're right. Let's leave Leo out of it for now."

"Does he have any other good friends besides the mayor?"

"The police chief." Faith chuckled humorlessly. "This job is his best friend, I'm afraid."

"Why don't you run home to see what's going on?"

"Who's going to cover for me?"

"The three of us can handle things until the engine

returns. Won't take you long. If we get a call, you can catch up."

She hated the idea, but concern for her dad overrode her worries about work. "It'll take me fifteen minutes, tops." Faith hurried out of Joe's office to her car.

A short time later, Faith was back at the station with no answers. There'd been no sign of her father at home, nothing unusual or out of place. His truck was missing, so he'd obviously gone somewhere of his own will. The question was where?

BY EIGHT O'CLOCK THAT evening, Faith and the rest of the guys had just returned from an unexciting trash fire. Her dad still hadn't shown up at the station, and her concern had ebbed into anger, whether justified or not. Who was the parent here? Who did he think he was to disappear and worry everyone?

And what if he was in serious trouble and here she was being petty?

She started helping the guys clean up the truck and refill everything, but distraction pulled at her, made it tough to concentrate on the job. She met Joe's gaze and he walked over to her.

"Heard anything?"

"My phone's inside."

"Go check. I'll take care of this."

She hurried off to retrieve her messages, and when she heard her brother Paul's voice, her shoulders sagged in relief.

"Dad's okay, Faith. Well…yeah. He's *going* to be fine. Call me and I'll fill you in."

She clicked on her brother's speed dial number,

puzzled by the somewhat ambiguous message and that he'd called instead of their mom.

"Hi, Faith."

"What's going on, Paul? Where's Dad? And Mom? Why couldn't she call me?"

"Don't you want to talk to your favorite brother?"

"Of course," she said impatiently. "Tell me. Is he okay or isn't he?" The rock was back in her stomach even though apparently her dad was alive.

"He's fine. Mom found him on the boat."

"The boat? What the hell was he doing there?"

Paul sighed, and she pictured him taking his glasses off and rubbing his forehead. "He was passed-out drunk."

It was like a bad soap opera.

"Mom had to rouse him and take him to the E.R. They're probably about done there. Faith, I'm sorry. You said he was losing it, but I had no idea.…"

"Yeah, well, who would guess the model citizen would go off the deep end and turn into a binge drinker?"

"This wasn't the first time?"

"Not the first time, no. So you're sure he's going to be okay?"

"He had some mild alcohol poisoning, but they pumped some fluids through him and he's mostly co-herent now, according to Mom."

Only thirteen hours after he was supposed to be at work. Faith kicked a spare helmet that had fallen on the floor.

"Mom's still with him?"

"Last I knew. She said she'd drive him home. Do I need to fly back?"

Faith blew out a frustrated breath, tempted to say yes, but… "No. I'm beginning to realize there's nothing anyone can do. He's determined to screw up his life. Who are we to try to stop him?"

"You don't mean that, Faith."

"Oh, I do," she said. "Thanks for calling, Paul. I'll go see him as soon as I'm off duty."

"Keep me posted, please."

"Yep."

She ended the call and paced back and forth in the hallway for a couple of minutes, fuming and trying not to show it. Jaw locked, she finally headed back out to the garage to help with cleanup.

"We've got it taken care of," Penn told her as she walked up. "You look like you could kill someone."

"And here I thought I'd calmed down. Thanks for covering my share of work tonight."

"You owe me one." He said it with a smile, and Faith nodded, distracted, then made a beeline for the door.

IF JOE HAD ANY QUESTION about Faith's state of mind, it disappeared the second he entered the exercise room. He admired her form as she beat the living hell out of the speed bag, hoping it wasn't his face she was imagining.

She must have gotten news about the chief.

Joe leaned against the wall near her and waited for her to take a break. She hadn't bothered to change out of her uniform into workout clothes, and sweat was starting to soak through her T-shirt.

After another couple of minutes of pummeling, she

stepped back, breathing hard. Her arms had to be ready to fall off.

"Did you hear from your dad?" he asked.

Faith didn't look at him. She walked over to the hanging bag and threw a couple vicious side kicks at it.

"I heard from my brother. My dad is okay."

She kicked the bag hard enough to send it flying each time. Joe made a mental note not to piss her off. He waited for her to say more, but she was determined to destroy the bag or die trying.

"That's all?" he said between her sequence of punches and a flurry of roundhouse kicks. "You going to tell me what's going on?"

Finally, she turned and looked at him. The hair at her temples was soaked with sweat. She mopped her forehead with the bottom of her shirt, and if he wasn't so damn honorable—yeah, right—he would've enjoyed the view of her bare, flat abdomen.

"Telling you would only serve to drag you farther into the Peligni family drama."

He fought not to show how frustrating she could be. "I'm asking, Faith."

"As my captain?"

He pushed himself off the wall and closed the space between them. "No. Not as your captain." Their eyes met and held, and for a moment, he saw beyond the tough, pissed-off-woman act to the scared daddy's girl.

When she blinked, tears appeared at the corners of her eyes, evoking an unfamiliar something in Joe.

Faith sat on the bench that ran the length of the wall, her shoulders sagging. Joe settled next to her.

"I don't want to put you in an uncomfortable position,

knowing stuff about my dad that maybe you shouldn't," she said after a prolonged silence.

"We can pretend I'm not an officer for a few minutes." He had no idea what he was doing, but for once he wasn't going to overthink it. He was compelled to be a sounding board for Faith, if that's what she needed.

"My dad went on another bender," she said quietly. "Drank himself into unconsciousness. My mom found him on the boat, still docked in the marina, thank God."

Joe swore under his breath and fought the urge to touch her. "Do you need to get out of here? Go see him?"

"That sounds strangely like something a captain would say."

"Probably so. Scratch that. Anything I can do, Faith?"

"There's nothing any of us can do, apparently. I've tried. I *am* going to have words with him, though."

"I wouldn't want to be in his place."

She narrowed her eyes at him. "Didn't we establish on the beach the other day that we couldn't do this kind of thing?"

"What kind of thing?" he asked, knowing full well what she was talking about.

"I'm not supposed to be chatty or casual. You're not supposed to be nice. We're not supposed to exchange more than orders and yes sirs."

"I could do without the sir," he muttered, standing up and halfheartedly punching the speed bag once. "We did. I tried. Turns out it's too late."

"Too late for what?" She eyed him suspiciously. Tiredly.

"Keeping it strictly business. There are lines I can't cross, but talking to you about something besides safety drills and hose sizes isn't one of them."

She continued to stare at him, nodding. "Do me a favor, will you?"

"What's that?"

"Give me some advance notice if you change your mind again."

"I'm not going to change my mind again. I like you, Faith. Whether that's wise or not."

She stood, her arms crossed. "Just don't let anyone know it, okay?" She smiled briefly. "I'm heading to the shower."

She walked off and left him standing there with all kinds of uninvited, unwelcome, erotic as hell images in his mind.

CHAPTER EIGHTEEN

"GOOD," her mom said when Faith walked in the door of the Peligni family abode after her shift ended the next morning. "You're home."

"So are you." Faith knew on some level she was being foolishly hopeful with that statement, but was momentarily thrown by her mother's appearance in the kitchen.

"No. I'm leaving for home now," Nita said pointedly. "He's threatened to go in to work, but I think he needs a day off. *Sober*."

"She's divorcing me and still trying to run my life," Faith's dad said grumpily. He sat at the kitchen table with a steaming mug of coffee in front of him, as if everything was totally normal.

With her mom there, Faith could almost make herself believe it was.

"You won't die if you miss two days of work in a row," Nita told him. "Unless you pull a repeat of yesterday. If the alcohol didn't kill you, I would."

Just the thought of what her father had put them through had Faith's blood pressure shooting up again, and the rage she'd suppressed all night threatened to blow.

Her dad looked chagrined. He raised his hands, palms

out. "I'm not going in to work and I sure as hell am not drinking anything but this coffee."

"Okay, then." Nita glanced around the kitchen—it appeared she had tidied up. "Sweet rolls will be done in a couple of minutes. I'll let Faith handle you now."

"I don't need anyone to handle me." Her dad's voice lacked conviction. Overall, he seemed subdued. He glanced at Faith with some trepidation.

"Goodbye, Mom," Faith said, having bitten her tongue since she'd arrived. She walked to the door to see her mother out.

"Go easy, Faith."

"I'll talk to you later," Faith said.

Once her mom was gone, she walked calmly—deceptively so—to the oven, removed the tray of cinnamon rolls and set them on the stove to cool. She leaned against the counter tensely, facing her father.

"What were you thinking, Dad?"

"I've heard it all from your mother, Faith. I don't need another round."

"You know what I don't need?" Her voice grew louder. "I don't need to spend the day at work wondering what the hell my dad is doing and whether he's alive. I don't need to have people asking where you are, or to try to think of a PC way to say who the hell knows."

"I'm sorry to put you in that position."

"Don't put *yourself* in that position, Dad! When did my father, my idol, the fire chief, turn into an irresponsible drunk?"

He dropped his gaze to the table and his shoulders fell at her words. Even that pissed Faith off, because he'd never been the type to back down from a challenge or an argument and, dammit, she just wanted her dad back.

"I'm not handling anything well lately," he said.

"No, you're not. And I get that your life has been ripped out from under you, that you're hurting. I'm sorry as hell about you and Mom. If there was anything I could do to change it, I would in a heartbeat."

"I know that, princess—"

"But you need to buck up and handle that Mom is gone. Put your big-boy pants on and deal. Self-destructing is not an option."

He stood and walked to the sink, staring sadly out the window. Faith felt herself softening some.

"I know you don't understand," he said.

"I do understand. It sucks." She picked at one of the steaming cinnamon rolls, blew on it and popped the bite in her mouth. "Maybe it would do you some good to hit the punching bags at the station for a bit. Work out some of your anger at Mom."

He didn't respond immediately, just kept staring outside at the bay. He shook his head slowly. "If I could be angry at her, maybe that would work."

"If you're not pissed, I'm mad enough for both of us."

"No." Her dad turned to look at her. "You can't be mad at your mom."

"Oh yes, I can."

"It's not her fault, Faith."

The urge to shake him was overwhelming. "She quit the marriage, Dad. I can't believe I have to remind you that *she* walked out on *you*. Pretty safe to say it's her fault."

"I guess it probably looks that way from the outside."

"I'm not on the outside. I'm here in this house, living with you, watching you piss your life away. Trying to find something to help you, anything to get my dad back to the person he's always been."

He walked over to her, palmed the back of her head to tilt it forward, and kissed her forehead. "That means more to me than you'll ever know, princess." He shuffled tiredly to the table and sat in his usual place. Leaning both elbows on the surface, he ran his hands over his face. "But there are things that've gone on in our marriage that you haven't been privy to."

"I know how much you guys argue about me. My career."

"That's not it. Well, that may be a very small piece of it but it's all part of a much larger issue. *My* career."

"Not a secret, either, Dad. You've fought about that longer than you've fought about me. Mom's always hated how much time and dedication it takes."

"Yes. Rightfully so."

"It's your career. You support the family. You're the fire chief, for the love of God."

"It *is* my career. And I've chosen it repeatedly over my family."

"Sometimes there is no choice. You do what you have to do. That'd be true with other jobs as well." Faith strode over to the table and sat down hard in the chair next to him. "Why is that so difficult for her to understand?"

"She understands that. The problem…" He ran a hand through his thick graying hair and sighed. "The problem is that I've screwed it up. Pushed it. Too many times.

There are instances when I had no choice but to go into work at an inconvenient time. Nights when I couldn't get around working an extra few hours. But they're few and far between."

"Like I said, you're dedicated."

"Stop defending me, Faith!" He smacked his palm on the table, his voice booming now. "Your belief in me has always meant the world to me, but this time you're wrong."

She swallowed a protest, because something in his eyes, some kind of conviction she hadn't seen there for weeks, stopped her. Made her sit there quietly and wait for him to say more.

"I could probably count on both hands the times it was justified. Staying late. Running out of here at all hours for work. I nearly missed your brother's birth. Holidays. Canceled family vacations. Hell, Faith, I was late to your high school graduation. So many of those times, I could've told the people at work no, I can't do it."

"But that's what makes you so good at your job. You make sacrifices."

He nodded sadly. "I'm afraid one of those sacrifices is my marriage, princess."

"So you're giving up?"

"You're the one who told me to move on. Something about big-boy pants."

"Quit drowning your sorrows in beer, sure, but give up?"

"I gave up weeks ago, Faith."

"Why would you do that? You love her, don't you?"

"Of course I love her." He shoved his chair back and

stood again. Walked over to the counter, his back to Faith. "How long ago did you leave the house, go off to college?"

"Eight years."

He nodded, and when he turned to face her, he was biting down on his lip. "Eight years ago, when it was down to just your mother and me, she warned me. Told me that if I kept running off to work at every opportunity, this would happen."

"She threatened to leave you? That long ago?" Faith's voice rose almost to a squeak.

He nodded somberly.

"And you, what, didn't believe her?"

Her dad shrugged. It struck Faith how beaten down he looked and how that contrasted with his tall frame, his wide shoulders, his usual proud stature.

"I blew it."

"So you knew she could leave you at any time, and you still kept on working long hours? Going to fires in the middle of the night just because? Allowing the mayor to call a meeting at dinnertime?"

"It's hard to break some habits, Faith."

Something snapped inside her. She popped up from the chair and spun around. The weeks of trying to figure out what to do for him, of babying him, giving him tough love—through all of it, she'd been blind. "Cry me a damn river, Dad. You've made your bed. She gave you every opportunity and you didn't even try to keep your marriage together. As far as I'm concerned, you let the family down. Knowingly."

"Faith, I—"

"I don't want to hear it." Beyond exhausted from a near sleepless night and twenty-four hours of worry, she stormed to her bedroom and threw some clean clothes into a large duffel bag. Grabbed the dirty uniform off the floor and stuffed it into a plastic grocery sack. Made a quick stop in her bathroom to get any essentials she could fit into the duffel. Headed through the kitchen toward the back door.

"Where are you going, Faith?" Her dad hadn't moved from his spot at the counter.

"Away. I'm staying somewhere else for a while. You can go ahead and finish self-destructing. Put your job first. You obviously couldn't care less about the family or anyone in it."

Fire blazed in his eyes suddenly and he straightened. Advanced slowly, step by intense step. "I may have made mistakes, but don't you ever, *ever* say that this family doesn't matter to me. My family means more than you can ever know. And you…you've always been a daddy's girl. I love you so much, Faith…it scares the living hell out of me to have you out there fighting fires. If anything happened to you again, it would kill me. *Kill me.* I have my best captain looking out for you, for God's sake. So don't tell me I don't care about you…or your brothers or your—"

"You have your best captain *what?*" Faith clutched the strap of the bag on her shoulder so hard her fingernails dug into the palm of her hand. Her insides sank to the bottom of her stomach.

Her dad's eyes widened briefly, as if he realized he'd said the wrong thing. "The point is that I'd do anything for my family, but I'm only human—"

"You asked Joe to look after me? Are you paying him an extra babysitting fee, too?"

"Calm down, Faith. It's not that I don't think you can do the job—"

"That's interesting, because from here, that's exactly what it looks like." Tears burned her eyes. She sounded semihysterical. And maybe she goddamn was.

"You know better than that, princess. You're good at the job. Damn good. But bad things can happen to anyone in our world. You know that firsthand."

She shook her head, blinded by her tears. "You were the one person who was behind me all the way, Dad, and now…now you've let me down in so many ways I can't even count them."

Faith swung the screen door open and walked out of the house she'd grown up in.

CHAPTER NINETEEN

LUCKY FOR JOE, his address wasn't in the San Amaro phonebook, which meant it took Faith a while to track it down. The station was nearly empty when she arrived, since the truck and ambulance had both been called out, and that gave her plenty of opportunity to poke around and find where he lived.

By the time she reached the door of his place—a modest, narrow, two-story condo in the center of town—the tempest in her had weakened slightly. His 4Runner was in the carport beneath his unit, reassuring her she was at the right address. She knocked and waited.

When he answered, she nearly swallowed her anger.

He wore only a pair of jeans, the button undone, the worn, soft material hugging his thighs. His body was… perfect. Chest and abs sculpted as if a famous artist had chiseled the ideal male specimen. Corded biceps, wide shoulders. She managed to work her gaze upward, and realized by the drowsy look in his eyes and slightly mussed hair that he'd been sleeping.

"Faith? What's wrong?" He blinked sleepily, still distracting her from the reason she'd come here.

"Can I come in?" she asked, fully aware of how visible his front door was from the street, should anyone they knew drive by.

He opened the door wider and allowed her to enter, then closed it behind her.

"Is your dad okay?"

The mention was all it took to snap her back to her pissed off place. "So he ordered you to look out for me, huh?" She fought to keep her voice from slipping back into hysterical mode.

He closed his eyes and dropped his head. Scratched behind his ear. Studied her. "What happened?"

"He told me he asked you to watch out for me. Is that what everything is all about? The kisses, the being nice to me? You were stuck babysitting me anyway, so you might as well make the most of it?"

"Whoa. Calm down, Faith." He took her by the elbow and led her toward the big denim-blue couch in the living room.

She shook her arm away and spun to face him. "Are you going to answer me?"

"I thought we'd sit and have a civilized discussion, but I see that's out of the question. Kissing you has nothing to do with your dad."

"You must think it's amusing to have the chief's little girl in your charge. What better way to butter him up for that promotion."

Joe started laughing then. Howling so hard he threw his head back. Faith narrowed her eyes and shook with the need to conk him over the head with a heavy object.

"Really?" she said through clenched teeth. "You're laughing?"

He sobered, his dark eyes intense. Disbelieving? "Think about that for a minute, Faith. Butter up the chief by getting involved with his daughter? If you believe that, you don't know a thing about men."

"What's that supposed to mean?" She knew plenty about how stupid and proud and clueless they were.

"Cardinal unspoken rule. You don't screw the boss's daughter."

"Who said anything about screwing?"

"You know what I mean." Joe stepped closer, his eyes taking on a different mood altogether. "Besides, correct me if I'm wrong, but I'd say we were about two steps from crossing that line in my room the other night."

She couldn't correct him. He wasn't wrong. And the way his dark, smoldering eyes bored into hers right now with such heat…

"I've kissed you because I wanted to, Faith. Because there are times I can't *not* kiss you. Because something about you, about your stubborn determination, the heart you put into everything you do…those damn kissable lips…" His gaze lowered and Faith involuntarily moistened her lips. "When I kiss you, it's in spite of your father. In direct opposition to my career aspirations. It's begging for trouble. Not paving any damn road."

Her annoyance leaked out like water from a barrel with a hole in the bottom.

"I get it," she said, lowering her gaze. "That accusation was one of the dumber things I've said."

"I wasn't going to be so blunt, but yeah."

"I'm still pissed." She crossed her arms emphatically. "Just not at you."

Joe grinned and took her elbow again, leading her to the couch. He pulled her down inches away from him.

"You know as well as I do that you don't need anyone watching over you."

Faith drew her knees up to her chest, hugged them to her, saying nothing. She felt Joe's eyes burning into her and avoided meeting his gaze.

"Right? Faith?"

She swallowed hard, unable to choke out an agreement.

He extended his hand and wove their fingers together. "Where's the kick-ass Faith with Texas-size confidence?"

She drew in a shaky breath. "She got crushed in a building collapse."

He squeezed her hand gently and shook his head. "She's still in there somewhere."

Before she could process what was happening, Joe slid one arm under her leg, the other behind her back, and scooped her onto his lap.

"What the…? What's that for?"

"To get your attention." He settled into the corner of the couch with her.

Faith sat stiffly, unsure how to act with Joe being so openly affectionate. His caresses up and down her thigh gradually relaxed her. Convinced her there was nothing to fight here.

"After what happened to you," he said, "it's okay to take a while to get back up to speed."

Surprised, she turned, stretching her legs out across the couch so she could see his face. "You think?"

"You don't think?"

She reached down and took off her work shoes, dropping them on the floor as she considered his question.

"Maybe a little while, I guess. But you're not supposed to tell me that."

"What am I supposed to tell you?"

"Captain stuff. 'No excuses. Get over it and do the job.'"

"When have I ever given you the impression that's how I work?"

Of the three captains in the department, Joe was the most compassionate. Probably the most respected and best liked, too. He was one of those rare people who could lead without condescending. Teach without talking down.

But she didn't need to tell him that and give him a big head.

"You're the meanest. Strict, unbending. All the guys detest you."

He chuckled. "I don't care what all the guys think of me. Only the girls."

"The jury's still out. You're welcome to campaign, though."

"I'll definitely keep that in mind." He lightly grasped her forearm, becoming serious. "What it comes down to, Faith, is that you need to trust yourself. The rest of us already do."

"My dad doesn't."

"Faith." Joe stared at her until she looked at him. "Is your dad in his right mind now? Does your dad normally go out and drink himself unconscious? Does the real guy miss even a day of work?"

She shook her head reluctantly.

"He's got serious problems, but I don't need to tell you that. You know better than anyone."

"I guess so."

"Okay, then. Let it go. In his eyes, you're still his little girl."

Faith fought a grin. "Which makes it twice as twisted that I'm on your lap."

"I said in *his* eyes. There's nothing little girl about what I'm seeing." Joe's voice lowered and went sexy, making Faith's heart skip a beat.

"It's the uniform," she said, grimacing. She hadn't had a chance to change after finishing her shift this morning.

"It's more than the uniform."

He pulled her toward him and kissed her. The warm softness of his lips drew her in. He was thorough, gentle. Too damn gentle. Faith needed more.

She turned to face him fully, her knees falling on either side of his thighs, and deepened the kiss. Her tongue pushed inside his mouth greedily. She craved this man, burned for the sensations she knew he could give her. The escape.

Running her hands up his solid, sculpted chest, she kissed her inhibitions goodbye and let out a low moan of appreciation.

Joe needed no encouragement. He met her urgency, his hands on her butt, pulling her body into his hardness.

He kissed her hungrily, his tongue playing with hers, swirling, exploring…taking what he seemed to need. Giving exactly what she wanted.

He untucked her uniform shirt and slid his hands up her torso. The size of them dwarfed her body. Made her feel sexy. Feminine. On fire. While he took his time working his way upward, she whipped her T-shirt over her head and tossed it to the floor.

He stopped kissing her long enough to lean back and take in her lacy zebra-print bra. "Do you always wear hot little numbers like that under your uniform?"

Faith laughed. "Numbers? I don't think there's anything mathematical about it."

Joe growled, running his thumbs over the tips of her breasts, covered by the thin material. "I don't know…there's the possibility for a study of proportions. Symmetry."

"Nice intellectual touch." Her breath was uneven, shallow. "As for hot, not always. Sometimes I go with a demure yellow mesh, a simple, light pink heart motif. Depends on my mood."

"You're killing me," he said huskily into her ear. "I don't think I can work with you again. Not without trying to figure out your 'mood.'"

"It's important to know a woman's mood."

"Right now I think I've got a pretty good handle on it."

Their lips came together again. He reached behind her and unfastened her "hot little number" with one hand. Faith arched toward him, aching to feel the heat of his skin on hers.

"You're beautiful," he said, cupping both her breasts, molding them with his palms.

She rose on her knees so he could draw her into his mouth. His tongue swirled around her nipple, teased it, shot a tight ache deep inside her. Faith ran her fingers through his coarse, dark hair, cradling his head to her.

Without warning, he pushed to the edge of the couch

and then to his feet, still holding on to her. Faith threw her arms and legs around him to avoid falling.

"I've got you," he said in a low voice.

"That you do."

He kissed her the entire way up the stairs, down a short hall, to his bedroom. She slid down him when he stopped in the middle of the room, and he wrapped his arms tightly around her, making her feel safe. Desired.

He walked her slowly backward until her legs hit his bed. As he strode across the room and closed the blinds on the back side of the condo, she slid onto the king-size mattress and crept up till she reached his pillows. The blankets were twisted and she could smell his scent on the sheets.

She watched him hungrily as he crossed back to her. Before joining her, he unzipped his pants and drew his jeans down his legs. Either he peeled two layers at once or he'd been commando, because now he was naked and, oh yeah, the rest of his body was just as impressive as his upper half. And then some.

Joe joined her on the bed and brushed her cheek with his knuckles. He pressed a tender kiss to her lips.

"Do you want this?" he asked, then trailed his lips along her jaw.

She wound her arms around him and ran her hands over his back, shoulders, ass. "I thought we weren't supposed to do this." She couldn't help smiling wickedly.

"Do you want to stop?"

"Does this feel like I want to stop?" she asked as she grasped the hardest part of him.

He moaned and undid her pants. Slid them down her

legs and dropped them over the side of the bed. Then he took intense interest in her matching zebra bikini panties, tracing the design before peeling them off as well.

Faith playfully propped herself up on one elbow, breaking all contact and smirking. "What about you? Do you want to stop?"

In an instant, he was on top of her, covering her with his wide, solid body. "Not for a few hours, minimum."

"If you think you can last that long," she taunted.

Joe quieted her by kissing her and doing deliciously naughty things with his hands.

Faith surrendered willingly. Enthusiastically. "I love it when you get all prove-a-pointish," she murmured when he trailed his lips down to the hollow of her neck and lower.

"I may have exaggerated on the time thing. You have this way of making me lose control."

"Yeah?" She slid her knees up, opening herself to him, and rubbed her body against his. "Maybe it's your age. They say a man reaches his prime at eighteen—"

Again, he cut off her words by slipping his tongue inside her mouth, making her laugh.

"That was the wrong saying," she finally said, breathlessly. "What I meant was with age comes expertise."

He drew his fingers downward from her breasts, inching lower, until he touched the part of her that throbbed for him. "That's not even the saying."

"Maybe not." Her breath caught. "But it feels right on about now."

When he rolled away from her, she wanted to cry, but he didn't go far. He opened the nightstand drawer and withdrew a condom. Faith held her hand out and he looked at her questioningly. She took the packet from him, ripped it open impatiently. Tried to slide it on him but her hand was shaking too much.

Joe took the condom from her and sheathed himself quickly. "Experience," he said. "With age comes experience."

She laughed and then sucked in her breath as he pressed into her, filling her, stretching her.

He was tender and patient as her body adjusted. "You okay?" he said into her ear, in barely more than a whisper.

Faith melted a little at his concern. "Very okay." She matched his rhythm, then increased their tempo, thrusting her hips up to meet him.

Their tongues mirrored their bodies with a mating dance. Her need ignited. There was nothing gentle or gradual about it—it was like having a match thrown on a propane tank. An explosion of sensation that burned, consumed her, making her cling to him for all she was worth as she climbed toward release.

Just like his kisses, his lovemaking was somehow tender and yet urgent at the same time. He was an unselfish lover, as concerned about her pleasure as his own. He made her feel more than just what he was doing to her body, made her chest feel light, as if it was filled with helium and he was the only thing keeping her from floating away.

Joe said her name several times as she nearly lost her mind, as her body began to tingle, and then she slipped over the edge to ecstasy. He followed her, then looked down at her with sated, drowsy eyes. He kissed the tip of her nose, her lips, her chin and back to her lips, where his mouth lingered. The urgency was gone from his touch and it was all gentle adoration, making Faith melt a little bit more. He rolled to his side, taking her with him.

She smiled, her breath shaky. "Wow."

"Yeah," Joe said into her ear, wrapping his arms tightly around her. "Wow."

SO THAT WAS HOW IT WAS then.

There was *something* between them. Something special, beyond man parts and woman parts and biology.

Joe had been with enough women to know that sex with Faith Peligni was nothing short of incredible. *Wow* was an understatement.

And that was not good news.

Maybe it'd just been too long for him. He'd quit the meaningless, short-term affairs a few years back, when he got promoted to captain. He was usually too wrapped up in his job or working too much overtime to expend the energy. Maybe he needed to get back to meeting people, taking women out. To give him perspective.

Or maybe he only wanted Faith.

Well, he had her right now, and that was all he could have. He intended to enjoy every second with her in his arms.

Joe stroked her silky hair slowly, over and over, taking in her scent, light, floral...*Faith*. When her breathing deepened with the rhythm of sleep, he finally closed his eyes, smiling to himself. Though he was more content than he'd been in months—maybe years—and completely sated, he'd been determined to stay awake.

The last thing he needed was to give this beautiful woman another reason to call him "old man."

BROAD FREAKING DAYLIGHT.

Faith had left her car parked in front of Joe's house for anyone to see…in broad daylight.

She opened her eyes instantly at the realization. Checked the clock on the nightstand. Fabulous. She'd been here for over three hours. There was no acceptable way to explain that—except to say she'd been having the most amazing sex of her life, of course.

Joe's arm was slung protectively—possessively?— over her abdomen, so there was no way she could dart off without him noticing. But she had to get out of here.

Panic clawed at her, made it hard to get any air in as she imagined one of the guys at work commenting on her "career aspirations." It didn't matter that the chance of anyone she knew driving by—and knowing this was Joe's house—was slim to none. Lying there, she was convinced the whole world would be aware of her slipup. As if she'd hired a skywriter to broadcast the news.

She studied Joe to gauge how deeply he was sleeping. Even in her panic, his handsome face had an effect on her. She considered how easy it would be to slide back under his arm and wake him up with her lips all over his body. The images softened her. Weakened her—for a good ten seconds.

Faith wrapped her hand around his arm to see if he reacted. He didn't. She lifted his arm and slowly worked her way out from under him. It'd be much easier to escape quickly if she didn't have to explain to him what her rush was about. She shouldn't have to tell him, anyway. There was no question this was a mistake.

He slumbered on, breathing deeply enough that she could hear him as she gathered her underwear and pants from the floor. She put them on as she walked downstairs to the living room, picking up her T-shirt, bra and shoes there and dressing quickly. At the door, she stopped and straightened her clothes. Looked around for a mirror. The only one she could find was in the hall bathroom. She ran her fingers through her hair in an attempt to not look as if she'd just been thoroughly ravished. It didn't do much good, but her purse—with her brush and makeup inside—was in the car.

Screw it. She had to get out of here.

Before opening the door, she looked out the side window. Then the peephole. The other window at the front of the house. For what, she didn't know. She was acting like a sneaky teenager. Without a glance back, she opened the door, squinting against the blinding, late afternoon sunlight, and made her way toward the car, trying for all the world to look as if she'd just had a cup of coffee and a work meeting with her captain instead of…the truth.

An old Buick drove by as she walked down the driveway. Once she was in her car, she spotted an elderly couple strolling along the sidewalk on the opposite side of the street. Probably Joe's next-door neighbors. The kind he would chat with as he watered his flower bed—if he had one.

She started the engine and, with no idea where she was going or who she could stay with, got the hell off Blue Fin Boulevard.

CHAPTER TWENTY

"DID YOU MISS ME?" Faith asked flippantly after she shut the door to Joe's office.

He'd missed her like goddamn crazy. In his arms, in his bed, even just talking to her about things like the best way to coil a hose or how many miles on the treadmill made a good day's workout.

It had been a week since she'd crept out of his house like a criminal, and they hadn't spoken since, beyond the bare minimum necessary to work together. He'd seen her plenty in that time, but being closed in the office with her created an intimacy that had his blood pulsing with need within seconds. He gritted his teeth against memories of her in his arms and forced his focus back to the items in his hands.

"Tell me this is a misprint," he said, tossing the program for the next evening's auction to the edge of his desk nearest her. It was turned to the third page of items up for bid. Items and people.

"What?" She frowned, leaning forward.

"You. Being auctioned off."

"Oh." Her tone was suddenly less concerned. More defensive. "Yeah. It's for a good cause. I believe you've heard of the San Amaro Island Burn Foundation?"

"Don't be like that, Faith." She knew damn well his mother had been one of the founders.

"Don't think," she said, glancing behind at the closed door and lowering her voice, "that just because of… what happened, you can tell me what to do outside of this job."

"This isn't the place to discuss what happened, though it would be nice to have that conversation sometime."

Her bravado faltered. Only for a second. "There's nothing to discuss, Joe. Nothing changed, right? Still an impossible situation."

And that was the bitch of it. She was right. The bigger question was why was he hanging on to it? Why was he letting it get to him that she treated him like everyone else? That was the way he wanted it. Needed it.

"Did you really think about volunteering yourself for the auction, Faith? You work so hard to earn people's respect as a female firefighter and—"

"You think just because someone can bid on a date with me that I won't be taken seriously."

"It's a good possibility. Am I wrong?"

"Yes," she said. "You know this auction as well as I do. They do it every year. The bachelor-bachelorette bit is only a small part, but it brings in huge money. And what better way to say 'hey, look, there's a new game in town. Girls can be firefighters, too.'"

He felt the tic in his jaw as he studied her. He could just imagine all the jackasses who would jump at the chance to take out a woman like Faith. Plenty of them had money and could spend big bucks. She wasn't a piece of meat, and he hated the idea that the wrong person could win the bid for her time.

She lifted her chin and walked closer to the desk that

stood between them, grinning. "You're jealous, aren't you?"

Of course, she'd hit on the truth. But hell if he was going to admit it.

"Just don't want the department to become a meat market. What if one of your coworkers bids on you?"

The way her eyes darted to the side told him she hadn't considered that possibility.

"Starting bid is a hundred dollars. No one around here can afford that."

"You'd be surprised what these boys might save their pennies for."

She straightened. "It's only a date. I'll be fine no matter who wins. My biggest worry is whether anyone will bid."

Joe laughed. "Oh, they will." As much as he wished he could prevent the whole thing, she wouldn't lack for bidders. In fact, personal issues aside, it was a genius fundraising move. Ten firefighters up for auction, and what man wouldn't empty his bank account to get the one woman? The knockout, kick-ass woman with cool blue eyes and a killer body.

"I think you might be biased," she whispered. "But thanks for the vote of confidence. Come to think of it, maybe if no one else bids, you could save me from eternal humiliation."

"People will bid, Faith. They'll pay plenty to go out with you."

"But…" She perched on the arm of the chair, propping one foot up on the seat, and even though she wore unsexy navy-blue uniform pants, he had no trouble imagining—remembering—what that leg looked like bare.

"Suppose no one does. And it's all quiet in the room. Uncomfortable. You'd throw one out there, wouldn't you?" She tilted her head just so and had a tantalizing, flirty look in her eyes.

"You know I couldn't do that." Thank God he was certain that wouldn't happen, because it would kill him not to.

"Would you want to?"

Damn, he wanted her again. Still. He walked around the desk and stopped three inches from her. "You know exactly what I want to do," he said in a quiet, husky voice.

Faith's gaze dipped to his lips, then her long lashes lifted again and she met his eyes.

"And I know how you do it, too. Very well."

His pulse was already going double time and other parts of him responded to her now, too.

A knock sounded on the door, and it opened before Joe could react. Faith whirled around guiltily as they both faced the fire chief.

CHAPTER TWENTY-ONE

"WANTED TO GET YOUR opinion of some… Oh. Hey, princess," Chief Peligni said.

Joe's heart hammered and he thanked God he hadn't actually been touching Faith—yet.

"I was just leaving," she said curtly, giving Joe the impression that she and her father were still at odds.

"Wait, Faith."

She stopped at the chief's plea. Waited for him to go on.

"Are you doing okay?"

"I'm fine, Dad."

"You can come home anytime, you know." He glanced at Joe uncomfortably, and Joe wished he was somewhere else. Anywhere else, so he didn't have to watch the chief grovel.

"I'm staying with Nadia for a while," Faith said. "But I'm looking for my own place."

"I'm sorry, Faith. I'm working on things. Making some changes."

Joe could tell the chief's words had an effect on Faith. Her posture relaxed slightly and her face softened into something less than anger. "I hope so, Dad. I need to go help Penn with lunch."

Chief Peligni watched Faith walk out, and Joe did everything in his power *not* to.

"It sucks to let down the people you care about," the chief said quietly, almost to himself.

The words made Joe break out into a sweat beneath his uniform. If sleeping with the chief's daughter wasn't letting him down…

He strode back behind his desk. Coughed uneasily. "Do you know about the auction thing? With your daughter?"

Tony Peligni, who was still looking out the door after Faith, turned around and sighed. "The bachelorette thing? Yeah. She and I *discussed* that when she decided to participate."

"I'm sorry. I had no idea she was considering it. I would have tried to convince her otherwise if I had."

"It wouldn't have done any good, Joe. Haven't you figured that out yet?"

Joe tried to hide a grin, because he had a very good grasp of Faith's stubbornness.

"Faith will do whatever she damn well pleases," the chief continued. "Oh, she'll make nice about it and act like she listens to your arguments, but then if she wants to do something, you might as well stand back and watch her do it. She doesn't worry much about what anyone else thinks once her mind is made up."

"I guess I'm surprised she doesn't see this as a negative thing." Joe should probably drop it, he knew, so that her father didn't get suspicious and wonder why he was so concerned about it. But he couldn't get over the idea of someone else taking Faith on a date. An honest-to-God, pick-her-up-at-the-door date. Something he could never do.

The chief shook his head. "She insists it will bring

positive attention to the fact that there's a woman in the department. Between you and me, I think she's dreading the date part, but she's determined to make her point."

"Nothing you can do?" Joe asked.

"I intend to be there and do everything in my power to make sure no one from the department dares to so much as think about bidding on her."

"Don't want her dating one of us, huh?" Joe tried to make it sound like a joke, but he was testing the chief.

"Hell, no. You and I both know this career takes a lot out of a man. I want better for her."

Joe fought to keep his face expressionless. None of this was news to him. He'd never had a prayer of making a relationship with Faith work.

Hellfire, he didn't even want to contemplate why he'd just thought the word *relationship*. He dragged his mind back to the conversation at hand, trying to think like Faith's captain and not her lover.

"I guess you have to give her credit for believing in something so strongly," Joe said, wondering to himself if there was a cause he believed in enough to go against the opinions of the people he loved. He couldn't imagine doing something that would upset his mother. Even before she was sick. Making his mom proud had always been high on his list of motivations, for better or worse.

"Faith's a special girl," the chief said, looking hard at Joe, as if he suspected Joe might be too aware of that fact.

"Of course. She's your daughter, sir. Now, what was it you wanted to talk to me about?"

As THE CLEANUP after the auction went on around him, Joe heard scraps of conversation that claimed the evening was a roaring success.

At the moment, he couldn't care less.

He tried to listen to the conversation he was supposedly part of, with the chief and an older couple who'd bid big bucks and won some artwork by Evan Drake's wife.

"It's beautiful stuff," Chief Peligni was saying. "Your donation will go a long way at the foundation. We're glad you could join us tonight."

The four of them shook hands and said good-night. The couple moved one way into the exiting crowd, and Joe and the chief moved the other.

The ballroom at one of the local hotels was fully decked out for the occasion, with marble columns and velvet curtains adding a touch of class. The small stage was decorated with deep red roses and other elegant floral arrangements Joe couldn't identify. Round tables with ten chairs each made the room a maze.

He was beyond ready to get the hell out of there and peel his dress uniform off. He'd had enough of this night.

"Faith looked beautiful, didn't she?" the chief said proudly as they slowly made their way toward the nearest door.

Beautiful enough that Joe had spent a good portion of the auction hard as a damn chunk of granite. "She did. She's a pretty girl." He hoped like hell that was professional and nonchalant, because the storm that raged in him was anything but.

"My glare at the guys apparently worked. Not one of them was dumb enough to place a bid on her."

"It climbed out of a firefighter's budget pretty damn fast," Joe said through clenched teeth.

The chief smiled. "Sixty-two hundred dollars she made for the foundation. I'm going to have to check out the guy who won. Did you catch his name?"

"Yeah," Joe said as they cleared the last table. "I know his name and then some. Troy Vargas. He's my stepbrother."

The chief stopped and faced Joe. "Is he all right?"

It took everything Joe had to stand there and appear unaffected, as if he wasn't ready to bash his stepbrother's face in. "He's okay."

"What's he do?"

"He's a partner in my stepfather's law firm in Corpus."

Chief Peligni looked at him thoughtfully, then nodded once, as if that would do. "There's Nita," he said, peering out over the crowd of people. "I'm going to go say hi."

"Have a good evening, Chief."

Joe stood to one side of the crowded lobby, searching for Troy. Instead, he spotted Faith, and felt his temperature go up as if a match had been lit under his collar.

She stood about twenty feet away, surrounded by her girlfriends and mother. Her father's assessment that she looked beautiful tonight was a gross understatement.

Her gown was dark purple and sequined, with thin straps holding it up. It hugged her body, clinging to her slender waist and curving outward with her sexy hips. A side slit revealed her legs when she walked. Her hair was pulled up in a fancy do that made Joe's fingers itch to release it. She wore makeup, and though he was a big fan of her without it, she looked more gorgeous than he'd ever seen her. Teasing her cleavage was an antique-looking necklace with a large amethyst.

A night with Faith would be worth every penny of the sixty-two hundred bucks Troy had forked over…and more.

In his peripheral vision, Joe noticed the dark head of the man in question, tilting back in laughter. Bastard thought he was pretty slick. It figured that just as Joe was starting to see his stepbrothers as decent guys he might actually hang out with even without his mother, Troy would pull this. And of course, Joe couldn't say a word. Not here, anyway.

He turned his back on his stepbrother, not wanting to come face-to-face with him.

Matter of fact, Joe wasn't much in the mood to talk to anyone. He'd chatted with plenty of people before the auction started, and didn't feel the need to mingle anymore. He headed toward an exit, but felt a hand on his forearm. He knew who the unpainted, short fingernails belonged to without looking at the woman's face.

"Faith."

"You're leaving already?" she asked. Her words and tone were indifferent enough, impersonal, not giving away anything of their recent history. But when he looked into her eyes, she seemed to see deep inside him, as if she could discern more than everyone else. "Are you upset?"

He took his time answering. Made a point of trying

to keep every hint of anger out of his voice. "Why would I be upset?"

The knowing look she gave him made him want to punch something. Or take her into his arms and mark her as his, maybe carry her off so Troy couldn't get his hands on her.

"Gee, I don't know," she said sarcastically. "I happen to understand how brothers work, Joe."

He nodded noncommittally. "Anything else?"

"It's better than a stranger, right? We know he's okay."

The rage started its slow build up once more, like water beginning to boil. "That proves you don't understand a *thing* about how brothers work. I'll see you at the station."

Joe headed toward the long hallway that would take him to the lot he'd parked in, congratulating himself for not losing his cool in public. He couldn't make any promises about the next time he saw Troy.

CHAPTER TWENTY-TWO

"ARE YOU GOING TO TELL ME yet where we're having dinner?" Faith asked Troy, trying not to sound rude or ungrateful. He'd been secretive the entire drive, even when he'd taken the exit to Corpus Christi.

"At my stepmom's house. We're celebrating her birthday tonight. It was a couple weeks ago, but she was in the hospital. Now that she's been home a few days, we thought she'd be up for it."

Unease churned in Faith's gut as he pulled in front of a large adobe home with a grand-looking entrance. It wasn't the near estate status of the house that worried her, it was that Joe's 4Runner was parked in the driveway.

Before she could say anything, Troy was out of the silver BMW and opening her door for her.

"Troy," she said quietly, stepping onto the curb. "Joe's here."

"Uh, yeah. Look, Faith, I'll take the heat for this. I know you don't know me from Adam, but trust me, okay? He might blow up when he sees you, but it'll be all right in the end. I didn't do this to hurt him."

She studied him, wondering what the hell she'd gotten herself into. Maybe a creepy stranger winning a date with her would've been better, after all.

She saw nothing creepy in Troy's eyes, though, and

nothing that hinted at anything but friendship. What she did see was the blinds in the front window of the house moving, as if someone was looking out. "If you say so," she said, wanting to get whatever scene was going to ensue over with. Get the night over with, actually.

They walked side by side up the front steps. The door opened before they got to it, and Ryan appeared with a big grin. "You are one crazy bastard," he said to his brother. "Everyone's in the kitchen."

"Nice to see you, too." Troy brushed by Ryan, leading Faith inside with his hand at the small of her back. "Kitchen's this way."

Faith braced herself for their entrance. Just as she'd expected, Joe stood there, leaning against the counter with a bottle of beer in his hand. He was laughing with the woman filling wineglasses next to him. Ryan's wife, Faith realized, when he came in and put a subtle but territorial arm around her.

When Joe saw Faith, his smile disappeared and he swallowed. "Hello, Faith," he said evenly.

Hello, awkwardness. "Hi."

Joe's jaw ticked as he completely ignored Troy.

"Faith, this is my wife, Shelly," Ryan said.

The woman turned to smile at Faith and shake her hand.

"Welcome to the Vargas-Mendoza testosterone well," Shelly said, eyeing Troy and Joe. "It's nice to meet you. And to have another female here."

"Good to meet you," Faith said, trying to ignore the thick tension in the air. "What can I do to help?"

"Have some wine," Shelly said, holding out glasses for her and for Troy. "The cook has everything under control. The salads are in the refrigerator and the hot stuff is being kept warm in the oven. Why don't we go out to the sunroom, where Carmen is? Troy, do you want to introduce Faith to your stepmother?"

The fire that flashed in Joe's eyes made Faith shudder. This was going to be ugly.

"Why don't you, Shelly?" Troy answered. "I need to talk to Joe first."

Shelly looked surprised, leading Faith to believe she didn't have a clue what, exactly, was transpiring in front of her.

"Sure. Come on, Faith. She'll be thrilled to meet you."

Faith glanced at Joe, but he wouldn't meet her gaze. Fantastic. She hadn't asked for any of this. He must know she wasn't interested in Troy. Joe's stepbrother was a nice enough guy but…he was a lawyer, for God's sake.

JOE EYED HIS STEPBROTHER as the women walked out to the sunroom.

"Easy," Troy said. "There's smoke coming out of your ears."

"Not too bright," Ryan interjected, shaking his head. "Like waving a scarf at a bull, man."

Troy glared at his brother. "What the hell are you doing in here, anyway?"

"Think I'm going to miss this?" Ryan took a swig from his beer bottle and stood back, crossing his arms. "You might need a referee."

"We don't need a referee," Joe said.

"I'm not interested in Faith," Troy stated.

"Save it. I'm not going into this with you."

"There is no 'this' to go into. I'm not an idiot, and even though we're not brothers by blood, I wouldn't home in on your woman."

Joe glanced toward the French doors to the sunroom. "She's not my woman. She works for me. Take her out if you want to."

Ryan hoisted himself up on the counter as if the NBA playoffs were starting up in the kitchen.

Troy laughed. "Yeah. I took her out tonight to the tune of a very nice donation to the Burn Foundation. You don't seem to be handling it too well."

Joe pushed himself off the counter and headed toward the formal living room at the front of the house.

"Wrong thing to say, man," he heard Ryan tell Troy as he walked off.

Joe paced to the front window and looked out at the neighborhood of impressive homes. Though it was an upper income area, there were lots of young families. Obviously not a place too many firefighters called home. A group of grade school kids ran through a sprinkler a few yards down, and two teenage boys were shooting hoops across the street. Joe heard someone enter the room behind him, but didn't bother to turn around.

"Will you hear me out?" Troy said.

"Say whatever you want to say."

"I brought Faith here for you."

Joe scoffed—he couldn't help it. "Why the hell would you do that? I told you we work together."

"Yeah, yeah, you're her senior officer," Troy said in a singsong voice. "Which translates to you refusing to take her out."

"It's not an issue."

"This is me, here. I don't give a shit if you're sleeping with one of your coworkers or underlings or whatever she is to you."

Joe turned sharply toward him. "Who said I was sleeping with her?"

"I don't know if you are, and frankly, I don't care. But that night at the hospital your feelings were obvious."

"Faith and I can't be together, Troy."

His brother laughed, and Joe tightened his fists at his sides.

"I get that," Troy said. "More than you know."

Something in his voice made Joe look at him again, more closely, beyond the remnants of the grin. He waited for him to spill the rest, whatever he was so intent on saying.

Troy lowered his voice and turned to make sure Ryan was out of earshot. "I'm seeing Betsy Wellington."

Joe stared at him blankly.

"Wellington. Of Smith, Vargas and Wellington. The daughter of the firm's president."

"Congratulations," Joe said, still unable to admit anything about Faith. For all he knew, Troy was playing him.

"Not looking for congratulations. All I'm saying is I know it's a bitch to want someone who's off-limits. And if you're going to continue to stand there and act as if you don't care about Faith Peligni, then suit yourself. I'm not the bad guy you'd like me to be."

Joe studied him pensively. "So you're telling me you dropped more than six thousand dollars just for me to have a good time for a night?"

"I dropped six thousand dollars to support Carmen's pet charity. It just so happened I found a way to try to give you some time with Faith, no questions asked."

"I didn't know you were the selfless type," Joe said after a moment.

"Sometimes I'm not," Troy said, sticking his hand in the pocket of his dress pants and rattling his keys. "I'll admit it was fun watching you get your hackles up during the bidding."

"Asshole."

"But an asshole you owe a favor to."

"You really have no interest in her?" Joe asked, finally starting to believe that Troy's motives were just what he'd said.

"None. Hey, she's hot. Don't get me wrong. But I don't go for the type of woman who could kick my ass if I piss her off."

Joe nodded, thinking about the women he'd seen Troy with. Always a different one. Always blonde. Always the type who would cry over a broken fingernail. "Yeah, Faith could take you."

"In your dreams."

"So what do you think I'm going to do with this 'favor'? It doesn't change a damn thing for Faith and me...*if* I was interested in her. And *if* she was interested in me."

Troy shrugged. "That's your problem. I've done my part." He sat on a couch that looked as if it had never been touched before. "Tell me this. What's holding you back? Is it against policy in the department?"

"Not officially."

"Then what the hell?"

"Why do you keep your girlfriend a secret?" Joe asked.

"She works for the firm. Receptionist pool. There's a rule against it."

Joe nodded. "Have you seen the fire chief?"

"Big guy? Looks like he could kill someone with his pinkie finger?"

"That's him. He's her father."

Troy swore. "Good guy? Bad?"

"My dad was his mentor. He's acted as mine since Dad died."

"Ouch."

"Like I said, Faith and I can't be together. If she even wanted to."

"Seems like she wants to, from where I'm standing. So, what, you're worried about disappointing the chief?"

Joe chuckled without feeling any real humor. "Worried about getting a promotion. Keeping my job. Chief doesn't want his little girl with a firefighter."

"His little girl *is* a firefighter."

"He's made it clear on numerous occasions he would not be supportive."

"So you choose the job."

"I've known where I was going professionally since I was twelve. Everybody's known."

"Things change, dude."

Joe stood. "Let's go see Mom."

"And Faith. You better see plenty of Faith tonight. It cost me a pretty penny to get you two in the same room."

"You're not going to let me forget that anytime soon, are you?"

"Not damn likely."

"Hey," Joe said, pausing before they opened the door to the sunroom. "Could we not tell my mom anything? I don't want her to get her hopes up for Faith and me."

Troy frowned and shook his head. "Your call. You know, you're too much of a damn people pleaser. I reckon you ought to try worrying about what *you* want instead of what everyone else wants for you all the time."

Joe told him where he could go as he opened the door and they joined Ryan, Jorge and the women.

TROY WASN'T AS DUMB as Joe had thought.

His stepbrother had made a point of keeping his distance from Faith. Being courteous and polite but not too friendly. Not goddamn touching her.

Apparently he liked living.

They'd just sung a painful rendition of "Happy Birthday" and Shelly was cutting the cake—chocolate with white frosting, with purple and yellow pansies on top. No candles. Though his mom was feeling much better, she was still weak and her lungs weren't back to normal yet. She was such a fighter, though....

Joe's throat swelled up as he looked at her and recalled how puny she'd been in the ICU. Tonight her cheeks were pink and her spirits high.

"Biggest slice goes to the birthday girl," Faith said, coaching Shelly.

"Carmen gets this one. Two big sugary flowers."

Faith took the plate, grabbed a plastic fork and carried

it to Joe's mom. She helped Carmen prop herself up again so she could eat, and then she perched on the arm of the couch, watching Carmen closely in case she needed help.

Joe tried to act nonchalant, sitting on a folding chair on the other side of the room, but he wanted nothing more than to take Faith in his arms and kiss her in gratitude. Gratitude and other stuff, as well.

She'd dressed casually tonight, in dark blue jeans so tight they looked like leggings, a Kelly-green silk tank top and killer silver heels. Her ears, wrist and neck were adorned with trendy silver jewelry that jingled when she moved. He was dying to hold her.

Troy's phone rang and he excused himself to the kitchen.

"Here's a piece with extra frosting for you, Joe," Shelly said. "You need something to sweeten you up. You're quiet tonight."

"He'll try to tell you it's a deep intellectual quiet, no doubt," Ryan said, grabbing his own slice of cake and digging into it as if he hadn't just eaten enough slow-cooked ribs for a football team.

"No need for me to say it." Joe took a bite of cake, and once again, his eyes went to Faith. He couldn't keep them off her. He didn't know how this night was going to end, but he had to get her alone somehow.

She looked up at him then, laughing at something his mom had said, something he'd missed because he was lost in fantasies of Faith. Her gaze met his and the heat in it made his body react.

"Ryan never quite mastered the 'stay quiet to keep

them wondering' philosophy," Jorge said. "We never wonder what's on his mind."

"We sometimes wonder if *anything* is on his mind," Joe said. He ducked when Ryan tossed his fork at him with a howl.

"You men are too loud—your mother needs peace," Shelly said, scraping some extra frosting off the knife and licking her finger. She carried a slice of cake to Faith and sat on the chair next to the couch with her own piece.

Joe's mom shook her head. "It's wonderful to have the noise. This place gets so quiet sometimes. I hope Faith doesn't run away scared, though."

Carmen smiled warmly at her, and not for the first time, Joe was relieved he wasn't the one who'd brought her here. His mom seemed to like Faith, and he didn't want to disappoint her when things couldn't work out between them. Better that she never know there was any kind of attraction between them. The whole family held few expectations for Troy to ever settle down, so having him bring in a woman was a whole different ball game.

Troy ambled back in then. He went over to Faith. "I'm afraid I have to take off unexpectedly," he said, mostly to her. "Got a client who's in trouble. I'm sorry to bail on you, Faith, but I'm hoping my honorable stepbrother can take you home to the island for me." He shot Joe a look, and Joe instantly understood. It was a ruse. Troy's way of stepping aside.

Faith looked alarmed as she glanced from Joe to Troy.

"I'm really sorry," Troy said. "I'll owe you one."

Joe held his tongue to keep from saying *the hell he would*.

"It's okay," Faith said. "As long as Joe doesn't mind."

"I don't mind," Joe said. *At all.*

"Thanks, bro. I'd say I owe you a favor, too, but…"

"Get out of here," Joe muttered, checking his watch.

It was almost ten o'clock. Getting late for his mom. They should be able to say good-night soon without letting on that he couldn't wait to get Faith alone.

He sat back to wait—impatiently—for the moment they could leave.

CHAPTER TWENTY-THREE

"THIS WAS ONE OF the strangest nights of my life," Faith said as Joe led her down the front steps of his mom and stepfather's house after telling them good-night. The others had left a few minutes earlier, and the quiet of the evening took over. There weren't a lot of Vargases, but they were a loud bunch. They reminded Faith of her own family in a lot of ways.

"Want to make it a little stranger?" Joe took her hand in his.

The simple gesture sent a thrill through her. They hadn't touched all night. Being with him in a casual nonwork setting without letting on they were anything other than coworkers—for several hours… God, she'd longed to touch him. Her fingers had itched with the relentless urge.

They'd never held hands like this before, just walking along, side by side, hanging on to each other as if it was the most natural thing in the world. As if they didn't have to dance around their attraction. His hand was big, like the rest of him. Rough. Strong. Multitalented, she thought, pursing her lips to repress a private grin.

"What's stranger than starting the evening with one man and ending it being ditched by him and rescued by his stepbrother?"

"Don't forget being thrown in with the crazy Mendoza-Vargas family."

"Trust me, your family's got nothing on mine when it comes to crazy."

"Troy orchestrated the whole night so we could be together, you know?"

Faith paused, touched. "Really?"

"It's why he's still breathing."

She laughed and they continued walking. "That's really sweet of him. Where are we going?"

"Not *that* sweet."

Instead of continuing to the foot of the driveway where his SUV was parked, they'd taken a brick path around the side of the house. Wide steps led downward, presumably to the backyard.

"To my secret hideaway." She could hear his smile. There was no light back here and the moon was buried by clouds, cloaking them in relative darkness under looming trees.

A secret hideaway sounded...promising.

She hadn't planned to see Joe tonight, but now that they were together, she could think of all kinds of ways she'd like the evening to end. When he took out his keys and unlocked the basement door, though, she felt slightly disappointed.

"Cars?" she asked, taking in the three-bay garage beneath the main house when he flipped on the lights.

"More than just cars," Joe said, his voice coming alive. "Classics."

She walked to the closest one. "Don't take this the wrong way, but this looks particularly unclassical."

It was a heap of junk, with dents in the back, mismatched paint on the driver's door, a broken head-light.

"You're not looking at it right," Joe said, coming up behind her. She felt his heat all along her body and, swear to God, her knees went weak.

Faith turned to look up at him, so close her head brushed against his chin. His spicy, clean, man smell teased her nose, and she longed to bury her face in his chest. "How should I look at it?"

"As potential." With his hands at her waist, he guided her past the middle bay of the garage, which was full of workbenches and tools, to the far one. "To look as sexy as this."

An old-model red car with black stripes on the hood was backed in, the rear end jacked up slightly higher than the front, the paint shiny.

"Nice," she said, walking toward it and peeking in the driver's window. "Much more classic looking."

"*Nice*. You say that like only a woman could." Joe laughed. "This represents over two years of my life."

"Wow." She started to run her hand along the side, but he caught it in his.

"Your rings could scratch the paint."

Faith tried not to laugh, because she could tell he was dead serious. "Sorry, boss."

"You did not just call me that."

"I meant car boss. Not fire boss. So are you going to tell me what this is, exactly?" Without touching it, she gestured to his pride and joy.

"It's a 1965 Super Sport Chevelle with a...you don't care about the engine, do you?" He broke off, with slightly less enthusiasm than he'd started with.

"*Care* isn't the right word. Know a thing about…no. But I'm duly impressed, anyway. You did what to this? Started with a heap like that one over there and made it pretty?"

He laughed again. "That sums it up well."

"Can I open the door?" she asked.

"Sure."

He reached in front of her for the driver's door, but an idea had blossomed in Faith's mind. She opened the door to the back.

Without waiting for his reaction, she slid in on the leather seat. The old-fashioned, wide bench seat. "Nice in here," she said, running her hand over the smooth leather. "Roomy."

Joe bent over at the door, hands braced on the roof. "It's never looked quite as nice as it does now."

"Yeah?" She leaned back across the seat, resting her elbows behind her, her feet still on the floor by his legs. "How about now?"

"I've always liked black leather, but…green silk and denim is fast becoming my favorite."

"Sometimes it's even better to touch, rather than just look."

He ducked his head inside and covered her body with his, one hand on the seat by her head and the other on the floor. "You have a naughty side to you, Faith Peligni."

"You seem to bring it out of me, Captain Mendoza." She put her arms around his neck and drew him to her.

He kissed her hard, urgently, revealing to her he'd been as frustrated all night as she had.

"Any chance of someone coming down here?" she asked when they took a breath.

Joe shook his head and nipped at her lips. "They never come down. This is my space."

"I like your space." Faith touched her finger to his moist lips, and he caught it with his mouth. The move was erotic, intimate.

"I like you *in* my space." He pressed his lower body to hers, showing her just how much he liked it as he kissed the side of her neck, just below her ear.

Faith slid her knees up to bring their bodies closer.

"As much as I'd love to have you with nothing but those do-me shoes on, you have to take them off," Joe said. "Don't want to ruin the leather."

Grinning, Faith slipped the four-inch heels off. "Or scratch the paint."

He kissed the grin away, intensely, his tongue seeking hers, tangling with it. One hand slid under her top, to her flesh. Trailed down, under the edge of her jeans. "These have to go," he said, unsnapping them. Working the zipper down.

The heat built in Faith fast, and she needed him to quell the ache. She wriggled beneath him, working her jeans off with her thumbs. His body was in the way, so she switched her efforts to his fly. He lifted, giving her access—to unzip, touch him, run her fingers along the length of him. Joe moaned and backed out of the car enough to take over removing her pants.

"It'd be faster to cut these off," he said, heat in his eyes.

"Patience. Virtue. Yada." Faith arched her hips upward and did what she could to help him.

"You turn into cliché girl when you're naked."

"You talk too much when I'm naked."

He dropped her jeans on the floor of the garage and eyed her dark purple thong. Bending over her again, he kissed her inner thigh, then worked his tongue under the thin strip of satiny material.

Joe teased her with his mouth as she ran a hand through his hair and tried to breathe. She thought she would die of wanting when he finally peeled her panties down her legs. The coolness of the leather under her barely registered.

Faith arched upward as he drew maddening circles with his tongue, inching closer to the part of her that ached most for his touch. At long freaking last, he covered her with his mouth, and she nearly shot through the ceiling, so electric was the sensation.

She pulled him upward, shaking with need. "Want you inside."

They both worked at his jeans and the boxers beneath them. When they were down on his thighs, he gave up and pressed himself between her legs.

"Faith," he breathed into her ear. "We need to use something."

Her mind was fuzzy and she struggled to think clearly. "Timing is okay."

"You're sure?"

"Very."

That was all he needed. He entered her, eliciting an unfamiliar sound from deep in her throat.

IF ANYONE HAD TOLD JOE he'd end up having sex in the backseat of his prized Chevelle, he would've laughed and said, "Like hell." Everyone he knew gave him continual crap for his meticulousness about this car. He'd never even let anyone sit inside except in the driver's seat.

He'd gotten over that the second Faith had sprawled so sexily across the black leather.

As she clung to him, arched toward him, coaxed him—as if he needed any coaxing—he lost all awareness of where they were. They could be five feet from a raging fire…God knew it was hot enough. He wouldn't notice or care. All he knew was Faith. The way her dark hair fanned over the seat. Her scent, sweaty and female, with a lingering touch of her floral perfume. The sounds she made—sexy gasps and short breaths and, damn, the things she was saying.

His need for release built, climbed so high he could taste it. He lifted her legs, angling deeper inside her, and she sank her teeth into his shoulder as she came. Joe watched her, and that was all it took for him to shatter into a million pieces.

As he slowly came out of his personal nirvana haze, he did his best to keep his weight from crushing Faith. It was nearly impossible, so he slid his arm beneath her and rolled onto his back on the small seat, holding her to his chest. They both breathed hard. The temperature in the car had to be about a hundred degrees, but he wasn't ready to bail out yet. Wanted to hold her for a while longer. Maybe a couple of weeks.

Joe brushed her hair back from her face and pulled her head closer to his for a long, quenching, soul-satisfying kiss.

For those few minutes, he was perfectly content,

satisfied, at peace with everything in the world. He dared to let himself think how wild he was about this woman—only for a moment. Then he moved toward the door, telling himself it was just the combination of great sex and the backseat of the car he loved. Nothing more.

"YOU MAKE IT REALLY HARD to leave, you know that?" Faith said hours later. They were stretched out in his bed, the sheets twisted, but pulled up halfway against the middle-of-the-night chill. They'd made love twice more since driving back from Corpus.

"I'd say I'm sorry, but that would be a lie." Joe trailed his finger along the curve of her naked hip, up her side to her rib cage. "You could stay."

Her heart skipped a beat. Even though it was nearly four-thirty in the morning and the night was more than halfway over, this was big.

Scary.

If she stayed tonight, slept in Joe's arms, would she ever be satisfied to sleep without him again?

"But," Joe continued, and she expected him to cancel the offer. "Aren't you staying with your mom this week?"

"Yes." Nadia had family in town for a few days, and Faith couldn't let herself take up her friend's only guest bed. So she'd sucked up her pride to bunk with her mom temporarily. As temporarily as possible.

"Won't she wonder where you are?"

"She's well aware that I'm a big girl."

"Sure, but staying out all night? She wouldn't approve, would she?"

Faith laughed. "Of course she wouldn't approve. Does that mean I'm going to jump up and run home to her?" Faith kissed Joe slowly, tenderly, not trying to start anything. "No. I want to be here."

He studied her in the near darkness with a quiet intensity, and Faith felt it again—some new level of connection between them. A contented ease that settled in once their frantic physical hunger for each other was sated.

"That's one of the things I love about you," he said after a while.

"What is?"

"That you do what you want to do because you want to do it."

"Why else would I do something?" She touched his strong jaw, rubbed her finger back and forth, lightly, over the rough stubble.

"Troy said something to me earlier. Got me thinking."

"What'd he say?"

Joe hesitated. Rolled onto his back. "Accused me of living my life the way other people want me to. Not for myself."

"Okay. Do you?"

He looked at her pensively. "I care what others think, I guess. Maybe more than I should."

"That's pretty normal," Faith said.

"Do you care what your mom thinks?"

"That goes a lot deeper than just having her disapprove of what time I come home at night. She's disapproved loudly of my career choice for years. Before I ever got out of high school."

"But you became a firefighter, anyway."

"Wouldn't you? If you burned to do something and your mom didn't think it was a good idea?"

"I don't know."

"Come on. Really?" Faith propped herself up on her elbow.

"It's so far from what I've experienced. My family was always so deep into firefighting, there was never any question. My dad hung out at the station from the time he was in single digits. My mom, well, she jumped in with both feet when she met him."

"That's so cool. My mom married my dad in spite of his career."

"So it must've taken courage to tell her you were going to follow in his footsteps."

Faith shrugged. "Not that much. I was more interested in the chance to share it with my dad. So I'm probably not courageous at all."

Joe gave a low, sexy chuckle. "Trust me. You've got courage in spades."

They lay there in silence for a while, both of them lost in thought.

"If you couldn't be a firefighter, what would you do?" she asked.

"I don't know. I love my job."

"You know it will change a lot when you get that promotion."

"*If* I get that promotion."

"What if you don't like pushing paper, Joe?"

"I want the job."

"For yourself? Or is there something to Troy's comments?"

He didn't answer.

"What would your mom think if you decided not to go for assistant chief?"

"She'd be disappointed," he admitted. "But not for herself. Because she knows I've been aiming for chief for so many years."

Faith settled in next to him, her head on his thick chest, his arm around her. "Personally, I think you'd be good at whatever job you do for the department. But there's something I've noticed."

"What's that?"

"Whenever you talk about becoming the chief, going for assistant chief…you never use the word *dream*. Are you going for it because you want it more than anything else, or are you doing it because it's what's expected of you? What would make your mom proud? Make your stepbrothers respect you?"

Joe hugged her to him and kissed her forehead. "All of the above."

She turned to stare into his eyes.

"Really," he said.

"Okay, then. Just making sure."

He tightened his hold on her. "I care about you, Faith."

She swallowed hard. "I know. Me, too."

"Too much."

She nodded, smiling sadly. "Me, too."

"I've wanted you since the day your dad brought you into my office—"

"When I was seventeen?" she asked, with feigned shock.

"God, no. What would I want with a crazy hormonal

teenage girl?" He laughed. "Since your first day at
work."

"Oh, that."

"I mean all-out, can't-get-you-out-of-my-thoughts
wanting. Physical."

"I kind of noticed." She tried to keep it light.

"But there's more. I don't know...."

"Shhh. We can't go there, Joe."

He nodded, seeming to understand exactly.

There was more than physical desire on her side,
too, but she didn't want to think about it. Couldn't let
herself. Because with every minute she spent with him
she wanted it—*him*—more and more. And knowing
they were so close to almost having something, but not
being able to reach out and take it, hurt a hell of a lot
more than having a building collapse on you.

CHAPTER TWENTY-FOUR

As the engine roared up to the burning warehouse, Faith's nerves tangled in a tight bunch in her gut.

She should be over this by now. Over the trauma of the building coming down around her. She'd bet the other firefighters who'd been there were past it. Of course, those guys in San Antonio had probably been through ten times as many fires in that time, which gave them more opportunities to cope....

Screw that. No excuses.

She was on the verge of being the weak link, and if she didn't get over this hesitancy now, tonight, she had a lot of thinking to do about her future. You couldn't fight fires if you let your fear get the best of you.

"Faith, you're with Nate," Joe said. He pointed out their way in and told them what size hose to take. As usual, he'd come alive as they neared the site, though there wasn't any question they had "something" this time. When you were the third company called in, you knew there was a live one.

Faith busied herself in standard preparations. She turned her air cylinder on, put her mask up to her face and took a test breath to ensure it worked. Settled her Nomex hood and helmet in place. Adjusted her air pack at her waist and donned her gloves. Breathed deeply.

Her equipment was ready.

The question was her. Was she ready?

Joe came up beside her and walked with her toward the door. Nate was about ten feet ahead of them, not paying any attention beyond a periodic glance behind him to make sure Faith was coming.

Nate paused at the entrance and checked his pocket for his radio.

Faith felt the blackness, the dread starting to seep in. Her heart pounded and bile rose in her throat. She closed her eyes, fighting it. Willing it back. Telling herself she had to stop panicking.

"Faith," Joe said, his head close enough to hers that she heard him over the chaos around them.

She met his eyes. They sparked with excitement, but she was more taken with the calm confidence in them.

"You can do this. You've done it a hundred times," he reminded her. He grasped her wrist loosely around the heavy turnout coat, a professional, supportive touch. "I trust you completely." He nodded once and gave her a long look.

Joe trusted her. He knew she could do her job. He believed in her.

As he'd told her in the past, she needed to trust herself.

He let go of her arm and moved away to talk to another officer.

Faith wasn't sure if she truly trusted herself yet, but she decided if Joe believed in her, the least she could do was fake it.

To hell with the self-doubt.

"Let's go," she told Nate.

She followed him in with no more hesitation, giving herself a split second to savor the small victory before becoming fully engaged in the task at hand.

FAITH HAD NO IDEA how long they'd been in the building—all sense of time was nonexistent for her when she was in the middle of fighting a good fire—but she knew they were finally starting to make some progress.

She and Nate had just decided to move in order to get a better angle on the flames. Faith was ensuring the hose wasn't caught up on anything. She pulled in some extra slack, but the hose stopped before she got as much as they needed. She followed it back to free it, then held on to it as she again made her way toward Nate.

He'd just sent the message to the engine to give him water when Faith realized something wasn't right. Something was going wrong.

In half a heartbeat, she knew. Something was caving in on them. She ducked, doing what she could to protect herself, her mind screaming out in utter terror.

Excruciating seconds later, the deafening noise subsided, and it was back to just the usual roar of fire devouring a building and everything in it.

Faith opened her eyes and did a mental inventory for any pain messages from her body. There were none. Whatever had come down had missed her.

"Thank you, God," she said as she located her radio. Tears leaked from her eyes as a hysterical relief bubbled up in her. The radio was there. Her limbs were fine. She was okay.

She crawled toward Nate, noticing he hadn't said anything. Hadn't checked on her. She'd made it only a few feet when her path was cut off by what looked to be a beam of some kind. As she stood up slowly to check if she could see Nate on the other side, something caught her eye to her left.

Shit! Nate was down.

Faith assessed the situation as quickly as she could, trying to fight off her panic at seeing him. She squeezed her eyes shut tightly against it, but instead of erasing the cold fear, she was taken back three months to when she'd been the "man down."

She shook herself and opened her eyes again. It appeared the beam or column was on top of Nate's left leg, possibly pinning him to the floor. She made her way toward his head and bent over him. He didn't acknowledge her, but at one point he moved his head slightly to the side, letting her know he was alive.

She checked the progress of the fire. It was creeping closer. She grabbed her radio and reported the situation to dispatch.

Without waiting for a response, she bent down again and tried to free Nate. She needed to get him out of there, to Scott and Paige at the ambulance, but his left leg was wedged beneath the beam.

Her brain moved on automatic then, creating a plan to get her colleague to safety. She had to fight the urge to wrestle with the beam by herself. Equally pressing was the advance of the fire.

She picked up the hose, which was lying a foot or so from Nate's feet, and opened it on the flames, waiting for help to arrive, and battling the urge to yank Nate out of danger.

Before she could make much progress with the fire,

Clay and Olin got to work freeing Nate. Joe had sent in Evan to help Faith on the line.

Every so often, she glanced down to her left to check on Nate. It seemed to take them forever, but again, she had no real concept of seconds or minutes in here.

At last they managed to move the fallen beam and carry Nate out. She couldn't see whether he was conscious. Turning away and saying yet another prayer for him, Faith made her way farther in to knock out the flames in this part of the building, Evan on her heels.

"YOU DID EVERYTHING RIGHT last night, Faith," Joe said as they walked out to the parking lot just after nine the next morning. "And that's no surprise to anyone but you."

She squinted against the blazing morning sun and pulled out her discount-store shades from her bag, attempting to act nonchalant. In reality, Joe's praise had her soaring, along with the realization that she had, indeed, made the right decisions during the fire. She'd overcome the memories and the fear, and hadn't let herself or her colleagues down. Nate reportedly had a fracture in his leg, but the injury was minor compared to what it could've been.

"Thanks, Joe." She glanced behind them to assure herself there was no one within earshot. "For...you know. The personalized rah-rah beforehand. It helped."

He shook his head. "I'm not taking any credit." They'd arrived at his SUV, and he turned toward the driver's side, while Faith kept going. "Go home and celebrate with a twenty-hour nap."

Bed for twenty hours sounded like just what the

doctor ordered, but it wouldn't be her bed, and she wouldn't be alone if she had her way. Unfortunately, her way was off-limits—she and Joe had agreed they had to see each other outside work as little as possible.

"A short nap, maybe, and then Assistant Chief Jones's retirement non-party." The bar gathering was the department's way of working around his very vocal opposition to a big formal celebration.

"Might see you there," Joe said, and Faith tried not to allow herself to daydream about meeting him at the Shell Shack tonight…or leaving with him.

She climbed into her Subaru and sat there without starting the engine. She watched Joe back up and drive out of the parking lot. As he waited at the exit for a car to pass on the street, he looked in his mirror and their eyes met. He shot her a private smile, then drove away. Faith's heart raced.

She leaned back against the headrest, closed her eyes and soaked in the moment. Overcoming her hesitancy at the fire scene. Conquering her fear by forging ahead in spite of it—without being reckless. And yes, trusting her instincts in the middle of an emergency. Pour on top of those Joe's professional and personal approval, and she was certain the only thing keeping her from floating away was her seat belt.

She laughed aloud as she started the car and drove out of the parking lot. Instead of going to Nadia's house, she headed to the public beach parking lot. It was still early enough in the day that the lot was more than half-empty. She stopped the car and got out.

Several clusters of people were scattered along the sand, but most were gathered in front of the hotels.

Faith had changed into workout shorts, a tank and Nike flip-flops before leaving the station. The day was going to be hot; the humidity was already climbing and there wasn't a single cloud in the cyan sky. The waves reflected the color, looking brighter, more turquoise than usual today. As she walked toward the damp sand, she scanned the shell bits in front of her out of habit. A large piece caught her eye and she picked it up. A white-and-yellow snail shell, almost perfectly intact. She slid it into her pocket and continued toward the jagged foam line where the waves currently ended their journey ashore.

Faith stretched out on her back, knees bent upward, her toes just out of reach of the water. Her clothing would get damp from the sand, but she didn't care. She lay back and stared up at the breathtakingly clear sky. Smiling.

A weight had been lifted off her shoulders just as surely as Clay and Olin had pried the column off Nate. She'd made it through a critical moment, one of chaos and confusion in the heart of a fire scene, and she hadn't let anyone down. Hadn't let herself down.

Somehow in that burning warehouse she'd found what Joe had insisted she was lacking. Trust in herself. She didn't really know if she'd had it before the beam collapsed, or if she'd faked her way through, but now she was sure—her mojo was back.

Hell, yeah, she could depend on herself in a fire. Her colleagues could depend on her, as well.

She'd always strived to work smart, and in the five years she'd been in San Antonio, she'd honed her instincts as well, so that when chaos broke out during an emergency, the two would hopefully work together—brains and instincts. She wasn't sure which she had stopped trusting when the roof had fallen on her. It didn't matter anymore.

All that mattered was that she felt better, mentally, than she had in months. And she was done hesitating before heading into a fire.

Faith noticed the waves had crept up higher when cold water hit her butt and soaked the edge of her shorts. She sat up, but didn't move out of the way. Instead, she kicked her feet in the shallow water, splashing herself even more. Laughed. Threw her head back and let the brilliant sun beat down on her, warm her. In her peripheral vision, she noticed a little boy to her left, staring at her. She grinned at him and winked.

She didn't care what people thought. And it went beyond the strangers on the beach.

Most of the guys in the department had started to respect her. Some of them would never get over her gender. Others might eventually come around, but the thing was...*it didn't matter*.

She got that now.

She'd been fighting for their approval since her first day on the job, but that would never replace trusting herself.

Her dad had had to work to convince the others on the hiring committee to take her on, sure, but Faith knew she was the best person for the job. Mired in self-doubt, she'd let herself forget it, but that was over.

Maybe she would've gotten to this point soon anyway, but there was no question in her mind that Joe had helped her along.

Joe.

He was the perfect man for her. A delicious combination of respected, don't-mess-with me fire captain and caring, patient teacher. He was looked up to and admired by just about everyone, so very good at what he did, and yet the private side of him had enough chinks to make him human…and endearing. Faith had seen the real man, vulnerabilities and all, and she loved him for who he was.

Loved?

Did she love Joe? Did she want to?

Did wanting to matter?

Because she did love him. She knew it almost instantly. Faith wanted to be with him, to know him even better. To fight his battles with him and have him at her side for hers. He understood her, really got her passion for her career and shared that passion. He was so loving toward his mother and Faith wanted to be loved by him, as well.

She knew he was concerned about what being together could do to his career, but Faith knew her dad. If they went to him and made him understand that what she and Joe shared was real, with long-term potential, he wouldn't punish Joe professionally. He wanted his daughter to be happy, didn't he?

Her objections to pursuing a real, in-the-open relationship with Joe were history. She wanted him more than she wanted to stop people from assuming the worst about her. They could think what they wanted. She knew that whatever she accomplished in her job would be due to hard work and dedication. Not because of who she was sleeping with.

She was ready to move forward with Joe and go

public. The next step was convincing him his career would be just fine—he could have her *and* the job of his dreams.

CHAPTER TWENTY-FIVE

JOE HADN'T BEEN HOME an hour, hadn't even gone to bed yet, when the chief called, wanting him to come in to the station to discuss something.

Something.

The assistant chief position, he'd bet.

He felt generally upbeat, ready for the news. Knew he'd given it his best. He and Roland Schlager had different strengths, so who would get the job depended on what the committee valued most. He couldn't change who he was, he thought philosophically as he climbed back into his 4Runner.

If he wasn't the chosen one, there would be another chance someday. Chief Peligni wouldn't work forever. Schlager was a few years older than Joe, so if he got the job, there was the possibility of him retiring early. Joe didn't know anything about the third, outside candidate for assistant chief, but he could easily be closer to retirement, as well.

Joe scoffed at himself and cranked the volume of the Metallica CD in the player.

To hell with all the positive mumbo jumbo. *He wanted the goddamn job.*

He was forty years old and he'd been waiting for the position to open up for several years. He wanted to make chief before he was a senior citizen. While he was young enough to still care so passionately about the department.

He pulled up to the curb at the back of the station and hopped out, not bothering to lock the door. It looked like everyone was across the street at the training facility; the halls were empty, quiet, as he made his way toward Chief Peligni's office.

"Thought you just left, Captain," Flo, one of the admin ladies, called out from her office.

"Figured you missed me."

"Always do." She cackled and her chair squeaked as it rolled across the thin carpet.

Chief Peligni's door was open, so Joe knocked on the jamb and went in.

"Close the door," the chief said.

Joe searched the older man's face for a clue about what he wanted to discuss. He seemed a little harried, but that was nothing out of the ordinary. It was impossible to discern anything. Joe sat on the worn vinyl chair facing the chief's desk.

"Tell me about the fire last night."

He'd called Joe in to rehash what he'd already written reports about?

"Nate okay?" Joe asked, thinking a turn for the worse would cause closer investigation of how the incident had been handled. But he'd just broken his damn leg. He was already home.

"Last I heard. He'll be out of the action for several weeks, of course."

Joe explained what had happened at the fire in as much detail as he knew. Which was the same amount he'd included in writing. He gave the chief no extra insight on Faith or what a personal victory the fire had been for her. To do so would reveal that Joe knew her better than he was supposed to.

"Faith did well, huh?" her father said, his pride showing through in his tone.

"Are you surprised?" Joe asked.

"Not in the least. She's my girl." He tapped his pen on the desk. "Saw you and her walking out this morning."

Something in his voice put Joe on alert—and the Catholic boy in him bowed under the weight of guilt.

"We were discussing her performance." *Performance?* Oh God, bad choice of words, considering that he already had to force himself not to fidget.

"She looks up to you," Chief Peligni said. "Respects you."

"I respect her. I've told you before she's got the potential to be one of the best here."

Chief nodded slowly, and Joe's possible promotion hung in the air between them.

The promotion that would suddenly become impossible if the chief were to hear about his and Faith's... involvement...from an outside source. Or worse, see them together in a compromising situation.

Joe bounced his leg repeatedly. Stared at the plaques on the wall without seeing them.

"Chief, you and I go way back," he finally said. "Our families. I'm going to level with you because I respect the hell out of you." He hoped to God this wasn't a career-killing move. "I have feelings for your daughter."

"You do." It wasn't a question. The chief's expression

didn't waver, didn't show signs of surprise or even anger—at first glance. When Joe looked more closely, though, he noticed the older man's nostrils were flaring. "She's an amazing girl."

"Yes."

The office suddenly got too hot. Joe forced himself to stop with the nervous knee motion.

Chief Peligni pushed his chair back as he stood. Paced to the windowed wall. Looked out at the employee parking lot, his back to Joe.

Joe tried to figure out what to say. How to handle this. He may have just screwed himself to eternity.

The chief turned around and leaned against the sill, crossing his legs at the ankle. "I called you in here to discuss a different matter."

There was no way he would drop the subject that easily, Joe thought.

"Wanted to talk to you about the assistant chief position," Chief Peligni continued.

"Yes, sir."

"There's been a…development. As of this morning, the decision has been made to discontinue the position, effective in conjunction with Bill Jones's retirement."

Joe blinked, thinking he'd misunderstood.

"The budget has been cut again. It was decided to slice a layer off the top tier."

Joe's pulse pounded in his head and his fists tightened against the urge to let loose and damage something. "Why wasn't this decided before now?" He knew the answer before he finished asking.

"Budget time is right now," the chief said. "Funds were cut. City revenue is down. Same story everywhere."

Joe leaned forward, supporting his elbows on his knees. He ran his hands over his face as he tried to absorb what this meant to his career.

"I hate to see it myself, because I know how much work Jones does. Know how much you wanted that position, as well."

Joe couldn't speak. Just nodded dumbly.

The chief walked back behind his desk and sat slowly in his chair. "This isn't for public knowledge yet, but I've made a decision regarding my own career." He tapped his hands on the surface. "I'm retiring at the end of the calendar year."

Joe's head shot up. "Retire? You?"

The chief chuckled, but it had a nervous undertone to it. "Me. It's time." He leaned forward. "Time for me to rebuild my marriage."

Joe immediately thought of Faith and how relieved she'd be. Then he pushed her from his mind. The job had to be his main concern.

"Your absence will leave a big hole."

"About that." Chief Peligni paused dramatically. "The position will be opened up, of course."

Joe nodded. It was a no-brainer that he'd be going for it himself. Competition would be fierce, as there would be interest from all over the state and beyond. But fire chief was his lifelong aspiration; he'd give it everything he had.

"Though the hiring committee will select my replacement, they've assured me that my recommendation will carry some weight." Chief Peligni loosely pinched his lower lip between his thumb and forefinger, studying Joe intently. "You know you've always had my support.

You would even if I hadn't promised your father I'd look after you."

Hope lurched in Joe's chest. Was he understanding the chief correctly? "That's been appreciated, Chief. More than you can imagine."

"I wouldn't hesitate to recommend you for the job, Joe."

Joe nodded once, grateful and yet…wary. There was more coming, he could tell.

"But you need to make a decision," Chief Peligni said with authority. "Fire chief or my daughter."

When Faith appeared in his mind's eye, Joe shut her out. He was on the verge of making thirty-plus years of dreams come true. Of realizing his biggest goal in life.

There was no guarantee he'd get the position just because the chief was behind him, but that kind of support was beyond golden.

"You know I want the job, Chief."

"I don't question that. But you just told me you also want my daughter."

Joe cringed to hear those words come from Faith's father. He made it sound so crude.

"You're dedicated," the chief said. "Like me. You'd do just about anything for this department. That's why I'd recommend you."

"I appreciate that." He couldn't help but notice the chief's use of "I'd" instead of "I'll."

"You're an honorable man, Joe. I want someone like you for my daughter. What I don't want for her is the fire chief. You might have a vague idea how much this job can require to do it well. But I'm living proof of what it can do to a marriage."

Joe wasn't sure what to say, so he said nothing.

"I know what you're thinking. You're thinking you could do it better. All it takes is some balance."

"No. I'm thinking all kinds of things, but that isn't one of them."

Joe had never considered his ideal job in such black-and-white terms before.

Job or woman. Job or family.

In his view of his future, the details had always been blurry. The job was clear—it was always the fire department. One day the chief. But the rest…there'd been an amorphous idea of a wife and kids floating around in his vision, but they were a consideration for later. Who knew when. And they sure as hell had never had faces.

Until now.

But he couldn't let a couple of nights of excellent sex sway him. Faith was beautiful and competent. She had her own bright future. They'd never discussed anything beyond the here and now, and that said something about her intentions—or lack of them.

"The job comes first with me," Joe told the chief. "It always has."

"I don't want you hurting my daughter. Is this going to hurt her?"

"You'd have to ask her, sir. But we're not deeply involved."

Chief Peligni nodded. "The longer it goes on, the more it will hurt her. Just talk to my wife."

"I understand."

"We're clear then?"

"We're clear."

Chief Peligni stood and held his hand out. "No guarantees what will happen, but I'm behind you one hundred percent."

"Thank you, Chief," Joe said as he rose and shook hands. "I won't let you down."

CHAPTER TWENTY-SIX

IT WAS A BAD IDEA to come here tonight, Joe thought to himself.

As a captain, he'd had to show up, but he should've toasted Assistant Chief Jones two hours ago, then cut out early.

Instead, he was still sitting here at the table in the corner of the Shell Shack patio, half listening to Ed Rottinghaus rattle on about his ex-wife, and trying not to watch Faith.

Which was next to impossible.

She sat on the concrete wall, her back to the Gulf, her blonde friend next to her and a group of firefighters around them. Some of the married ones—Derek, whose wife was working behind the bar, Evan, Olin—and a couple of single ones that Joe felt compelled to keep an eye on.

As if he had a say in who Faith could interact with. He'd made his decision earlier, surrendered the right to be involved in her life in any way.

Even if she didn't know it yet.

That was the bitch of it…he'd seen her looking his way numerous times. Caught the heat and longing in her eyes. Had to pretend he hadn't noticed.

He'd always thought she was hotter than hell in her drab SAIFD uniform after working a fire for ten hours.

Tonight, she was nothing short of stunning. Her normally straight hair had a tousled-looking curl to it. She wore a spaghetti-strap black tank with rows and rows of small ruffles and sparkles that should've looked ridiculous but were sexy as hell. With black jeans that made her legs look even longer and more slender, black and silver-studded stilettos and lots of silver jewelry, she'd turned just about every head in the place at some point tonight.

And yet she met *his* eyes across the patio. Again.

FAITH HAD STOPPED DRINKING an hour ago.

She'd had only three beers, but with each one, she'd found it harder and harder to stay away from Joe. Though going public no longer worried her, she knew his feelings about it and would respect them until they had a chance to talk. Hopefully, he would see her rationale and agree to come clean with her dad.

Hyperaware of everything Joe did, Faith tried hard to pay attention to the conversation around her. Laugh when appropriate. Answer when spoken to. Damn, he was distracting.

It was nearly ten-thirty when Nate showed up, awkwardly making his way toward their group with a large cast and crutches. Everyone greeted him loudly, a little extra enthusiastically.

"Surprised to see you out and about already," Derek said, pulling up a chair for him.

A waitress came over and asked Nate for his drink order. "Shot of vodka. Make it two." When she took orders from the rest of the group and left, he said, "Sometimes you've got to self-medicate."

Everyone laughed and a few told him they were glad he was okay.

Nate leaned forward to look around Nadia's legs at Faith. "You," he said. "Thanks for not letting me lie there and die last night."

Faith hid her surprise and smiled nonchalantly, as if he hadn't been her biggest doubter in the past. "Olin and Clay deserve the credit. They did all the heavy work."

The waitress handed him his shots and distributed the rest of the drinks. Nate held up one of his glasses as a salute to Faith. "You kept your cool, got them in there and kept all of us from being barbecued. I'd fight a fire with you by my side anytime."

Faith raised her cup of water and tapped his shot glass, then they drank together.

As she drained her cup, Joe stood up across the way. Her heart inexplicably sped up, as if he might come over and talk to her group, but he didn't even look at her. He said something to the people at his table, something that looked like goodbye.

She watched him walk away. Watched for a sign, a subtle signal that he was hoping she would follow him, but saw nothing.

She waited fifteen minutes, assured herself Nadia was fine on her own, congratulated Assistant Chief Jones one more time, then followed Joe, anyway.

"IT WORKED," Faith said without preamble when Joe opened his front door. He'd been home just long enough to grab a beer.

"What worked?"

"The playing-hard-to-get thing. I followed you home like a puppy."

"So I see." Two days ago, that would've made him a happy man. Today it was torment.

He looked behind her, checking for a car or someone who might recognize them. The street was empty of both.

He opened the door farther and let her inside. An awkward silence descended on them as his mind flipped through his options. He had to find a way to have the discussion they needed to have without touching her. Being tempted by her.

"Are you busy?" she asked nervously, looking around his living room for who-knew-what.

When she finally turned her gaze to him again, their eyes met. Held. God, he wanted to kiss her. As if reading his mind, she moved into his arms, and though he knew he should fight it, he couldn't resist one last touch.

They kissed, lightly at first, like a couple who'd been together for years and away from each other for the day. Then he was drawn in, like a hummingbird that had gotten a taste of the nectar and needed more to live.

He throbbed with need for her even though their only contact was their lips, her hands around his neck and his at the sides of her waist.

"Joe," she whispered between kisses. "Can we talk about something?"

It took him several seconds for the message to get through to his brain, for him to pull back and respond.

"Yeah. We need to talk." Before he got any more carried away. "Let's sit down." He gestured to the couch. When she sat on the end cushion, he took the chair at a right angle to it in an attempt to put space between them.

Both of them leaned forward over their knees. Faith reached out and took his hand in hers. He had to restrain the urge to draw her hand to his mouth and kiss it. He watched her thumb nervously trail back and forth over his fingers.

"I think we should tell my dad about us," she began.

Hell, that wasn't what he'd expected at all. He didn't know what he'd thought she might say, but she'd blindsided him by bringing up her father. "I thought you didn't want anyone to know."

It was a stall, he knew. He was a coward. Finding the words to tell her about his meeting with the chief was proving a challenge.

"I didn't. But that was before." She launched into an explanation of how the fire had affected her, that he'd given her the boost she'd needed to figure out how to trust herself again.

"You did that yourself, Faith."

"A little push never hurts. I was worried about what people thought. Needed to prove myself without people concluding any success I had was because of you." She smiled and his stomach knotted. This wasn't the talk they were supposed to be having.

"Faith."

She stopped short as she was about to say more, as if finally sensing they weren't on the same wavelength.

"We can't be together anymore," he said bluntly. Best to rip the bandage off quickly, for both of them.

To her credit, her expression didn't change. Showed nothing. She stared at him for several long seconds, then stood. Walked to the TV cabinet on the opposite wall. Picked up the framed photo of him and his mom and studied it. Set it down.

Her silence was killing him.

Joe got up, closed the space between them. He stood behind her.

She spun around and looked up at him. "Am I allowed to ask why?" Now the hint of vulnerability showed in her eyes.

"Chief called me in today, right after I got home from work. This isn't for public knowledge yet."

"Okay," she said slowly.

"They aren't going to refill the assistant chief position. Budget cuts."

"What?" She touched his forearm. "Joe, I'm sorry."

"Have you talked to your dad lately?"

She shook her head. "I'm not ready to yet. I know I need to...."

Damn. Joe hated to break the chief's news to her, but he didn't know how else to explain the situation.

"Maybe you should sit down."

"What's wrong, Joe? Is he okay?"

He nodded toward the couch.

"I'm not sitting down," she said. "What's going on?"

"He's fine. In fact, I think you'll consider at least some of it good news. It's not my place to tell you this, but it's relevant to us. You and me." Joe hesitated. "He's decided to retire this year."

"My dad? He's quitting his job?"

"Retiring. To rescue his marriage, is what he said."

"He and my mom are back together?" Her head

tilted in question, eyes searching. "The smarmy man is history?"

"I don't know the details. You need to talk to him about all that...."

She was thoughtful for a moment, then returned her attention to him. "So they'll have to hire a chief. And you're interested."

"Yes."

"Okay...and?"

Joe paced back to the chair and sat on the edge of it, so damn worn-out. Faith stood in front of him.

"What, Joe?"

"I admitted to your dad that I had feelings for you."

THE WEIGHT OF THAT finally made Faith sit on the couch again. "Feelings for me." One and one were not adding up to two here.

"You know that, Faith," Joe said, weaving their fingers together loosely on her knees.

"I don't know anything of the sort. You just told me we can't see each other. Stupidly, I thought things were going pretty well, and then wham! Is this supposed to make me feel better?"

"Your dad gave me an ultimatum." He said it as if that explained everything, but Faith didn't understand.

She pulled her hand away from his and rubbed her temples.

"He'll recommend me for the position," Joe said quietly. "But only if I'm not involved with you."

Faith shot off the couch, the urge to break something, anything, pounding through her. "He made you choose? Really?"

"He's afraid I'll hurt you, Faith." Joe was suddenly standing right behind her and she spun away.

"Ha. Hurt me? Yeah, I can pretty much imagine that in vivid color. Did you tell him you already were?"

Joe's eyes closed briefly. "I don't want to hurt you, now or later."

"Too late." Her damn voice wavered when she said it. "Why would he do that?" she asked, focusing on the anger at her dad to avoid letting that hurt seep in.

Joe let out a long shaky breath, making her wonder if maybe he wasn't totally okay with this.

"I'm a lot like your dad, Faith. Professionally, I take that as a compliment."

She nodded, unable to disagree.

"He's afraid I'm like him in his personal life, as well."

"Meaning?"

"Relationshipwise. Says I'm the kind of guy to put the job before a marriage."

Faith laughed at the absurdity. "We've not even come out of the closet about seeing each other and he already has us divorced? Do you know how stupid that is, Joe? How dumb it is to let him dictate what we do?"

"I told you before, I love my job, Faith," he said simply.

"That's great. How do you know you'd love being chief as much?"

He studied her. "You think I'm making a mistake, don't you? Going for these promotions?"

She stared back at those dark eyes that still stirred her. "That's not for me to say. You have to figure that out yourself, Joe. You have to figure everything out for yourself." She swallowed hard, trying to will away the emotion that was causing a lump in her throat. "All I can tell you is this. I care about you. A lot. I know we haven't known each other that long, but I haven't felt like this in—maybe ever."

"I care about you, too, Faith. Don't doubt that."

"But not enough."

"I've planned this my whole—"

"Your whole life. I know, Joe. And that's fine, if it's what you want more than anything else. If you truly want to be fire chief for your own fulfillment, more than you want to have someone to fall asleep with every night, then I'll wish you the best. If you're doing it because you're supposed to, because it's what your dad wanted, or your mom, or my dad, or anyone else...I'll be very sad for you."

His jaw and shoulders stiffened and he looked away. She had her answer. Regardless of what his reasoning was, he was going with the job.

Her chest ached as she took one last long look at him. "I hope you get the job, Joe. I hope it's worth it."

FAITH SWUNG THE DOOR OPEN so hard it crashed into the wall. If her father hadn't been awake before, he would be now. Which was her point.

"What in the name of God is your problem?" her dad said. He stood in front of the kitchen sink with a sponge and a bottle of kitchen cleaner, acting as if it was noon instead of midnight and he was used to doing housework. It was a sight so foreign to Faith that she stared for several seconds.

Then she snapped out of it and remembered why she was there.

"As if you didn't know." She closed the door, again less than gently. "I just talked to Joe."

"Do you know what time it is, Faith?"

She glanced at the clock on the microwave. "Eleven forty-seven Peligni time. That thing's been three minutes fast for months."

"I don't appreciate you slamming in here at almost midnight like this."

"I don't appreciate you butting into my personal life."

He threw the sponge in the sink and gave her his full attention. "What did Joe tell you?"

"Everything I needed to know. You're retiring. You and Mom are getting back together. You made him choose between me and the job."

"Your mom and I are taking it slow. Working on it. I'm cooking her dinner tomorrow."

That explained the midnight cleaning expedition.

"You don't know how to cook."

"I'm grilling. Making salads."

On some level she was thrilled they were trying, but she wasn't in the mood to give him a pep talk or congratulations.

"That just leaves the retirement and the ultimatum. If I can make a suggestion, you might try telling your family you're retiring from your forty-some-year career before you spread the word to others. Assuming that you're turning over a new leaf and putting family first."

He met her eyes. Nodded. "I deserved that, I suppose.

As for Joe knowing first, it wasn't my choice. He won't tell anyone else until I make it public."

"Would've been nice to hear it from you."

"When have you been around for me to tell, Faith?" His voice climbed in volume. "I screwed up with the drink-a-thon. I understand that you're still mad. But don't go throwing around blame at me for not talking to you when you won't *let* me talk to you."

"Two topics down," she said, grabbing the sponge from the sink and the bottle of cleaner. She sprayed the counter and went after it with everything she had. "That just leaves the running-my-life one."

"Stop cleaning and let's discuss this like adults."

"This place is a pigsty. You need help."

If she didn't scrub at the stains on the counter from the past two weeks, she might end up throwing a plate or crushing a glass. Just for kicks.

"I don't want you to get hurt, Faith."

"What a coincidence. I already have been. Thanks to you."

"How involved are you two?" Her dad ran his fingers over his eyes as if this was giving him a headache. *Him.*

"Involved enough that I'm here at midnight to tell you what I think of you trying to ruin a chance at happiness for me."

He had the gall to look pained.

"Haven't I proved that a man dedicated to that job has a tough time handling his home life?"

"Joe isn't you, Dad. He may be the best captain in the department, as dedicated as you are to the job, but that doesn't mean he'll make the same mistakes as you."

"But he might. And I can't stand the thought of anyone putting you through what I've put your mother through over the years."

"So you thought you'd rush in and save the day. Save your daughter from potential heartbreak. Or was it that you wanted him fully focused on the job? With no outside distractions?"

"Speaking as the chief, as someone who's put everything I had into that department for so long, hell yes, I do want him fully focused on the job. But more than that, I want you to find someone who will be devoted to you first, princess."

The nickname had her gritting her teeth. "I'm twenty-six years old. I can take care of myself. I've taken care of you for the past three months. And now you think you're in the position to take Joe away from me."

"Faith." He stepped closer to her, as if he was going to comfort her.

She straightened her spine and backed away.

"I didn't force Joe to give you up. I merely laid out his options." Her father's voice was calm, quiet now. "He's the one who chose the job."

Next came the twist of the blade that seemed to be slashing through her heart. Overwhelming physical pain seared through her, had her limply tossing the sponge back into the sink. She leaned on the counter, her face in her hands.

He was right, of course.

Faith had been so angry at her dad that she hadn't allowed herself to face the truth. That Joe could have said forget the job and chosen her. And he hadn't.

Didn't that just say it all?

Slowly, she nodded. Tried to pull herself together long enough to get out of there.

"I'm sorry, Faith."

"It's fine," she said, straightening. "Guess you saved me some time and future heartache."

When she finally worked up the courage to look him in the face, his pained expression—on her behalf—nearly did her in. He held out his palm, and she pressed her hand to his warm, protective one. She sucked in an uneven breath as her dad pulled her close for a hug. After a few seconds, when she was afraid she'd embarrass herself by bawling like a little girl, she drew away.

"I need to go." She forced the words out.

The compassion in his eyes belonged to the dad she'd always known and loved. Idolized. "You have a room here, princess. This is your home."

At those words, she realized nothing sounded better than the comfort of her pink bed, just down the hall from her dad.

Faith nodded. "You're right. This is where I need to be. Think I'll shower and go to bed."

After another heart-wrenching look of sympathy from him, she hurried to the hall bathroom, turned on the water and prayed he wouldn't hear her cry.

CHAPTER TWENTY-SEVEN

SPRING TRAINING BEAT the hell out of sitting at home questioning himself. Even if it *was* the Astros.

"You going to pass the bag of peanuts over here?" Troy said to Ryan, who sat on the aisle, opposite Troy.

"Told you to get your own damn nuts."

As a vendor walked up the aisle, Jorge stood and flagged him down. "Need some more nuts, please." He handed the guy cash and threw a bag of peanuts at Troy. "The two of you never change."

"Where are my nuts?" Joe asked, amused.

His stepfather attempted a stern look but ended up cracking a grin as Joe's stepbrothers chuckled. "If you don't know by now…"

"Explains a lot about why you don't have a woman," Ryan said.

"Damn well better have a woman," Troy said, taking a swig of his overpriced beer. "How's Faith?"

A crude word slipped out before Joe could stop it. "I imagine she's fine."

Troy, who was slumming in jeans and a polo for the game, groaned. "No. It's not over already."

"Afraid so."

Instead of the smart-ass remark Joe expected, Troy said, "I'm sorry, bro."

"Seemed like you two had it going on," Ryan said.

Joe nodded, watching the action on the field as if he'd never seen anything so enthralling. Unfortunately, they were only warming up a different pitcher.

"I owe you an apology," Joe said to Troy on an exhalation. "I was a prick the night you showed up with her."

Troy smiled cagily. "I could've handled it better. Might've wanted to get a rise out of you, at least a little."

"Thanks for setting it up so we could have some time together."

"Hope you made good use of the night," Troy said.

Joe couldn't allow himself to think about that. "Pitcher's looking decent."

"Astros are going to spank your Rangers this year," Jorge said.

That was all it took to get away from the subject of Faith. Relieved, Joe picked up the verbal sparring and took on all three misguided men.

He was still doing an okay job of not thinking about Faith by the middle of the sixth inning. The beer was helping, and so was the company. He'd decided last-minute to join his stepfamily on this trip, hours before they'd left, just yesterday. He'd paid a fortune for the airline ticket and had to share a hotel room with his stepfather, but he was glad he'd come.

After the scene with Faith, two nights ago, he'd needed to get the hell out of the house. Out of town. And for once, he'd decided to spend time with Jorge, Troy and Ryan because he wanted to. Not because it'd make his mom stop worrying. Not out of some pseudofamilial obligation, but because he was starting to actually like these guys. Overpaid suits that they were.

At the end of the row, Ryan let out a howl as he looked at his cell phone. The next thing Joe knew, his stepbrother was holding out a plastic shot glass.

"What's that for?" Joe asked.

"Pass it to Troy."

Joe did as he was told. Troy leaned forward to question his brother wordlessly.

Ryan handed another "glass" to Joe, one to his dad, then took out one for himself. Rustling around in an interior pocket of his windbreaker, he pulled out a silver flask.

"What the hell's going on?" Troy asked, setting his empty beer mug on the cement.

"We're celebrating." He poured a golden liquid into his own cup, then passed the flask to Jorge. It went down the line, with all of them obediently filling up.

"Tequila," Jorge said, sniffing. "This better be the good stuff. I'm too damn old to drink the cheap garbage."

"What are we celebrating, dumb-ass?" Troy nodded at the woman in the row in front of them when she turned to glare at him.

In reply, Ryan handed his phone down the line, a black-and-white photograph filling the screen. Jorge looked at it. Shrugged. Joe took it and smiled.

"What the hell?" Troy said, leaning over to see.

"Should we be congratulating you?" Joe asked.

"For what?" Troy took the phone from him.

"I'm going to be a dad," Ryan said, beaming so much he could light the stadium if the game went too long.

"Ho-ly shit," Troy said. "What is this?"

"It's the ultrasound photo," Joe told him. "With all that higher education you've got, you should know that."

Jorge slapped Ryan on the back. "I'll be damned. Didn't think either of you two bozos were going to figure out how to reproduce with a good woman."

"She is that, isn't she?" Ryan said, grinning widely.

"She went to the ultrasound without you?" Joe asked.

"I was there. Two days ago. Just took her a while to send me the photo. Had to text her to remind her, so I could show off my future stud."

"It's a boy?" Troy asked.

"According to that." He gestured to his phone. "She's nineteen weeks along. Supposed to be fairly accurate."

"Nineteen weeks and you're just telling us now?" Jorge asked.

"I wanted to tell you right away. Shelly was nervous that something would happen. She wanted to make it halfway through, but she's worried someone will notice she's getting fat."

"Not fat, son," Jorge said. "Never say fat."

"Pregnant," Ryan corrected with false sincerity.

"To another generation of Vargases." Jorge held up his liquor.

"God help us," Joe added as they all toasted.

Two more rounds emptied the flask. While Troy became louder, Joe turned oddly introspective. Though he was genuinely enjoying the day, an emptiness was starting to nag at him.

Nothing another beer wouldn't cure.

He headed up to the concession stand for one and was on his way back down to their row when the batter hit a foul ball in his direction. Not close enough to go for. Joe had left his mitt under his chair, anyway.

He watched a younger guy, probably Faith's age, grab it and high-five the guy next to him. Without deliberation, Joe headed in their direction.

Five minutes later, after making small talk and a deal, Joe returned to his seat. He tossed the ball to Ryan.

"That's for your son. From his uncle Joe."

Ryan looked confused for a moment. "Is this the ball Robertson just hit?"

"I'll even get it signed for you afterward," Joe told him.

"How'd you get it? I didn't see you catch it."

"Cost me a small fortune. But I figure he's my first nephew. He deserves it. Even if it is just an Astros ball."

Ryan looked the ball over and stuck it in the pocket of his jacket. "Thanks, man. You'll be his favorite uncle."

"The hell he will," Troy said. "He'll look just like me, be an Astros fan and grow up to be a lawyer."

"What if he wants to go the cool route and be a firefighter?" Joe said.

"Enough of the crazy talk." Ryan took out a candy bar and ripped it open. "You want another firefighter in the family, you have your own kid. Mine's going to be one of the next generation of partners at Smith, Vargas and Wellington."

"Wouldn't that be something?" Jorge said. "Bet he'll be a trial lawyer just like his grandpa."

The three law-heads engaged in a debate of what kind of law the kid would be interested in, but Joe stopped listening.

Another firefighter in the family.

Have your own kid.

Not two days ago, he'd assured himself he didn't need that. Didn't need Faith or a future that might include a family. Didn't need anything but the job.

It hit him now, like a brick to the head. He'd been dead wrong.

An image, uninvited, appeared in his mind—of Faith holding a child. Her child. Dammit, he wanted it to be *their* child. Not today. Not right away. He wanted to spend a good year in bed with Faith, practicing to make that baby first.

But he wanted to be the father of her children.

And while a boy would be cooler than hell, the picture in his imagination was of a little girl dressed in a pink dress and wearing…a kid-size fire helmet.

The crowd became noisy as someone got a hit. Belatedly, Joe stood like everyone else, but he was only half aware that there was even a game going on.

The job stood in the way…the possibility of the promotion. Fire chief.

His life's goal.

He liked his current position, he reasoned with himself. No question about that.

Would he really like being the top dog as much? He knew there was a load of bureaucracy to reckon with. Politics. City budgets. Endless paperwork and meetings.

No fires.

But he'd be running the department. Making changes that needed to be made so firefighters could do their jobs more effectively. Save more lives and buildings. He had innovative ideas.

So he would, what, move up in the department and make a difference for a few years and…then what? Retire to a garage full of cars?

Let the Mendoza family line come to an end?

Go to sleep by himself every night? Without Faith.

Joe excused himself and went back up the concrete steps, then wandered off to the right behind the stands, lost in thought. The farther he walked, the fewer people were around, which suited him fine. At the end of the line, he leaned against the wall.

His mom would understand if he didn't put his name in for chief. She'd been telling him as much for months, but he hadn't really heard her words until now. She wanted him to be happy, and in the past, he'd thought a promotion was what would do that for him.

Faith would make him happier.

He'd been miserable without her for the past two days. They hadn't been able to spend a lot of time together before, but knowing he'd put an end to any possibility of being with her, his house had vibrated with the quiet. The loneliness.

But what about his dad? The man who'd done everything in his power to pave the road for Joe, including elicit a promise from Chief Peligni to help him go far in the department. As far as Joe wanted to go.

You have to figure everything out for yourself.

Faith's words rang out so clearly in his mind she could've been standing next to him.

What did *he* want?

He wanted Faith. And he still wanted the chief's job.

And regardless of his reduced chances for the promotion when he threw away Chief Peligni's support, he was prepared to fight for them both.

CHAPTER TWENTY-EIGHT

SEVEN IN THE MORNING had been the earliest flight Joe could get out of Florida. He'd gone to the airport last night after the game, hoping like hell he could change his ticket and catch the last flight of the day, but it had been full.

He'd thought hard about renting a car and driving all night to get home, but the tequila and beer had made that a dumb idea.

As he drove up to the Peligni house, he spotted the chief in the backyard, on the side that overlooked the bay.

"Morning, Chief," he said as he walked across the small lawn.

The older man was perched on a short stool, pulling weeds out of a bed of bright yellow and red flowers. He stood, looking perplexed.

"Morning, Joe. What brings you here? Thought you were on vacation."

"I'm back. Wanted to speak to you about something."

"On a Saturday? Let's sit. I'm old. Retirement age," he joked, gesturing to a set of weathered, white lawn furniture near the water.

Joe walked with him and sat on one of the two chairs at angles to the bench.

"What's bothering you, Joe?"

Joe gazed out at the calm, shallow water. A gull swooped low and grabbed at something on the surface. Halfway across to the mainland, a pair of kayaks glided parallel to the shore.

He waited for the nerves to set in, for some kind of nagging anxiety over what he was about to do, but he was as relaxed as the turquoise bay water.

"It's about the job opportunity, sir."

Chief Peligni's head whipped toward him. "For fire chief? You change your mind?"

He crossed a leg over the opposite knee. "Did a little soul-searching on my trip."

The chief frowned. "Chief's what you've talked about for years. Since you were four feet tall and hanging out at the station after school."

Joe chuckled, thinking back to the days when he would've given anything just to get inside a fire. Some days, when they knew it was a pretty routine call, the fire crew would let him ride in the truck to the scene. "It's the coolest job on the planet. I want to be just like my dad."

"And your chances are good. So why are you here?"

"Because I want Faith in my life, as well."

"I told you where I stand on that."

"Yes." Joe rose and walked to the edge of the embankment. "I chose wrong the other day. I want Faith more than I want the promotion."

The chief appeared next to him. Nodded expectantly.

"I understand your stance, Chief," Joe said. "I intend to apply for the position with or without your backing."

He looked straight into the other man's eyes. "Faith will always be most important, whether I'm a captain or the chief. And without your recommendation, I know I may still be captain for years. But I have to do what will make me happy. I have to try."

"That's a lot to take on. Faith and leading the department."

"I don't take it lightly. But I figure if I start to screw up with Faith, she'll set me straight."

"She'd have some help from me, as well." The chief's expression remained impassive.

"I get it," Joe said. "I hope Faith will give me the chance to show you both I'm up for it."

"You probably know what a stubborn woman she is."

"I'm acquainted with that part of her personality, yes."

"She's not always willing with second chances."

Joe had spent the flight home debating with himself on that very point. What if she was so hurt by the decision he'd wrongly made that she wouldn't give him the time of day?

"She gave me one, though," the chief admitted.

"A second chance?" Joe asked. "You two made up?"

The chief pointed over his shoulder. "She's inside. Probably just waking up, if you want to try your luck."

The moment of truth.

"I don't want to wake her."

Chief Peligni stared at him with mock disgust. "You didn't cut your trip short just to sit here and shoot the shit with me. Get your ass in there."

Joe started to head inside, and then paused.

"Are you and I cool?"

The chief took his sweet time replying. "I admire your determination. As long as you understand I'll tear you apart if you hurt my girl, we're cool." His features slipped into something just short of a grin and he nodded once, almost imperceptibly. "Good luck, son."

Joe didn't miss the handle. The chief had never called him "son" before.

FAITH HAD SKIPPED her morning run for the past two days, too drained to motivate herself. But today she was determined to get over it and make up for the days she'd missed.

She'd slept in later than usual and hurriedly dressed to get outside before it was too hot.

When she opened her bedroom door to track down her MP3 player, she nearly jumped out of her skin to see Joe heading straight for her.

"Morning, sunshine," he said, smiling warmly as he looked her over.

She hadn't brushed her hair yet, hadn't showered. Thank God she had the compulsive habit of brushing her teeth first thing every morning.

Why was he smiling at her?

"Hi," she said. "Are you here to see my dad?"

"Already saw him."

The tiny glimmer of hope that he'd say he was there for her crashed and burned. "Where is he?" She craned her neck to see into the kitchen. Her dad's chair was empty.

"Outside."

"So you came inside to…?"

He'd reached the hallway. Stood two feet away from her, leaning against the wall in a very noncaptainlike way. Casual.

"Talk to you. You're better looking."

She glanced down at her purple sports bra and black running shorts. Bare feet. The tangled ends of her hair. "I need to take a shower."

"You're perfect the way you are."

That stopped her short and she looked up at him, her heart hammering. Stupid body part. She was not going to forgive him just because he buttered her up with compliments.

"Not perfect enough. Why are you really here, Joe?"

"To grovel."

She crossed her arms and leaned against the cold wall. He must've figured out how awkward work was going to be the next time they shared a shift.

"It's fine. You don't have to apologize for your feelings. I can be mature about the whole thing."

"I was an idiot, Faith," he said quietly. "I screwed up."

She stared at him, searching the depths of his eyes for his meaning. "Screwed up what?" She didn't dare to breathe.

"The biggest decision of my life. I blew it. I was stuck on what other people thought I should do, not what I want more than anything."

The hope she'd been stifling since she'd seen him in the living room took wings. Still, she needed him to spell it out. "Which is?"

"You. And the job. In that order. Without your dad's

recommendation I don't know if I have a chance at the second one. And I'm waiting to hear whether I have a chance with the first."

He took her hand and pulled her to him. "I'm sorry, Faith. I know I hurt you, and that's something I never want to do again. I was so afraid of letting everybody else down that I didn't let myself think about letting *me* down. And you."

"You're stubborn," she said, unable to keep the smile off her face.

"I've been told that a time or two. I can also be persistent. So you could put me out of my misery right now and let me kiss you, or—"

"Make you grovel some more? Is that what you called it?"

"That's what I called it." He wrapped his hands around her bare waist. "I may be dense and slow, but I want you in my life. If you'll have me."

One thing kept her from jumping into his arms. "What happens if you don't get the job and realize it's because of me? What if you resent me because you're stuck at captain?"

"I won't. You made me reconsider what I want most. I want you. I want to raise our own company of little firefighters. Or doctors. Bartenders. Hell, lawyers, if that's what they choose. I want to spend my life with you. I love you, Faith."

He loved her.

She'd been determined not to forgive him, and all it took was five minutes of him saying the right things, like that he loved her. Call her easy. And over-the-moon happy.

Faith wrapped her arms around his neck and held on for all she was worth. "I love you, too, Joe."

He slid his hands down to the backs of her thighs and pulled her up off the floor. Into him. He kissed her, and his lips were like cool, lifesaving water to a woman who'd been dying of thirst. Their kiss was thorough, unhurried, as if they had the rest of their lives to love each other. Which, suddenly, they did.

Joe pulled back and gazed at her with the most tender, adoring expression in his eyes. He brushed his lips over the tip of her nose. "Do you think we can live together *and* work together?"

She smiled. "Do you think you can avoid the whole special treatment thing until we're off the clock?"

"I'll do my best," Joe said, "if you'll stop worrying about what everyone else thinks of you."

"Already done."

"Then this might work out," he said lightly, "as long as…"

Faith pulled her head back to question him. "As long as…what?"

"I seem to have acquired a couple roommates…."

Faith frowned, trying to imagine who Joe would take in and where they would sleep and, most important, how she would ever have enough privacy with this man.

"They're fuzzy, but they're small. Shouldn't take up much room. One's black, one's gray…"

Faith threw her head back, laughing. "Cinder?"

"And Smoky. I found places for the rest of the litter, but those two kittens need a home."

"If it's your home, I'm in, Mr. Soft Heart." She

pressed her lips to his, thinking she would never get enough of kissing him, loving him.

"You can call me whatever reputation-ruining names you want," he said between kisses. "But you're wrong about one thing. It's no longer my home. It's ours."

"Yes, sir," she said, laughing. "That sounds perfect to me."

A sneaky peek at next month.

Cherish™

ROMANCE TO MELT THE HEART EVERY TIME

My wish list for next month's titles...

In stores from 16th December 2011:

☐ The Tycoon Who Healed Her Heart – Melissa James

& Daring to Date the Boss – Barbara Wallace

☐ Beauty and the Wolf – Lois Faye Dyer

& Their Miracle Twins – Nikki Logan

☐ Donovan's Child – Christine Rimmer

In stores from 6th January 2012:

☐ The Prince's Texas Bride – Leanne Banks

& The Reluctant Princess – Raye Morgan

☐ Master of the Outback – Margaret Way

Available at WHSmith, Tesco, Asda, Eason, Amazon and Apple

Just can't wait?

Visit us Online

You can buy our books online a month before they hit the shops! **www.millsandboon.co.**

12

Have Your Say

You've just finished your book.
So what did you think?

We'd love to hear your thoughts on our
'Have your say' online panel
www.millsandboon.co.uk/haveyoursay

- Easy to use
- Short questionnaire
- Chance to win Mills & Boon®
  goodies